THOR
DAUGHTER OF ASGARD

By the Author

My Date with a Wendigo

Olivia

THOR

DAUGHTER OF ASGARD

by

Genevieve McCluer

2021

THOR: DAUGHTER OF ASGARD

ISBN 13: 978-1-63555-814-2

This Trade Paperback Original Is Published By
Bold Strokes Books, Inc.
P.O. Box 249
Valley Falls, NY 12185

First Edition: January 2021

Credits
Editor: Barbara Ann Wright
Production Design: Stacia Seaman
Cover Design by Jeanine Henning

Acknowledgments

Thank you to Jessica, Danny, Alexandra, and Kassandra for all of your support and help, and to my editor, Barbara. And a special thanks to Alice, without whom I wouldn't be alive, and who inspired a character.

PROLOGUE: RAGNAROK

The day had gone dark. Where the sun had lit the world on her chariot ride through the heavens, in her place lay an empty blackness, darker than any night could ever be. All these years they'd spent waiting for it, fearing it and struggling to prevent it, but the end of days had come at last. Fenrir had eaten the sun. Ragnarok had arrived.

Light sprang up from the ground, casting long shadows over the battlefield, each mote a spark from one weapon striking against another. As the warriors adjusted to the new darkness, the clashing weapons rang out more and more, producing enough sparks to light up the entire realm, blanketed as it was in battle.

In this luminescence, Thor stood dwarfed by the great serpent, Jormungandr, its body coiled around the world, its great strength causing fissures in the Earth beneath Thor's feet. He resigned himself to his fate and leapt upon the mighty beast. It lunged for him, spinning the world beneath it, its body flying through the air to meet the god. Thor avoided the serpent's strike and flung his hammer, felling the beast in a single blow.

After only managing to walk nine paces from its still-warm body, before Mjolnir could even return to his hand, Thor fell, never to rise again, killed by the venomous blood of the creature he'd slain.

CHAPTER ONE

Hannah slammed her shot glass on the table, letting out a satisfied sigh. It was her twenty-second birthday, and her sorority was celebrating it in style. Since she shared it with April, the president of Beta Kappa Sigma, they always did more lavish parties, but this time, it was quite focused on her. April was staying on and starting grad school, but in just another week, Hannah would graduate and be off in the real world, away from the home they'd shared for the past four years. Even if it was just on the other side of town.

They'd rented out the VIP room of the Ragnarok Club and invited several other houses and a few of the more interesting people from the community. Not the least of which was the man now offering them coke.

"I'm good," Hannah said, turning to the bartender to order a beer. It was on the sorority house's card tonight, and she was certainly not going to complain.

"Coming right up," the woman behind the bar replied, grabbing a glass big enough to tide over even Hannah, at least for a moment.

She had been rather distracted by the festivities until that moment and hadn't even noticed what the bartender looked like. She was four drinks in and was clearly insane to have missed her. The bartender had long blond hair cascading down her back in a gentle curl and was wearing a short black top that showed off impressively toned abs. "Hi," Hannah managed, forgetting she was already talking to her.

"Hi." The bartender grinned, sliding the glass over. "Was there anything else you wanted?"

"No. Sorry. I was just saying hi. Um, I'm Hannah," she added, a bit louder than she'd intended, as she extended her hand. She could always say that she was trying to be heard over the club's loud music.

"It's on the tab," the bartender shouted back.

"No, I'm trying to shake your hand, to introduce myself." Gritting her teeth, Hannah decided to snatch her drink and take her losses. She'd been a waitress long enough to know how creepy it was having someone trying to pick her up at work. She could try finding the bartender later? No, that would be even creepier. With a heavy sigh, she drained the drink and felt a good deal better about herself. So what if she didn't have cute bartenders throwing themselves at her? She had a 3.8 GPA, an internship over the summer that she couldn't wait to start, and a week left to spend with these crazy bitches before she would never see some of them again. She should focus on the present, on enjoying that time and appreciating how great her life was, not on some bartender with zero interest in her.

Deciding to follow through on her own advice, she joined Megan and April on the dance floor. She could have some fun, get way too drunk, and then she'd still have all day tomorrow to study for her art history final. She had only needed two classes this year to graduate, but she'd been sufficiently curious about art history for it to be worth keeping her full-time status.

After a few songs, Megan shouted something in her ear.

"What?" Hannah asked.

"I need a drink," she screamed.

Hannah had to rub her ear to stop the ringing, but she nodded, and after an eager thumbs-up from April, they left her with the newest guy to fawn all over her, his hands running through her platinum hair.

Megan ordered two gin and tonics, and Hannah didn't care enough to argue. It wasn't her preference, but it was perfectly palatable when the bill was already being covered. As they turned to find a table where they could keep an eye on their friend, a sudden sound drew Hannah's attention. Someone had called her name.

The bartender waved her over. With a quick glance around, Hannah did as she was told. "Do we owe you?" she asked. Maybe the tab wasn't quite enough.

"No." She giggled, showing a smile that Hannah could swear stopped her heart. Though that could have been the drinks and exertion. "I didn't realize what you were saying until after you left. It's really loud in here. You said your name was Hannah?" She motioned at the speakers, then back to her ear. "I'm Emily."

Emily. It suited her somehow. "Nice to meet you." Beaming, she held her hand out. "Oh, and yeah, I'm Hannah," she added. It was a miracle she was getting out full sentences.

"This is a gay thing, right? You're not just being weirdly friendly with a bartender?"

This time, Hannah was the one to giggle. Had she heard that right? She'd never been quite so forward, but maybe that was why she'd only been with one other woman and hadn't had a date in the last year. It was nearly impossible to make people realize she liked them when she looked so femme. "It's a gay thing," she said, barely loud enough to hear. What if Emily had said that it was a "hey" thing? Hannah was fairly certain that that wasn't an expression, but taking the chance was still terrifying.

"Good." Emily scribbled something on a cocktail napkin and shoved it into Hannah's hands. "Call me tomorrow."

"I will."

"You'd better. I'm not supposed to be hitting on customers."

Managing to hold it together long enough to nod, Hannah turned around and then, grinning ear to ear, she ran to her and Megan's table, almost spilling her drink in the process. "Holy shit," she muttered, taking a sip of the gin and tonic.

"Good, right?"

"Yeah. Best I've ever had," she had to admit. She could barely taste it, but anything would taste like heaven right about then.

"Did she give you her number?"

"What?" Hannah's eyes went wide, knowing that she must look like the cat that swallowed the canary.

"I saw you run back there. She's cute. I think you should be with someone with higher goals than being a bartender, but who knows, maybe she's in school during the day."

"Yeah, not everyone's parents can pay for their education," Hannah replied, sounding more accusatory than she'd meant. Megan had at least slightly softened the jab at Emily, albeit still missing the bigger issue with her assumption. She didn't need it rubbed in her face.

"I know. I didn't mean it like that. She's cute. I'm happy for you. It's been way too long since you've had a date. Just make sure you tell her that if she breaks your heart, I'm breaking her."

Megan had always been more aggressive, and Hannah believed that she'd follow through. She hated the image, but she appreciated the thought. "Thank you."

"So what do you know about her?"

"Her name's Emily, she's a bartender, and that's about it. It's pretty hard to find out much here, and she's working, so I don't want to pester her."

"But I want to know."

"I do too."

Setting her glass down, Megan rose from the seat. "Well then, you better tell me everything after you go out. I'm gonna grab another drink. Or would you rather be the one to talk to her?"

"Nope, you can go." She was trying to steel her nerves for the call the next day and didn't have it in her to keep talking to Emily the whole night. There were just too many chances to blow it either through sheer awkwardness or even worse, inexperience and ineptitude. No, she was good right where she was, where she could drink in relatively worry-free peace. "Grab me a beer, please."

A few beers later, while she could've gone for a few dozen more, Hannah was desperate to not make a fool of herself in front of Emily, so she gave Megan a tight hug—April had already left—and took a cab home. This was the best birthday she'd ever had. She just hoped the call would match.

CHAPTER TWO

Hannah stared at her phone, the screen taunting her for the last ten minutes. Emily's name was displayed brightly above her number. All she had to do was push the number and call. Just seeing it, Hannah could already feel her heart in her throat. It had been so long since she'd last been on a date, and she was beyond nervous to try this. What if Emily wasn't really interested? Or even worse, what if she was interested, but then she realized how boring Hannah really was? It was safer to just not call. At least she knew that she still had it in her, that she could get a number if she really wanted. It didn't mean that she had to act on it. Besides, she was so busy, and she'd be starting that internship soon. She'd never have time for a relationship. It just didn't make sense to call.

She tapped the numbers and heard ringing in her ear. She tried to will herself to either toughen up or actually chicken out rather than hyperventilating on the other end of a call.

"Hello?" She recognized the voice from the bar. So there went any chance that it was a fake number.

"Hey. This is Hannah from Ragnarok last night. I mean, you work there, you know where we were. Sorry."

"Hannah." Her laugh was sultry, and it melted Hannah in more ways than she'd care to admit. She had always had such a weakness for blondes; maybe this really wasn't a terrible idea. "I was wondering when you'd call. I realized after you'd left that the party was for a girl named Hannah. I assume that was you?"

Biting her lip, Hannah scooched back in her bed, pressing against the wall. Her anxiety was starting to die down, but she could feel her cheeks burning. "Yeah. It was my birthday."

"Well, happy birthday, then. I forgot to get you a present."

"I'm sure you can make it up to me." Hannah could scarcely

believe she'd managed to say that. She pumped her fist in victory. She wasn't a complete wreck. She could at least figure out how to flirt, even if she was likely coming on a little too strong. "How about I take you out for dinner tonight? That sound like a good start?"

Hannah's mouth went dry as butterflies seemed to be having a rave in her stomach. This was so much more terrifying than calling had been. It was an actual date with a really cute girl, one who likely hadn't been sheltered in college and school all this time since she had an actual job and looked a couple years older. Her mouth opened and shut again, her words seeming to fail her.

"Maybe around seven?" Emily suggested. She was sounding nearly as nervous as Hannah felt.

She had to give an answer. It wasn't fair not to. How would she have felt in the same situation? She'd have actually died. "Seven sounds perfect. Any chance you could pick me up? I don't have a car."

"Sure. Where do you live?"

"Off the park blocks, by PSU, if that helps. I'll text you the address. It can be really annoying to drive to, from what I've heard." She'd tried giving directions to her parents a few times when they'd come up to visit and had found out driving those streets was much more complicated than walking them.

"I'll manage."

"All right. Then I guess I'll see you in like five hours," Hannah said, still too scared to breathe.

"It's a date."

Was this what heart attacks felt like? Maybe it was a panic attack instead? They hung up, and she somehow managed to send Emily the address, but she wasn't sure how to handle this. After the disaster her sophomore year, she'd decided that dating could wait until after graduation. That was in a week, but it still wasn't now, so she was absolutely making a mistake, and there was no way this could go well. She tried to ignore the fact that she'd be equally petrified if she'd waited that extra week.

After an hour of trying to talk herself either out of or into the date—she couldn't manage to stay on either track for long—she used her remaining hours to get ready. She wanted this to go as perfectly as it could, and she had absolutely nothing to wear.

❖

At 6:45, Hannah was waiting outside the sorority house wearing a teal crop top with a blue and black flannel shirt unbuttoned over it and a pair of faded jeans, both of which she'd borrowed from Megan, with sneakers and her bright red hair up in a bun. It was so hard to get used to pants. They just never felt right. She'd tried a few dresses but didn't think she looked gay enough, and Megan's argument that she didn't need to convince Emily she was gay when she was already on a date with her did little to dissuade her of that concern. Earlier, she'd swiped a button-up blouse and slacks from April but managed to spill someone else's drink on the top, which she took as a sign that she shouldn't be dressing up anyway. It was a first date, and she didn't need to be dolling herself up, despite having gone all-out with her makeup to match one of the outfits she'd originally decided to go with.

Emily was early. The black Nissan pulled up to the curb, the passenger window rolling down as she leaned across the seats. "Hey there, beautiful. Love the top."

Hannah would have to steal it from Megan on a more permanent basis. "Hi," she managed, tugging on the shirt, trying to breathe like a normal, functioning person. It was easier said than done.

"Get on in. I've got the perfect place picked out."

When she climbed in, she was relieved to find that Emily was wearing jeans and a T-shirt, her long blond hair cascading freely down her back. Hannah had been worried that it was going to be something fancy and that she'd completely messed things up with her final outfit. "Where are we going?"

"Not one for surprises?" she asked, giving Hannah a playful wink.

"I can wait." Hannah actually loved surprises. It was the whole dating part that was throwing her. With friends, or even strangers, she was nothing like this, and she was terrified about giving the wrong impression, but she had so little experience in this area that it was tough not to feel nervous. She'd been on one date with a guy in high school and had hated it, and then only a handful with the girl she'd dated when she was nineteen. She decided to look at this as practice. Emily seemed way too cool and confident to end up with her, but this date could give her experience so the next time, she wouldn't end up sticking her foot in her mouth. At least not quite as much.

"Oh?" Emily smiled, looking surprised. Hannah was a little annoyed to find she was still shorter when they were sitting. "I had expected I'd have to tell you. And look at me, I didn't even think to bring a blindfold."

Hannah was one hundred percent certain that her cheeks were quite red. "I can just close my eyes."

"You don't have to. Unless you know this whole city like the back of your hand, I doubt you've been there before. I hope you don't mind someplace a little seedy." She headed toward the highway.

In truth, seedy places were not an area Hannah had any experience in, but this was supposed to be a learning experience, so she'd make it work. "I've only lived in Portland for college. I moved here from Washington, so I definitely don't know most of the places around here too well. The seediest place I've gone is Voodoo Doughnuts at, like, three a.m. after a night of drinking."

"I want to say that that doesn't count, but I've been there at three a.m., and it kinda does."

Hannah found herself beaming. She seemed to crave Emily's approval, though she wasn't sure why she wanted it so badly. At least this meant she wasn't quite as sheltered as she often felt like she was. Growing up as a spoiled rich girl had some complications, but they weren't interesting ones. "Yeah, one of my sorority sisters refuses to go alone there anymore, which is likely why I've gained about ten pounds this year."

"Well, it's working for you," Emily said, smirking before a red light.

"Aren't you supposed to tell me I'm not fat?"

"You're not, but you look gorgeous as you are, so that's what I'm gonna go with."

It was hard to argue with that logic. Hannah leaned back, staring out over the Willamette as they crossed and doing her best to keep her nerves under control. She so rarely left downtown that it was still a novelty to see the water beneath her, even though she used to get a closer look at it quite regularly.

"We're almost there," Emily said, stirring Hannah from her reverie.

"Sorry, didn't mean to go all quiet."

"It's fine. I like watching it too."

The words relaxed Hannah far more than they had any reason to. *Oh wow, you like to look at water. Clearly, we're soulmates!* Maybe it was only because of how silly it made her feel that it did relax her. Clearly, Emily was putting a lot of thought into her behavior, so maybe she was nervous too. "To be honest, I haven't been on a date in a while," she admitted, in the hope of clearing the air and maybe feeling out how much of a chance she had at things progressing anywhere with the drop-dead gorgeous woman.

"Seriously? How? I mean, have you *seen* you?"

With lines like that, Hannah wasn't sure they'd make it through dinner before she pounced. It had been as long for that as it had for dating, so she might have been on a bit of a hair trigger. "I've been busy with school," she muttered, feeling the need to justify herself.

"Yeah?" Emily asked, glancing over as she pulled into a parking spot. "What're you studying?"

She should have expected that question. She hated talking about her major with other people. They never seemed to understand why she'd like it. "Aren't we going inside?"

"Yeah, we are. Am I not allowed to know?" She flicked the button on her seat belt, her hand moving to the door to leave, her blue eyes still on Hannah.

"Accounting," she muttered, throwing open the door and stepping out.

"What's wrong with accounting?" Emily asked, chasing Hannah as she tried to lock the car. "You're going the wrong way."

"Oh." She'd only gone a few steps, but apparently, the larger restaurant was not the correct place. As if she could even be more embarrassed.

"Why are you acting so weird about being an accountant?"

"Everyone makes fun of me for it."

"Then everyone you know is an ass."

The laughter came harder than she'd expected, and it quickly grew into a hearty guffaw, but Emily joined right in, so it alleviated her embarrassment rather than adding to it. "April's not an ass," she insisted, far too late for it to be believable. Megan could certainly be one, but April barely counted as such. "She can't wrap her head around why I like it. She's convinced it's only because it's a stable job, and I mean, it is, you can get really consistent work with an accounting degree, but I like making the numbers settle themselves. It's not, like, my big passion or anything, but I'm pretty sure you can't major in drinking."

"You are going to be so happy with this place if that's your passion. It's like a three-hundred-level class in intoxication."

"I think I need graduate courses at this point."

"Well, then, it'll be an easy A." Her teeth flashing in a playful grin,

Emily took her hand and began leading her toward a hole-in-the-wall-looking joint.

Hannah tried not to read into the fact that they were already holding hands. The bar was a bit less seedy than she'd expected from Emily's words, but it was a little on the gaudy side, with a retro sign out front and a garish color scheme on the patio. "I promise, the food's better than you'd think, and the drinks are amazing and reasonably priced."

"Far be it from me to doubt a bartender on her alcohol."

Inside, a photo booth took up a substantial portion of the small room with two pool tables. "You play?" Emily asked.

"Not much, but I'm happy to let you teach me." She'd played pool quite a bit when she was younger, and they had one in her sorority house, but it had been a while, and she was more than willing to let her rustiness shine.

"You hustling me?"

She held a poker face the best she could and said, "Only one way to find out."

"Well, I already said I was taking you to dinner, so I'm not sure what to bet then."

"Loser gets first round." Her charade was already fading. She wasn't sure what she'd been expecting, other than a clichéd lesson on how to hold a cue while Emily's arms were wrapped around her. In fact, that was exactly what she'd been expecting. She couldn't help but be competitive when given the chance.

"And here I was going to suggest strip pool."

Blinking, Hannah stared, trying to see how serious Emily might be. It wouldn't be the first time she'd lost her shirt in a bar, and if she had her way, it wouldn't be the last. She was starting to feel more confident now that they were in her environment, though she didn't want to think about what a bar being her environment said about her. "Maybe back at my place. We have a pool table there."

"Probably not the best thing to tell me when you're trying to hustle me."

Giggling excessively as she grabbed a couple of cues from the wall, Hannah said, "I'm a terrible hustler."

"Now you're trying to hustle me at hustling."

"Wait, what?" Her eyes narrowed as she tried to figure out precisely how that would even work.

"You break."

She did and earned her place as solids. She was downright dreadful at pretending to be bad at pool. There was no way she could've kept it up for an entire lesson. It was three more shots before Emily even got a turn. Emily was surprisingly good and made it all the way to the eight-ball before Hannah had another turn, but she still managed to come back with a narrow victory. Emily bought them mason jars filled with beer.

"Rematch?" Emily asked, sweeping a strand of hair behind her ear. Watching her sip from the jar, Hannah was reminded of how sexy she was.

"Think you can take me?" Hannah managed, trying to hide herself in bravado.

"I almost did last time."

"Let's save it for my place." She swallowed, masking her hesitation with a large swig. She shouldn't be so presumptuous when their date had barely started, no matter what sort of thoughts Emily might be sending through her mind. "I haven't eaten today."

"Well, then, I suppose I ought to remedy that." Emily gestured toward a table and slid a menu to her. "It's happy hour. Their grilled cheese is amazing, though I was thinking of getting the pulled pork sliders. We could get both and split them? Or more, if you're hungry."

"I could eat a horse."

"I think the closest they have is cow, unfortunately."

Rolling her eyes, Hannah glanced at the menu. "Both of those and some tacos?"

"Throw in some chicken sliders too. I forgot to eat lunch, now that I think about it." Emily bit her lip, staring at the pool tables. "I may have been a little nervous. I haven't been on a date in a while myself."

"You could've said that earlier. It would've made me feel a lot better."

"Yeah, but I was trying to look cool." If there was any chance Hannah was going to manage to be mad at her, then that cocky grin certainly eliminated it.

"You're lucky you're hot."

Her cheeks coloring slightly, Emily flagged down a waitress and told her their orders.

"So how'd you find this place?" Hannah asked, looking for something more to talk about.

"Wow. I should have thought ahead for this." She looked like a deer in headlights, searching desperately for a good excuse. "Well, fuck. It makes me sound like a horny schoolgirl, but they have a women's arm wrestling contest here sometimes, and I came to watch with a friend. So many gay girls. It was amazing."

"Sounds like fun." Why had no one ever informed her there was such a thing? She'd have been here ages ago. Saying that out loud seemed a bit scarier after Emily thought it made her look bad to be interested in it.

"It is. Maybe we…well, that'd sound weird."

"Asking me on a second date already?" she teased, finding that this whole thing was a lot less scary than she'd built it up to be. If it was only pool and drinking, she should've been dating this whole time.

"Let's not get ahead of ourselves," Emily mumbled, burying her face in her drink, clearly trying to hide her blush.

"How long have you been a bartender?"

She looked relieved to be let off the hook. "A little over a year. I mostly like it and not just 'cause I can get booze out of it. It's fun with a schedule that doesn't require I be up at normal-people hours."

"I hear that."

"Accounting doesn't have that benefit. Though if it's your calling, I assume you can manage the schedule."

"I'm still hoping there's some secret night shift accountant job."

"You never know. So how about you? How long have you been in college?"

"This is my fourth year. I'm about to graduate," Hannah said as their waitress returned with heaping plates of food. It smelled amazing and looked even better. It also did a fantastic job of reminding Hannah how hungry she was. She took a bite of the grilled cheese right away, and it was at least as good as she'd hoped. Though she might have just been starving.

"Good, right?" Emily asked, grinning as she grabbed her own slice.

They made it through all the food as well as two more massive beers before they had any inclination to leave. Emily was proving to be pleasant company, and Hannah was enjoying getting to know her. That strip pool game was sounding more and more appealing by the moment.

"Wanna get out of here?" Hannah asked, hoping she didn't sound too insistent.

"I'd love to."

Outside, the pavement shimmered, and the whole place smelled mildly of rain. They must've missed a shower while they were inside. It was Portland, after all. "You sure you're okay to drive?" Hannah asked.

"Probably," Emily said and promptly slipped in a puddle.

Hannah caught her, taking advantage of the misstep to sweep her off the ground and hold her in her arms, blushing as she met those light blue eyes again, noticing the flecks of green for the first time. "I got you."

Emily stared before returning her gaze. "Wow." Her hand rested on Hannah's shoulder, and she made no effort to be released. "You're really strong." She squeezed her bicep playfully.

"I work out."

"It shows. What the hell do you do to manage this?" Her feet dangled, almost kicking Hannah as she laughed.

"I do reverses from twenty every morning. It's the perfect hangover cure."

"I have no idea what that means, but I am one hundred percent certain that exercise is the opposite of a hangover cure. That would just make your hangover worse."

She was starting to feel like she should've set Emily down a while ago, but not having her in her arms sounded dreadful. "I learned it as a warmup when I rowed crew freshman year, and it always worked for my hangovers."

"Why'd you quit rowing?"

"I was hungover every morning and didn't want to get up at four."

That smile again. It was hardly making setting her down more appealing. "I can't argue with that logic." She let out a shaky breath, licking her lip. "Wanna go back to your place? We can skip the pool."

She really did. "Absolutely."

CHAPTER THREE

The loud knocking at the door drew Hannah's attention and caused Emily to groan and throw the comforter over her head. Hannah pulled it back off and hopped out of bed. Clearly, Emily wasn't handling the previous night's drinks too well, but she felt fit as a fiddle. Throwing on the first clothing she could find, which ended up being Megan's jeans and Emily's T-shirt, she opened the door, stepping into the hall to limit Emily's torture.

"I take it the date went well?" Megan asked, seeming barely able to contain her mirth as she rolled on the balls of her feet, biting her lip to keep from grinning. "She still in there?"

"She's trying to sleep."

"April made pancakes if you want to come downstairs and tell me about it."

She had worked up a good appetite over the long night. "Yeah, all right, I could eat. Any bacon?"

"There's tofu bacon," Megan said as if there was no possible way that could be an acceptable breakfast food.

"I thought that was pretty good the last time she tried going vegan. You know how much she loves breakfast food, so I'm gonna support that." Rolling her eyes, she moved past Megan to head downstairs. That judgmental attitude was not helpful when she knew how much veganism meant to April.

"Sorry. She's just a way better cook than I am, so it sucks when she stops cooking actual food."

"Your cooking is fine," Hannah said, giving her a quick smile and ignoring the latest jab at April.

In the kitchen, Megan took a seat in front of a half-eaten stack of flapjacks, digging back into her food with undisguised glee. Apparently, the vegan pancakes weren't as big an issue as the vegan bacon.

"Morning, Hannah," April said, setting a plate in front of her. "I tried cooking the bacon in brown sugar this time, and I think it made a big difference. You up for being my guinea pig? No one else in the house has been up for trying it."

"You know I'll eat anything you put in front of me."

"Yeah, I could hear that last night," she shot back with a playful giggle. "I'm glad to hear your date went so well. It *is* the girl from the party, right?"

"Yes," Hannah said, trying her best to keep her voice down. "What, do you think I found some other girl in the middle of my date?"

April shrugged. "It has happened."

"It has not," Megan said. "How would that even end up happening?"

"It just does," April said, taking a bite of still-sizzling bacon as she set a fresh plate on the table and turning her attention back to Hannah. "See how much better this is?"

"It's amazing." She finished her second strip, sadly realizing she only had another week of April's cooking left.

"Nice deflecting," Megan grumbled, trying to wipe a drop of syrup from her dark brown hair. "So, Hannah, what happened on your date? She take you anyplace interesting?"

Hannah reflected on the previous night, thinking of how she'd felt that connection with Emily, how naturally it had all come together. "We went to this cute little dive bar and had a bunch of mason jars of beer."

"Mason jars?" April asked. "I've never seen a bar do that."

"Yeah. It was pretty great. Their food was good too, but I don't know what it was about last night. I sure as hell had no idea what I was doing—other than at pool—but talking to her was so easy and wonderful. I've never had that happen before. And she's so beautiful, and I didn't have to try when I was with her, like she just sort of got me. Megan, you were right, I could've worn a dress."

"That mean you're going to let her see you in one today?"

Hannah tapped nervously on her fork as she considered. It was so rare that she was actually read as gay, and she didn't want Emily to think she was anything but. This wasn't an experimental thing. She'd felt this way her whole life. She supposed that after the previous night, she'd probably persuaded Emily, but it was still a little intimidating. "Maybe a skirt and top. That could at least look a little queer if I went for the right shirt."

"I have a denim shirt if you need it."

"I will consider it." She hid her shame with a forkful of flapjacks. She hated that she did this—she knew gay people could look any way they wanted—but it was something she was still really sensitive about and hadn't had enough time to grow accustomed to.

"Hannah?" a voice called from the stairway.

Both Megan and April stared excitedly at the bottom of the stairs. They'd already seen Emily the other night, so Hannah wasn't sure why they were making such a big deal.

"Oh," Emily muttered, stopping short a few steps into the kitchen when she found several sets of eyes watching her. "Hi. You are allowed to have guests, right?"

"Of course we are," April said, pulling out a chair. "Are you hungry? There's some more bacon, and I have more batter if you want pancakes."

"They're delicious," Hannah added, biting her lip as she warred between jumping up to hug or kiss Emily and sitting there trying to maintain her cool.

Before she had the chance to decide, Emily hooked her leg behind her chair and pulled her into a quick kiss good morning. She sat, looking pleased with herself while Hannah tried to hold on to what little composure she had left. "I would love some."

"It's tofu bacon," Megan warned.

"I would love some *pancakes*."

April tsked, clearly losing a few points of appreciation but hiding it the best she could. Emily didn't seem to notice. "Of course. I'll make you some."

Emily grinned, turning back to Hannah. "I was a little worried when I didn't see you in bed."

"It's my bed. It's not like I'm gonna run off and never come back."

"It wouldn't be the first time. Though I suppose I could've waited another hour that time. She may have still been too drunk," Emily said. "Speaking of, thanks for driving. I was definitely in no shape to, and I'm still not quite sure how you were."

"I can hold my alcohol."

"She can," Megan stated firmly, nodding. "She won a drinking contest with a bunch of douchey frat boys. They were knocked out, and she was barely stumbling."

"It's a useful skill at parties. Lets me keep an eye on you."

"And yet you don't need to." Megan rolled her eyes. "I can take care of myself."

"You literally threw up in the coat closet at the last house party you went to."

"Only because the line for the bathroom was really long," she replied, grumbling.

"Yeah and then you passed out in someone's bed!"

"One time, someone actually did that in the coat check room at work," Emily said, coming to Megan's rescue. "The throw-up part. We're still not even sure how they could've gotten back there, and there was no one there when Jill found it."

"You must have so many amazing stories." April set the pancakes before her. "From what I've seen at parties, I can barely imagine some of the horror stories you get when you work at them."

"Hmm." Emily paused as she dug in. "Well, there was this one time, like last week, these two guys showed up in Viking armor and started a bar fight."

"Like some overenthusiastic fans after one of our football games?" Hannah asked.

"Go Vikings," Megan and April added half-seriously.

"I guess that could've been it, but they actually had swords. It was a little scary."

"Oh, babe, I'm sorry," Hannah said, reaching an arm protectively toward her, then quickly pulling it back. "Wait, can I call you that? Like, what are we?"

"We can have that conversation when we're alone and not having breakfast."

Megan shot a quick glare but thankfully remained silent.

Emily gave her own. "I'm gonna say yes, if she's asking."

Hannah blinked, staring in disbelief. "Oh. That makes things way less scary. Want to go have that conversation now?"

"Let me finish my food first," Emily said, stabbing her fork into the sizeable fraction still remaining. They really hadn't given her much time to eat.

"Okay, but we get to interrogate you later," Megan stated in a tone that brooked no further discussion.

"Sure, as long as she's cooking lunch for it."

❖

Hannah sat on her bed with Emily a few feet away as she nervously cleared her throat, trying to figure out what she wanted to say. "Last night was amazing," Hannah finally managed.

"It was," Emily agreed, staring intently at the gray carpet and letting out a nervous chuckle.

"So you want to keep doing that then?" she tried, her tone raising with each word as she worked to keep her hopes in check.

"I would love to. I'm still here, aren't I?"

"Well, yeah."

She squeezed Hannah's hand, pulling it into her lap. "You doing anything today?"

Hannah shrugged. Looking into Emily's light blue eyes, she could scarcely even remember what day it was. "I don't think so."

"How about I take you out again? Maybe someplace a bit less intoxicating. We could go hit up some food carts or something."

"I haven't gone to the pod on Tenth in a few months. I could go for that. Though I'd rather also get drunk, but with your tolerance, I can see why you'd want to go easy today." With a taunting wink, she pulled her hand back, beaming, daring Emily to take her up on her challenge.

"I'll have you know that my tolerance is just fine. In fact, I've been told by more than a few people that it's quite impressive." She rose, placing her hands on her hips, staring, clearly ready to put their tolerances to the test despite how badly she would lose. "I don't think I've ever had a girlfriend who could keep up with me when I was really trying."

"I'm sure you're very impressive for a drinker in your league…" She realized the implication of Emily's last few words. It shouldn't have been surprising since Emily had all but said that was what she'd wanted over breakfast, but hearing it like that was still something for which she was unprepared. "Wait…girlfriend? Like, that's what you want me to be? But I mean, we barely know each other."

"I know how you taste, and I already know your friends. I figure everything else will come with time. I take it you don't agree?" Emily asked, looking more nervous by the second, her confident posture fading as she shrunk, trying to meet Hannah's eyes, probing for an answer.

"I'm not saying I don't want it," Hannah insisted, leaping to her feet and moving to her…that was the question, wasn't it? "Well, we're going out today, and you've met my friends, so maybe I could meet your friends? I'd just rather at least have done that before we're official."

Emily groaned, her teeth showing in a pained flash. "You're gonna think I'm so weird."

"You don't have any friends?"

"No! I do." The offended look on her face guilted Hannah into taking her hand. "I have friends. My best friend is just my..." She paused, groaning. "My hairdresser."

"Wow, and I was worried I was too femme."

"There we go."

"I'm kidding. Have you seen your hair? I'd be her best friend too. Gotta have my...You." Hannah gulped. The word was so terrifying, no matter how amazing it sounded. It had just been so long. And Emily was so awesome. "Looking this amazing," she finished, hoping the hesitation hadn't made her sound too bad.

Emily visibly relaxed, tracing her thumb along the back of Hannah's hand. "It's *them*, actually. So you want to meet them?"

"Like, there's more than one?"

"No. I'm so glad we're having this conversation first. Alys is nonbinary."

"Huh."

Emily rolled her eyes. "You know how you're a girl? And how supposedly some people are guys, but I can't really understand why anyone would accept that fate."

Hannah giggled and nodded. "And some people are neither or both. I've heard of it. In orientation. And online. I've never met a nonbinary person, though. I've always wanted to. At least, I really hope I haven't met one or else I've been really rude to somebody. But her name's Alice?"

"*Their* name."

Hannah nearly smacked herself in the forehead, but that always hurt way too much. "Right. Sorry. I know. I'm trying."

"It's okay. I know it's weird when it's new, but I promise that you can get used to it. Just try to be respectful. If I'm gonna be showing you to them, then..."

"I will be," Hannah insisted, squeezing Emily's hand a bit harder than intended. "I don't understand it, but I can be nice. I have to make a good impression with my potential girlfriend's friends."

"Right," Emily agreed nervously. Hannah hoped that she'd be able to ease those doubts before too long.

CHAPTER FOUR

Letting out a shaky breath, Hannah followed Emily into the beauty salon. They'd grabbed some shawarma and poutine from some nearby food carts on the way over, and now Hannah was both concerned that she was going to make a fool of herself in front of her not-quite-girlfriend's best friend and that her breath must smell terrible. "You'll be fine," Emily said reassuringly, her hand resting on the small of Hannah's back.

"Right." She cleared her throat, taking in the little shop with its collection of hair products against the wall and a woman with multi-colored hair rapidly mashing buttons on a computer while finishing a discussion with another woman. A few other women were farther back either cutting hair or getting a haircut. Maybe one of them was Alice? There were a few more milling about in the front reading magazines and playing on their phones. When the colorful-haired woman handed the customer a receipt, she thanked her, and as she turned to leave, the colorful woman's eyes landed on the newcomers.

"Emily!" she squealed. Hannah noticed the name tag that said Alys, which had to make this Emily's friend, and made a note to try to switch her understanding to "person" rather than "woman," as she initially assumed, as the name was spelled differently than she'd expected, but it made sense with what she'd been told. Alys ran toward Emily to drag her into a hug. Hannah noted the nose ring and the fact that the left side of their head was almost completely shaved. "I haven't seen you in far too long."

"It's been maybe a week since I came in for a haircut."

"Yeah, and then you canceled movie night."

"I had to work a party."

Guilt panged at the back of Hannah's neck. "Sorry about that. It was my birthday party, and my sorority rented out the private room and kinda needed a bartender."

"Well, at least you chose well." Alys beamed down at Hannah, making her wonder why everyone she interacted with lately was so damn tall. "So who's this?"

Emily glanced at Hannah, biting hard enough on her lip that the impression stayed. "Well, we're kind of dating, and I thought maybe she should meet my best friend."

"Wow, you're at that point already? When's the U-Haul?"

Emily chuckled. "Not until at least tomorrow. This is our second date. We're taking it slow."

"Excuse me?" Hannah asked, staring in shock. She managed to collect herself before she made a bigger deal out of it and tried to turn her consternation into a joke. "I don't move out of my sorority house for another week, so it can't be before then."

"I'll put it in my calendar. 'Move in with that cute redhead from the party,'" Emily said, tapping something on her phone. "June thirtieth work? That's a little over a week from now, so I figured it was long enough."

She swallowed. "Better make it the first of July."

"I'm working that day."

"Thirtieth it is, then."

"I'm Alys, by the way," they announced, extending their hand. "I have an opening in half an hour if you want a haircut. My treat."

"Why?" Hannah asked, still feeling suspicious and a bit behind on what was going on.

"So I can interrogate you, of course."

It seemed it was a requirement that best friends made that joke. "Sure. See if you can do anything with this mess of curls. It doesn't like cooperating."

"I'm sure I'll manage." They flashed a grin before turning to an older woman sitting in a nearby chair. "Sorry about the holdup, Clarice. I'm ready for you now."

"It sounds like we have a half hour to kill," Emily said, gesturing toward some empty chairs in the corner.

"Yeah, seems so," Hannah agreed, following her lead and taking a seat. "So…Um…" She stared at her knees. Obviously, they had been joking. Asking about it would be stupid. But Emily had put it in her calendar. Would she have done that if it was just a joke? This was such a terrible idea. There was no way she'd been serious. "So...We're not actually moving in together next week, are we?"

"Oh." That response didn't give Hannah much to go with. How badly had she just stuck her foot in her mouth? Should she walk right out the door and accept that she'd ruined everything? "I..."

"Forget it," Hannah shouted, way too loudly judging by how many people turned to stare.

"We could," Emily finally said.

Hannah's jaw dropped.

"I'm trying really hard to convince myself that I shouldn't put the offer out 'cause I still barely know you. I'm not sure if we're even a couple yet, but it does sound really nice. Do you have anyplace else you were planning on moving?"

"I was gonna move in with Megan, but every place she found is so tiny. Rent in Portland is not cheap, and neither of us has even started getting paid yet."

"My rent's actually really cheap. I live in a basement, and it's not the best neighborhood, but the place is huge, and it has a washer and dryer and everything."

"Wow."

Emily nodded, not quite meeting Hannah's eyes. "I've never done anything like this before. I don't know why I'm so into you." Emily finally faced her, and she resisted getting lost in those gorgeous blue eyes. "Not that there's no reason to be into you. Obviously, there is. Are. There are loads of reasons. You're amazing. I just mean, it's early."

Hannah took a deep breath. "We're really doing it?"

"I'm sure there's a very compelling reason not to, but it seems to be escaping me."

Hannah rolled her eyes. "That's hardly reassuring."

Clasping her hands in hers, Emily leaned in to eye level. "Move in with me."

Any rational thoughts fled. "Okay." Lesbian time was certainly real. That had to be the only explanation for this. Why else would she agree to move in with a girl she just met? But it felt so right.

"Well..." Emily trailed off, then her expression changed, looking almost awed. "So, I guess this makes us a couple."

"Oh, shit."

"Always what you want to hear when you just said you're together."

"No, not that." Hannah groaned, finally realizing what it was that she was supposed to be doing. The excitement and terror of the day had done a terrific job overshadowing it until now, but that new terror must've finally cleared her head and reminded her that she had a final she desperately needed to do well on. "I'm beyond thrilled, but I just remembered I have a test tomorrow. I meant to study today, and well, you're very distracting."

"I don't want to make you fail your class. Maybe I can help you?"

"That wouldn't be, like, the lamest date?"

"I don't mind."

Despite that not being reassuring, Hannah spent a bit of time getting the site to work on her phone before downloading the study guide the professor had uploaded. "Wanna go over this with me?"

"All right, but I'm not stripping when you get the answers right."

"I guess I'll live," she said as she tried to drudge up any elusive art history knowledge she must have absorbed at some point during the semester. "Let's do this."

They spent the next twenty-five minutes going over the guide. At the start, Hannah was having far too much trouble focusing to remember the likely intention of the artist as represented by the iconography of the Standard of Ur or in what ways the lamassu was intended to be viewed, but Emily's hand holding hers helped her relax enough that she started remembering lessons from earlier in the quarter, and she soon found herself able to answer most of the questions with only a minor hesitation. By the time Alys was ready for her, she felt the slightest bit prepared for her final.

❖

"How long have you known Emily?" Hannah asked as Alys checked the water temperature with their hand.

"Lean back." They lathered shampoo into her hair, massaging her scalp. "She's been coming here for around nine years. Though we've only been friends for about eight, if that's what you meant."

Emily sat idly in a nearby chair, watching them, looking far more relaxed than Hannah had been in her situation. Her fingers tapped rapidly on her phone before she began sliding through something that Hannah couldn't see. Emily hadn't actually even tried to add her on social media yet. It seemed weird to already be moving in together when they weren't even friends online, no matter how wonderful the moving in felt. She needed to remember to ask about Facebook soon; then she wouldn't have any nagging thoughts.

Her hair thoroughly rinsed, Hannah sat up, stretching the kink out of her neck. "How'd you end up being friends?"

"Aren't I supposed to be interrogating you?"

"You can ask me next."

"Get in this chair." They spun the chair around and wrapped a cape around her. "She mentioned that she was planning on going to pride, and since my former partner and I had broken up about a month before, I didn't have anyone to go with, so I asked if I could join her."

"Were you two…" Hannah trailed off, not wanting to presume.

"You just won't let me ask my stuff, will you?"

"It's part of the same question."

"No, we weren't. Not really my type." They snickered, circling once to take a look at her hair. "Just a trim, or do you want me to do anything interesting?"

"Like, how interesting?" she asked, eyeing them askance.

"Well, I wasn't planning on giving you a mohawk or anything."

Emily glanced up from her phone, looking Hannah up and down. "I think she could pull it off."

"I like being able to do things with my hair," Hannah grumbled. "It's really nice being able to throw it up in a bun or braid it or do whatever I feel like. Plus, I play with it a lot."

"Short hair would be a lot less work," Emily offered.

"Em, you're not allowed to tell anyone to get short hair. You've had your hair down to at least your ass the entire time I've known you."

"All that means is I know what I'm talking about," she said, returning to her phone, sounding done with this conversation. "Besides, I was going to have short hair until you talked me out of it," she added before returning to being done.

"I stand by my decision."

"Just give her something cute."

Hannah's gaze darted between the two of them. She was a little concerned that they might pick a radical hairstyle, and by the time she realized what they were doing, it would already be too late. "Please let me still have long hair?"

Chuckling, Alys pulled out their phone and clicked on a few things before turning the screen so Hannah could see it. "I was thinking something like this." On the screen was a woman with a similar hair texture to Hannah's, though a darker color, with it long and styled for some event on a red carpet. "You like?"

She nodded. "You sure you have the time to do all that?" Hannah was starting to worry that she might not have the time to look after it herself, but it seemed inconsiderate to say that when seated next to Emily.

"Let me work my magic." They gripped Hannah's hair and went to work. The picture had put Hannah's mind at ease but only partially.

"I have a big corporate job that I'm starting soon. Otherwise, I'd totally be up for something more interesting," she said. They were gonna think she was boring. Everyone always did. Her dream was to be an accountant. She could at least pretend to be cool.

"I'm not trying to convince you to do anything. I just want you to be happy with the results before Emily drags you back to her place and messes up all of my work."

Emily ignored that comment. Hannah tried to do the same but found her mind wandering back to the previous night…and a good deal into the morning. They'd fallen together so naturally. It was like they knew every button that would drive each other mad, almost like they'd known each other for years but with the frenzy of new lovers. She'd never felt anything quite like it.

"How old are you? How badly is my girl robbing the cradle?"

"She's not. I'm twenty-two." It was only then that Hannah realized she had no idea how old Emily was. She hoped the age disparity wasn't as creepy as Alys was acting.

"She's twenty-seven."

"That's not that bad," Emily cut in.

"I guess." Alys shrugged. "It's not like she's a few thousand years old or anything."

"Right," Hannah agreed, somewhat confused by the comparison.

"She mentioned meeting you at that party, so I already know how you met at least. That girl can never resist redheads."

"Why would I want to?" Emily asked.

Hannah sighed. She remembered enough of that from the guys—and a few girls—in high school. It was a big part of why she'd waited until college to start dating. When she was young, people had made fun of her for being a redhead, quoting *South Park* and in general being little pricks. Then when she was older, they switched to fetishizing her and acting like a trait that millions of people had was somehow exotic. "Gee. Thanks."

"Huh?" Emily asked, sitting upright to meet her eyes in the mirror. "Sorry. Did I say something wrong?"

"It's nothing," Hannah said, doing her best not to let her anger show. It wasn't a big deal. She really liked Emily, and it wasn't as if she'd made a big deal of it. Besides, Alys might have been joking. Maybe they'd talk about it later, but she needed to not let it get to her.

The scissors snipped near her ear, almost making her jump. "What's this corporate job you're starting? I'm not sure I want my friend dealing with someone who's already selling her soul to capitalism at the poor young age of twenty-two."

Her eyes flashed in the mirror, but she didn't allow her annoyance to show anywhere else. She wasn't selling her soul. This was what she wanted to do. What business was it of theirs…Hannah forced a smile to her lips, meeting Alys's gaze. "It's an internship with the local branch of this big company. I probably shouldn't say anything more until it's official. I'm not sure what all I'm allowed to say." In truth, she knew full well that her working there wasn't any sort of secret, but with how Alys was acting, she was pretty sure there wasn't a company on Earth that would be an appropriate answer. Maybe Doctors Without Borders needed an accountant.

Alys's easy smile made the whole exchange seem more like idle chatter than any sort of test. It was possible Hannah was misreading the situation. "Sounds like you'll have some serious zeroes on your checks. I'm certainly glad Emily found someone who can take care of her."

The internship itself was minimum wage, but the job that theoretically followed would pay well enough that she was willing to take that internship in the meantime. She neglected to mention any of this as well. "Well, we are apparently moving in together. Some wife I'd be if I wasn't willing to support her." It was so much easier still treating it as a joke.

"You didn't say she was funny, Emily." A smile showing off perfect teeth met Hannah in the mirror. "I don't think Emily would ever be willing to be a housewife."

"It's not like bartending is my passion," Emily said.

Alys quirked an eyebrow, their scissors-hand resting on their hip. "You adore it. You've told me time and again how much you do. Unless you were going to run off and start a vineyard or a brewery, I can't possibly see you abandoning it."

"Hey, since we're apparently eloping, wanna go start a brewery with me?" Emily asked, smirking at Hannah's reflection.

"In every way, yes," Hannah replied, surprised by her own enthusiasm. She was pretty sure she was going to enjoy her new career, but running a brewery—especially with a beautiful woman at her side—seemed like a dream come true. It was also probably the only field for which she was more prepared than accounting. She knew her beer.

"Thanks for the suggestion, Alys. I don't think we could afford running a business in Portland, so I guess we're going to have to move out of town."

"Like hell you are."

"Maybe we'll have some places that would buy from us here so I could visit you when we're making deliveries." Wait, was this a real thing? Hannah had thought they'd been joking.

Alys's green eyes narrowed and they took a step forward, towering over Emily. "You're staying in Portland where I can keep an eye on you, and that's that."

"You're no fun." Emily gave a forlorn sigh. "Guess I'll just have to bartend."

"Good." Alys turned back to Hannah, making a few quick cuts to her hair. "Okay, I have one important question before I'm willing to approve of your marriage and new business with my best friend."

"Okay?" Hannah asked, wondering how serious any of this was. Would either of them actually be willing to do it if they thought the other was serious? It was pretty clear that she and Emily were rather passionate about their hops, but she doubted they'd divert their life so dramatically on such a silly little whim. Then again, they were already moving in together. She should really specify that she still wanted to be an accountant, but that look in Alys's eyes was way too intimidating.

"Do you eat meat?"

"Yes?" She offered hesitantly, worried that this was another long gag after she'd already had to put up with enough of Megan's crap on the subject that morning.

"Cool. We're having a barbecue Wednesday—it's Emily's day off—and you are officially Emily's plus one." They turned. "No, you don't get a say in this, Emily."

"It's fine, oh god of the grill. I wasn't going to turn down your offer."

"Great, so I'll see you both there." With one last clip, they set the scissors down and took a moment to admire their work.

Hannah checked out her reflection. She didn't look bad, though she hardly struck the same pose as whoever had been on the red carpet in that picture. "I take it I don't have a choice, either?"

"Nope. Now hold still. I need to clean you off and blow-dry you."

When they were done, Hannah had to admit that she was a little in love with her reflection. "I look amazing." She'd studied Alys's process as they had fixed it all up, and she was more than willing to put in the effort if the results were going to be this good. She looked like a model, with a wave of red falling to the middle of her back, the normal curls minimized to barely more than an attractive bounce.

Emily seemed to appreciate it as well. "Wow," she mouthed, looking her up and down. It would be well worth the work every day if it kept earning that response.

"Thank you," Hannah said, barely able to contain her joy. She managed to keep her feet on the ground and not squeal, but it was a close call. "Seriously, this is amazing."

"I know. I'm the best."

"Sorry for hogging so much of your time," Emily said. "I know you have other clients."

"It's fine. I'm paying myself well for your visit. You crazy kids go have fun before my four o'clock kills me."

As it was now a little past 4:30, neither Hannah nor Emily put up a fight, instead bidding their good-byes as quickly as they could manage and rushing out of there. "So about that strip studying?" Hannah asked as they headed back to Emily's car.

"Well, I wouldn't want to risk you failing because I kept you busy all weekend. I suppose I don't really have any other option."

With Emily's assistance, Hannah was more than ready for her finals.

CHAPTER FIVE

Alys waved to the two remaining stylists as they followed their last appointment of the day out. They'd already cleaned up their station, but Miriam always wanted to stay around talking. Today was too important, and they'd wasted far too much time on her. But at least now, Hel's plan could finally start.

Whistling as they made their way to their car, they felt a slight smile tug at their cheeks. It would all be worth it. It had to be. She'd promised.

The drive back to their place was a short one, but it gave them more than enough time to ponder what awaited them. Now that Hannah was there, everything was finally in place. Soon they would be able to stop wearing this disguise; they could be themselves; they could do anything.

And maybe when it was all over, Emily would be able to forgive them.

The second they closed the door, they dropped their façade, letting that weight off their chest as their body shifted to be more androgynous. Their house was as empty as ever. It had been so long since anyone besides Emily had even set foot in it. Having Hannah would be so weird. They wanted to clean it up, to busy themself, to have something else to do, but it was already immaculate. Well, there were a few dishes in the sink, and their cast iron pans could do with a new seasoning, but that seemed far too minor to be a worthy distraction.

They'd just have to go ahead and do it. They'd been looking forward to this since they'd met Emily. It didn't matter what it would cost, they couldn't start doubting now. It was so close.

Alys opened the basement door and flicked on the light. The stairs were carpeted, and the light came from several covered ceiling lights. The place looked cheery. It hardly seemed appropriate for calling the goddess of the dead.

There was no circle in the center of the room. Such magicks were far too new for them. They traced a handful of runes in the air, and the room shimmered, revealing a woman in a plain black dress sitting before a long dinner table in an empty hall. One side of her was decayed and sunken, while the other would've been pretty if it wasn't so severe. The room stretched so that Alys was at the other end of the table, an empty plate before them.

Hel smiled. "Alys. So good to hear from you."

It took eons for dinner to be finished in Hel's hall. She was almost always at her table. Or at least she was whenever they tried to call. She had to be elsewhere sometimes. Didn't she? "Good evening."

"Is that the time? I believe the entrée may get here by tomorrow." She chuckled, a small smirk on her lips. "I trust you've news?"

Alys nodded. "Yes. They've finally made contact." Talking like this made them feel like a spy. It was far better than feeling as if they were betraying one of their only friends in the entire world. "Thor's name is Hannah. You were right. They weren't able to resist each other. They were trying to joke, but they're already talking about moving in together."

"Is that not normal for their kind?"

There were so many different ways Hel could be stereotyping them, between them being women, gods, humans, and lesbians, that Alys didn't care to guess which. "You don't sound surprised. You've only ever told me to wait for a redhead to meet her and to let you know what happened. I did, time and again, and each time, you were disappointed that it wasn't the right person. So you did know who you were expecting? You know Em…" They cleared their throat and hardened their tone. "You know Sif trusts me. If you needed them to meet, I could've set things up."

"It wouldn't be proper," she said, as if that was any sort of answer. "Things have to happen as they will. All we can do is nudge from the shadows. Thor will never trust us, no matter how innocent he may appear."

That only made it sound all the more like she knew more than she was letting on. Alys hadn't said anything about how innocent Hannah seemed. Or how wrong it felt to be lying to her. They hated lying to everyone. When had that ever stopped them? They shook their head. "Of course."

"Then the time is finally coming." She let out a contented sigh as a single slice of bread was placed on her plate. A servant stood behind her, who Alys had dismissed as a statue. "Good. If there's one thing living here has taught me, it's patience. And yet, I do so relish the idea that I may have life again."

Alys nodded.

"Tell me, what is Thor like?"

"She seems to be...*he* seems to be...nice. He's in a sorority, wants to be an accountant." They tried to focus on that. She wanted to go work for some giant corporation. She couldn't be that innocent. "He's very timid. I didn't see anything of the boisterous countenance I've always read in myth. He seems young and in love. He'd probably do anything for Emily."

"Good. We'll use that if we must. Very good. Let me know when you learn anything more. I'll be in touch." The room shimmered, and she was gone, taking the table along with her. Alys stared at the fish tank bubbling against the wall.

Well, they had a barbecue planned. They'd learn more there.

❖

"Oh. Wow. You really meant barbecue," Hannah said, staring at the smoker in the backyard.

Most people just called grilling barbecue, and it ruined any capacity for proper conversation. Alys was not most people. They intended to allow their brisket to speak for itself, and based on the look on Hannah's face, it was doing just that. Grinning, Alys tossed her a beer from a cooler and let out a low whistle when she caught it.

"Good catch. I was kind of expecting I'd bean you in the face."

Emily grabbed her own beer. "Play nice. I don't want you injuring my new girlfriend. She's still in mint condition."

"Girlfriend?" Alys asked, staring. Emily had never been one to move that fast or to say anything like that. Was this because of who they were? Perhaps a few centuries getting to know each other did justify moving quickly this time.

Emily scratched her head, an unconvincing smile plastered on her face. "I was gonna tell you."

"Right..." It was good news. How surprised should they act? What wouldn't be suspicious here? "Well, I'm happy for you. You two are just so cute together." Hopefully, that wasn't laying it on too thick.

Hannah scratched at the label on her Full Sail amber lager and chewed her lip. "I haven't told my friends yet either. Hell, they don't even know we're moving in together."

Alys stared at her, not blinking.

"Technically, we did tell you that one," Emily said.

"I thought you were joking."

Hannah chuckled nervously.

Emily stared at her beer. "Sorry."

At least they weren't the only one keeping secrets. Why didn't that make them feel any better? They'd be in the same place, and there was no chance of them breaking up. Whatever Hel had planned, this was good news. They needed to change the subject. They had no excuse to be hurt by Emily keeping things from them. "Did you want your brisket as a sandwich or just a plate, Hannah?"

"That's it?" Emily asked.

Alys shrugged. "Congrats?"

Hannah stared at them, and for a long moment, Alys was worried that they had been found out, and a way too beautiful Thor was going to kick their ass. "Can I have both?"

Right, the brisket. That was all that was on her mind. Of course, she was Thor after all. "Sure, there's plenty to go around."

Emily grabbed Hannah's hand. "You don't think we're rushing into it?"

"If it's meant to be, it's meant to be," Alys insisted, almost too fast.

Hannah giggled. "I think they like us together."

Great, they were actually going to have to talk about this. At least they didn't have to lie. "I want my friend to be happy, and based on how much she was glowing when you two showed up at my salon the other day, I'm pretty sure you're at the very least giving her some amazing orgasms, and it sounds like maybe even more than that." They unwrapped the brisket now that it was done resting, and the smell almost distracted Alys enough to stop studying Hannah. "Damn, I'm a good cook. Moist or lean?"

Both women answered moist, and Alys was polite enough to not make a sex joke out of it.

They needed to not be too invested in Hannah and Emily's relationship, but they should probably try to talk about it more. "Really, though, I think that you two could be great for each other." They handed a plate to Emily. "There's some vinegar sauce on the table if you still insist on your heresy."

"I do," Emily replied, her teeth showing in a playful grin.

"You cool with normal human sauces?" Alys asked.

"Made from humans, in humans, or by humans?"

"By humans. I'm not wasting my perfectly good bodily fluids on cooking."

"Then yeah, I'm fine with it." Hannah took her food, the paper plate holding up remarkably well to the mountain of meat.

"There're rolls on the table, and there's some sauerkraut if you want." They served their own food and joined the others at the glass-topped outdoor table, sitting in one of the vinyl chairs. "Oh, was there anything else you needed? I hope there are still a few beers left."

Hannah and Emily exchanged doe-eyed looks. "No, I think we're good."

Alys looked between their guests. They were supposed to be Emily's friend, and yet they never really could be, could they? At least they could still cook for her. That had to make the betrayal go down smoother. They forced a grin. "Fantastic. Now we can eat."

Chapter Six

I can't believe we're not gonna be able to do this much longer," April cried, sipping her mojito and wiping away a few tears. The three of them were commiserating over the end of the school year at the Cheerful Tortoise. It was the main bar on campus and had discount Jell-O shots every day, though after the last time April had taken advantage of it, they'd all but sworn off that particular deal.

"It's not like we're vanishing off the planet," Megan insisted.

"Hell, we're not even leaving Portland," Hannah added.

"Yeah, but we won't all come here," April said. "I mean, think about it. You two won't be living downtown anymore, and you're certainly not going to want to come up to PSU to get a shitty steak."

"You take that back. This steak is amazing." Hannah stabbed the teriyaki steak appetizer with her fork, glaring daggers. "I would come back here for their New York strip any day."

April rolled her eyes. "Hannah, honey—"

"Yeah, no, I heard it. I'm sorry. Don't praise the meat, you're vegan again."

"It's okay." Her eyes crinkling in a jovial smile, she drained the rest of her drink and rose. "This is my round. What do you two want?"

"Jack and Coke," Megan said.

Hannah indicated the mostly empty glass of stout. "Another of this thing." It was dollar beer night, and she intended to get more than her fair share of drinks from it.

"You sure? It's my treat."

"Then get me three. It's still cheaper than hers."

Holding up her hands in surrender, April retreated to the bar to give their orders. Hannah took a bite of the celery from April's plate and washed it down with the last of her beer. A moment later, April returned, somehow managing to balance five drinks in her arms without spilling them.

"I was joking."

"You never joke about beer."

Hannah opened her mouth to reply but instead tilted her head, conceding the point. She was almost certainly going to go through at least that much that night, and having it already at the table wouldn't hurt her at all. "I feel like we should be doing something crazier. This is our last night together."

"Don't say that. Besides, if you want to get really crazy, we could see if they're doing karaoke tonight," April said.

"I'm good. Sane sounds fine."

"I've heard you sing. You have a lovely voice." April stared incredulously at Hannah, and fiddled with the straw of her daiquiri. "I think you should do it."

Megan glanced toward the stage. "They don't have it tonight, anyway."

Hannah gave an incredibly forced smile as she reveled in her victory. Emily seemed to like her voice all right too, but she had no intention of singing in front of everyone, at least not without a lot more alcohol. "How'd your talk with the office go, anyway?"

April sighed, a look of relief washing over her. "I'd been so worried about it. I didn't want to have to find a new place to live so soon. But they managed to arrange it with the building's owner so that I could stay there when I'm staying on as an adviser. It's such a relief. Especially since as busy as I'll be with grad school, I wasn't too keen on not having a chef anymore."

"But you're the chef," Megan insisted.

"No, I just always cook for you."

"I think I've eaten your cooking more than I have the actual chef's, so I'm not entirely convinced that we have one."

"That would be because you don't come down to dinner until seven, after everything has already been eaten."

Hannah finished off her steak. She was only marginally better about actually making it to dinner on time. "How exactly are you going to manage when you start work? You have to be the least punctual person I've ever met, Megan."

"It's a lot easier to want to show up when you get to carry a gun," she said, grinning madly. "All I get for showing up now is more food or more accounting."

"I like accounting. And I love food."

"Have you two figured out where you're going to be living yet?" April asked.

Megan shook her head. "I've found a couple places I wanted to check out, but Ms. 'I just got a new girlfriend' over here has been a little too busy enjoying that to actually check any of them out with me."

Hannah let out a worried squeak. She'd should've told Megan ages ago. Megan was going to end up homeless, and it would all be her fault. "Um…About that."

Megan stared at her.

"I'm…" She could say this. It wasn't difficult. She just had to get the words out. "Um." That was not closer.

"You're…" Megan said, motioning for her to continue.

"MovinginwithEmily!" She spluttered it out as a single word.

They both stared at her.

"You're what?" Megan asked.

"Hannah, you've known her for less than a week."

"More than a week now."

"Okay, a week and a day," Megan said. "That's not better. And you've just been standing me up this whole time without a word? When did you decide that you were moving in together?"

Lying would be so much easier. "Almost immediately. But I knew it was probably dumb, so I didn't want to say anything in case…" In case she came to her senses? In case they broke up like people who barely knew each other were prone to do?

"In case what?"

She shrugged. "In case it changed. I'm sorry."

Megan sighed. "They're not throwing me out of the sorority house for at least another week. You know how lax they are with that shit. Katie had a boyfriend living there for most of a month before anyone even noticed."

"I noticed," April said. "She just wasn't willing to do shit about it until I started talking to higher-ups."

"Such a narc," Megan grumbled.

"You're a cop."

"Not yet." She flashed a playful grin.

April crossed her arms, glaring at Megan.

"Hey, Hannah's the one we're upset with right now."

Her eyes narrowed. "Oh, I have plenty of reasons to be mad at you too."

"Yeah, but she's moving in with a girl she just met." Megan jerked her head toward Hannah.

"I am well aware." April turned her authoritative gaze on Hannah, prompting an involuntary shudder. "What are you even thinking? You barely know this girl."

Obviously, that was true. No one with any sense would do this. Even by lesbian standards, this had to be a little fast. "I know. But it's almost like I've known her for forever."

"Yeah, that's called the honeymoon period."

Hannah shrugged. She was trying so hard not to take this personally. They had reasons to be worried, but they didn't understand. "Maybe. I haven't been in many relationships, so I guess I don't really know. But it doesn't feel like that to me. It's more like we've been together for years. I just know that I can trust her. And I…" She wanted to say it. That one simple word could explain her feelings. But it would only make her sound crazier. "I can trust her. And besides, Megan will totally still let me move in with her if things fall apart."

"The hell I will. I'm getting a one-bedroom now."

Hannah stared, trying not to look too hurt. It wasn't unreasonable. Hell, it was smart. "You really wouldn't?"

Megan crossed her arms as well. This was starting to look more like an intervention than a fond farewell. "Hannah, this is a really bad idea."

"It's not."

April sighed. "It kinda is."

"You've met her," Hannah cried. "She's amazing. We're gonna stay together. I know we will. And her place is nice and super cheap. And she's gonna let me use her car to get to work, so it'll be even faster than if I moved closer and had to rely on the bus."

"Hannah…" Megan said.

"I'm doing it," she said firmly, glaring. It didn't matter how crazy it was, her friends should support her. "Please don't make this harder."

Megan shook her head. "I can't stop you. But if she even thinks about hurting you, then I'm arresting her."

"Exactly why you shouldn't be a cop," April said. "Though just this once, I might allow it."

With a smirk, Megan said, "And you can tell her that."

Hannah drained one of her beers. "Fine," she growled. They just cared about her. She shouldn't be getting so riled up. But they were treating her like a child. She could make her own decisions.

"And you can stay at my place if something happens," Megan added.

She faltered, slumping in her seat. She hadn't even realized she'd been halfway to standing. "You mean it?"

"Of course I do. I think you're being an idiot, but I don't want you to end up homeless, or staying in a bad situation just because I'm too much of an ass."

April gave a relieved sigh. "If she didn't, I'd have figured out a way to square it with the owner."

Hannah sniffled, swallowing the lump in her throat. She had been getting so mad. She almost stormed out. She should've known better. Her sisters would never turn on her. "I'll get the next round."

Chapter Seven

The big day had finally come. Hannah could scarcely believe it. She wished she could sit with her girlfriend or sisters—at the very least to make sure Megan followed through and actually showed up—but she was ready to do this. As of today, college was behind her. She could enter the real world. Her internship started soon, and she couldn't wait, but she was also scared. She'd only ever been a student, aside from a few months working part-time as a waitress, so going right into a full-time office job was going to be a massive change. And she was moving in with her girlfriend too. It was a lot of firsts.

"Olsen, Hannah," the speaker called. For a moment, Hannah almost didn't recognize her own name, but she figured it out and ran up to the stage, her steps catching on her gown. She'd expected something more, but she was just handed her diploma, shook someone's hand, and then had to file past. She supposed there wasn't time for more if they didn't want the whole affair to take all day. Still, April had gotten to speak, and that hardly seemed fair.

Megan actually had showed up. Hannah watched as she took her diploma and dashed offstage as quickly as possible. She was one of the last in the class, with only a handful following her. After the ceremony, she found Megan again and tugged on her sleeve.

"Hannah!" Megan hugged her tight. It was almost as if they hadn't seen each other that morning. "I'm so glad that's over."

"It wasn't that bad."

"It was painful. I wouldn't be here if April hadn't made me."

"It's our last day at PSU. Aren't you going to miss it?"

Megan stared at the field before them. "I guess. It hasn't really hit me yet. Maybe I'll miss it in a few months, but right now, I'm just glad to be leaving."

Hannah huffed. "Well, I'm gonna miss it."

"You won't even notice you're gone. You'll be so happy living with Emily."

Hannah tried not to prove Megan's point, but she couldn't help grinning as she thought about that imminent reality. "Any chance of things happening with that guy from the last party?"

"Jim? No, he was fun, but he's moving for grad school, and I'm not sure I want anything long-term anyway."

"Well, I hope you find someone soon." Hannah always worried about her there. Megan had even worse luck dating than she did. Especially after that guy she really liked freshman year ghosted her.

"I'm gonna be too busy for that. So unless there's some super-handsome guy who sweeps me off my feet in combat training, I'm not finding it too likely."

Hannah frowned. "I just want you to be happy."

"I *am* happy. I want you to be happy too, but you found some weird accounting internship."

She narrowed her eyes. "I'm very happy about my job."

"Then you get it." Her grin made Hannah realize that she'd proven yet another of her points. Since when was Megan the one to trick her into this sort of thing? She must be tired.

"You still helping us move?"

"Do I still get pizza?"

"Yes."

"Then yes." Clapping Hannah on the shoulder, Megan dragged her along. "Let's go find your girlfriend. I want to get out of here already."

"But shouldn't we say good-bye to a few more people? We'll probably never see them again."

"I'm hungry. I want that pizza. We'll have time at the sorority house to say good-bye to everyone when they get back."

Before Hannah had the chance to reply, they found Emily. Her face lit up when she saw them. Hannah could practically swoon seeing her face. She looked so beyond happy to see her. It had only been a week, but it was just so real. She must've been looking all over for Hannah after the ceremony had finished. Now, if only her parents had been able to make it to graduation, then she could introduce them, but at least they'd be there in a couple weeks.

"Congrats," she said, freeing her from Megan's grasp and pulling her into her own. "I'm proud of you, honey."

"Thank you." She leaned against her, smelling the soft scent of her lavender conditioner. She had spent so little time at Emily's place that it was weird to think that she'd be living there starting that night, but she was still excited. She should be scared, hell, terrified. She'd known this woman for a week, but it felt so right. Hannah was falling hard for Emily, and she was pretty sure those feelings were returned. She laced their fingers, staying where she was, pressed against Emily's shoulder, for as long as she could manage to drag out this moment.

"Come on, already," Megan whined, dragging her out of her reverie.

Looking up, Hannah found Emily's blue eyes smiling down at her. "I rented a pickup. Let's do this shit."

With one last look at the field and doing her best to savor her last fleeting moments at the school where she'd spent the last four years of her life, Hannah followed her girlfriend and her best friend to see her home for the last time.

Carrying a stack of cardboard boxes taller than she was, Hannah blindly searched her way down the stairs to Emily's foyer. She'd had to weave past the owner of the house's car to reach the back door with only her memory and the occasional shouted warning from her friends to guide her. She could, of course, have carried fewer boxes, but she could handle this many easily, and she wasn't going to make more trips than she had to, damn it.

The boxes thudded to the ground past the landing. "I still don't know how you did that," Emily muttered, setting her own smaller box next to the stack.

"Yeah, our girl's a monster," Megan said, dropping a big plastic bin where she stood. "Can we please grab food before the next trip?"

"Yeah, okay," Emily agreed. "Sorry. I didn't want to leave with an empty truck."

"I get it, but I'm starving. I didn't have time for breakfast before the graduation ceremony."

"And whose fault is that?" Hannah asked. "It was your last chance to enjoy having a chef make all your meals. I can't believe you skipped out on it."

"You're the one who suggested we get pizza instead of eating lunch there."

Unable to provide any argument, Hannah climbed the stairs. "Let's get the last of the stuff."

Emily and Megan shared the second bin as Hannah managed the last two boxes, which was still enough to completely blind her. They'd tried to talk her out of it, but by the time they'd reached the truck, she was already carrying them.

Their task accomplished, they all filed back into the truck, with Megan squeezing into one of the tiny fold-out seats, and they made their way toward Hot Lips Pizza. It was almost on the way, and since Megan wasn't going to have a car, she was convinced she'd never see it again, as Sizzle Pie would be closer to her new apartment.

At Emily's expense, because she was the best girlfriend ever and Hannah was absurdly grateful for her, they each had their own pizza, along with some of the fresh baked cookies and the store's special sodas. Emily justified it by saying that Megan would have to stick around to help unpack since she'd have food to reheat, but Hannah was pretty sure it was that she was really nice and made enough money from tips to splurge.

The greasy monster of a pizza was exactly what Hannah needed, and she devoured slice after slice. She had only had a small breakfast that morning, as she'd been too nervous about graduation. She wasn't sure what she'd been expecting, but she'd always had stage fright. "Did you two come here often?" Emily asked around their third slices. "God, that always sounds like a bad pick-up line."

Giggling, Hannah said, "Not really. It's too expensive, and I liked the boba tea place next door, and the bar another block or so over, so I never really went on my own, but when parents came to town, it was pretty universally agreed that we had them take us here. One time, Jackie's parents visited, and she brought back some Pizzicato, and we revolted."

"It was still good."

"It's not as filling."

Emily chuckled. "I've had them a few times, but this is my first time here. I think I like them. Plus, this soda is basically crack. I could drink twenty bottles of it."

"Same," Hannah said.

Megan drank hers in agreement.

"So you all brought food back for each other?"

"Mostly, it was the three of us," Hannah said. "But we tried to bring enough to share with more of the others if we could, and it ended up as a bit of a tradition. Eventually, parents learned that they had to buy a couple pizzas for the house if they wanted to visit."

"Must've been nice," Emily said, taking another swig. Hannah immediately regretted bringing this up. She knew better.

"Okay, I'm gonna actually buy us another round of these on the way out."

"I mean, they *must* be good for Hannah to get one instead of beer," Megan chimed in.

"I think what she means is, you don't have to get her a second one."

"No, I want one."

Ignoring them, Emily stuffed a slice of pizza in her mouth before wiping off the grease on her chin.

"Did your parents take you out much when you were in college?" Megan asked.

Hannah's eyes widened, but Emily waved her off from trying to talk for her and met Megan's gaze with a decidedly less friendly expression. "No. They didn't," she said, her tone clipped.

Glancing between the two of them, Megan seemed to take the hint. "Sorry."

"It's fine."

They grabbed some boxes from the counter along with a six-pack of sodas and headed back to the truck. Finding parking had been a bit of a bitch, but they'd managed to grab a spot close enough that they weren't out of time on the meter when they pulled away to head back to the sorority.

As soon as they came through the door, April threw her arms around them, dragging Emily into it by association. "I thought you'd left," she shouted into their ears. "You didn't even say anything."

Failing to pull out of the hug, Hannah said, "We wanted to hurry and start moving the stuff over."

"I would've helped."

Hannah could almost hear the gears in Megan's head turning as she tried to decide if stuffing someone else in the back with her was worth the slightly reduced workload. "Well, then, come help," she finally said. "We still have another load or two and then my place."

"Oh crap," Emily said. "I have work tonight, but I'll leave the keys with Hannah so you can finish up if we're not done. I forgot we were moving your stuff too."

"I didn't want to make a big deal of it."

April finally released them. "Well, then, let's get working. You've already eaten, right? Lunch is still on the table."

"We grabbed Hot Lips."

"I hate you."

"I'd let you have some of mine, but there's meat on it," Megan offered as penance.

"Mine too," Hannah added.

"Mine had mushrooms and bell peppers. You're welcome to a few slices if you want."

"Emily, you don't have to do that. I just ate here. It's fine."

"I'll save you a slice when I have dinner, then."

Hannah was thrilled to see how well Emily was getting along with her best friends. Especially after how they'd reacted the previous night. Clearly, she should marry her already.

Their energy restored and more assistance gained, they loaded the remaining contents of Hannah's room into the truck. As Megan dragged off the last box, Hannah searched for anything she'd forgotten and found the room empty. It hadn't been her room the entire time she'd lived there—this was her first year with a single after rooming with Megan before—but it still felt like a big part of her life had been destroyed as she stared at the empty room with nothing more than a few bits of trash on the floor and a bare mattress. Her old life was really over. She had to be a grown-up now.

Trying to shake the existential angst, she followed the others, finding the truck overloaded. She'd thought that seeing the three most important people in the world to her would have helped, but she still felt her heart breaking at the departure.

Her parents would be in town next week to meet Emily and buy anything else that she was missing, but she felt as if she had a new independence she'd never experienced before. Her parents had both been busy this week and more than a bit freaked out at the idea of her running off and moving in with someone they insisted was still a complete stranger, no matter what Hannah said, but April had managed to help cool them down. As much as living in a sorority house had felt like she was finally moving out and having her own life, it had still been in the confines of college and a very controlled environment. Now, she was going to be living on her own with her girlfriend. Granted, it was in some old guy's basement, but it was still a place of their own. She even started her job soon. She really *was* entering a whole new world. She hoped she could survive it.

CHAPTER EIGHT

"How do I look?" Hannah tugged at the skirt of her dress, staring at her reflection in the mirror. She'd done her makeup, styled her hair the way Alys had taught her, and done everything society and her mother had ever taught her a proper young lady should do in the morning. Unfortunately, this still left her with far too much time to worry.

"Pretty straight."

She glared at Emily. "Straight, huh?" A few steps and her hand was on Emily's hip. "Well, if I look straight, then I guess it doesn't mean anything when I do this." She rubbed the bone with her thumb before sweeping her hand back and cupping an impressively firm ass. "Or this." She traced Emily's supple thighs with her other hand.

"I've always wanted to fuck a straight girl."

"Sorry. I'm straight."

Before she had the chance to pull back, Emily pinned her hands against the bedroom wall. "Such a tease. You still have half an hour. Maybe I should make sure you're soaked by the time you make it to work."

Hannah let out a nervous squeak. That was so hot, and if it was any other day, she'd take her up on it, but it was her first day at her dream job. "That sounds really uncomfortable."

"It'll be worth it."

Her cheeks heated, but she did nothing to free herself from Emily's grasp. "Now who's the tease?"

"Oh, I'll absolutely follow through."

"How about when I get home?"

Emily finally let her go and gave her a quick peck on the lips. "So long as I did a good job distracting you."

Hannah sighed. That had been a few minutes where she wasn't

stressing over what her boss would think of her, how she'd actually be at accounting under normal work circumstances, if she could even handle being awake this early every day, and every other possible eventuality. "It did."

"Good." Another kiss, more forceful, her hand on the small of Hannah's back as she pulled them flush. "Though it's also gotten me a bit riled up. Maybe we *should* have that quickie."

"When I get home. My makeup is perfect, and I am not showing up for my first day all smeared." She took a deep breath, trying to calm her libido before she went back on her word and just pounced on Emily.

Emily sighed. "Fine."

Hannah started pacing again but caught herself and leaned against the pillar in the middle of their bedroom. The architecture of the place made it abundantly clear that it was not intended to be used as someone's home, but the lack of windows in the bedroom was an absolute blessing for a morning hangover or for trying to sleep after a night out. Or for someone who worked nights, which was probably why Emily had rented the place. "What if I'm not good enough?"

"I'm still not a hundred percent sure what being an accountant entails, but you actually want to do the job, and that's more than most of the people there can probably say."

"Yeah, but they have experience."

"This is an internship. If you had experience, I'd be a bit confused. You'll have experience soon, and then you'll be the best damn accountant there." Sitting on their bed, Emily faced her, likely not wanting to risk another bout of accidental foreplay, looking at her with as much affection, pride, and confidence as a human could possibly radiate. It was hard to feel too stressed looking at that face, but by God, Hannah was finding a way.

"Maybe if I'd paid more attention in class—"

"Hannah, you had a 3.8 GPA, as you have mentioned several times in the week I've known you."

"Only because April made me. If our grades weren't good enough, we risked being kicked out of Beta Kappa Sigma."

Emily took a deep breath, still staring. Hannah could see she'd only proved Emily's point, but she wasn't about to admit it. "You still did it. You can't have almost all As and also claim you didn't pay enough attention in class. Hell, you also tutored Megan, and with our study sessions, I even managed to learn a thing or two about accounting. Don't worry, I've worked very hard to forget it."

"But—"

"You're going to do amazing." Emily approached her and rested her hands on her shoulders. "Honey, I promise, you have nothing to worry about. They're going to love you. You'll probably be running the accounting department by next year."

"I really doubt that."

"They'll still love you."

"What if they're homophobic?"

"Well, then, it's a great thing you're straight now." She smirked.

Hannah playfully swatted her shoulder.

"If they're dicks to you, I'll beat them up. Hell, I may be able to get every bartender in town to refuse to serve them, and as many accountants come to bars, that's really hitting those assholes where it hurts."

"I want to say that that's an inaccurate stereotype, but our fridge is half beer."

"Exactly."

Hannah reached for one of the hands on her shoulder, trying to borrow what strength she could. "You really think you could do that? Make everyone refuse to serve them?"

She shrugged. "I've never tried. This is Portland, though. There aren't too many homophobic bartenders. I could probably talk a lot of people into it."

"That would be amazing, babe."

"Well, then, it's a promise. If they're awful to you, I'll make them pay…by not letting them pay anyone for alcohol. So accept that you're going to do great, and worst-case scenario, you can find a new job while they'll all have to find a new bar."

It wasn't enough to make her feel confident about the day, but it was nice to be reminded of how much Emily cared. She just hoped it wouldn't come to that. "I know it's still early, but can we leave now? Maybe once I'm actually at work, it won't be so scary."

"Sure. I'll leave my phone's sound on so you can call or message if there's an issue. I'm just exhausted, and it's past my bedtime."

"Thank you. Should I drive myself? It's late, and you really should sleep."

"But I wanted to drop you off since it's your first day."

"Yeah, but then I can go somewhere for lunch."

Emily considered this, eyeing her. "Fine. Take care of it, and get some gas if you can. The tank's pretty low."

"Of course."

"It'll be fine, honey. If you don't need me, I'm gonna get some sleep. I'm really proud of you, and I know for a fact that you're going to do amazing."

In truth, Hannah did want Emily to drive—she was concerned that forcing herself to show up would be too much for her—but she'd forgotten how tired Emily had to be after a full night of work followed by dealing with the crazy girl running around their apartment getting ready. "Get some sleep. I'll see you when I get home." She swallowed, trying to feel as confident in herself as Emily did. "And I'll be back to report how fantastically I did."

"That's my girl." She kissed her, holding her tight as their lips met. "You're gonna be amazing."

Emily dropped into the bed like a sack of particularly sleepy potatoes, and Hannah grabbed the car keys. She could do this. She knew she could. All she had to do was prove it.

❖

It only took ten minutes sitting in the parking lot before Hannah managed to gather the courage to go inside. Emily was right. She could do this, but it required actually being in the building. Which required getting out of the car. She took a deep breath and did just that.

Having never seen the place before, Hannah was almost taken aback by how beautiful it was. The familiar sight of the Willamette flowed behind the very modern, angular glass building. A few people were on the bike trail in front of it, one sneaking a cigarette and two others huddled together, shackling their bikes to the employee bike rack. The parking lot was full of Mercedes, against which Emily's beat-up old Nissan stood in stark contrast, further emphasized by the bit of black duct tape on the bumper. This did little to make her feel more at home.

One of the cyclists waved, and she responded in kind as she walked inside. The email had said to talk to the receptionist in the lobby. She'd been expecting something small, maybe even a little dingy, not...whatever this was. The pretty, chic, oddly backlit desk area looked more like something from a mid-century depiction of an airport than any truck-manufacturing plant had the right to. It looked so nice that it almost went all the way around to being unsightly but stopped just short. Hannah should've dressed up a bit more; judging by the disco ball-like lights off to the side, her dress from the sorority's last seventies theme party might have been more appropriate.

Too distracted by the screens showing advertisements for a few dozen different things, including her school's mascot—go, Vikings—it took Hannah several seconds to notice the woman waving her over. "Good morning. How may I help you?"

"Hi, yeah, I'm supposed to be starting my internship here. Good morning. I'm not really sure where to go? It's for accounting."

"Orientation is going to be right this way," she said, gesturing off to the side. "There's breakfast there. When you're all done, you'll be split up to your own departments."

"All right, thank you so much. I'm really nervous. What was it like for you?"

She offered a warm and substantially more genuine smile, the robotic facade cracking. "I'm still pretty new here, but it's been really nice. I think you're going to like it, though I don't really know anything about our accounting department. If it helps, one of our lounges looks over the river, and it's an absolutely gorgeous view. It's how I managed to sell a friend on working security here."

"That does help a little." At least there was something that offered some familiarity and comfort, both of which were far too scarce. "Well, I should find the orientation before I'm late."

"You'll need to go straight down the hall, and it'll be on the left. You can't miss it."

The first thing Hannah noticed when she turned into the open doorway was the tray laid out with croissants, bagels, English muffins, and an assortment of Danishes for the handful of interns milling about. The three-month internship program was apparently held yearly and was a big part of their recent recruitment and, of course, a way to take advantage of paying minimum wage for fully qualified employees. Hannah grabbed a couple croissants and probably too many Danishes and found a seat with a blond boy and another red-haired girl. Despite what TV and movies said, there actually could be more than one redhead in a room at a time.

As soon as she took a bite of her food, the lights dimmed, and a projector lit up the back wall with the introductory page to a slideshow bearing the words "Welcome to Muller Trucks."

The following hour and a half was spent going over the conduct code, sexual harassment rules, corporate policy, company goals, and how they were to conduct themselves as representatives of Muller

Trucks. Hannah listened, rapt by the barrage of information. As it was her first time really dealing with this sort of thing, since her old waitressing job had involved none of it, it was an exciting novelty.

When the presentation finished, Hannah sent a quick message to Emily, letting her know how everything was going and how excited she was before she followed the presenter's directions to the accounting department.

A thin man wearing glasses, the picture of an accountant, called her over. "Ms. Olsen?"

"Yes. Nice to meet you. I'm Hannah Olsen." She held her hand out.

He glanced at her before turning back to his computer. "Okay, the program will walk you through everything. You've got a cubicle right there." He glanced to the empty stall next to his. "Ask if you have any questions."

She didn't even know what she didn't know. She'd never professionally accounted before. She hadn't even amateur accounted outside of school and wasn't entirely sure what that would entail. She'd done her own taxes the previous year, but that hadn't involved much since she hadn't been working. "You don't have any other instructions for me?"

He eyed her again, looking more annoyed. Apparently, questions were a sure way to make her eventual review go poorly. She would have to figure everything out herself. Maybe someone else would be more accommodating if she needed anything. Without another word, she took her seat and attempted to log on only to find that she didn't know her password.

Should she ask him or try to figure it out?

A rapping sounded on the cubicle wall not occupied by her grumpy supervisor. "Don't mind him," a woman's deep voice said with a slight accent she couldn't quite place. Hannah wheeled her chair back to see her neighbor. Glinting brown eyes and black hair poked around the corner, along with a playful smile. "I'm Isabel. I take it he didn't bother to give you your log-in info?"

She shook her head. "Oh, and I'm Hannah."

"Nice to meet you. Give me a minute." Her chair slammed back against her desk as she strode the few feet to the still-unnamed man. "Mate, she kind of needs the log-in info if you want her to work. You can't expect people to do everything without a word. I swear, Miranda is gonna kill you when she gets back from maternity leave."

Hannah heard a huff and could imagine his eyes rolling behind those thick lenses. "Fine, whatever. I think it was emailed to me. I'll forward it to her."

"You don't see the problem there?"

"Then I'll forward it to you."

Hannah could almost hear the words the woman wanted to say. She even took in the breath to say them. Something to the effect of "That's a serious breach of security, and you know full well that it's against company policy," but she must have thought better of it and she let him do as he wished. "Fine." A second later, the wheels of her chair squeaked, and she was grinning at Hannah again. "I'll have your info in just a minute. I'm so sorry about him. This isn't even his department. He's from marketing, but he's got the most experience with the internship program, so they wanted him to help you."

"He's not even an accountant?"

"Not to my knowledge. I know, you'd really think he would be."

Hannah stared at the wall preventing her from seeing the annoying man. "Huh." She should've known she couldn't judge a book by its cover. But maybe that meant the real boss would be nicer.

"Right." Her computer dinged, and she clicked a few times. "Here we go." She pulled herself into Hannah's cubicle and gave her the info. "Let me help get you set up and then you can take care of things. He was right about one thing, the computer really does walk you through everything."

"Thank you." With Isabel's help, everything grew much easier, and Hannah made it through the rest of her first day as an accountant with no real struggle. She made one minor error in the math that would've resulted in them owing ninety thousand dollars, but she caught it before it could've caused anything, so she was counting the day as a success. She couldn't wait to do it again. It still hardly felt real, even eight hours in. She was finally an accountant.

A few minutes after five, she joined Isabel at the elevator. "Any big plans?" she asked, trying to fill the empty air.

"Not really. I just want to grab Chinese and get some sleep."

"I may have to suggest that to my girlfriend." She almost caught herself. If she'd just stopped a second earlier, she could've said partner or played it off the same way straight girls used it, but after an awkward pause, she was certain she'd left no doubt as to the meaning.

"Don't worry about it. My best friend's gay."

Breathing a sigh, Hannah resisted hugging her. "That's a relief."

"The company's great about it, so probably don't worry, but I get wanting to keep your head down when you're an intern. Great work today, by the way."

"I was so worried, but it's a lot easier than I thought it would be."

"Or maybe you're actually a trained accountant or something, love."

Before the words had time to resonate and her new status could properly sink in, someone screamed down the hall. Someone else called for security, and she heard another voice say, "Sir, this isn't the renaissance festival. I'm going to have to ask you to leave."

"Want to take the back exit?" Isabel asked, peering nervously down the hall.

Hannah nodded, and they walked down the Willamette until they reached the side of the building.

"Hurry to your car." Isabel glanced at the entrance. "I don't know what was going on, but I don't want anything to happen to you on your first day. I'll wait to leave until I see you're safe."

"You don't have to. I can take care of myself." Except she didn't want to have to hurt anyone, but she knew she'd never get in a fight. That would just be crazy.

"I insist." Isabel gave her a quick hug before climbing into her Mercedes.

Hannah was starting to feel some serious car envy, but having a car at all was enough of a novelty that it wasn't too bad. Hers was back by the entrance since she'd come so early. She'd been too caught up talking to Isabel, her first ever work friend. Hopefully, security had taken care of whatever was going on inside.

She heard heavy footsteps to one side. "Father?" a voice asked somewhere behind her.

As she was no one's father, she ignored it. The beeper for the car had been on the fritz that morning, but it seemed to work fine now, and she heard the car unlock a couple dozen feet away.

"Thor," the voice called.

A hand snatched her wrist, and Hannah turned, staring at the massive form of a heavily armored man. "What the fuck?" she asked, trying desperately to pull away.

His eyes didn't show anger or malice, only a strange recognition and possibly even affection. It made him all the more disconcerting.

"See, Modi? I told you it was him. Look at that hair. I'd recognize it anywhere, just like Father's old beard. I don't know why he lost the beard, though. I always loved it. It was how everyone knew him."

"What?" she asked, too confused to even try fighting him off.

"Brother, please," another voice said behind her, his footsteps thudding on the asphalt. "You're clearly frightening him. I don't think he knows anything."

"But Mimir said—"

"I'm sure dying is quite disorienting."

"But—"

The man holding her was looking at someone over her head. His grip slacked. Using all of the strength she'd built up from years of working out, she threw her open hands at his chest, pushing him away, and wrenched free of his grasp. Without looking back, she ran for her car, ignoring the confused shouts, and started it before her butt was even in the seat.

As she closed the door, a horn blared next to her as Isabel drove up.

Hannah didn't look back as she pulled out, narrowly avoiding hitting one of the nearby cars. That would've cost a fortune.

Her heart still thudding, she sped down the road, only obeying the speed limit a few miles later. What the hell had that been about? Were they the same people Emily had seen? She needed to know but had no idea how she could possibly find out. What had they been planning on doing with her?

Her heartbeat started to slow again, but she could still feel it in her throat. What would have happened if she hadn't fought them off? What about Isabel? She'd left her there. What would they do to her? She pulled out her phone and realized as she stared at it that she didn't have Isabel's number. She felt like the worst friend, even if they barely knew each other. She'd check on her at work the next day; it was all she could do.

Back home, Hannah tried to think of what to tell Emily. She heard her in the shower, and she didn't want to ruin their night with the strange news of her recent encounter with the asshole LARPers, but hiding it didn't seem any better of an idea. She took a seat in their kitchen and sipped a beer. If only Emily didn't have work, they could stay in and order pizza. She wanted to cower in their apartment, but she had to go to work the next day, and she wasn't willing to lose this internship. "Fuck," she muttered, draining the rest of the bottle in a single swig.

"That you, honey?" Emily called from down the hall.

"Yeah, I just got back."

"All right, give me a minute. Unless you wanted to have that quickie we discussed earlier. I have to head to work pretty soon."

"I don't think we have time." She wasn't at all in the mood, but she didn't want to worry Emily. But she should tell her. Why was this so difficult?

"You just keep saying that." Still glistening from her shower, Emily rounded the corner and gave her a quick kiss. Hannah found her eyes drawn to the toned abs, perky breasts, and ample hips of the woman she was falling for. Though at this point, the abs were all the more impressive, as she'd never seen Emily work out once, and she tended to eat nearly as much as Hannah did. "Did work go okay?"

Say yes. That was all she had to do. But doing so would be giving in to her fear, and she was stronger than that. "It…" she started, searching for a way to explain.

Emily's brow creased. "Honey? What happened?"

Hannah glanced between her abs and her eyes. Neither one quite helped. "There were these weird guys. I think they may have been the ones you saw in the bar before. They were wearing armor and had swords."

Emily gulped, her jaw dropping. She knelt. "What happened?"

"They came at me after work." She sighed. "One of them grabbed me, but it wasn't a big thing."

"What do you mean they grabbed you?" Emily growled, her blunt fingernails digging into the arm of the chair as she stared intently.

"You don't need to be angry. It's really nothing. One of them grabbed my wrist, but I don't think they were trying to harm me. They seemed confused and like they wanted to talk," she said. "I pushed them off and drove away. Nothing happened. You don't need to worry."

"Something clearly *did* happen. He grabbed you. Don't tell me not to worry!"

"Babe, it's okay." Hannah took her hand, pulling it away from the chair with some coaxing. "You don't need to worry. Security kicked them out of the building in the first place, and I think they were just crazy. They were babbling some nonsense about Thor or something. I'm fine. And I'm safe now."

"And I'm about to leave, and you'll be stuck here alone."

"They were crazy people on foot. They didn't follow me here."

"But…" Emily sighed. "I really don't want to have to call the cops. But we probably should."

"And tell them what? That one touched me and then let me go and said weird things? I pushed him a lot harder than anything he did. I don't think they were trying to hurt me." She'd seen the look in his eyes, heard his voice. He seemed confused, but how could she possibly explain that to Emily?

"Should I call out of work? I'm really okay with it."

"No. I'm fine. If you want to do anything, maybe order some pizza?"

Emily crossed her arms. "Is food all you think about? They could've done anything to you. And I wasn't there to protect you."

"But they didn't, I'm fine, and now I'm hungry, and you don't want me to go out."

Emily rolled her eyes. "Fine. I'll do that. Can I at least call Alys? I don't want you to be alone."

Hannah took her hands. "I promise. I'm okay. I don't need a babysitter. And besides, I barely know them, and I don't think they like me. Just go to work."

Emily's eyebrows furrowed. "Hannah…" She sighed. "Fine, but if anything at all happens, call the cops. Promise me."

How could she argue with that? Hannah smiled, trying not to let any fear show. The two men hadn't seemed like they'd wanted to hurt her, but that hadn't made it any less terrifying. "I will."

"All right. You're sure you don't want me to stay?"

"Yes." Hannah gestured to the bedroom. "Go, get dressed. I'll be okay. Thank you."

Emily nodded, still watching her. "Fine. Call me if you need anything, and I can duck out early. You matter more than my job."

Hannah tried not to tear up. She'd wanted her job for so long, and even if it wasn't quite the same for Emily, she knew she liked bartending. Would Hannah be able to say the same? The answer came so easily, she almost wanted to laugh at herself. She'd give up just about anything for Emily, no matter how crazy that sounded.

The next two days passed uneventfully. Emily kept checking on Hannah, no matter how many times she insisted she was fine. Though since they worked opposite shifts, it was hard to be too upset by the brief quick glimpses of concern.

Emily finally had a day off, and Hannah was thrilled to actually get to spend time with her. Just, hopefully they could avoid focusing on that incident the other day. She tried to think of something special to do that would be properly romantic, but the best she came up with was that bar they went to on their first date. It wasn't near their apartment, but cheap beer and delicious food was a hard prospect to beat. The nostalgia only added to that.

They sat at the same table they'd sat at on their first date and ordered a beer they hadn't tried before. They were promised that it was rich and hoppy, and that sounded like the perfect way to begin the day. Hannah drained hers immediately, feeling a good deal cheerier.

"Has work been okay?" Emily tried.

Hannah rolled her eyes, although she couldn't help but grin. It was hard to be annoyed when Emily's concern was so sweet. "Babe, I love that you're this worried about me, but I'm really fine."

"I wasn't—"

"You were. And it's sweet. No, they haven't showed up again, like I told you when you asked after I first got home. Other than that, work has been great. I'm making the numbers add up. Haven't lost the company any money, and I've been talking to Isabel a bunch too. It's been really nice. I think I actually made a new friend. Even if I still feel awful about running off on her."

"You didn't run off. She was in a car too."

"She said the same thing." Hannah sighed, the merest speck of regret breaking through her cheer. "She left right behind me, and she was fine. She gave me her number, so if anything like that ever happened again, I wouldn't have to worry. I just feel bad."

"I know, honey. I can't believe that happened. What do those armored assholes even want with you?"

Hannah shook her head as she shrugged. "I don't know. Something about Thor? They seemed so confused, but it was really scary."

Emily still looked terrified. "I know. I've been worried sick about them showing up again. I won't let them hurt you," she said, taking Hannah's hand and squeezing it. The gesture was reassuring, even if it didn't match her expression.

"It's okay. I don't think they meant any harm. They were just kind of intimidating."

A gruff voice came from just beside them. "I really am sorry about that."

CHAPTER NINE

Emily and Hannah turned to find the subjects of their discussion standing a few feet away. They looked downright bashful; the taller of the two was even staring at the floor and softly kicking at the ground with his leather boots.

"What?" Emily asked.

"We didn't realize that you remember nothing. We were only trying to get your attention. Both of you. We have been for months," the other said. He sounded more confident, his calm gray eyes meeting theirs with only a slight reluctance. What the hell was going on? None of this made any sense. "We thought if you saw us, then you'd want to talk, but people kept stopping us. It never occurred that to you, we must look like raving lunatics off the street."

"Sorry, Father. Sorry, Mother," the other added, still not looking up.

"What the fuck?" Emily looked between the two of them. How long had it been since she'd last blinked? Not a word of this made any sense.

"We left our swords outside, if that helps at all."

Hannah chewed her lip, staring, the fear on her face seeming to give way to curiosity. "Okay. If you're apparently not 'raving lunatics'—which is very ableist, and I'm still not entirely convinced of—then who are you?"

Emily stared at her. Her reaction was just as crazy as what was happening.

"My name is Modi," the smaller—relatively speaking—one said. "My brother here is Magni. Apparently, you don't remember us, but you're our parents."

"Come again?" Hannah sounded shocked but nowhere near as much as Emily felt.

"You're Thor and Sif," Magni muttered.

Emily finally blinked, but she didn't wake up, and nothing made any more sense. "I'm sorry?"

"What?" Hannah asked.

"You're our parents. You're Thor." He pointed to Hannah. "And you're Sif." He pointed to Emily.

Emily let out a nervous laugh. This was so ridiculous. What did that even mean? "So raving lunatics sounds about right."

"You *do* know I'm a woman, right?" Hannah asked.

"That threw me off at first too," Magni replied. "But Mimir seemed quite confident. You've been brought back. We were so excited that we rushed down to Midgard to find you. Our parents were alive again, but then…" He trailed off.

"You found out we aren't your parents?" Emily suggested.

Modi shook his head. "We found out that you didn't know who you were. We intend to fix that."

How crazy was this guy? Emily would remember if she gave birth, and a thorough examination proved that Hannah had no way to knock her up. What was he going to do if she didn't play along? A chill ran up her spine. "And what do you mean by that?"

"Sorry, that did sound threatening, didn't it? I didn't mean it like that. I meant that we want to jog your memories. Does anything seem familiar about us, Father?"

Hannah shook her head.

He nodded, looking as if he was on the verge of tears. "What are we to do, brother?"

"There must be some way we can prove it?"

"Do you want to leave?" Emily asked Hannah, not taking her eyes off the men. They needed to get out of here.

"Wait, no, please," Magni insisted. "Give us a chance. There has to be some way we could remind you of who you used to be. This must be the work of Hel. Why else wouldn't you remember?"

"Or not have a beard?"

"What?" Emily asked.

"I've got it," Modi shouted. "There are two things Father could never fail at. If she can do them, then not only will my doubts be assuaged, but hers may be as well. No mere human could best Father in strength or drinking." He gestured toward the horn hung from his belt, a sloshing sound coming from it as he moved.

"Hey, if you're buying, I'm in," Hannah said.

"Are you crazy?" Emily asked. Why was Hannah going along with this? She was starting to sound as mad as they were. No matter how broke they were and how much alcohol they were going to go through that night. Okay, she had a point on this one spot.

"I'm still really hungry, and we haven't had dinner yet." The waitress was doubtless too scared to come out and deal with these men. Emily glanced around the room. Several people had leapt under tables and a few others seemed to have fled to the bathroom or the back door. One person had their phone out, recording them. "But if we're having a drinking contest, we're getting drinks from here. I don't trust whatever you might have in that horn thingy." Wow, at least she'd thought one part of this through. Hannah was way too smart to be acting like this. She didn't actually believe them, did she? Emily took another look at the two giants. Could they really be her kids? No, of course not, how could she even think such a thing?

"Hannah, are you sure about this?" Emily asked, flinching as one of them made the slightest move, but he didn't take a step toward her.

Hannah shrugged. "They keep following us around. I want answers. Don't you?"

"They're clearly delusional. That isn't enough of an answer?"

Hannah chewed on her lip, looking between Emily and the lunatics. "What alternative do we have? They're not hurting us. They're just confused. Let's prove them wrong, and they'll leave us alone."

It sounded like there was more to it, but Hannah apparently wasn't going to say, and Emily certainly wasn't leaving her alone here. "Fine, but if they kill us, it's your fault."

Hannah shrugged. "I can live with that. Let's get drinking."

Magni slid a chair over. He seemed reluctant to sit in the booth, maybe trying to give them some degree of space. It was a welcome change. "First things first. Since your death, I am the strongest living being in the universe. If you can even come close to me in might, then that should show you something."

"Well, if I don't know how strong you are, that doesn't tell me much." Hannah offered a cheeky grin. Emily stared. Had she run off and had a few dozen beers when she wasn't looking?

"Very well. Look out that window." He pointed to a car on the street. The chair shrilly squeaked as he moved, heading outside. He stood next to the car, a perfectly normal sedan. Then it was suddenly several feet in the air in one of his massive hands.

Hannah stared her mouth hanging open. "That can't be possible. And they think I can do that? It's ridiculous."

Emily blinked repeatedly, trying to wake herself up from this dream.

The car's alarm started blaring as he set it down. He strolled back inside and took his seat again, a self-satisfied smirk on his lips. "I don't know why that thing is making that noise, but are you convinced? It hasn't cursed me, has it?"

"Can we shut the alarm off?"

"Um," a voice sounded from under a nearby table. "Okay." A man peeked up and pressed a button on a key fob, and the alarm ended with a chirp.

"There's no need to fear," Magni insisted. "I intend no harm to anyone. Please, beer wench, come back out and serve."

"If I'm your mother, I raised you horribly," Emily spat back.

This was met with a mighty laugh that echoed through the little establishment. "Everyone, please, relax and enjoy your food and drink. I shall pay for all of this, and any damage we cause." Producing a heavy cloth bag from inside his armor, he tossed it onto the counter. "I believe that should cover everything?"

The bartender climbed up from behind the bar and untied the bag, causing a gold coin to spill out onto the ground. "I'll have to ask my manager."

"Very well."

"Can I call them?"

"Of course." There was a very good chance that he didn't know what phones were.

The bartender pressed more than three buttons on his cell phone, so it was likely he wasn't calling the cops. He probably just wanted that tip. Emily could hardly blame him. She was tempted to grab that fallen coin. "How do you want to test my strength?" Hannah asked. "I'm not really a fighter."

"Now, those are words I never thought I'd hear my father say." Another laugh bellowed forth from his belly. "Modi, sit and watch while I show you the truth of Mimir's words. This is our father. I would know those eyes anywhere. I trust you know how to arm wrestle?"

Emily leaned back, rolling her eyes in disbelief. Somehow, it always came back to arm wrestling in this bar.

Hannah nodded slowly. "I have no idea why I'm going along with this. You're lucky I love arm wrestling and drinking."

"That's our father," Magni said.

With a groan, Hannah thudded her elbow on the table and held her hand out, staring into the gray eyes of the man who claimed to be their son. There was no way she could win. She couldn't lift a car. But at least she could prove him wrong, and then they'd stop harassing them. Right?

"Are you ready, Father?"

"I'd be more ready if you stopped calling me that."

He paused as if only now realizing how weird that must sound. "Then, do you have names? It would feel strange to call our parents such, but if that is your preference, I believe we can accommodate you. Can we not, Modi?"

He nodded. "We can, brother."

"I'm Hannah," she said, her hand already extended.

"Are we seriously doing this?" Emily asked.

"These guys keep showing up places. It's just all too ridiculous. I need answers."

Groaning, she shrugged. "Fine. I'm Emily."

"Hannah, Emily, it's nice to meet you." Magni took Hannah's hand, his grip looking likely to crush the tiny girl's. Emily dared not breathe.

"I'm glad we can be civil now," Modi said. "I wish we'd known this all from the beginning. It really is a pleasure to meet you, and I hope that we haven't offended you too gravely."

"Nah, it's okay," Hannah said, sounding far too eager for the little contest. "Let's do this." Magni's face tensed, his lip trembling as his hand pushed against Hannah's. She didn't move, and she appeared as cheerful as she had a moment earlier. Hannah was weirdly strong, but this man had just lifted a car. "Are you holding back?" Hannah's voice was soft, almost scared, but with a strength that reassured Emily. Whatever was going on, no matter how crazy this was, at least Hannah would be here. And having a super strong girlfriend was hardly the worst fate in the world.

"A little," he admitted, his voice sounding strained. He looked to be redoubling his efforts, as veins popped out on his head and arm, and sweat beaded on his forehead.

Hannah met his strength, letting out a chuckle as she leaned in, gritting her teeth. Emily's annoyance gave way to staring at her girlfriend's biceps with undisguised lust. "Well, I am too." Emily swallowed, not believing the words. She really wasn't struggling? This wasn't possible.

Modi's hand thudded on the table, the wood splintering under them as Hannah jumped to her feet and cheered.

He stared at her, his jaw dropping. "But you don't even have your belt."

"What a weird response to having your ass kicked." She laughed. "Does this mean I have lightning powers?"

"What?" Modi asked. "No. You're not Zeus or anything."

"Is Zeus real?"

He shrugged. This was only raising more questions.

"You were just hustling her, right?" Emily asked, unable to move her gaze from Hannah's arm.

"No." Magni panted, falling back in his chair and almost sliding out of it. "I was giving that my all. She is Father…I mean, she is Thor."

Hannah smirked.

"This still doesn't mean I'm a goddess," Emily said, her voice weak.

"That is much harder to prove." Modi took a seat next to his brother, clapping him on the shoulder. "Mother—that is to say, Sif—er, Emily. I'm sorry this is so difficult. Her hair. It was the most beautiful thing in the world, to the point that even a golden veil was considered a poor substitute for it."

"Your hair *is* amazing, babe."

"You are going along with this way too easily." Emily finally tore her gaze away to stare at the men claiming to be her children. "Having amazing hair doesn't make me a god."

"I don't know how else to show you."

She looked pleadingly at Hannah. "This doesn't make any sense."

"I know it doesn't. I still can't believe it, but I just won an arm-wrestling match with someone who could lift a car."

Biting her lip, Emily stared at everyone. Was that really all Sif did? In the movies, she at least fought and then disappeared forever. Wow, was she really that insignificant? But she was Thor's wife, apparently. Was that why she'd felt so drawn to Hannah? She'd never been like this with anyone before, but with Hannah, they'd come together almost instantly. They'd even moved in after only a week. She'd assumed she was finally living up to lesbian stereotypes, but could there be more to it? "Fuck it. Clearly, Hannah can beat up both of you if you're trying to pull something, and I make it a rule to never turn down free drinks." Her mouth was dry for so many reasons, and she was trying to go along with this, but what was she supposed to do? And more importantly, really? All she got was amazing hair? Hannah got superstrength, and she, what, got pretty hair? Damn, at least Alys hadn't let her cut it.

"Then it's time for my test." Modi grinned. "Thor could outdrink anyone, even other Aesir and Jotunn. He once drank the ocean down several feet when it was turned into beer."

"What?"

"I assume it was the term 'beer wench' that offended you? What should I call her instead?"

"Hey, could we get about thirty rounds here?" Hannah called. She was already back to going along with it. Then again, it was Hannah and free beer, so at least one thing in the world made sense.

"Wait," Emily said.

"What's the matter, Moth—Emily?" Modi asked.

Emily strode across the room to the guy recording them. "Hey, uh, I didn't mind so much when it was just crazy guys, but I'd really rather my girlfriend not go viral, so…" She held out her hand.

"Huh?" The man replied.

She snatched the phone and deleted the video, then scrolled through to make sure there weren't any others. "Did you send this to anyone?"

He shook his head.

"Then great." She grinned. "Enjoy the free food and I guess the free show. No flash photography or recording, anyone," she shouted as she headed back to the table. Now she was acting as crazy as they were. But Hannah had superpowers. She couldn't let her end up dissected in some lab. The whole reason they'd agreed to this contest in the first place was so crazy people would stop following them. If footage got out, that would only ensure they would keep following them.

She took a deep breath. It looked like she was gonna have to go along with this insanity. "All right. Let's do this."

After twenty-five drinks, Modi's head hit the table, and he seemed unable to continue. Both Emily and Magni were given a single drink from the remaining five, but Hannah took the other three for herself. Emily's head was swimming, but she wasn't anywhere near gone yet. So she got minor drinking powers? She'd always been able to hold her liquor, at least around anyone who wasn't Hannah. But even there she got a better power! Hannah drained the three drinks and continued keeping pace.

Soon, Emily found herself unable to continue. "I'm tapping out."

Magni hiccupped. "Does this prove it yet? No human could handle what either of you two did."

"I've seen humans drink a *lot*," Emily insisted.

"Well, those humans belong in Val…" He trailed off, his eyes growing distant and sad. "I should take this pitiful fool back home. We have much to tell the other Aesir. We'll find you again soon."

"Okay. This has been…" Hannah paused, seeming to search for the right word. "Interesting."

"So we're Norse gods, whatever," Emily muttered. She must have been drunk if she was starting to believe it.

"I bid the both of you a good night. I believe Modi's coin should be good for a bit of food if that contest built up an appetite. It should only be a few days." Hoisting his brother over his shoulder, he walked out the door, leaving them with a great many unanswered questions and a hell of an appetite.

The waitress's attention was already on them, so it took no effort to wave her over. "Could we get five orders of nachos, two orders of pulled pork sliders, two grilled cheeses, and two burgers?" Hannah asked.

They enjoyed their food and the rest of their night, but every time Emily tried to bring up what had happened, Hannah brushed her off. It worried her, but she could wait. Not everyone could process something this big so quickly. Or maybe she was just drunk.

Either way, Emily savored the chance to reaffirm how very not-straight her girlfriend was. She could see how familiar they were, how well everything fit together. It felt like they'd known each other for centuries.

CHAPTER TEN

None of this made any sense. Hannah sat at the desk a few feet from the bed she'd been sharing with Emily for the last week. She'd barely been able to sleep. She'd tried so hard to keep her cool. The guys really didn't seem like they meant any harm, and she didn't want to piss them off, and they were pretty convincing, but it was just all so insane. Maybe she could accept that she was a god. Maybe. But what did it mean for her relationship? It couldn't be that she was predestined for this. That had nothing to do with it. Right? She'd just met a beautiful woman and fell for her.

And moved in with her barely a week later.

Because the timing had worked out. Why wouldn't she? She was graduating college and following her dreams, and she'd met the most amazing woman who was absolutely her type—

"Right," she muttered, blinking away the tears she'd been trying to hold back. Of course Emily was her type. They'd been together for centuries. Millennia? How long ago had everything happened? No wonder she'd fallen in love the second they met. It wasn't her doing it; it was just Thor.

She stomped out and yanked on the bedroom door. With a wretched creaking and the sound of metal straining, it popped clean out of the wall. The room didn't have any windows, but the light filtering in from the hallway was now unobstructed, and she could see the hinges hanging from the hunk of wood in her hand.

A confused noise came from the bed. "Hannah?" Emily asked, the words muffled by sleep.

"It's fine," she spat back, choking down more sobs.

This was why she hadn't had a bedroom door as a kid, wasn't it? She remembered having one when she was much younger, but when she was ten or eleven, she vaguely recalled it breaking somehow, and she didn't get it back for years. Her parents had never really talked to her about that. Did they know?

What if they did? What if that was how those two weirdos had tracked her down? Why wouldn't they have told her anything? What could they have been thinking? Had they hidden everything from her?

No, that didn't make sense. Her mom had been so worried when she'd talked about Emily.

But that didn't mean she knew Emily was Sif.

Hannah wanted to scream. Why was she treating this like it was real? She dropped the door and sprinted to the hallway by the kitchen, dropping to the floor to start her push-ups.

She was strong because she worked out. That was all.

And sure, she'd been strong before she'd started crew and hadn't really worked out until then, and she'd had to learn to hold back to keep pace with the other girls, but that didn't mean she was Thor.

Even if crazy old guys in armor insisted she was. Even if she fell in love with a woman they thought was Sif. It didn't make it true. None of it had to be real.

She tried to focus on her breathing, on the exercise, on the feeling of her muscles straining. But they never did.

Could she really lift a car?

She couldn't stop thinking about it. She'd watched that man pick up a car with ease, and then she'd crushed him in arm wrestling. But that didn't mean she could do it. Did he throw the game? But she'd seen the strain on his face. She'd felt how hard he was pushing against her. It didn't seem like he was faking.

She'd finished her third round of sit-ups and was working on the matching set of jumping jacks and couldn't get the image out of her head. He'd picked up a fucking car! It wasn't possible. No one could do that. Right?

When she finished the last set, she could almost feel it calling to her. It was like a gravitational pull that she had to resist, tugging her toward the stairs and the door, trying to take her out front to Emily's car. But there was no way.

She stared at the car. She barely even remembered walking outside. That hopefully meant she hadn't ripped the doors off the wall. How much was Emily's security deposit anyway?

She squared her feet and crouched beside the Nissan, adjusting her stance as she tried to figure out where to grip it. Where had he grabbed it? The axle? She didn't know much about cars.

Oh, well, it was old, and insurance would probably cover any damage. She took a deep breath and, making sure to put all the weight on her legs, gripped the bottom and started to stand. She'd expected it to be a strain, to feel her body protest and the car to resist, but it came up with her. It was heavy, sure, but it didn't feel much heavier than all those boxes when she'd moved in. The only difference was that the car was a bit more awkward to hold.

Hannah raised the car straight above her head, and her biceps trembled. Finally, it felt like a bit of a workout. So this was what everyone else always whined about? All the other girls on her team had complained about the pain and aches of rowing, and she had never really gotten it. Sure, after eight or ten hours it would start to get to her, but it was never that bad. But now, holding at least a ton over her head, she could feel it. It was exhilarating.

And it meant her sons—no she couldn't call them that, it was too crazy—those armored assholes were right.

The joy drained out of her, and a pit formed in her stomach. With a good deal less grace, she set the car down, and it bounced on its tires. That probably wasn't good.

"Fuck." She wanted to scream it, but she only dared to whisper. It was all true. She was Thor. And that meant Emily had to be Sif. And that meant it wasn't Hannah's choice to be with her. This wasn't about her meeting an amazing woman and falling in love; it was some preordained bullshit. She was only with Emily because she'd always been with her, and she hadn't had a choice in the matter.

No wonder she'd asked Emily out, and no wonder it had worked. She never flirted with staff anywhere. It was super creepy. And Emily hadn't thought it was weird. All because it was supposed to happen.

The world blurred as the tears came again. Her entire life was a lie.

Even being a god didn't put a great spin on that.

No wonder she ate so much. She was actually a giant Norse asshole. And a guy. Was that why she was gay? It had been such a scary thing growing up. Megan had sure freaked out when she'd told her. And her parents hadn't been weird about it at all. Because they knew she was Thor? She loved them so much, she wanted to trust them, to believe that they were as in the dark as she was, but how could she? How could she trust anyone now?

She hurried inside to the bathroom, convinced she was going to throw up everything she'd eaten last night, but nothing came. She felt so sick, and nothing was working to stop it.

After a quick shower, she felt no better. There was beer in the fridge, but she'd end up drinking all of it, and she had work in a few hours. She almost wished Emily hadn't had the day off, as then, she wouldn't have had to wake up next to her feeling like this.

And she hated that thought. She loved Emily so much. How could she want to not be around her? Shit. She really did, didn't she? Her stomach dropped, and her blood ran cold. Probably not literally, but she was a god, so how was she to know at this point? That wasn't what mattered. She loved Emily. She'd tried so hard to hold it back. It was too soon. Didn't that just prove it was Thor's emotions? But it didn't feel like Thor's. She knew her feelings, at least, she was pretty certain she did. It wasn't just Thor's love for Sif. It was hers for Emily. Wasn't it?

But how could she want it either? Not when she knew none of it was real. It was all just some old creepy god's feelings for his wife, and she was just along for the ride.

April was probably awake and wasn't likely doing much. Her summer courses hadn't started yet. Hannah could call her and talk about it. But what could she tell her? What would she believe?

Megan wasn't any better an option.

Clearly, she should tell everything to Isabel at work. She'd known her for like three days, and if Isabel thought she was insane, she could easily have Hannah fired. It was the perfect plan.

So she had no one to turn to. Except Emily. But she couldn't bring herself to do that. Not now. Not yet. Not when she hadn't sorted out her feelings. But she couldn't do that without someone to talk to.

It was easier to rid herself of temptation. She threw on a professional-looking dress and grabbed Emily's keys. She'd buy doughnuts and coffee and take the time to think before work. Maybe by the time she was finally home, she'd be ready to talk.

❖

Work had done nothing to ease Hannah's troubled mind. Isabel had tried striking up a conversation, but Hannah couldn't focus on anything. She was lucky the accounts were all so easy, or she'd have been in some serious trouble the way her mind was. She couldn't keep going like this. This job was the dream that she'd worked toward the past four years, and all she had to do was make it through an internship, and it was hers. If she couldn't even focus on that, then she'd lose everything. She couldn't let this stupid god bullshit take everything from her.

As she pulled up in front of their apartment, she yanked the car into park and barely breathed as she watched the gearshift. When she pulled her hand away, it stayed in place. She hadn't broken it. Probably.

The car didn't move, so it was in park. That was a good sign.

Hannah held in her tears and hurried around the back of the house to go into the basement apartment. Emily's apartment. She wasn't even on the lease. Which meant she could get out of this if she needed to. But was that what she wanted?

Not even twenty-four hours earlier, she wouldn't have questioned it in the slightest. She knew how much she loved Emily, how much she trusted her. Now she didn't know anything except that she was the Norse god of thunder. And didn't even have lightning powers. It was such bullshit.

"You're home," Emily called from the living room. She sounded so relieved. So happy Hannah was there. How did she not feel the same dread that Hannah felt? The same loss of free will? Why was she fine with this?

"I am," she called back, trying to sound appropriately chipper.

"Everything okay? I didn't hear from you all day. And I messaged you after I saw the bedroom door was broken. It wasn't those guys, our...sons again, was it?" She sounded worried now. Apparently, Hannah hadn't managed to fake it at all. "Something happen at work?"

She could lie. Say it was that and run off to the bedroom, but Emily didn't have work that night. With a heavy sigh, Hannah grabbed two beers from the fridge and began the arduous trek to the living room. The fifteen or so feet felt like the longest hike April had ever dragged her on. She had to face up to this. She had to talk to Emily. There wasn't a way around it.

"Hey there," Alys said as Hannah rounded the corner. They were draped nonchalantly over Emily's recliner and swirling a mostly empty beer over the side of the chair.

Hannah stared. "Hi..."

They flashed a quick grin.

"What's up, honey?" Emily asked, patting the spot next to her on the couch.

"Uh..." Hannah glanced at Alys.

"Oh!" Emily grinned at Hannah. "Don't worry. I told them."

Hannah blinked, but those words didn't make any more sense, so she tried again.

"Being gods, pretty badass," Alys said.

"For her maybe," Emily grumbled. "I get what, perfect hair and a green thumb? I barely even eat vegetables. I mean, I could try starting a garden or something, but it's such bullshit."

Hannah stared at her. That was the part that troubled her? She had a pretty low bar for bullshit. "It's not like it's amazing for me either."

Emily rolled her eyes. "Please, you get superstrength. I mean, hell, when you picked me up on our first date you had me then and there. It's not like I could've just flashed my golden locks to win you."

"But you did," Hannah shouted and felt their eyes on her. They didn't know what she meant by that yet, but she'd already started. She couldn't just leave it there. "It didn't take a thing for me to fall for you. Because you're Sif, and I'm Thor. We're supposed to be living our own lives and following our dreams, and then I fall madly in love with you, and it turns out it's because I was meant to. Because Thor wanted me to. Hell, how am I supposed to know that he didn't want me to be an accountant too?" She wanted to sink into the couch and let it envelop her, but Emily was right there, and she wasn't ready for that. And she couldn't exactly throw herself into Alys's lap, now could she?

"What are you talking about?" Emily asked, staring. "You..."

Hannah shook her head and let her arms droop, the sloshing reminding her that she was holding beers. She tossed one on the couch next to Emily and popped the cap off her own, taking a long swig. It did nothing to clear her mind. "I'm Thor. You're Sif."

"Right," Emily said. "I get that you're freaking out. I was too. It's why I invited Alys over." She kept watching Hannah, biting her lip, looking like she wanted to say something, but Alys beat her to it.

"And why I pointed out how awesome it is. Seriously, it doesn't have to be a bad thing. You're gods. That's cool as hell," Alys said, clearly trying to lighten the mood.

"And apparently, those two were ancient lovers meant to be together or something ridiculous like that."

Alys studied her. "They weren't necessarily meant to be together in the myths."

"What do you know?" Hannah asked, regretting her words immediately. Alys wasn't the one she was mad at. Hell, Emily wasn't even the one she was mad at. It was Thor. And she was Thor.

"Well, I've read every single major text on the subject in English. I never managed to learn old Norse. So I think I know a few things at least." They sounded so hesitant. Had her words hurt that much?

"Oh." Hannah slumped all the more and finished the rest of her beer.

"If we weren't meant to be together, what does it matter?" Emily asked. "Or hell, even if we were."

"There's not really any destiny with it that I recall," Alys said. "I could do some reading if you want, and I mean, Sif literally means wife, but beyond that, she's not even the only person Thor was with, and he's not the only one she was with. Thor even had a kid that wasn't hers."

"Well…It still matters," Hannah muttered. "How am I supposed to know that this is real if it was all Thor?" She stared at the woman she loved. "I've fallen for you in a way I didn't even know I could. It scared my friends, and it even scared me. You're my world. And I've known you for like two weeks. That doesn't worry you?"

Emily shrugged. "We're gay." She glanced back to Alys, shaking her head. "My name really means wife? I am the worst god."

"Still!" Hannah stomped her foot, cracking the wooden floor. "I need to know that this isn't someone else's choice. I need to know I'm in control of my life."

Alys cleared their throat. "I'm sure it's nothing like that."

Emily held up her hand. "I can handle this." She stood and reached for Hannah's free hand, but Hannah didn't give it to her, so she dropped hers to her side. "I love you too."

It was the first time she'd ever said those words. It should've felt amazing. But it just added to her dread. "How do you know that?"

"I feel it. I know it when I see you, when I think about you." She reached again, and Hannah didn't resist this time, her heart skipping as Emily traced along her knuckles with a thumb. It felt so nice. So right. And that was precisely the problem. "I've never felt like this for anyone else. I know it's only been a couple weeks, but I can't imagine not being with you."

"Exactly." Hannah pulled free and stepped away, facing the wall and rubbing her eyes. She could still feel Emily's touch. How right it felt. "It feels too good to be true. Because it isn't true. It's not *us*. It's them. It's Thor and Sif's feelings."

"It doesn't feel like an old married couple to me."

That stopped her for a moment. She wanted Emily all the time, and their opposite schedules were so painful. All she wanted each morning was to wake up and see her. And maybe do a few other things to her. Would Thor feel that way about Sif? Especially when they'd been together for probably centuries? She really needed to learn about mythology now. She had no idea how long they might've been together, but gods were old, so centuries seemed a safe bet. "Well, we hadn't seen each other in like twenty-seven years or whatever."

"And it doesn't feel like that. At least not exclusively that. I know my feelings. They're no one else's."

Hannah shrugged and sniffled, not bothering to stop the tears running down her cheeks.

The old leather of the recliner creaked. "How about I talk to her?" Alys asked. "I'm an impartial observer who already knows who you two are and is well-versed in Norse mythology. I'm the perfect person for this."

"But—" Emily started.

"I know. You want to comfort her, but you only seem to be scaring her. Come on, Hannah. I'll buy you dinner, tell you about Norse mythology, and you can vent to me about the whole thing."

Hannah wanted to say no. But that dinner was hard to pass up. She and Emily both ate a lot—apparently because they were gods—and she hadn't received her first paycheck yet. "Pizza?"

"Sure."

She turned around, sizing up Alys. "I can pick the place?"

They nodded. "Fine by me."

Emily said, "I can—"

"Emily." Alys squeezed her shoulder. "She's freaking out over you. Let me take care of it. I promise, it'll be okay. I'll bring her back safe and sound by curfew."

Hannah crossed her arms and rolled her eyes.

"As long as she's back by midnight," Emily joked, though she didn't sound into it.

Alys flashed a wink. "After you, then." They gestured toward the door.

Hannah nodded, dabbed at her eyes, and marched to the door. At least she already had her shoes on.

CHAPTER ELEVEN

By the time Hannah finished inhaling her entire pizza without saying a word, Alys was beginning to wonder if they were actually going to talk about any of this. Damn it, they were so bad at this junk. They had years of experience manipulating people. Why was this so much more awkward? Hannah was cute, but not short-circuit their brain cute.

"It's really cool that you're Thor," they finally tried. Could that have possibly been lamer? At least she'd never suspect that they were secretly trying to control her life for the goddess of the dead, as they were far too incompetent for that to make sense.

Hannah shrugged.

"Seriously. I know you think it's some horrible fate, but it isn't." They remembered when Hel had first told them they were Loki. They'd been homeless at the time, begging for food, and Hel had appeared before them. They'd thought the hunger must've finally gotten to them after only managing to scrape enough together for a bag of chips and a gas station hot dog a few days before. Hel had offered them power, the ability to do anything. They'd stolen a feast's worth of food and had changed their entire appearance and had eaten like royalty for the first time in months. "It's gotta be a little liberating, right? You have superpowers. You're a god. You don't have to worry about all that human stuff anymore."

"I'm an accountant," she said. "That's all I want. I don't want to deal with this stupid god stuff. I want to settle down with the woman I'm madly in love with and have a nice boring life. It's all I've ever wanted. And now I don't even know if that's me wanting it." She sniffled, a tear running down her cheek.

Great, she was crying again. Alys really was hopeless. "Even if it is Thor who wants it, that's still you. Just because you're not the same as Thor was described doesn't mean there are two separate people inside you. You just have a longer past than you thought. That's all that's changed."

"What do you know?"

Their jaw dropped wide enough to fit the foot they they'd just shoved in there. How were they so bad at lying? Sure, they'd never had to lie that much, just misuse the truth and work a few spells, but still. "It's how I'd feel."

"Well, it's not how I feel. I had some crazy assholes claiming to be my kids show up and insist I was a god."

"That's certainly never happened to me."

Hannah harrumphed. "Can we get out of here? I need some fresh air."

"Yeah. Sure." They needed to fix this. There had to be something they could say. If Hannah left Emily, then Hel lost half of her leverage. And Alys was Emily's friend, not Hannah's, so it wasn't like she'd keep talking to them after a breakup. There was no way they could keep things going if Hannah did what it looked like she was thinking.

That was it! Not the being way too desperate for them not to break up for their own good, but Alys needed to get a handle on what Hannah was thinking. "I get that this whole thing is freaking you out," they said, opening the door for Hannah. "But what exactly are you planning?"

She looked up at them. She really did have beautiful green eyes. Alys could absolutely see what Emily saw in her. "What do you mean?"

They offered a weak smile and a shrug.

"I don't know." Hannah kicked some litter on the sidewalk as they walked outside. "I just want to have the choice. To not feel like it's all something I was forced into. To feel like I'm me and not some ancient god."

Alys felt the urge to grab her hand but resisted. They needed to be Hannah's friend for Hel's sake, but they couldn't let themself care too much. They didn't know what Hel might have in store for her. "I've read enough mythology to know Thor isn't controlling you. You're Hannah…what's your last name?"

"Olsen."

"Nice. Very Norse." Shit, that was a terrible thing to say right now. They were so excited to finally be able to talk about Norse mythology that they kept doing this. Next, they were going to say the reason they both ate so much was because they were Norse gods, and then they'd have ruined the whole scheme just to geek out about mythology. "You're Hannah Olsen. You're a dorky accountant lesbian, and Thor was none of those things. Hell, he was a transphobic asshole who constantly referred to his best friend with slurs that there aren't even proper translations for in modern English, and I've never heard you say a single transphobic thing."

"Huh?"

They were identifying with Loki. Openly. While talking to Hannah. How were they this stupid? Fourteen years of doing this, and a cute redhead was all it took to make them leap into volunteering that information. "Loki may have been a trans woman. It's not a super debated thing, but I read a doctoral student claiming it on Tumblr years ago, and it's always stuck with me. Basically, they're consistently referred to as 'ergi,' a slur that was used for the ancient Norse equivalent of trans women, and they don't take offense despite it being a massive insult considered legally worth killing over. Also, they jump at the chance to castrate themself with the slightest excuse. It's nothing major. Like I said, I like Norse mythology. I'm not sure if Emily has made this clear yet, but I'm a massive nerd." They were trying so hard to pull away from the topic. They couldn't let it seem like they were Loki. They took a deep breath, trying to get themself to calm down without being too obvious about it. "I probably know even more crazy theories about *Doctor Who*. Which I'm sure I could also discuss the trans representation in and have read obscure Tumblr posts on, but that's not really the point I'm trying to make. Thor was an asshole. You're not. You're an amazing, fun, caring weirdo who actually wants to be an accountant. And Emily is lucky to have you."

"Don't thank luck, thank Thor," she spat, speeding up, and Alys was glad their legs were so much longer.

"That's what I'm saying. Thor clearly doesn't control you. He *is* you. It must be hard to think of yourself as having been a different person, but that's the thing, you're not. Thor is as much Hannah as Hannah is Thor. I know you don't like having this strange past you didn't know about, but it's only part of who you are. And there's so much more to you." *Now just say you're Loki and that you get it. That'll go over well.*

"But I'm not. And it doesn't work like that. I didn't influence him, but he influenced me. How can I know that anything about myself is really me?"

"It's all you. You drink like a god, you can apparently bench-press a semi—which is badass as all hell—and all of those things make you Hannah. It's all you. You didn't fall in love with Emily because of your past. You fell in love with her because she's perfect for you." That might be a little too close to the destiny idea, but at least it wasn't quite there. They should've said because Emily was Hannah's type or something. They wanted to kick themself, but that would just be awkward.

Hannah took in a sharp breath and ducked down an alley, covering her face with her hands as she slumped against the wall. "How can I trust that? How can I trust anything I think or feel now? Any of it could just be Thor."

"And that's you. You're not possessed by him. You used to be him. I know it doesn't sound that different, but it is."

Hannah shook her head. "I keep flip-flopping between anger and sadness. And I want to hit someone, but I can't do that. And I want to be mad at Emily, but it's not her fault. I want to be mad at Thor, but that's apparently just me. I don't have anyplace to point my feelings. I don't even know who I can trust anymore."

"You can trust Emily. She's in the same boat as you." Alys wanted to add that she could trust them. It was the perfect time for it. Hannah would believe them, and they could use it. Why couldn't they bring themself to say it?

Hannah shrugged. "Maybe."

Alys hesitantly put their hands on Hannah's shoulders and bent at the knees to meet her eyes. "I promise. I get that this is all crazy, and we don't really know what's going on, but we're all just as confused." That was a straight-up lie. So they could bring themself to lie to her after all. "But we'll be here helping you. I know how scary it must be to talk about it, and I know we're not that close, but I'm more than happy to help."

Hannah stepped away, their hands fell from her, and she shook her head. "Why are you so okay with this? It doesn't even affect you, and yet you're so cool about it. What, are we an exciting show for you? Just more myths to read? Or are you so unfazed because…What? Have you met other gods? Why do you even believe it? I watched a man lift a car yesterday and proceeded to do so myself this morning, and I barely believe it."

"You what?" How strong was she? And without the belt?

"Exactly."

They had to come up with something. Hannah couldn't get too suspicious. What could they even say? "I don't like doubting people. I know Emily, and she wouldn't lie about this. Plus, I saw the door you ripped off its hinges." Wait, they'd already moved away from that point. They were changing the subject. Did that make it even more suspicious? Their mouth went dry. Was the jig up? No, they could save this. "And I don't think you'd lie either."

Hannah walked down the alley without a word, and Alys ran after. "Hannah?"

"I don't fucking know," she shouted, rounding on them. "This is all so crazy, and you're so cool about it. And of course, you're such a good friend to Emily and now to me. And my life is so perfect. And it all makes it feel all the more insane. I have nothing to be upset about, and yet I feel like none of it is mine."

"Well, then, I'm sure you won't mind handing it over," a voice behind them said. It sounded masculine, gruff, and maybe a little drunk.

Hannah looked around Alys. "I'm sorry?"

Alys turned slowly and saw a gun in the hands of a scruffy-looking man in a dirty jacket and jeans. There but for the grace of Hel… "How can we help you?" they asked, trying to sound calm but unable to stop a nervous burst of laughter.

"Evening, ladies." He offered a grin, showing rotten teeth. "I don't want to hurt you, but this is my alley, and there's a toll for using it for your screaming matches."

"Oh, we're not—" Hannah started, but Alys silenced them with a panicked look. "And they're not a lady."

Alys glared at her. What the hell was she thinking?

He stepped forward, clicking his tongue. "Portland, I swear, but all right, I won't be unreasonable. Just all the cash you have. It's so much kinder than pickpocketing. You won't even have to cancel your credit cards."

"Yeah, you're a swell guy," Alys said.

Hannah stared at him. Alys had been wondering the entire evening just what was going through her mind, but now it seemed especially pressing. They didn't want to get shot, but they suspected they could recover without much difficulty. But Hannah couldn't. Would Hel be able to bring her back again? How would that work? *Is it a* You Only Live Twice *sorta thing?* Why were they thinking in Bond movies now? Why not a limited regeneration joke? That would be so much more in character, but there was a gun pointed at them, and it made thinking hard.

Hannah on the other hand, didn't seem to be struggling with it. She seemed fed up. "Look, I'm going through some shit right now, and

I'd really appreciate it if you bothered someone else. Or, you know, no one. That would probably be best."

Both Alys and the mugger stared at her.

"Hannah…" Alys said, but the gun jerked, and they didn't so much as breathe. There was no sound. No bullet piercing their body. They were okay. For now.

"Hannah, is it?" he asked. "I don't know what you think this is, but if you don't want me to shoot your girlfriend, reach in your purses and hand over all the cash. I have places to be, and I'd really rather not shoot anyone, but I'll do it if I have to. I've done it before."

Alys stared at him. Did they look like they had a purse?

Hannah took a step toward him, glaring hard. She had said she wanted to hit someone…

The mugger stared, his grip tightening on the gun.

Alys felt like their eyes might pop out of their head. Hannah was going to get them killed. What the hell was she thinking? She was staring him down like an idiot…like Thor. Not that the two were different. "Hannah," they pleaded.

The mugger grabbed Alys's wrist. Their blood ran cold. All they had to do was grow some spikes, and he'd lose those fingers. But they couldn't do it in front of Hannah. "Listen to your girlfriend. Just hand over the money, and I won't have to hurt her."

She lunged. The gun went off as she knocked it from his hands. Alys looked around, the sound still ringing in their ears, but no one seemed to be shot. They looked down but didn't find any blood pouring out of them.

"They're not a girl," Hannah shouted. She shoved the man hard enough that he crashed through the alley wall, sending powdered brick everywhere, the remains of the wall propping up his motionless form. Hannah stopped and stared at her hands, shaking. "No," she said. "No."

"Hannah?" They were closer, but they didn't remember moving. The mugger wasn't moving, and his dark red blood was running down the wall. Someone on the street seemed to be screaming. People would come investigate in a matter of seconds.

"It's okay, Hannah. He's still breathing." Another lie.

Tears streamed down Hannah's face. "No. I'm better now. I had so much therapy. I don't get angry like this anymore. I don't. I don't. I can't."

"Hannah?"

"It's Thor. It wasn't me."

And there went all of the progress they'd made. "Get out of here. I'll tell the cops we were mugged. It'll be fine."

She shook her head but made no other movement.

Alys grabbed their keys and stuffed them into her hands. "Hannah, take my car and drive home. You're in no condition to talk to the police."

"But Megan's a cop. I can call her."

They couldn't deal with the cops. There was a dead body; there'd be too many questions. They'd arrest Hannah, and she'd end up revealing her superstrength. It would go terribly. That left one option, one of the first spells Alys had ever learned and the main way they'd gotten this far with their limited lying ability. It required a susceptible target, but as broken as Hannah seemed, it wouldn't be too difficult. It might even last the whole trip home. They traced their fingers in a quick rune behind their back. It felt far too much like crossing their fingers. "Take my car and go home."

Hannah took the keys and started walking.

"Other way." The voices were coming from the closer street. Hannah would have to duck around back. The car was that way anyway.

Hannah did as she was told. Alys stared at the body and willed their clothes to change into a fitted suit and their face to a knock-off Duchovny. They'd pull jurisdiction and say it was an FBI investigation, then vanish the body. It wouldn't be the first time.

Chapter Twelve

Hannah stared out the car's window at the house. She didn't remember driving home. Where was Alys? What had happened? She shook her head, trying to clear the fog. The mugger! Was Alys okay? She found her phone still in her purse, which was still on her shoulder. She hadn't even thrown it in the back while she drove.

"Alys?" she asked as soon as the ringing stopped.

"Hey, Hannah. You get home okay?"

Hannah stared at the phone in disbelief. Why were they so nonchalant? "Um, yes?"

"Cool. I was worried about you."

She stared at her hands. She'd attacked that man. He was a mere mortal, and she was a god, and she could've killed him. She sounded like a lunatic. "Are you...did everything go okay?"

"Oh, yeah, it's fine. I told the cops what happened, and they said they'd call me if they had any questions. I kept you out of it."

"But—"

"It's all fine. You don't need to worry. Go talk to your girlfriend."

Hannah nodded. Something seemed to be missing, but she couldn't put her finger on it. Was this trauma? She hadn't felt like this the last time. She still had her senses; she was just scared. Why was this time so different? "Are you okay?"

"I'm fine." They chuckled. "I'll get a cab over there and pick up my car. I just didn't want you to have to deal with that with the state you were in. You were barely talking. You did manage to drive home in one piece, right? My car's okay, and you know, you are?"

"I already said I did," she snapped. There was that temper. All those years getting it under control, and she lost it like this. For what? Because she was freaked out over her relationship? Or because that dick misgendered her new friend? Probably both. She sighed. "Thanks for worrying about me. I can't believe I was such a wreck."

"It was scary. I'm sure I'd have been blubbering too if I didn't have you to look after."

Hannah took a deep breath and opened the car door. Everything felt off. She could taste her tongue. It felt like she hadn't been in her body for a few minutes. Was that what an out-of-body experience was? But she didn't remember anything. "All right. Thank you. I'm sorry you had to deal with all that. And you're sure you're okay?"

Another laugh. "Hannah, relax. I'm fine. You kept me safe. My hero. It was kinda sexy."

Hannah's cheeks warmed, and all she could do was shake her head. What the hell was Alys talking about? "I..."

"Right. Sorry. I'll talk to you later." The phone clicked, and the call ended, leaving Hannah at an utter loss for how to process anything that had just happened. She had to talk to Emily.

Hannah hurried around the side of the house, trying to stop thinking for a minute. She wanted to drown all of her fears in alcohol. Normally, she'd run to Emily, but that still sounded too terrifying. What if it was only Thor who wanted that?

Alys's words crept back to her. Thor wasn't a separate person, just her. But that didn't make any sense. Hannah caught her fist in midair. It was mere inches from the wall on the side of the house. She was standing under the carport, and she'd nearly destroyed her landlord's house in the middle of her panic. She couldn't do that. She'd taught herself years ago not to do that. But something had snapped in her with this revelation, and it was almost like she had to start over from square one.

Hannah took a deep breath.

Let it go. She let the breath out, trying to release her anger.

Within me is a peacefulness that cannot be disturbed. She ignored just how disturbed that peacefulness felt. She hadn't needed to do this since high school. She was better now.

That only sent her rage burning up again. She repeated the mantras, breathing in and out. She couldn't change what she'd learned. She couldn't change anything that had happened, not even hurting those people. But she could take control now. She could accept her life as it was, godhood and all, and the strength that went with it, and not use it to hurt people. She could be better.

Hannah opened her eyes, swallowing down the last of her fear, and strode boldly to the apartment she shared with her girlfriend. She still didn't know what she was going to say, but she knew that the way she had been handling it wasn't working.

"Hannah?" Emily sounded so scared that a pit of guilt welled in Hannah's stomach. She'd put the woman she loved through so much. And for what? Because she was a god? Wow, talk about a real struggle.

"Hey, babe," she managed. Hannah couldn't face her just yet, so she grabbed a six-pack of beers, then forced herself to round the corner into the living room. Emily was still sitting on the couch, a movie paused on the TV.

Emily cleared her throat and looked at her but didn't say anything.

"I'm sorry," Hannah said.

Emily shrugged, but Hannah could see a tear run down her cheek. "You didn't do anything."

"I did. I hurt you." And that poor bastard. Nausea bubbled up, and she set the beers down, opening one and draining it in a single swig. It did nothing to settle her stomach or her nerves, so she offered one to Emily and checked to see if a second bottle did any good.

This time, when Emily patted the seat next to her, Hannah took it.

"I love you," Emily said.

Hannah nodded, unable to hold back the tears. "I love you too."

"You don't have to say that if you're not sure. I get that this whole god thing has thrown you. It's fucked me up too. I mean, I'm, what, some useless wife god who can't do shit? That sucks. But it doesn't suck quite so much if it means I get you."

"You do," she whispered.

Emily pulled her closer, and Hannah felt lips trailing down her cheek. When they finally reached her lips, she gave in, pulling Emily to her with a loud "ooph" and deepened the kiss, savoring it, hardly even having the energy to care what part of her wanted this. She had time to sort that out. Hell, she was probably immortal now. But she wasn't ready to give this up. They had known each other for far too short a time for how strongly she felt, and that scared the hell out of her, but Hannah loved Emily.

She pulled off Emily's shirt, hearing it rip, and pressed her closer. She needed this.

❖

Hannah held Emily close and felt the simultaneous urges to flee and to stay right there forever. She ran her hand over Emily's bare belly as her lip trembled. Just what was she going to do? Was this really okay?

"I can almost hear you worrying." Emily turned over, her face mere inches from Hannah's, and took her hand. "Honey, please, talk to me. You don't have to stuff down all of your feelings."

If only that was true. "I don't know if they're my feelings, though."

"That's what I told Alys. I thought they'd think I was crazy, but somehow, they really got it. Sif isn't some separate entity from me. Which is, you know, super annoying. Can you really see me as some boring farmer of a wife? Like, come on. Me? I'm cooler than that, right?"

Hannah giggled. "Goddamn it."

"I think you mean *you* damn it."

She rolled her eyes. "Is this what Thor was into? This badass, butch, sorta cocky—"

"Very cocky, excuse you."

"Is that what Thor was into?"

Emily sat up, staring and pulling the sheet over her chest.

"I'm not saying that I'm not," Hannah shouted, pulling herself up beside Emily. "I'm sorry, I was saying it stupidly. What I meant was, that's so my type. You're absolutely perfect for me, but from what I've seen in movies, I don't know that Thor would really be after that. So is it me wanting you, then? I'd like to think it is, but you were still the woman Thor loved, and it's scary."

"Like I said, we can't really think of it that way. Though, hey, at least the movies didn't completely misrepresent you. Sif was a total badass in everything I've seen, but instead she's a damn farmer. It's like I'm back in North Carolina or something."

Hannah wrapped an arm around her and pulled her close. "I don't think I can see you farming."

"Then I guess I'm not just Sif, am I?"

That threw her. Hannah stared, unsure of what to say for a long moment.

Emily leaned in and playfully bit her lip, then pulled back, smirking. "I love you, Hannah. I don't think I'd have been into Thor. He's kinda a big burly man and not my femme bodybuilder."

"That doesn't help."

"You're not Thor. You're Hannah. And you're the woman I love.

I don't care if it's some weird destiny thing or if it was just chemistry. It doesn't matter to me. All that matters is I can't imagine not having you here. Christ…Odin? Damn, I need to figure out how to swear now. Fuck. That works. I've only known you for a few weeks, and yeah, that's weird. But it's also gay. And just, I know that I want you here. I want to share this apartment, my shitty old car, hell, my life with you. I've never fallen like this for anyone, and if that's because I've known you for centuries, then all that does is tell me that we already know it can work."

Tears trailed down Hannah's cheeks all over again. "Don't you want to know that you're your own person?"

"I am. You already said that. I'm not this weird farmer bitch from mythology, but I also am. I can deal with that. Mostly. I really hate how not cool it is. But you're a big badass god and my dorky accountant."

"I'm not a dork," she muttered.

Emily wiped Hannah's cheeks and planted a soft kiss on her eyelids. "You are. You want to be an accountant. No one wants to be an accountant. That's literally the plot of both *The Tick* and *The Producers*."

Hannah grumbled.

"And that's not very Thor now, is it? But it is Hannah. It is one hundred percent the woman I love."

She nodded, fighting back a sob.

"So let's just try to take this as it comes. We found out we're gods. That's weird, but we'll deal."

"But doesn't it change everything? God, Alys and I were mugged, and I put the guy through a wall. This isn't a human thing. These aren't the kind of problems I'm supposed to have. I wanted a normal, boring life. With you," she added. It was still true. It shouldn't be. This all should have sent her as far away from Emily as she could reach, but how could she want to be anywhere else?

Emily's eyes widened, and her mouth opened, then closed before she finally managed, "You were mugged?"

"It was nothing."

"You were mugged?" Emily licked her lips, glancing around the dimly lit room. Hannah was almost glad she'd ripped the door off, since she wouldn't even be able to see now that the sun was down. "I should've been there. I shouldn't have let you go off like that. I could've protected you. Are you okay? Is Alys okay?"

Hannah nodded. "We're fine. It really wasn't anything that bad.

Okay, I guess it was. He did pull a gun on us, but I'm Thor." She hated how good that felt to say. "I saved the day, and then Alys told me to head home and that they'd talk to the cops. I was kind of freaking out."

"I can understand why!" Emily hugged her tightly, as if she was trying to make sure Hannah was really there.

"Not that." Hannah had to gently pull herself free to breathe. Suffocating like that would be a good way to die. "The mugger didn't even really scare me that much. Like, yeah, it was scary, but I just needed to stop him...to..." Those damn tears returned. "To put him down. I shoved him so hard, he went through a wall. I wanted to kill him. I would have for misgendering Alys, but as soon as I saw what I had done..." It was too much. She wouldn't face that thought again. "But it's all okay. We're fine. We're safe. Everyone lived."

"I'm so glad. Holy fuck. Why didn't you tell me?"

"I didn't want you to worry."

Hands clasped her cheek, those oceanic blue eyes searching hers. "Please don't scare me like that. I need to know that you're safe. I love you."

"I love you too."

Emily leaned in, kissing her hard, and Hannah lost track of any thoughts in her head. This was exactly where she needed to be.

Chapter Thirteen

They're going to be here any minute," Hannah squealed, and Emily couldn't tell if it was out of fear or excitement. For herself, it was mostly fear.

She glared at the rows of beer in the fridge. She wanted to drink a few dozen to calm her nerves, but she was pretty sure that would be the exact opposite of helpful. She'd met precisely one girlfriend's parents before, and it had gone about as amazingly as trying to smoke a pig indoors. And she only came up with that comparison as there actually had been a fire. What were they going to think about the older woman Hannah had moved in with?

Hannah threw herself onto the couch and let out a low mournful moan. "I'm not ready. Can't they come tomorrow? We still need to go over everything. What if they're weird about us sharing a bed? They never said anything about it before, but it's not like I ever really gave them the chance. They probably think we're already sleeping together, right?"

"Honey, it's fine." Emily did her best to sound soothing as she ran her hands through Hannah's hair. "You don't need to worry." She hoped.

"Are you good with parents?"

She faltered but recovered surprisingly quickly. "I'm a quick learner."

Before Hannah could react to that cop-out of a response, her phone chimed. Saved by the cheery pop music. Emily could faintly hear a voice on the other end. "Wait here," Hannah said as she leapt to her feet. "I want to see them first."

"Worried I'll make a bad impression?"

Hannah didn't bother answering, so Emily was left stewing in her own nerves as she waited. This had to go better. But how? She'd never learned how to interact with parents. Her own wanted nothing to do with her.

She tried sitting. Then standing. Then pacing around the place. It couldn't have been more than a few minutes, but she settled on leaning against the wall, then realized that looked weird and went back to sitting on the couch.

"And you feel safe here?" she heard someone say as they opened the first door. Hannah's mother, she suspected. "Even having to use this back door? Do you trust your landlord?"

Hannah had the tact not to mention that they'd heard a gunshot a few blocks away the other night and that their landlord had already entered their apartment once since she'd moved in without any sort of notice or even bothering to knock. Hannah said, "Of course. The place is super safe, and our landlord is a great guy. He even gives us extra food sometimes."

"'Our,' 'us,'" her father repeated. "Are we finally going to meet this girlfriend of yours? You've barely told me two things about her."

Emily hurried over, realizing that sitting on the couch might make her look like a slacker. "Now, that's the setup for a great entrance if I've ever heard one," Emily said, opening the door to the Olsen family. She was wearing a nice button-up blouse and slacks, as she'd refused Hannah's suggestion of wearing a dress, with her long hair pulled back in a ponytail. "Name's Emily Johnson." Extending her hand toward Hannah's father, she added, "You must be the parents of the amazing woman I'm living with."

"We would be that exactly. I'm Mark, and this is Cheryl," he said, a goofy grin on his face as he shook the proffered hand. "She's pretty. You really lucked out, Hannah."

The elbow to the gut from his wife did little to dispel his good spirits. "How old are you?" Cheryl asked as she also shook her hand. That wasn't a great sign.

Emily's smile grew more forced. "Well, as young as you look, I must be older," she tried.

Unfortunately, that seemed to be the exact opposite of what Cheryl wanted to hear. "So how old is that? I just want to make sure my little girl is safe."

"Cheryl," Mark muttered.

The door to the main house and the attic apartment opened, and they took it as an opportunity to shepherd Hannah's parents through the second door and downstairs. Emily hoped Cheryl would forget what they were talking about.

"So you were saying?" she asked.

Holding her hands up in surrender, Emily replied, "I'm twenty-seven. I assure you, I'm taking fine care of your daughter, and the only thing my age means is that I was old enough to rent a truck so she could move in more easily."

"Well, I—"

"Kiddo, Emily, do you think you could grab us a drink? It's been a long drive, and we're both parched."

"No problem," Emily said.

"Sure," Hannah added, as they dashed to the kitchen. "Grab waters. I think my mom might have a heart attack right now if she realized I'm old enough to have beer."

"She doesn't know you drink?"

"Oh, she knows. She bought me my first drink when I was fourteen, but there's a big difference between that and accepting that the girl you're still trying to baby is an adult who can buy her own beer."

"Yeah, I get that." She opened the fridge and grabbed a couple of bottled waters. "You want to give these to 'em? I'm a little worried your mom might think I'm trying to poison her or something."

Hannah glanced around them as if she was looking for any eavesdroppers. "Don't give her any ideas. But it should be fine. Even if they know I'm Thor."

Emily stared. Hannah hadn't said anything about that. "You told them?"

"No. I'm just...Don't worry about it. I'd rather they not overhear this. And I'm probably being crazy."

Bearing the water bottles, they found Hannah's parents sitting on the torn-up leather couch. Cheryl looked a lot calmer. What had Mark said to manage that? Emily handed them the water. "I hope Aquafina's okay." She took a seat on the beige recliner. The lever had come off long ago, but it was still a perfectly comfortable chair.

"It's fine, thank you," Cheryl managed, taking a sip.

"Did you want us to show you around town?" Hannah asked, sitting between her parents.

"Sure," Mark answered, a warm grin on his face.

"Emily knows the area better than I do," she said, gesturing toward her. Now if Emily could only live up to that, it might finally be an opening to win some trust. "I've only been living here for the past week, though there's this amazing taco cart by the grocery store. Any idea where you'd like to go, babe?" She emphasized the last word, looking right at her mother.

"Yeah, actually. It's prime rib night at this place near here." Emily gave Hannah a quick glance as if asking, "that's what parents eat, right?" She was woefully out of her element here, but Hannah gave her a smile and a quick nod. "Most of the other stuff around here is dive bars and fast food, unless you want to go up toward Stark. I've only been to this place once, but I recall it being pretty good."

"That sounds great," Mark replied quickly.

Cheryl nodded. "Do they have a senior discount?"

Emily's smile grew more forced. "I have absolutely no idea."

"I suppose you wouldn't." With a light chuckle, Cheryl climbed to her feet, wincing slightly. "All right, let's go. My treat."

❖

"It's a bar." Cheryl's derisive sneer doubtless put the fear of God into the little restaurant. Or Odin? Damn, this was even throwing off Emily's dumb jokes. "First those streetwalkers on the way over, and now this."

"Honey, your favorite restaurant is a bar," Mark said.

"Well, yes," she said, glaring at the placard displaying the specials. "But it's not like this. It's much nicer."

A few minutes later, they were seated, but Cheryl was nowhere near finished complaining.

"The prime rib looks fantastic, dear," Mark said, pointing to the little handout that showed the day's special.

"It does, but everything is so expensive."

"Come on, it really isn't. Especially not compared to Seattle."

She fixed him with a gaze that brooked no argument. "I don't mean for us. Our poor Hannah is only an intern, and she's got her student loans. How is she supposed to afford anything in this city?" Looking like she just came up with an idea, she turned to Hannah and said, "Are you sure you wouldn't rather come live with us?" Could that have been her trying to keep Thor a secret? But then why send her off to college in the first place? "We won't charge you any rent, and you can start working on saving up for your future."

"Mom, I'm sure. I have an internship with a huge company here, and it's likely to end up with a full-time job after this summer. I wouldn't be saving up for my future. I'd be throwing it away." She squeezed Emily's hand hard enough that she had to stifle a pained whimper. "Besides, all of my friends are here—hell, my whole life is here, and I—" She stared into Emily's eyes, and Emily's fears vanished. It didn't matter how this went, she still had Hannah. She could relax. She wasn't going anywhere. "And I love Emily. I'm not going anywhere."

"You what?" her mother asked.

Emily gulped. There was no way she was going to win Cheryl's approval at this rate.

Mark held his hands out, looking between them. "Ladies, why don't we all figure out what we want to eat first? I'm sure we're all really hungry, and we'll feel better once we have some food in us. How about we get these bacon cheddar chips? They have a star next to them, so I'm sure they're delicious." He seemed so harmless. Maybe even nice. He seemed like an actual proper dad.

"I got them last time, and I loved them," Emily said, squeezing Hannah's hand. She searched her face for a second before she continued, "And I love your daughter. Possibly even more than those chips."

Hannah elbowed her.

"Definitely more than the chips. I love her more than…Hell, more than I've ever loved anyone. I completely understand why you'd be suspicious of me. I'm five years older than her and a bartender, and I even have a tattoo, so I'm sure I'm everything you were scared she'd find on her own, but I swear, I'm taking good care of her, and I will do everything in my power to never hurt her." Not that anything could. Hannah was Thor, after all. But this was getting to her too much. Maybe it reminded her of her own parents, or maybe Hannah freaking out the other day already had her too terrified of losing her. She felt something run down her cheek. Damn it, was she really? Since when did she get this emotional? "Now, if you'll excuse me, I need to splash some water on my face because I am not crying in the middle of a bar." She kissed Hannah chastely but with enough force to seal her words, and said her order in case the waiter came around.

As Emily walked away, she could hear Cheryl asking, "Is that true?"

"Is what true, Mom?"

"Is she taking good care of you? Do you love her?"

"She is, and I do. I didn't move in with her because it was convenient, as much as we love to pretend that's the case, and as cheap as the rent is, I moved in because I can't imagine not seeing her when I wake up. I want to be with her so badly. I know how scared you are, but I need you to understand that she means the world to me."

Emily had heard more than enough and far more than she should have, but with a massive grin, she ran to the bathroom. As painful as this was, it seemed like what Emily expected normal moms to sound like. She'd only seen them on TV, but this seemed like an overprotective parent, not someone trying to keep a secret about their god child. Hopefully, Hannah was realizing the same.

A minute later, she returned, her hair and the collar of her shirt clinging to her where the water had splashed. "They come?" she asked, pretending there was no greater concern on her mind than her prime rib.

"Yeah, I ordered you that stout we tried the other week."

"Sweet. It was delicious." So she did get beer in front of her parents? Emily was all the prouder. She wished she'd had the courage to be so open with her own. Not that it would've gone half this well.

"What's your family like, Emily? Should we be expecting to meet them over the holidays?" Mark asked.

Emily was increasingly convinced that he was trying to beat Cheryl to any insensitive questions, but he was probing in what was without a doubt the most sensitive recesses of her psyche. It had been planned as an emergency topic of conversation—their secret weapon—if Cheryl reacted as badly as she'd ended up doing. It looked as if they didn't have a choice but to deploy it. Hopefully, it would eliminate any remaining coldness on Cheryl's behalf.

Emily sighed. She hated talking about it. Hannah had been incredibly touched by the fact that she was willing to discuss it with them at all. Sucking on her teeth to buy a bit of time, she glanced at the table, hoping their drinks had magically arrived. "They're not great. I haven't talked to my family in six years. So, no, I doubt you'll be seeing them."

"You don't talk to them?" Cheryl asked, sounding genuinely concerned. It was a welcome change from her previous tone.

"No. They really didn't appreciate my coming out. I moved away from North Carolina shortly after. I couldn't put up with them anymore. Or that whole state. Not with how they treated me after I came out. The food is the one thing good about it, and I have a friend here who can make it just as good."

"You're from North Carolina?" Mark asked. "You don't have any accent."

"Yeah, I worked at that for a while."

"Oh, Emily, I'm so sorry," Cheryl finally said. Hannah's eyebrows shot up. Their secret weapon had been even more effective than expected.

"It's okay. My life worked out pretty well." Beaming, she planted a kiss on Hannah's temple.

"Well, I promise," Cheryl said. "Despite how I sounded, I'm nothing like them. We're so proud of our daughter for being who she is…and…and I guess if you're going to be such a big part of her life…" She hesitated. Saying this clearly pained her. "Then I'm happy to welcome you into the family. I don't want to be another person rejecting you."

Emily's worst fears came true. She cried in the middle of the restaurant. Hugs, beer, and some napkins did a good deal to counteract it, however, and by the time they left the place, they were all laughing and chatting as if they'd known each other for years, one big happy family. This had gone so much better than she'd feared. Before the senior Olsens returned to Seattle, they even made Thanksgiving plans together. Despite the weird godly hang-ups, her new life with Hannah was looking to be a perfect one.

CHAPTER FOURTEEN

"Y^{ou} sure you still want to go to Alys's tonight?" Hannah asked, exhausted from a long day of work. The one other intern in the accounting department had made a massive enough mistake that he was no longer with the company, and she and Isabel had had to go through all of his work, trying to sort out what went wrong. They'd expected a decimal point being in the wrong spot, which happened to everyone sooner or later, but instead, it seemed he'd just given up and was making the numbers up whole cloth. Isabel had joked that he'd be a great accountant for the mob. After all that, Hannah was absolutely in no mood to leave the house. That would involve clothing, and she was enjoying the freedom from that that living with her girlfriend entailed.

"Come on, hun. You know you're a slut for their cooking, and besides, they're the only person who knows about us."

That was, sadly, difficult to argue with. Alys's food might actually be worth putting clothes on. She hadn't had a home-cooked meal since she'd moved out. She had been too much of a coward to tell her own friends, so she'd been dodging April's repeated offers. This was the last day of Emily's weekend, Magni and Modi still hadn't been back, and as busy as Alys had been, they weren't likely to be able to meet up again until the next Wednesday. "But I'm tired."

"Please." There was something in Emily's tone that Hannah couldn't quite place.

Hannah rubbed her arm, glancing at Emily. How was she supposed to explain this? She didn't want to deal with being a god. She was just an accountant. And if they went over to see someone who was clearly obsessed with mythology and knew they were gods, then how was she supposed to not think about it? But they were also Emily's best friend. "Babe…"

Emily squeezed her hand. "What's wrong?"

Great, she really did have to say it, didn't she? "Can't we just stay here?"

She looked so concerned. Hannah either had to fess up or come up with a really good excuse. "Honey, what? Do you not like Alys?"

"No, it's not that." She sighed. "I just don't want to deal with this stuff. I don't have to be a god all the time."

The hurt didn't seem to go away. Emily turned slightly, not quite facing her. "I need someone to talk to about it. It's a big thing. Especially when you get all the cool stuff, and I get nothing. Come on, it's not like you hate it. You seemed to really enjoy showing off your strength."

"Yeah but I always did that." That wasn't much of an argument. Fine, Emily needed this, she supposed it was worth it. "Did they smoke some meat?"

"I'll call and ask."

A few minutes later, under assurance that there were leftover ribs and that they would be delicious, Hannah agreed.

"I don't want to get dressed," she complained.

"I know, honey. I don't want you to get dressed, either."

"How long do we have?"

"They get off at eight."

It was only five-thirty, so that gave them enough time for sex and getting dressed. Maybe even a shower if they hurried. "Well, then, I think you need to be getting *out of* your clothes."

Emily's face lit up. "Yeah?"

"You dork. When am I ever not up for having my way with you?"

"I have my way with you plenty."

"Yeah, but I'm a god."

She quirked an eyebrow. "So, dear Thor, mightiest of the gods, is it your intention to overpower me?"

"Would you like that?"

The reddening of Emily's cheeks, along with the almost inaudible squeak, seemed to suggest that she would very much like that.

"All right, then, get out of those clothes, or I'm ripping them off."

Emily clearly didn't need to be told a third time. Her clothes were on the ground in a matter of seconds, and Hannah scooped her up in a single hand, supporting her by her firm ass.

"Did you know you were this strong?"

Hannah shook her head, but conversation was the last thing on her mind. She kissed along Emily's collarbone and began trailing down to increasingly alert nipples. They did not end up having time to shower.

❖

"You smell like sex," Alys said, as soon as Hannah and Emily walked through the door. Hannah hadn't had the chance for a good look inside the last time she was here, which was surprisingly nice and cozy. All she'd seen before was the bathroom, and she'd been in quite a hurry. There was bric-a-brac everywhere: little toys, instruments, lights, and a few plastic figurines. It looked homey and eclectic. She liked it far more than she would have thought, had it been described to her. It made Alys seem more human, where before they were always this weirdly judgmental figure that seemed to tower over Emily. Only metaphorically. Emily was a couple inches taller.

"I figured you'd rather we get here earlier than later."

They shrugged. "I mean, it's not awful or anything."

"Yeah, you like the scent?" Emily asked, giving a playful smirk.

Rolling their eyes, Alys gestured toward another room, which Hannah soon discovered was a living room with plush couches covered in blankets that someone could melt into. She tossed herself into one, beaming at Emily and Alys. "I love your house."

"Thank you. I actually just finished paying it off."

"Then help a girl out," Emily said.

"I'll think about it. I assume you two want beer?"

Emily bit her lip, seeming to mull that over for the first time since Hannah had known her. "I don't suppose you have mead? Now that we're Norse gods, I feel like we should try it out."

Hannah glared at her.

"How appropriate. That's actually why I invited you over."

"To show off your mead? Damn, great minds do think alike."

Alys chuckled. "What on earth made you think I had some in the first place?"

"The swords on your bedroom wall."

"Hey, it's one sword and one ax."

"Nerd. But I rest my case."

They departed to the kitchen and came back with mead, along with a wooden board containing some food Hannah couldn't quite place. "What's that?"

"Venison with cheese and crackers. I figured if we were going with a themed meal, then I'd go as all-out as my lazy ass could manage."

Hannah pouted. "But ribs."

"Fine, let me preheat the oven. This is just an appetizer."

Hannah scooped some deer meat onto a cracker and took a bite. It was stronger than she'd expected, with a strange bitter taste that she drowned in mead before having another bite. By the third cracker, she still wasn't sure if she liked it, but she seemed incapable of stopping. "This tastes weird."

"Yeah, I can tell you hate it," Emily said, sinking into the cushion next to her and grabbing her own cracker. "It's a bit of an acquired taste, but I love it."

"I'm glad to hear that," Alys replied, returning with a soft smile on their face. Having their food complimented seemed to always work for them. "I cold-smoked it over the weekend. I hadn't done that before, and I'm really pleased with how it turned out."

"That doesn't even make sense." Hannah took another bite.

"You cure the meat—I used a dry brine—and then you keep it under ninety degrees while you let in smoke from another chamber."

"This isn't cooked?" Hanna stared at the food. She'd already had enough that it likely couldn't do any further harm. It was probably worth it, she decided, stuffing the rest of the cracker into her mouth.

"Nope. But I made sure it was safe. You don't need to worry." They sat in a felt recliner that actually had a working leg rest. Hannah tried not to be too jealous.

"There was kind of a reason for all this. This is going to sound strange."

"Try us," Hannah challenged. "I mean, you believed us about being gods with zero evidence. I don't think we have any room to judge."

They nodded, licking their lips. They looked so nervous. They scratched at their cup rather than actually drinking from it. "You know how you found out? The same thing happened to me." They took a slow breath, seeming to study them. "It was over the weekend. I wanted to tell you, but I wasn't sure how you'd react. My…" They hesitated. "My daughter said that I'm also a god."

Hannah had absolutely known they were going to have to talk gods, but this managed to throw her. How many gods were there on Earth? Or just in Portland?

"Oh?" Emily asked, setting down her food. "Which god are you? I'd bet Apollo?" Her normal confidence wasn't in her voice, and it was clear that she was trying to keep her cool.

They drained their cup before filling it again. "Anyone want any?"

For once, both Hannah and Emily shook their heads. They promptly changed their minds and took Alys up on it, but it was still saying something. Hannah wasn't sure she'd been this surprised in at least a week.

Once they'd finished pouring the drinks, Alys sat back down and said, "Promise you won't tell your kids this?"

"Okay?" Emily said, sounding more confused than ever.

"I'm Loki." Not that Hannah had been staring at them or anything, but she noticed that their breasts were gone, though nothing else seemed particularly different. She could swear they'd been there a second ago. And they'd definitely still had them the other week. "My daughter taught me some basic magic. I was scared to reveal it because it's just so strange, but you know me. I always hated those things." They gestured at what Hannah had absolutely not been staring at.

"That's amazing. I'm so happy for you."

That was not the response Hannah was expecting. She stared at Emily. Magic was real. There were even more gods. All of this insanity kept following them. And Emily was just fine with it.

"Did your daughter tell you anything else?" It sounded so strange to hear both of them talking about their kids. She'd never had a kid. She'd sure as hell never been pregnant. And now they were casually throwing around talk about their children, who were all fully grown gods. How were Emily and Alys handling it? Hannah looked between them. They both seemed totally fine. Like it was all just a normal thing.

Alys shook their head. "Nothing like that. It was mostly about what I could do. Magic and the like."

"Can you teach me?" Emily asked.

"I don't think so. It seems to be more of a Jotunn trait. Oh, Loki, which I guess is me, was not an Aesir like Thor and Sif. The singular is Ass, so enjoy that."

"You're an ass," Hannah chimed in. Ironically, she wasn't willing to act like one. It didn't matter how weird this timing or crazy the coincidence was, they were still Emily's best friend.

"No, you both are, though." Alys snickered. Hannah had walked into that. "Jotunns seem capable of wielding magic, while the Aesir aren't. Odin had to sacrifice a lot to gain the ability to use runes, giving up half of his life, and Heimdallr is a very complicated case. I could try to teach you, but I wouldn't get my hopes up."

Someday, Hannah would have the barest understanding of what any of those words meant. Probably. Maybe.

"Then what the hell good does being a god do for me? I don't have any powers."

"And they said I didn't have lightning abilities. The movies sure make it look like I…like *he* did." Even if Hannah was accepting that she was Thor, and she was only mostly convinced that she was, referring to the mythological figure as herself felt wrong.

"Hmm." Sucking on their teeth, Alys seemed to consider these points. "I'm not sure. I suppose there is nothing explicit about Thor having control over lightning, but he was called the Thunderer. As for Sif, well, you could take up gardening or show off your hair more. I'm so glad you kept it now that I know you're Sif. Those locks of gold. Some claim that's literal, so I guess you could take your hair to a pawn shop or a jeweler."

Emily cocked her head.

"You also live longer. You are probably stronger than a human, and it would explain your metabolism and why you're so fit despite never doing anything. So it definitely has a few advantages."

"How come she gets all the better stuff?"

"Sorry," Hannah muttered. She'd give her strength to Emily if she could. It was fun to play with, but it was too much trouble, especially if it made Emily jealous.

"I'll look into it and see if I can find out anything else. I was kinda busy with all the Loki research." A beep sounded from the other room. "I'm gonna go put the ribs in. I'll be right back."

Was that why they'd mentioned Loki before at the bar? But they hadn't known they were Loki until this weekend.

"They're taking this better than we did," Hannah said once Alys was out of earshot.

"Well, yeah, it's kinda their thing."

"But still."

"Still what? They're a nonbinary person who can shapeshift. They ended up with basically the perfect powers." The "unlike me" was implied.

Hannah shrugged. "I guess. I don't know, it's just bugging me. They really only just found out? But they mentioned Loki last week."

"Yeah, because he was a shapeshifter. They've always been into him."

Hannah took another bite of venison. Maybe she just didn't know Alys well enough. She supposed there wasn't really anything suspicious going on. Maybe it was because as little as Hannah knew about mythology, she'd never heard much good about Loki. She decided to keep her thoughts to herself for now. She'd already said all she knew, and Emily trusted Alys. Hannah didn't want to piss her off and end up making it into a fight. After last time, the idea of her temper flaring was too terrifying. Especially with Emily. She was better than that, and Emily deserved better.

"The ribs should be like twenty minutes. I don't want them to lose their tenderness, so I have to take it slow."

Hannah giggled and was surprised to find that no one else found that funny. "Almost sounds like you're romancing the ribs," she said, trying to explain.

"Yeah, they're married," Emily said.

Loki—Alys—Hannah had no idea how to refer to anyone now—the nonbinary person over there smirked. "You gonna go off to Asgard?"

"I'm not sure," Emily said. "Modi and Magni said that they'd see us soon, but it's been over a week. Maybe they're busy setting that up. What about you?"

"I don't think I'm welcome there. That's why I'd really like it if you would keep quiet about me."

"Yeah, that's no problem."

"But why would they hate you?" Hannah asked. "I mean, you're one of them…of us."

"The old Loki was a bit of a traitor. I'm, of course, nothing like him." Their hair was suddenly a bright green. They seemed to be enjoying their newfound freedom. "But they won't understand that. I'm sure they're plenty weird about you two already, given that you're twenty-something women rather than the gods they're used to, and I'm not ready to try to deal with that. Please let me be separate for a while. Maybe once they're accustomed to you, we can talk about it, but at least for now, let me be hidden."

"Okay, fine," Hannah relented. She supposed that all made sense.

"Oh, while I'm asking favors, if they let you get some apples from a tree there, would you grab me one too?"

"Why?" Hannah asked, her suspicion piqued again. Seriously, how did none of this bother Emily?

"They make you not age. They're likely to give them to you, but I would rather not age if I could avoid it. Being immortal sounds nice, so pretty please? I'll cook anything you want."

"You'll make me brisket again?"

"I'll make you a whole cow. Hell, get your special goats, and I'll make them every day if you need."

"What?"

"Cow it is, then."

"I have special goats?" She looked at Emily for support but only received a shrug. "Okay, fine, we'll grab you one."

"Yeah, it'll be no problem," Emily said. "So we're not immortal without them? But aren't we gods?"

"Norse gods are weird. We're longer lived, but we'll still age without Idunn's apples. Keep an eye out, and if they give you any, try to grab one for me too. Other than that, well, enjoy being a god, and I'll try to find out everything I can about your powers."

"Anything you can find would be great," Emily said.

"I really wanted lightning powers," Hannah grumbled.

Chuckling, Alys took a sip of mead. "Well, I'll see if you can have them. Now, let's make like Norse gods and get wasted and eat way too much meat."

Hannah giggled. "There's no such thing as too much meat."

They drained the entire bottle of mead, as well as an assortment of beers, and devoured all the ribs and another helping of venison. Hannah's suspicions waned, and she genuinely got drunk for the first time in far too long. It was absolutely worth putting clothes on.

CHAPTER FIFTEEN

A blinding pain, along with the sound of someone shouting numbers, roused Alys from sleep. They blinked, trying to will the world to make sense. They were in the living room in their recliner. They pushed a button to turn it back into a chair, the sudden motion sending another jolt of pain through their head.

The table in front of them was covered in dozens of empty beer, mead, and whiskey bottles. There was even a tequila bottle among them. They had drunk everything.

"Oh, I'm sorry," a girly voice squealed from somewhere beside them. They'd remember who it was in a minute. "Did I wake you? Was I counting too loud? Sometimes, I get kind of into my morning exercises."

"It's fine," they muttered, raising their hand and sloppily sketching some symbols in the air. Their head promptly cleared, and they could breathe again. It was so nice to finally be able to do that around someone else.

"What was that?"

"Just fixed my hangover." They chuckled. Not only could they do it, but they could even show off. "You need one?" they asked, finally turning to face Hannah's perkiness. Perky was right; she'd apparently lost her bra at some point in the night. Alys did their very best not to notice.

Hannah shook her head. "No. I'm fine. My hangovers are never that bad."

Alys looked over the table again. "Are you sure?"

"It's really fine. I can handle it. My exercise already took care of most of it."

"I really don't mind. I'd be happy to help." Alys rose, looking into those green eyes to see if they could understand the issue. If Hannah was scared, Alys didn't want to force it on her, but if she was just being awkward, then they would be more than happy to spare her any pain.

She stared back, hesitating, but she finally nodded. "If it's not any trouble."

"It's not at all." More dexterously than their previous attempt, Alys traced a series of runes in the air before tapping Hannah's temple. The flutter in their stomach and the sudden desire to cup her cheek were nothing but a strange aftereffect and meant nothing. It couldn't happen. It wouldn't.

Hannah's overeager grin sent another ripple through them, and they had to take a step back. It was only because they'd never been open with anyone before. It wasn't anything more than that. It didn't even make sense. They were using Hannah. Nothing could happen with her, and they didn't even want it to. They'd be lucky to even keep Emily as a friend when all of this was through, but even in the few weeks they'd known her, they'd seen that Hannah was far too innocent to ever understand. She didn't know what it was like.

"Something on your mind?" Hannah asked, the goofy smile only growing.

Swallowing the lump in their throat, Alys shook their head. "No. Just still waking up. Weird dreams maybe."

"Oh? Anything fun? Was I in them?" She giggled, and that same thought came back.

"Were you in them?" Alys asked, trying to find any explanation for that that didn't play into the same demented thoughts that seemed to be running through their mind.

She shrugged. "I dunno. Just seemed like it."

"Right." It hadn't been her hoping, just suspecting. They'd need to be more subtle. "I was going to make breakfast. Probably something bacon-y. You want anything?"

"Yes." She grinned. "Can I help?"

"It's fine. Let me know if Emily wakes up, and I can fix her."

"I'm not going to watch her sleep. I've done that enough. Let me help. I'm not bad in the kitchen."

Biting their lip, Alys tried to consider the request fairly. It wasn't as if they had a good reason to say no. And they would enjoy the company. "Sure. You can grind some pepper over the bacon while the oven preheats. I was going to make omelets, but I'm really craving grits right now. You okay with that?"

Hannah blinked. "What are grits?"

"It's like cornbread soup, basically. Think oatmeal but with cornmeal instead. You'll like it. And be careful with my pepper grinder. It can't handle your superstrength."

"You know, I've been using my muscles my whole life and never accidentally...*rarely* accidentally broken anything. Damn, how did I never realize I had superstrength? In my defense, phone screens are really fragile."

Alys did their best not to laugh. They failed and laughed into the fridge as they grabbed the bacon and butter. "Cookie sheets are under the oven. Put some parchment paper in it and start seasoning."

The two of them set everything up in a companionable silence, and Alys absolutely hated how much they loved it. Those dreams really had not helped. How had they been that obvious that Hannah had been in them? They should have called a cab to take her and Emily home instead of getting completely wasted with them. They were so close, and it was way too risky to let things slip like that. "What time do you have work?" Alys asked, not at all looking for a reason to get rid of Hannah.

"Nine, but it's on the other side of town."

"I can drive if Emily still isn't up."

"Oh. I figured I'd take Emily's car and either pick her up after or have you drop her off. Your way is probably better. But I didn't think she'd mind being stranded here. Damn, I really didn't think this through."

More chuckling. That was not a good sign. "I have work later, and I'm sure she won't mind picking you up. Let me drop you off." Wait. Why were they offering? Emily could take a cab. Hannah needed to get away. If they kept getting closer—humanizing her—it would only be that much harder for Alys.

"If you're sure," Hannah said, biting her lip.

"I am." If only they knew a spell to wipe her memory. That would solve everything. Why hadn't Hel ever taught them anything of the sort?

Hannah grabbed a beer from the fridge and held another out for them.

"Morning drinking. Wow, no wonder Emily loves you."

"That mean you don't want one?"

"It does not. I'm still a Norse god." Damn, did it feel good to be able to say that. They reached out, but Hannah pulled back.

"Hold on." She set her drink on the counter and grabbed the top of Alys's bottle, popping the lid off barehanded before handing it back. "You know, I have a bottle opener," Alys said. They'd seen the trick already. It didn't make it less impressive, but they weren't going to fawn over it. Again.

"Yeah. Me." She did the same to her own drink and took a quick swig. "I'm starving. The grits ready yet?"

As if on cue, the timer went off. Hannah's face lit up, and Alys did their best to ignore it. At least food would keep them from sticking their foot in their mouth.

When they'd finished their meal, and the several helpings that followed, Emily still wasn't awake, and it was growing late enough that Hannah would have to hurry. "Let's go," Alys said. It was their last chance to change their mind, but that didn't seem to be happening.

At least they managed not to say anything stupid on the drive. They simply let Hannah talk about accounting and her coworkers. They couldn't imagine why it was so damn endearing.

When they got back, they needed to check in with Hel, but they couldn't risk Emily catching them. That might have to wait until after work. Their daughter would be expecting an update, no matter how patient she claimed to be.

They opened the door, expecting to find Emily still sleeping. As nocturnal as she was, it would be a miracle if she was even awake before they left for work. Instead, they found her eating grits on the couch, watching Netflix.

"Anything good?" Alys asked, hiding their surprise.

"Some action movie."

"You say as if you watch anything else."

She rolled her eyes. "I do." With a slight groan she added, "With you or Hannah. This one has that guy you liked from that space thing, though."

"How specific."

"You know the one."

"I do not."

"You will when you see him."

If there was popcorn, Alys would've thrown it at her, but there wasn't time to make it, and the grits would be too messy.

"The food is delicious as ever, by the way," Emily said, patting the seat beside her.

Alys flopped onto the couch and stole a piece of bacon. "It should be. Your girlfriend helped make it."

Emily grinned, a bit of grits still stuck to her upper lip. "Yeah? You didn't seem to like her at first. I'm glad you two are getting along."

"It wasn't that I didn't like her." How the hell could they explain this? "It was just that I didn't want to like her."

"Oh," Emily said. Alys studied her. What was she assuming? And why had they even said that? "Because of last time?"

Grinding their teeth, Alys sat back. It wasn't entirely wrong. They shrugged. At least it was noncommittal.

"You do have a bad tendency to fall in love with my girlfriends, don't you?"

"What can I say, we have the same type. Fortunately for you, yours tend to be too gay for me."

"Sorry."

"There's nothing to apologize for."

"Sharon was still awful about your gender."

Alys shrugged. "And you dumped her for it. And you were even cool when we both dated Claire."

"Still feel bad about it."

"Don't."

"Does this mean you're crushing on Hannah?"

"No," Alys shouted, far too vehemently.

Emily smirked, lacing her hands behind her head. "Let me know when that answer changes."

Alys crossed their arms, promptly losing their huff. "Think I can get away with not putting these things back?" They gestured to their chest. They'd almost added, "for once," which would've given the game away. If only they didn't trust Emily. Emily certainly shouldn't trust them.

"Huh. I hadn't thought about it. I'd say it's worth it. What are they gonna do? Say you didn't have top surgery?"

They nodded. "You're right." They'd grown too used to lying. They'd forgotten how few consequences honesty sometimes had. On rare occasions. "I have work soon. Are you gonna stick around?"

"I was gonna finish breakfast."

"That's fine. Take all the time you need. My home is yours. You know that." They'd just tell Hel after work. It wasn't like there was much to report. The plan was finally on. Thor and Sif knew who Alys was and trusted them. It would work.

CHAPTER SIXTEEN

Saturday afternoon, Hannah browsed Facebook while Emily slept with her head on her chest. "I have to go to work soon," Emily muttered, stifling a yawn and planting a soft kiss on her pillow.

"That tickles." Hannah giggled.

"Should I bite instead? Maybe suck?"

Rolling her eyes, Hannah swatted Emily's bare ass. "Go shower."

"But I have better plans right now."

"You have work in an hour."

Emily's teeth found a newly excited nipple.

"Babe, work. We do not have time."

"You're no fun," she groaned, tossing the sheet from her legs and crawling out of bed. "Want to at least join me in the shower?"

"The last time we did that, we ran out of hot water, and I still ended up late for work."

"Third time's the charm."

A knock sounded from the top of their stairs. "Go shower. I'll see who that is," Hannah said, grabbing her clothes from the floor.

"Father! I mean Thor...Hannah. Emily. We have returned." The voice carried through the door and likely through the entire house. At least they weren't selling drugs or anything. Calling people Norse gods at five o'clock in the afternoon was hardly grounds for an eviction.

"I guess I don't get a shower or morning sex," Emily said.

"It's not morning."

"I'll call in sick. See what our crazy kids want."

"They're not our kids," Hannah said, much louder than she'd intended.

"Are you getting the door or not?"

"Fine." Stomping up the stairs, Hannah threw open both doors and promptly had two pairs of arms wrapped around her. "Ugh," she managed, patting each of them on the back. "Let go."

"Sorry," Modi said, pulling back.

"It's really nice to see you. We've missed you a lot."

"Even if I am Thor, which I'm still not…" She hesitated, looking at the wistful faces before her. "I'm sorry. I know you miss him." She needed to stop denying it, no matter how much it sucked. She didn't want to hurt them.

"It's okay. It's not your fault." Modi smiled at Hannah and patted his brother on the back.

"Do you want to come inside?" The other week, the idea of inviting the armored stalkers who had been showing up around town into her house would have seemed the dumbest thing she could possibly do. Now, it seemed rude not to. It still felt wrong. It still felt crazy. Hell, it was crazy. But she was starting to accept that maybe, possibly, these might be her sons. And she needed to find out what that meant.

"Yes, thank you."

"Is there beer?" Magni asked.

"Loads."

Hannah cracked open four bottles, and Emily returned from the bedroom, now clad in a tank top and cargo pants. "My boss is pissed, but I've got the day off. What's up?" She took one of the proffered drinks.

Modi sipped the beer and gave it an appreciative look. "This is good."

"It's local."

"Is there more?"

"Not cold."

"Cold is a novelty that I'm not used to. I'll happily take warm beer."

Hannah grabbed one from the cabinet and set it before him. Emily had taken the third chair, so Hannah sat in her lap. It was a surprise how strange it felt doing that in front of people who were at least, in most ways, not her children. "What did you find out?"

"We want to take you to Idavollr," Modi said.

"Which is?" Emily asked, draining her own beer before glancing between Hannah, the cabinet, and her now empty bottle.

"The home of the gods. It's where Asgard was before it fell."

"Ah." Emily sounded thoroughly unimpressed.

"The other Aesir doubt that you're really you," Magni said. "Even my claim of your strength wasn't enough for them. We want to show you to them, to let them see how 'you' you really are."

Hannah was justifiably skeptical of how convincing her appearance would be, but she held her tongue.

"So we're leaving Earth?" Emily asked, still sounding as if she was talking about a trip to the corner store. Hannah couldn't understand how she acted so blasé. Granted, she acted that way about most things, but this was going to another world. And they were talking about it as if they were going out of town to visit relatives. She supposed they were.

"Yes, we'll be leaving Midgard," Modi said.

"Glad I called out."

Hannah swallowed her fears. She needed answers, but she wasn't willing to put her life on hold for them. "How long will we be gone?"

"Shouldn't be more than a day. Unless, of course, you want to stay there?" Magni looked so hopeful. He clearly wanted his family back. Hannah could imagine how she'd feel if something happened to her parents, and she was told that someone else used to be them. She would probably want this connection just as badly. She doubted that Emily would agree, but it explained why she felt so bad for disappointing them.

"What should we bring?"

"You shouldn't need anything. We'll take you to the Bifrost, and then it's a few hours' walk from there to the main city. Without Heimdallr, we can't control the bridge, but it seems to have taken pity on us. It's very near."

"Is there overnight parking near it?" Hannah was not willing to risk losing the car for a trip to some magical land. She had to be able to get to work.

"Sorry?"

Emily sighed. "We'll find out. Do you know where it is?"

"We can direct you," Modi suggested. "It's around a dozen miles from here. It should only take a few hours."

"How about we drive? I'm sure we can find parking."

"What do you mean?"

"Hannah, I believe we're going to have to teach our children about cars."

"They don't even know to look both ways before crossing the street. Clearly, we were very neglectful parents."

"So you do believe us, then?" Magni asked, that same hopeful expression all the clearer.

"I don't know what I believe," Emily said as she stood.

Hannah yelped and clambered to her feet. Pouting, Hannah looked up but accepted that it was time to leave. "Let me throw on some pants. Should I bring a jacket? Is it cold?"

"It is quite warm."

"Do you even have pants?" Emily asked, her voice lilting mockingly.

"I have a couple."

"Prove it."

She could tell by the look in Emily's eyes that she wished she'd challenged her on this ages ago. She knew she looked amazing, and Emily was only proving her point. "I love those jeans."

Hannah smiled victoriously, ignoring the fact that they belonged to Megan. It was absolutely worth wearing them.

"Right." Modi cleared his throat. "Are you ready?"

"Can we grab more beer for the road?" Magni asked.

Hannah put her hands on her hips. Far too much of their budget went to beer, and they couldn't afford two more people with bottomless appetites. Was that a god thing? It would explain Alys. "Don't you have beer in Asgard?"

"It's not Asgard anymore and not like this."

"Do you have more of those gold coins?" Emily asked.

"Of course."

"Sweet," Emily said. "Hand some over and we can stop at Fred Meyer on the way."

❖

"Roll the windows up," Emily called as they approached the statue the Asses had mentioned. Maybe she really was their mother. She was certainly acting the part. Hannah tried not to laugh.

"How?" Magni asked.

"I think we just hit the button," Modi replied, promptly unlocking his door.

"Just pull your heads in, and I'll roll them up. Christ, it's like giant armored Labradors."

"That sounds adorable," Hannah said, grinning back at their strange dogs.

"Don't encourage them." Emily rolled the windows up and came to a stop at a red light. "It's by the statue of Mimir, right?" After a few minutes of them attempting to give directions that didn't involve street names or landmarks and included the word *fathom* at least once, Emily had looked up the statue on her phone.

"It's right next to it. Maybe three paces away."

"Great." She found a parking lot nearby that offered overnight parking. "You sure this will only be a day? I'd rather it not get towed while we're gone."

"You could stay for longer," Magni said, hope clear in his voice.

Emily and Hannah exchanged looks. Hannah tried to silently convey that they absolutely could not. This was all still crazy, and if they stayed too long, she might not make it back for work, and it sounded dangerous, and scary. She hoped her point got across.

Emily shook her head. "We should probably just do the one day. But I'm sure we can come back later."

"It's still a bit of a walk," Magni said. "A day might be tough."

"These cars make travel much more convenient. Do you think it could drive on the Rainbow Bridge?" Modi asked. "You could carry it there, brother."

"Or perhaps Father…Hannah could. She's stronger than I am." Hannah eyed the car. "I managed to lift it once, but I don't know if I could really carry it very far. I don't want to risk part of it coming off." She still wasn't sure nothing had broken the last time, especially with how the car had bounced. She'd been trying to keep an eye on it when she drove, but it was so old it was tough to tell.

"You better have enough gold to buy me a new car," Emily said. "Maybe a Jaguar."

Shrugging, Hannah bent and gripped the car where she'd grabbed it before. She lifted it up over her head again, bracing herself to carry it, and the metal only yielded slightly under her hands. Those dents were totally already there.

Magni applauded. "Yes, Father. I knew you could do it."

"I already had," Hannah said, trying not to sound too cocky, but that was hard to do when she felt like Superman.

"Do you need help carrying it?"

Hannah tilted her head from side to side. It had weight. It wasn't like holding up a balloon, but she still wouldn't call this heavy. "Not exactly."

"Okay," Emily said, finally sounding fazed. "Well, that's

incredibly hot, but how about we leave this world before people ask a bunch of questions?" Emily grabbed Hannah's bicep before darting out from under the car and turning to their kids. "Where's this bridge?"

A glint in his eye, Modi pointed at a fence between the branches of a couple trees just off the sidewalk. There was a house past the fence. It didn't seem like there could be a whole world there, but now that Hannah was staring, there seemed to be a shimmer, almost like light reflecting off oil. "After you," she said.

"Of course." Modi and Magni led the way, with Hannah following and Emily a few feet behind. Hannah wondered if Emily was checking out her ass as she had to support this thing.

Even carrying a car, it was difficult to believe this was real. She was Thor, her kids were other gods, and her girlfriend was another. It was like a dream or maybe a nightmare. She was walking right at a fence holding a car. She almost hoped she was being tricked. At least then, she wouldn't have to wonder about what it meant.

But it worked.

"Holy shit." Hannah stared at a mighty tree that looked to dwarf any skyscraper she'd ever seen. She hadn't even realized she'd stepped over; she'd been so focused on the car and her thoughts. It hadn't felt like anything had happened. She couldn't even see where the tree ended from her spot on the bridge crossing two of its branches. Emily bumped into her, and she had to scramble to not drop the car.

"Hey…Oh." Emily seemed just as transfixed by the sight. "Where are we?"

"This is Yggdrasil, the world tree," Magni said. "Her branches support the nine realms."

"Holy fuck."

A whole new reality unfolded before them, and lifting a metric ton of metal and having random, fully grown children no longer seemed like the strangest things. Hannah's normal life was so far behind her. She would say worlds away, but that was too literal. It sent a chill up her spine. "It's beautiful."

"If you set the car down, we'll head up this road, and then there's a well-worn path that should guide us to our home once we're in Idavollr."

Unable to find the words or a reason to argue, Hannah set the vehicle on the solid ray of colored light, and they all piled in again. They were driving on a rainbow. Hannah could hardly believe that the car wasn't passing through it.

She was worried the car seemed to be riding lower than it had been but hoped that was her imagination. "Buckle up," she muttered as Emily started to drive. It seemed worth saying. Though if they went over the edge, she doubted seat belts would save them. The bridge was tragically not OSHA compliant.

It only took an hour of cautious driving, as the path past the bridge could only be called a road when speaking very generously, before they found the edge of a strange city. There were stone houses with thatched roofs and a castle in the distance, but describing it as medieval seemed woefully inaccurate. Hannah was far from an expert on architecture, but she didn't think they could or would have built houses so large and winding. Even the smallest hovel here would be an estate compared to present-day houses on Earth. Or would that be Midgard? The material seemed shinier and, if she had to guess, sturdier than any masonry possible in medieval times. Yet she saw people in scratchy-looking clothing tilling fields and looking the very picture of medieval peasants, save for the handful wearing glasses. It didn't seem anachronistic, since it didn't look like bits of her present—aside from the car—were impeding on the village. It seemed like a place that could never have existed. The handful of giants meandering around did little to diminish this appearance.

Everyone seemed to be taking a particular interest in them, but no one moved toward them. Hannah wasn't sure if that was a good sign or a bad one.

"Wow," Emily said, gazing out the windshield with a look of complete bewilderment mixed with fascination. "Where do I go from here?"

Modi pointed straight ahead. Emily had to avoid a few fields of crops, as ruining them would cause a poor impression, but she managed about as straight a heading as could be expected of a lesbian. Soon, Hannah realized they were driving to the imposing castle that seemed to tower over the countryside. It looked almost Victorian, not in the steampunk sense of top hats and gears, but in that it seemed to rely less on the medieval technology of the outskirts. There was no steam coming from it, so if they had engines, they weren't steam powered, but the gate lowered itself, and there didn't seem to be a crank on the inside.

A few minutes later, they parked in the middle of a courtyard and emerged to find a handful of archers training arrows on them. Of course they wouldn't welcome them with open arms. Nothing about being a god had been great so far, why did Hannah expect it to be now? With a twinge of fear, she wondered if she was arrow-proof. She stepped in front of Emily on the off chance that she happened to be more durable. She wouldn't let anything happen to Emily if she could avoid it.

Modi and Magni managed to clamber out of the car, struggling as their armor caught on everything, but they held their hands up. "Wait," Modi called. "It's us. And we've brought back Father and Mother, just as promised."

"Where's his beard, then?" one of the archers asked.

Was that really all that separated her from Thor? Hannah had always assumed that she had to look more feminine than an old Norse god. The way people always looked at her and how dresses hugged her figure would certainly suggest that. Maybe Thor was just a lot more feminine than she'd been led to believe.

"He seems to have lost it," Magni said. "But I assure you, I'd know my father anywhere. This is him. We have our proper king."

Hannah stared at him. She was an accountant, and that was all she wanted. She didn't have time for a second job, and being king— or queen, however it would work—seemed really demanding. "Wait, what? That wasn't what we discussed."

He offered an apologetic grin before turning back to the increasingly confused archers. "Come now, you know us. Where are the others? They must see them. I'm sure Baldur will be thrilled to find his brother."

A murmur echoed through the ranks as their bows lowered one by one. "Very well. Erik, would you go alert the regent? We have guests, and I'm certain they'll need a feast." The man doing most of the talking was dressed differently than the others. Hannah guessed he was a captain or some other sort of military rank. "Pray tell, what is this contraption you've arrived in? It's a strange carriage."

"Tiny horses," Emily said. "Like ten of them in there."

Modi stared at the idling engine in awe. "Truly?"

She shrugged.

This was not the time to try to explain internal combustion. Hannah highly doubted that either of them were capable of that explanation either way.

"All right, well, come with me." He slung his bow on his back and waved for them to join him. "I trust you're tired after your travels?"

"No, I'm good," Emily said.

"Definitely up for that feast, though," Hannah added. Perhaps she should start thinking of herself as Thor while she was here? Thor followed. No, she hated it. As much as she might be Thor, she refused to stop being Hannah, even for a moment. "We brought beer."

"Oh, I forgot it," Magni cried, running back to get it from the car. He looked startled when the car beeped as Emily unlocked it and then did it again as he carried the crates from the trunk. "Strange horses."

"We really need to explain that later," Hannah said.

"You're welcome to try."

There was a lot more of the courtyard than Hannah had expected, but soon they found doors several times her height or even the height of Modi and Magni. Servants or guards, she wasn't sure which, opened the doors and revealed a hall that could have fit Alys's entire house inside. Torches on either side lit their path, but the hall seemed to go on for miles. Hannah was starting to wish they'd brought the car.

It took them almost an hour to find the dining hall, but they were promptly met with a feast. Was it really going to be this simple? They'd just show up, say they were gods, and have a feast? She'd expected something more.

"I thought you said Thor was here?" a voice asked from the back of the dining hall. It seemed to come from the raised row above the rest of the tables. If April's historical dramas had taught Hannah anything, that was where the king would be sitting. Or was it regent, since it sounded like they didn't have a king?

The room was half-full of people. Their clothes looked medieval but clean and maybe even pressed. None of them looked dirty, and several had flowers braided into their beards or hair.

"She is," Magni said.

"Did his beard run away along with the last two feet of him?"

Several of the other Asses laughed at what was apparently the height of godly humor.

The insults were getting ridiculous. Hannah was comfortable with her height, and she was one hundred percent comfortable with her gender. She loved dresses, and she sure as hell didn't want a beard. She just wasn't used to being made fun of. "All right, if any of you doubt who I am…" she found herself bellowing in the deepest alto she could manage. "I've brought enough beer to start out-drinking you, and I'll arm wrestle any of you fuckers who decide you'd like to tussle with the god of strength." God, she hoped Thor was actually the god of strength.

That boast would really backfire if he wasn't, but Magni had made it sound like he was. She was? Pronouns were very confusing when your past-self was a god. She wasn't even sure why she cared so much. Maybe she just didn't want to disappoint Modi and Magni? Or maybe she wanted more answers.

"Okay, that might be Thor," someone at one of the low tables stated.

Hannah showed her teeth in what she hoped was an intimidating smirk directed at whoever this asshole was. She had not expected that to work. She had mostly hoped to get to the drinking.

"Come now, you can't expect me to believe those are Thor and Sif," a man to his side said.

"If that is Thor," the regent said, "that trick isn't going to satisfy me. How do we know she's not simply a Jotunn in disguise? It wouldn't be the first time."

"Jotunn means giant, right?" Hannah whispered into Emily's ear.

"I think so."

"Do I look like a giant?" she asked loudly. She was trying so hard to prove herself to these people. It was just like how hard she tried to prove to Emily that she was gay. That was it, wasn't it? She couldn't stand the idea of hiding part of herself, no matter how crazy that might be. She wasn't willing to uproot her life, she didn't want to be Thor, but she was him, and she needed to know what that meant.

The lower tables laughed again, but the high table, which she was starting to assume was comprised of the other Aesir, only watched her with unamused looks on their faces.

Save for one. A blond near the center looked quite tickled by the joke. "Look at his…her eyes. I'd know my brother anywhere." He rose, his fair features lighting up with a massive grin as he hopped down, ignoring the stairs, and sprinted to Hannah, wrapping his arms around her. "Oh, how I've missed you. Clearly, my son has had far too much to drink today if he can't recognize his own uncle. I do hope you haven't forgotten me."

Well, that was convenient. Hannah pulled away, looking into the fair features of the man in front of her. He had pale blond hair and eyes the same light blue as April's. The regent looked a lot like him, though his features were a few shades darker. "It doesn't work like that, unfortunately. I still don't know how this happened, but I can't remember a thing."

"Well, you always did take a few too many blows to the head. Do *you* at least recognize me, dear Sif? It's your brother-in-law, Baldur."

Emily shrugged.

"Well, that should prove it for you, Forseti!" He turned to the regent, flashing an impressive smile. "If they were Jotunns, I just gave them more than enough reason to lie, and it wouldn't have cost them a thing. Why would spies do such a poor job pretending to be Thor and Sif? It's them, I'm sure of it."

The regent—Forseti, apparently—looked them up and down before whispering to a woman to his left. She was wearing silver armor with wings and seemed to be listening intently before she nodded and said something back. He turned to Modi. "Your guests may stay the night, but without proof, we can't accept them as who you claim."

"You're just scared they'll take your throne," Magni cried.

"Brother, please." Modi's hand rested on Magni's chest. He didn't need to hold him back quite yet, but he looked perfectly prepared to do so should the need arise.

"Forseti, I swear, I would know my brother anywhere," Baldur insisted. "You wouldn't doubt me, would you?"

"I'm sorry, Father." The younger man, who still looked substantially older than even Emily, shook his head, looking sadly at the blond. He ran his hand through his own sandy hair, leaving a faint trace of grease from the bird he was eating. "I've been entrusted with keeping Idavollr safe. I want to believe this is truly Thor returned to us. But why wouldn't he have come back when you did? Why would he be a woman? I can't believe it yet, and even a display of Thor's might would do little to quell those doubts."

"Well, what can I do?" Hannah asked.

"Why do you even care that much?" Emily muttered.

She wished she knew. A new job didn't sound that enticing, she didn't want to rule—she didn't even want to leave Earth—but she'd just found out that she was a god and could lift a car without breaking a sweat. How could she not want to know more? Maybe she didn't need to convince these Asses, but why shouldn't she? They were her family, weren't they?

She sighed, meeting the steely gaze of the man above her. "I don't want anything from you, but if I'm Thor, then I want to know it as badly as you do." She did kind of want that apple, which was maybe reason enough, but she knew the rest was true too. Immortality just sounded cool. "I'm not trying to take over. I don't want your throne. All I want is to know how I could be some old Norse god. Until the other week, I thought I was a normal accountant from Seattle. Then these guys came up and insisted they were my children, and all of a sudden, I'm a superpowered god in another world. If you don't believe I'm Thor, then at least believe that I'm as confused as you are."

"Well, now I know you're not Thor. He couldn't give a speech like that to save his life. Especially not sober."

"Maybe the beard made me dumb."

Finally, she managed to get a chuckle out of His Excellency. She had no idea if that was how you addressed a regent, but she hoped it wasn't. "As I said, you can stay for the feast. You're welcome to join me at my table. I want you to be Thor. In fact, I'd want it even more if you *did* want to rule, but I won't let an impostor harm those in my charge."

"We don't want to hurt anyone," Emily said, stepping up to face the man as well. "We just want answers. This was sprung on us, and if I'm a goddess, I'd really like to understand better. Like, maybe find out that I'm more than just pretty hair?"

He nodded somberly and gestured, causing a servant to bring out two more chairs for them. Hannah hoped the servants were paid well. If they were slaves, she would absolutely get rid of that if she was in charge. She shook her head. She didn't want to be in charge, and entertaining the idea was asking for trouble.

"Please. Sit down. Magni, Modi…grab a cup and explain why you thought this was true."

"We talked to Mimir," Modi began once they were seated and enjoying cups of godly beer. It wasn't quite as good as the stuff they'd brought, but that could wait for later. "I asked him if any prophecies mentioned the Jotunn continuing these recent raids. He said there wasn't anything about them, but he suspected they would. Then Magni said he wished Father and Mother were here, that they'd know how to keep our home safe, and Mimir…" He stared at his plate as if he was trying to remember the exact words. "He started to say something about how they'd both fallen and offered advice on how to move on, like he did the last time Magni said it, but then he stopped. He didn't seem sure how he knew, but it was as if there was a whole new prophecy. He said that we'd find the ladies Thor and Sif—that's how he phrased it—in Midgard, in the very city the Bifrost had connected us to. We went to Midgard, but we couldn't find them. We looked for a week."

"Then we went back to him," Magni said. "He told us that he'd heard that Mjolnir would be able to find Thor if we were in Midgard. He wasn't sure how, but it was supposed to work. So we took it with us, and we found her. Mjolnir wanted to return to her hand. It was like every time Father had thrown it. It knew it needed to return to his grip, and now it knows it for Hannah. If that's not proof, I don't know what is."

"Why didn't you tell me that?" Hannah asked, staring in shock. "Why did I have to prove it?"

Forseti shook his head. "He was hesitant because he knows full well that doesn't mean anything. First, why would Mimir know they were back? It doesn't make sense."

"He knows everything."

"Well, his knowledge has seemed quite shaky since Sif died."

Magni's face fell. Hannah supposed that meant Sif really was his mother, despite what Alys had said. It was clear she meant the world to him.

"The hammer will return to anyone who throws it."

"I was the one holding it. It wanted to return to her because Thor threw it to kill Jormungandr, and it never returned to him. It never completed its task."

"Then it could be a spell. Loki used to love stealing the hammer at every opportunity. I see no reason to think she couldn't be him."

"I would know Loki anywhere," Modi insisted. "That traitor got my father killed." Then it would probably be a bad idea to mention Alys. "This isn't a spell. Mjolnir recognizes its wielder. If that's not enough, they came here on the Bifrost. For Odin's sake, Forseti. The Bifrost takes us to the very city she's in. Why do you think it's been there? How does none of this prove it to you?"

"Just because you want to believe it…" He sighed. "No, I can't accept it. Please, eat. Perhaps we can try this Midgardian beer your friends have brought."

That was that. Modi and Magni seemed unwilling to attempt any further discussion. Magni tried once but was promptly shut down by his brother, so Hannah took the hint. They were not getting any apples today. They'd have to try again later.

CHAPTER SEVENTEEN

"We'll figure something out." That was all Modi and Magni had left them with once they returned to Emily's car in the morning after spending the night in the softest bed they'd ever felt. They'd been that close to immortality, to answers, to being actual literal gods, and instead, they were left to stew in their own ignorance.

"I guess we're not getting those apples, then."

"You think?" Before the words had even left her lips, Hannah regretted them. She was snapping at her girlfriend, which she'd sworn she wouldn't do again. It wasn't who she was anymore. It couldn't be.

Emily stared, her mouth slightly open. She didn't even know that Hannah could have a temper…at least, Hannah hoped she didn't know. She was pretty sure she'd never let it show around her.

"I'm sorry," Hannah said.

"You really wanted that immortality, didn't you?"

She shrugged. It hardly seemed to matter at this point. "It doesn't seem fair that we're not getting it. We're gods too, right? I mean, I carried a car yesterday."

"It's okay." She laced her fingers with Hannah's.

"I just hate how this went. I thought for sure we'd be accepted immediately."

"You've never really had to face not being accepted. Most people don't come around to whatever you claim to be the second you tell them. Most people don't even come around eventually. I don't know if they will, but it's not like you're empty-handed. You have superstrength and the ability to drink your weight in alcohol. I have nothing."

"You have a girlfriend who can bench-press a semi." She hoped Emily would still want to be together. With Hannah's temper and her strength, she'd hardly blame anyone for not wanting to be with her.

Emily smiled softly at her. "I do have that."

"Even though I snapped at you?" Worriedly, she peered at Emily, barely willing to meet her eyes.

"Honey, I already said it's okay. Besides, that barely counts as snapping. You said something slightly flippant and then immediately apologized."

"But—"

Squeezing her arm, Emily rested her head against Hannah's shoulder. "I have no intention of leaving you. Hell, if what our kids are saying is true, we've been together for centuries. What could possibly come between that?"

Hannah bit her lip hard enough that it hurt. She couldn't share what had happened before. It would make Emily hate her. She knew exactly what her temper could cause, and she wasn't willing to risk it again. She'd control it. She had to. She hoped that it was enough.

"Okay. Fine. You're right."

"I always am." Heading around to the other side of the car, she opened the passenger door for Hannah. "Let's get out of here. We're clearly not wanted."

"We could try to steal the apples."

"I don't think they're a one-time thing. Besides, we still might get a second chance. Modi and Magni seemed pretty intent on making sure of it. Maybe next time, we'll even get to look around. For now, let's just head home."

"And do what?"

"Well, we should probably tell Alys what happened. I know they really wanted to get their hands on that apple. Can hardly blame them… the poor dear is almost thirty."

"Oh. I guess we can do that."

Emily chuckled. "Did you have something else in mind?"

"Thought I'd hold you with one hand and fuck you with the other."

The car almost swerved off the Rainbow Bridge and killed them both. "You can't say that when I'm driving."

"So I take it you want to do that?"

After a few moments of concentrating on driving, Emily finally said, "Yes. But then we see Alys."

❖

A few drinks in, Alys finally asked. "I take it that it didn't go too well?" Other than exchanging pleasantries, neither Emily nor Hannah had been quite sure where to begin and wanted to give the alcohol time to restore their brains from the scrambling they'd given each other earlier.

"I wouldn't go that far," Hannah said.

"I would." Emily sighed, stretching and setting her legs in Hannah's lap. "They didn't believe we are who we claimed. I can't really blame them on my account, but I'm not sure how they could come to that conclusion for Hannah…she could probably lift a mountain."

"Only if I really needed to."

"They let us stay in a room at the castle overnight and then more or less kicked us out. Modi and Magni say that they're going to figure something out, but I'm really doubting we'll be able to get your apple."

"Don't talk like that." They smiled at Emily, but it was pained. They looked almost desperate. "I know you can do it. You just need to wait for your kids."

"Why do you need it?" Hannah asked. "If you can shapeshift, couldn't you stop yourself from aging?"

Their eyes grew wide, but they shook their head. "I'd rather not have to, and I'm not really sure. But I mean, come on, how could I not want apples that give me immortality?"

"I thought you had to keep eating them? I looked into it some online before we came, and I'm not sure how one apple would even help you." Hannah leaned against the armrest. She understood wanting them, but the whole thing was just weird. Maybe the first one did more than the others? Alys certainly knew more mythology than she did.

They drained their beer. "I figured that one apple would buy me time to figure out how to get more. Especially if you stole them for me again. Or I could try growing them, but it's really not clear if it's special apples or if they only grow that way for Idunn."

That seemed to grab Emily's attention. "Wait, that's a power a god could have? I mean, it's not as showy, but I'd take being able to make immortality-granting fruit."

"Well, you're the goddess of earth, grain, love, and marriage. So you can make super-strong girls love you."

"I do appreciate that, I guess." She didn't sound like she did.

"And you could probably make her marry you."

Hannah nodded. "Yup, it'd work."

"Wait, what?" Emily sat up, pulling her legs away. "You? What?"

"I'm not saying we should do it right now, but that is well within your powers, my beloved goddess."

Her cheeks reddened. "Well…I…Thank you."

Hannah set her feet in Emily's lap. She'd worn herself out earlier, and while she wanted to get up and kiss her, that seemed like a lot of work. She probably just needed some food.

"See? You have great powers. You could also farm really well."

"I'm not farming."

Alys sighed. "Well, maybe you could make amazing wine." A smile spread across their face. "Or you could try making beer. You are the goddess of grain, after all."

"Huh." She chewed her lip, idly massaging one of Hannah's feet. "I could make beer." She nodded. "Yeah. I have to try that. How do you make beer?"

"Look it up. I'm your mythology expert, not your hops expert."

"I thought you knew everything."

"I do. I just don't want to have to walk you through this." They tried to sip from their empty bottle. "Speaking of, I need another. Anyone want anything?"

"Twenty beers and something you cooked?" Hannah asked.

"How about I just bring out the two six-packs I already have in the fridge and warm something up for you?"

"Yes please." She grinned, whimpering softly as Emily hit a callus. "That sounds amazing."

With them in the other room, Emily asked, "You were joking, right?"

"Nope." She closed her eyes, letting the cushioned armrest serve as a pillow while she enjoyed Emily's ministrations.

Emily made a strange noise that Hannah couldn't quite place but continued her work, and Hannah was more than content to enjoy it until there was food.

She must have fallen asleep because Alfredo pasta with grilled chicken was sitting on the coffee table next. "Hmm?" she asked, wiping sleep from her eyes.

"Morning, sleepyhead." Alys beamed at her. "I hadn't smoked anything recently, but I had leftover grilled chicken, so I threw this together."

"Yes, please." She swung her legs off Emily and grabbed the plate. It was as good as everything Alys cooked, and the sauce only accentuated it. She then realized that, other than Emily, she hadn't eaten anything today. No wonder she'd been so tired. "It's amazing."

"I know. Eat up."

Hannah did as she was told and saw that Emily's plate was already almost empty. How long had she been asleep?

"It did sound like you wouldn't be welcome there," Emily said. It must have been part of a conversation they were already having. Hannah couldn't quite tell. She was too busy stuffing her face.

"That's what I figured, and what I'd heard." Alys groaned, tapping the bottle against their teeth. "What did they say?"

"They were worried we could be you in disguise."

They nodded. "Yep. That makes sense."

"Sorry."

"It's okay. I wasn't expecting to be allowed in. Maybe back in would be more appropriate. Being reincarnated is weird. It's why I was hoping you could steal that apple."

"I'll try. I promise. Hmm." Biting her lip, Emily stared at the rug, something clearly running through her head. "Do you really think I could grow them since I'm the goddess of earth?"

"I kind of doubt it since it's Idunn's thing, but it's worth a shot."

"Right. Yeah. I guess we'll try it."

"Assuming we can get an apple in the first place."

"Oh, come on, there's no way Modi and Magni will let their parents die. Worst-case scenario, I'll have to grow one."

Their head tilted to either side. "Yeah. That could work." Fingers tapped the armrest of their recliner. They didn't seem too satisfied with this plan.

Hannah set the empty plate down and held back on asking if there was any more as she finished her drink. "I don't know why exactly, but I trust them. If they say that they'll figure something out, I think we should at least give them some time."

"Sure you're not just feeling lazy?" Emily asked.

Alys met Hannah's eyes, staring. Their eyes were a deep purple that day. That was different. Were they changing them all the time now? "They're your sons. If you trust them, then I do too. We can wait." Their eyes were distant as they nodded. "We can."

"It still seems so weird that I have sons."

"Hey, you two got to skip all the hard parts. That has to be nice."

Emily tapped on her drink. "I don't know. I feel like suddenly having kids in their fifties or sixties or whatever has its downsides."

"They're super rich," Hannah offered.

"They *are* super rich." Her foot thudded against the ground. "Shit. We forgot to get some gold."

"We'll do it next time."

"They owe us for the beer."

"We'll manage. My first paycheck comes in on the thirtieth, so I can cover rent if you're hard up."

"Thanks."

Alys chuckled. "You're married already."

"Have been for centuries, apparently," Hannah said.

Emily blushed again, staring away. For the goddess of marriage, the subject seemed to make her surprisingly bashful.

Hannah decided to let her off the hook. She turned to Alys. "You're like my brother, right?" That was what movies had taught her. She wanted to know a bit more about her family now that it had changed so much. "Like how they're our kids."

"What? No."

"Right, sorry. I guess I should say sibling. It always feels weird when people call me brother or father. But Thor and Loki were brothers, like Baldur. He wouldn't stop calling me that."

"No, Loki was only Odin's brother by a blood pact. He had no real relation to Thor other than a complicated friendship." They squinted, and one eyelid seemed to twitch. "Wait, what did you say about Baldur?"

"Is he not my brother either?"

"He is. But what do you mean you talked to him?"

Hannah cocked her head, trying to figure out what the problem was. "He was in Isa...Isengard."

"Idavollr, honey." Emily patted her shoulder.

"They only said it like one time."

"How was Baldur there?" Alys glanced between them. "You're sure it was Baldur? You couldn't have misheard?"

"It was definitely Baldur," Emily said. "What's the problem?"

They sighed, their foot tapping a discordant beat on the footrest. "I mean, he is supposed to be back, but why would he be there? That doesn't match what I've been told."

"Why wouldn't he be back?" Hannah asked. The whole problem didn't make any sense. How in depth did these myths go? She really needed to read them.

"No. No, no, no. Oh, of course." The footrest slammed back into the chair as Alys leapt to their feet, wide-eyed. "Holy shit. That explains so much."

"What explains what?"

"Oh, that bitch. That brilliant bitch. Of course she'd do that. I can't believe she'd betray me. I'm such a proud father." Their laugh was cold and bitter. "No one does that to me. That's my job…I'm the fucking trickster. She's just supposed to be the goddess of the dead." Another thud sounded as they kicked the chair. "Goddamn it."

Hannah watched, transfixed. What the hell were they talking about?

Alys turned to them, a wicked grin contorting their features. "Well, then. I suppose that settles that. If she really has Baldur there, she'd have her fucking apple and wouldn't be pulling my strings. Who knows what else she's lied to me about? Well, two can play that game. It seems you've got yourself a double agent."

"Sorry, what?" Hannah asked.

"What do you mean?" Emily asked. Hannah wasn't sure when she'd gotten to her feet, but she was standing a couple feet from Alys, staring like she couldn't believe what they were saying.

"This is fantastic." They breathed out a sigh. "I hated having to betray and manipulate you. I'm so sorry, Emily. I cared less about that with you, I'll admit, Hannah, but I was certainly willing to do whatever it took to not have to kill you, even if it meant I'd have to wait a few decades."

"I knew it!" Hannah was almost happier than she was upset. "I kept saying that you were suspicious, that you were reacting too well for this. I knew there was a reason."

"Alys, what are you talking about?" Emily closed the gap between them, taking their hand. "What do you mean you've been betraying me? Manipulating me?"

They sighed, wiping away a sudden tear. "It's a long story."

"I think we have time." Emily's tone didn't leave any room for further argument.

"Maybe we should have more beer." Alys turned toward the kitchen.

Emily gripped their hand harder, stopping them. "No. I need answers. How have you been manipulating me? For how long?" She swallowed. Hannah could see the magnitude of this claim slowly dawning on her. "You've known for more than a week, haven't you? Did you know before we met?"

Avoiding Emily's gaze, Alys nodded. "I've known since I was sixteen."

"What?"

Hannah had never heard Emily's voice sound so cold. It scared her.

"Look, I'm sorry."

"Alys, tell me what the fuck you mean."

Their mouth opened and closed, tears trailing down their cheeks. "I'm sorry."

"That's not an answer."

"Fine. Okay. I'll tell you. I've always wanted to. I just couldn't. It wasn't like I enjoyed hiding things. Sure, I befriended you because Hel needed me to, but you were the first person I ever really cared about, that I ever felt close to. It's been eating me up for years, you have to understand."

"You've had over eight years to tell me if it bothered you so much," she spat.

Sniffling, they nodded. "I know. She told me I couldn't, that I had to keep lying to you. You couldn't find out from me. It had to come from the other Aesir. It would happen so long as we were in Portland."

"That's why you didn't want me to move when my ex—"

"I didn't want you to move because I love you. You're my best friend, my only real friend." A shaky breath left their lips as they tried and failed to meet Emily's steely gaze. "Emily, please. I swear, I never would have hurt you or Hannah. I know how much she means to you."

"You said you would've had to kill her."

Hannah had never heard Emily so full of rage.

They winced. "Fuck. If you two couldn't get an apple, I was supposed to kill Hannah and take her place. She thought maybe I could convince them better."

"You wouldn't have my strength," Hannah said, her voice hollow. Any satisfaction she'd found in this was gone.

"Maybe I was supposed to get your belt. I'm not really sure. She only let slip that if you couldn't do this, I'd take your place. I think there was more to the plan, but she wouldn't tell me anything when I asked."

Emily let out a derisive snort. "She sounds so trustworthy. I can see why you'd betray me for her."

Their eyes finally met. Alys gritted their teeth. "She'd sure as hell earned my loyalty. Just because you had people you could stay with, money, a phone, and all that when you got kicked out of your parents' house doesn't mean *I* had anything. I was homeless, living on the streets for weeks before she found me. She told me what I was, what I could do, and that she could help me. It took work, and I had to keep the form I hated when I was in public, but I could be anything I wanted after that. And I could take anything I wanted."

"You never said—"

"Forgive me for not wanting to talk about…" They shook their head. "No. I'm sorry. Here I am feeling sorry for myself after everything I've done. I know our friendship was based on a lie, but I swear, it wasn't a lie itself. You mean everything to me. I've been trying to figure out how to tell you for years." Tears fell on the carpet with a light patter. "I'm so sorry."

"Alys—"

"You don't have to say it. I know you can't forgive me."

"Emily." Hannah stood, taking her free hand. "They didn't hurt me. They haven't done anything they can't take back." It felt strange being the one defending Alys, but she knew how important they were to Emily, and no matter how justified it was, she couldn't let Emily throw that all away.

"They've lied to me for years."

Alys jumped in. "I did. But I swear, I won't do it again. Please, Emily, I promise. You don't have to forgive me or even stay friends with me, but I swear, I won't lie or hurt you again. I'll turn against her. I'll do anything you want. Please don't leave." Their lip quivered, and they turned away, ripping their hand free. "No. That's too much to ask for. I'm sorry. I'll figure something out. I'll lie to Hel, say the Aesir killed you, whatever it takes."

"It's not like our sons were honest with us either," Hannah said. "They sure seemed to know a lot more than they've said before, and what was that about Mjolnir finding me?"

"They haven't had eight years to come clean," Emily snapped, turning those ice-cold eyes on Hannah.

For a moment, Hannah couldn't find her voice. She'd never seen Emily like this, and certainly not toward her. So that was what it felt like to be on the receiving end.

"Fuck," Emily muttered. "I'm sorry. You haven't done anything wrong."

"Well, it sounds like Alys hasn't had any real choices."

Alys cleared their throat. "No. I have. I could've told you at any time, and I didn't. I won't pretend otherwise. Hel certainly didn't want me to, but she wouldn't want me betraying her now either, so that doesn't justify anything. I should've told you years ago."

"Can you really blame Alys for that loyalty?" This was new. Having to talk someone else down when they were angry. At least she knew all the tricks.

"I can't forgive you."

"I'm not asking for forgiveness," Alys said.

"But I'm not willing to throw you out of my life, either." Eyes softening, she turned back to Alys. "I can't imagine what you've been through. You should've told me. And you should've told me what I was too. But I understand why you didn't."

Alys nodded, choking back sobs.

"I know how much our friendship must mean for you to be willing to turn against her."

"It means everything."

Emily sighed, starting to collapse back onto the couch but apparently changing her mind. "I need some time to process this. If you find anything out, tell me. I'll talk to you soon, but I can't be here right now. I promise, we'll tell you if we learn anything more. We'll…Right, I guess you're not after that apple for yourself."

"I'd still like it. I'd rather be immortal, especially if I'm turning against another god."

"Fine." Emily pulled Hannah toward the door. "We'll talk later."

"Bye," Hannah offered.

"Bye," Alys muttered back, falling into the recliner, tears falling anew. At least Emily was still going to talk to them.

Emily didn't say a word as she drove back to the apartment. Once there, she broke down sobbing in Hannah's arms. This was definitely not how Hannah had wanted the evening to go. She stroked Emily's hair, offering comforting words and soft kisses on her forehead and temples. They'd make it through this, and with a bit of luck, Alys would too.

CHAPTER EIGHTEEN

A lys stared at the credits on the screen. They couldn't remember a single detail of that episode. Well, that wasn't strictly true. They'd seen every episode of *Doctor Who* at least half a dozen times—maybe three for the classic series—barring the missing episodes, so they absolutely knew what happened, but they didn't remember having just watched it.

Maybe if they stopped staring at their phone, things would be a little different.

They checked again to make sure. Still no messages from Emily.

For the dozenth, twentieth, fiftieth time, their thumb hovered over the call button. "Fuck."

They slammed the back of their head against the excessively cushioned couch. It was so soft that it didn't feel like hitting anything. They almost wished they were tall enough to hit the wall behind it. Well, they could be...

Shaking their head, Alys stared at the phone.

It had barely been an hour. There was no reason for Emily to call. Or forgive them.

They sighed, slumping. "What the fuck am I doing?" they shouted to the empty house. "I could've kept my cool. I didn't have to come forth with the whole truth. I could've come around to their side without owning up to the whole thing." While they were fairly certain they hadn't literally turned into goo, they slid off the couch nonetheless, their knees hitting the coffee table. They didn't bother to move.

"It's not like I assumed she'd understand. I mean, I did. But I didn't." They'd hated lying to Emily so much, but it hadn't stopped them from doing it. "Maybe I deserve this."

The next episode started, though they could only kind of see it over their knees and the table. It wasn't like it mattered. They started to hum along to the theme tune but trailed off after a few notes. They didn't have the energy.

What could they even do? How could they earn her trust again?

Alys chewed their lip and idly watched David Tennant run. They could call Hannah. "No. Don't be ridiculous. No matter how fine Emily might have been with my little crush, I don't think either of them would take that well right now."

No. If they wanted to do something about this, they'd have to go to the source.

They'd have to contact the other woman they couldn't bring themself to reach out to. They'd even started sketching the runes earlier but had stopped. What would they even say? "Some double agent I am."

They could try smoking something? If they made that brisket again, maybe Emily, or at least Hannah... Alys sighed, slumping farther until they flopped over their side on the floor. At least their carpet was soft. They rubbed their cheek on the gray frieze fibers. Maybe they could just sleep there?

With another sigh, they tried to bring themself to their feet, failed, and just lay there, staring at the parts of Freema Agyeman's face that weren't covered by the table. They were fine like this.

What felt like hours later but had probably only been a few minutes—though the credits were rolling, so that wasn't a great sign—Alys sat up. Their cheeks were wet with tears, and they had to blink them away and rub their eyes. "I can hardly talk to her like this," they muttered.

Finally standing, Alys willed their appearance to change. They watched the reflection in the glass coffee table as their hair turned a bright green while their cheeks dried, and their eyes lost their redness. They took a few breaths to steady themself. "You can do this. Come on."

Groaning, they let out a nervous whistle. The next episode was a good one. Maybe they could...nope. They grabbed the remote and turned off the TV. They wouldn't fall for that trap. They had to do this. They had to talk to Hel.

Their clothes were a mess. They should change, shouldn't they?

A few minutes later, Alys stood nervously in front of the door, their new T-shirt and jeans seeming inadequate armor.

Using all their will, they grabbed the doorknob and stepped down the stairs. They could call Hel anywhere, but the runes and circle in the basement gave them hope that they wouldn't be spied on after the call ended. They blew out a breath. If they were wrong, if Hel was able to watch them and had heard their betrayal…they traced the runes in the air before they had any further chance to second-guess themself.

They could do this.

"Loki?" the familiar voice asked. The imposing figure stood in the center of their basement, the decayed flesh looking more horrifying than ever. "I was not expecting you so soon. Things are progressing well, then?"

Alys nodded. They could work with that. They really should have figured out what they were going to say first. Even with all the years of improvised lying, they'd never had to actually come up with much. Not mentioning the goddess they occasionally talked to was surprisingly easy. "Yes. They've met with the gods. They went to Idavollr."

"Good." Half her face gave a warm smile. "Then you have it?"

"No." They forced themself to stand still. They could do this. They just had to come up with a plausible story. "The gods want Hannah and Emily to prove themselves first." Lying by telling the truth might have been all they tended to do, but it wasn't all that useful when you were trying to be a double agent. "But it won't be long. I've offered to help."

"Hmm. So Thor couldn't manage it? Perhaps I made him too soft?"

Alys had to fight with every fiber of their being not to narrow their eyes. What did that mean? That Hel hadn't challenged Hannah enough or…They'd never quite allowed themself to wonder what all Hel had controlled.

"We may need to move on to alternative plans. She shouldn't be difficult to replace."

"No!" Alys's gulped. They'd been far too quick to say that. "She's useful." They kept their tone neutral, but it wasn't nearly enough to cover their enthusiasm. "We can dispose of her when the time is right, but I don't have her strength. What if we need it?"

"I'm sure you'll be able to fool them."

"Modi and Magni already trust her." Now was the chance. Should they take it? They hadn't finished ensuring Hannah's safety yet, but they also couldn't look too interested in it, and this information might earn Emily's forgiveness. "Baldur trusts them. Quite readily."

"Of course."

The answer gave nothing away. Alys needed to learn that skill.

"But you told me that you brought Baldur back as one of Hannah's friends. How is he there?"

Hel cocked her head. "Why should that matter? We'll accomplish our task, and then you can finally be who you want. You won't have to hide anymore. Is that not what you desire?"

"Of course. That's all I want." They already didn't have to hide anymore. Not since Emily knew. Was that all Hel thought she had on them? Was that why they'd listened to her for so long, even when they knew they were hurting someone they loved? Just because Hel would eventually let them be themself. Alys felt disgusted with themself. They were even worse than the Christianized myths made Loki sound.

"Then be patient. Next time, I hope you'll have more promising information. If not, we'll move ahead with the plan and dispose of him." The uneven smile, pulling away at the desiccated face, made the implication more than clear. Alys had given away too much. Hel knew they were protecting Hannah.

CHAPTER NINETEEN

The next morning, Hannah headed to work. While, apparently, some people could ignore their schedule and not get fired, she definitely lacked that ability and was not willing to risk losing the internship, let alone the potential job offer it could lead to. Even if she could have all the money in Idavollr, being an accountant was still her dream.

The first three hours went by quickly; there had been some recent major expenditures she needed to document, and by the time she'd finished, it was almost lunch. She pushed her chair in, stretching for the ceiling lights and finding herself far too short. She hadn't even noticed how much she'd hunched over her monitor.

Isabel nudged her. "I brought you lunch. I've seen you starve a few too many times for comfort."

"I'm waiting on that first paycheck," Hannah insisted. Not that she'd actually be able to afford food on that check, but she'd be slightly less broke. Emily had been struggling to cover everything. Modi and Magni needed to chip in already. They could look after their parents.

"Well, until then, I have leftover stir-fry."

"I love you."

"That's what I thought." Grinning, she held up a bag and gestured to the door. "I was hoping to eat outside if you want to join me."

"Sure, I'd love to." Hannah followed, finding a picnic table a few floors above the river. She stared out, lost in thought for a moment. The sight of the river really took her back.

"Earth to Hannah."

More like Midgard. She managed to avoid chuckling at her own terrible joke. "Sorry, I have a lot of fond memories on this river. Let's see the food."

Isabel had already set out two plastic containers, each containing shrimp and broccoli stir-fry. "Ta-da!" Her cheeks dimpled, as she smiled while displaying her culinary creations. "I hope you like broccoli."

"It looks delicious. A friend of mine is a vegan, so I got used to eating it with her." The first time April had gone vegan, broccoli had been on sale, and she'd included it with almost every dish she made. Hannah had never been one to turn down April's food, or apparently any other free food, as the current meal was showing. She'd have to ask Alys if that was a Thor thing.

"Well, I'm glad. Want to tell me about these memories? I mean about the Willamette. You were really zoning out there."

Sitting, Hannah took a fork and had a bite. "Mmm. This is so good." Why could everyone else she knew cook so well? Maybe her Thor genes were holding her back. "Back in college, freshman year, I was on crew, the rowing team. We did exercises on the river at least once a week." Watching the water flow below them, she found herself drifting back in time. "I shouldn't have quit, but mornings were really tough for me—I have no idea how I'm managing here—so I didn't come back for the second year. But I really loved it. It got me in way better shape that I've managed to keep and taught me how to work out. Plus, it's fun. Being on the water is great, and I love the feeling of my oar slicing through it, pulling me forward. If I get that job here, I'm gonna buy a kayak."

"Well, the only other intern in our department got fired, so I think you'll have it."

"They could still decide not to hire me. I don't want to make any assumptions. I know I should probably buy a car—"

"We get company cars."

"What?" Her jaw dropped, but she breathed out a sigh of relief. It explained so much. "That's why everyone drives Mercedes."

She nodded.

"Huh." She felt so much better about her broke ass. "I want a company car."

"Well, stay for a year."

"Can do." Grinning, she took another bite. "I can't wait. My girlfriend's car is okay, but it's definitely getting up there. It'll be so nice having something, well, *nice*." Probably not a good idea to take it to Ida…whatever, though. That would be hard to explain if it got damaged.

"I love it." Isabel smiled, a bit of broccoli showing in her teeth.

Hannah pantomimed to demonstrate the food, and it took far longer than either of them liked to admit for the message to come across and the offending morsel to be taken care of.

"You starting to get used to it here?" Isabel asked as she leaned against the railing.

"I think so."

"Any problems?"

Hannah shook her head. "Unless you can make us not have to start so early. Though I couldn't borrow Emily's car, then."

"Her name's Emily? You never said."

"I didn't?"

"Nope. You've always called her your girlfriend with me and they or your partner when we're in the office."

"Well, her name's Emily. Emily Johnson. And she's the best thing to ever happen to me." Superpowers included.

"I'm happy for you two. I really should put myself back out there. Men are just kind of terrible."

"Glad I don't have to deal with that." She chuckled and earned one in response.

"You're lucky like that." She glanced at her phone. "We should probably head back in. Want me to bring you food tomorrow?"

"Yes, please." She felt bad relying on Isabel for this, but she had a bottomless stomach, and not having anything to eat at work each day had been killing her. One of the downsides of being Thor. They went back to work, crunching numbers and filling out spreadsheets, and made it through the rest of the day. It had been nice having time away from all the godly stuff, although she felt a bit bad about hiding it from her new friend, but she needed to deal with her older friends first.

After she helped Emily cope with someone lying to her for way longer. No hypocrisy on her part there. Nope. Damn, she needed to tell her friends.

❖

What was Emily going to be doing? Probably lying in bed, refusing to get up, maybe with a bottle of whiskey to keep her company. She always went to whiskey when she was drinking to get drunk. Hannah tried to think of what she could do to help her. They had time for a quickie, barely, if that was what took, but she felt like getting some food in Emily would probably be a better plan. What would Emily like most? Hannah had never seen her like this before, so she had never had to figure out the best comfort food. Maybe something fried and some chocolate?

With sandwiches and a giant chocolate-covered doughnut in the shape of genitals in the back of the car, Hannah drove home. They definitely didn't have time for that quickie now, so she hoped she'd chosen right.

Locking the door behind her, Hannah climbed down the steps to their apartment, expecting to find the place quiet. Instead, she heard music coming from her right and smelled waffles. Well, at least that meant she'd chosen something in the right ballpark. "Babe?" she called.

"Hey, Hannah." Emily smiled at her from over the waffle iron. "Do you want any food?"

So much for her being all depressed and hiding under the covers. "I actually got you something."

Looking surprised, Emily turned, smile faltering for a fraction of a second. "Oh? What'd you get me?"

"Roast beef and cheese and a doughnut."

"Well, I'm pretty hungry, so split this waffle with me, and I can still eat all that?"

Hannah hadn't been able to afford a doughnut for herself, so that sounded pretty good. "Yeah, sure. You feeling okay?"

"Why wouldn't I be?"

Hannah stared. Should she say it? She didn't want to drag Emily back down, especially when she needed to go to work. "No reason, I guess?"

"I missed too much work over the weekend, so I wanted to make sure I had enough carbs to get through the day."

"Like you ever need that excuse."

"Waffles are good, okay?" She reached toward the iron protectively, keeping it safe from anyone who would dare criticize its importance.

"Yeah. That's why I'm eating half, remember?"

Emily brought it over to their little table and drizzled syrup on top. "Work go okay?"

"Yeah, it was fine. There was a minor issue from billing, so I had to actually look over the transaction myself and fix the error, but we caught it in time. Mostly, it was just a normal day." She grinned. For years, she'd been waiting for a normal day, and despite all the magical insanity going on in the background, she was thrilled to find that it was really happening. A nice accounting job and a beautiful woman to come home to. All of her dreams were coming true, and she had superstrength to boot.

"Where's the sandwich?"

Hannah set the bags by the waffle, and Emily tore one open. "Mine is the turkey with lettuce and mayo."

"Yep, this one's yours." She shoved it aside and reached for her own. "I'm glad your work is going well. I know how worried you were about it."

"I wasn't that worried."

Emily smirked. "Of course not. Well, I have a bunch of crazy drunks at Ragnarok to deal with pretty soon, so thank you for this."

"It's no problem."

"Really, honey…it means a lot."

Grinning, Hannah bit into her own sandwich. "Well, I'm glad I could help. I know how rough yesterday was for you, and I wanted to look after you." Shit. She had decided not to bring that up. Wow, it had only taken her five minutes to screw up.

"I told you, I'm fine."

"Babe—"

Emily held up her hands. "No. I'm okay. You don't need to worry. I'm a big girl, and I don't need you looking after me. I appreciate the food, really, but I promise I'm okay. Just let me be."

"But, Emily…"

"No. It's okay." She ripped off a chunk of the sandwich and swallowed it before adding, "A lot happened the last couple weeks. Found out that a lot of things I believe about myself were wrong, so it makes sense that the entire basis of my friendship with my best friend for the last eight years would be a lie too. I don't feel like dealing with it. I processed enough last night. I just want to shove some food in my face and go bartend."

"Are you sure you don't want to talk about it?"

"That's never how I deal with stuff. Now, please, can we drop it?"

Hannah didn't want to. She wanted to work through this and figure out how to make sure Emily's friendship with Alys could continue. Anger tearing things apart was never worth it, no matter how justified that anger was, so long as everyone still cared about each other. "Okay."

Emily sighed, turning her gaze from the bread-load of beef back to Hannah. "If I promise to talk to them on my day off, will it make it easier for you?"

"A little."

"Okay. Fine. I can do that. They might have some useful information anyway. They sure as hell know what's going on better than we do."

"Thank you."

"Since I have to do that, when are you going to tell Megan and April?"

Hannah's eyes widened, and she wished that she had gone with the quickie idea. She was trying so hard not to think about it, and Emily just had to bring it up. Food gave too much time for talking. "I don't wanna."

"If I have to talk to my friend after everything, then you can certainly do the same."

"But what if they think I'm crazy?"

"Hannah, you can lift a fucking car one-handed."

Hannah kicked the table, sending it a few feet away and leaving Emily with nowhere to set her sandwich. "But that doesn't mean the other stuff is any more believable."

"It convinced me."

With a sigh and another groan, Hannah shrugged. "I'll talk to them."

"Try to do it soon. I can say firsthand how bad it feels to have these secrets kept from you. It's already been a week. Don't make it any more than that."

"I'll invite them over."

"Please do."

Sinking into the chair, Hannah tried to avoid meeting her gaze. She'd been trying to make sure that Emily took care of herself and did what was best for her friendship. It was no fair having that turned around on her. She took another bite to avoid having to say anything more.

"You're wonderful, and I love you." Emily's voice sounded so soothing. She probably felt she'd gone too far by comparing Hannah's behavior to Alys's.

"Love you too."

Emily finished her sandwich and waffle, gave Hannah a syrupy kiss, and grabbed the doughnut box. "I'm heading to work. I'll eat this in the car. You have fun with Megan and April."

Hannah glared back.

"It'll be fine. Don't worry."

"I guess. Have a good night at work."

"I will. Have to get chewed out for missing the last two days first."

"Think you'll get fired?"

Emily shook her head, her usual confident smile returning. "Not a chance. I've been there for years, and they love me. I can miss the occasional few days without any problem."

"Okay." That made her feel a bit better. At least that fight with Alys wouldn't cost Emily her job or anything. They exchanged another kiss, and Emily left, leaving Hannah alone with her phone and the knowledge of exactly who she had to deal with. Eventually she'd be able to work up the nerve to call them, to confess everything, but first, she decided to finish her waffle and have a beer.

Chapter Twenty

Hannah stared at her phone. She couldn't for the life of her figure out why this was as scary as it was. Even coming out hadn't been this scary, though she had cowered from it for a long time and avoided letting anyone other than Megan know in high school. So maybe it was exactly as scary as coming out. "What do I even say?" she whined. "Well, turns out I used to be a guy…not like that." Groaning, she sank into the couch, trying to force herself to call, or at least text, her friends.

She had a few texts from both of them, as well as Facebook notifications, and an entire conversation in their group chat. It had been over a week since she'd last talked to the people who she'd rarely gone more than a day without talking to. They likely suspected it was due to her internship, and she'd wanted to let them continue believing that. But now she couldn't hide it any longer, not if she wanted things to go any better than they did for Emily and Alys.

Could you two come over tonight? It's important. She clicked send in the group chat before she had a chance to reconsider, grateful that in her haste, she'd managed to avoid any serious typos. She let the phone fall onto the hardwood and threw her arm over her eyes. She was beyond terrified. They were going to think she was insane.

The fact that she could prove her claim did little to make her feel better.

Grabbing another drink from the fridge, she put a show on and tried to pay attention. It didn't work for the first show or the second or even the third. She'd only made it a few minutes into each one, so she decided to see if the fourth time was a charm and drained the rest of her beer.

Her phone chimed. Almost too scared to answer it, Hannah stared at the screen on the floor. The preview at the top of the screen showed

April: *Of course! I've missed you. I can't wait…* Her desire to see the rest of the message overcame her increasing aversion to dealing with her friends—or perhaps all Midgardians—and she snatched up the phone. *…to tell you about everything that's happened. Life has been all over the place for me, but I'll tell you all about it in person. Want me to make anything?* the message continued.

It certainly beat having to cook. *Do you still have that vegan mac and cheese recipe? Make that. Also garlic bread.* Apparently, the sandwich and waffle hadn't been enough. There were some downsides to being a god, and it mostly went into the grocery budget.

Of course. The response came a few minutes later. *Haven't had it since that attempt. I may need to go shopping, but it sounds great. 7:30?*

As Hannah started typing that she didn't want April to go to any trouble, a message from Megan came in. *Garlic bread sounds great. 7:30 works for me. I can't stay too late though. Academy has been kicking my ass.*

For some reason, it was starting to seem less scary. Maybe she just needed reminding of the fact that these two had gone through everything with her and were likely to take this new revelation as well as anyone could possibly be expected to. *Awesome. I'll see you then.* She added several heart emojis and a smile and sent the message. Now she just had to figure out how to tell them.

The beer and TV didn't seem to have any answers. She tried looking online, but apparently, her situation was surprisingly unique. Lifting a car it was, then.

❖

We're almost there. Want to meet us at the bus stop? Damn it. Hannah had been hoping that Megan had a car already. Now what was she going to lift? Throwing on her shoes, she ran up to the other end of Lents park to wait for them. Fortunately, it was a short ride from the school, so at least the trip probably wasn't too bad.

After a couple minutes of pacing, the bus pulled to a stop in front of her, and after one other person, her friends climbed out. April threw her arms around Hannah, and Megan promptly joined in. "It's so good to see you. I've missed you so much."

"Work been keeping you that busy?" Megan asked as they pulled apart.

"Kind of." She was supposed to stop lying. Why was it so difficult to be honest about finding out that she was a Norse god? It wasn't like she was on drugs. Though it might sound like she was, and some drugs could give superstrength. That could be a problem. "What about you two? I went through the texts I missed. Congrats on those dates with the new guy, April. Three in one week? I'm impressed."

"Yeah, I think Ben and I may actually get together. I haven't had a steady boyfriend in a while. I'm kind of nervous."

"Oh, come on. It hasn't been that long."

"A month or so. Ben seems like the kind of guy that things could be serious with. I'm not saying we're running off and getting married or anything—"

Hannah chuckled. "Of course, that's more *my* style."

"If you and Emily eloped and you didn't invite me, I will actually stop being your friend."

"We didn't."

"And she didn't propose?" April stopped in the path, her eyes narrowing and planting Hannah in a withering glare.

"No. And before you ask, I didn't either." Hannah tried to sound annoyed, but she was grinning too broadly for it to be believable. It was so nice spending time with her friends again. She hadn't realized how much she'd missed them. "I promise, I wouldn't get married without you."

"Damn right," Megan said.

"You'd better not. And maybe I'll be able to bring Ben as my date." She was grinning even wider than Hannah. "We're gonna have 'the talk' soon. I want him to be my boyfriend, and I think he wants that too, and I'm very annoyed that you've been away, and I haven't been able to gush about him to you. I had to talk to Megan. She's terrible at this stuff."

"It's true."

They went around the back of the house, and Hannah let them into the apartment. "What about you, Megan? Any cute boys in your class? I'm sure you must've suplexed someone and had them go all crazy for you."

"We don't suplex."

"Really?"

"We have other throws." She collapsed into the couch. "But, no. No guys have been interested in me."

Hannah cocked her head, staring. "No *guys*? Not no *one*?"

Her cheeks colored. "Well, obviously, it was unrequited."

She grinned at her. "It sure doesn't look it."

"I'm not into girls."

"Well, clearly you fooled her."

April ran in from the kitchen. "I didn't have time to cook, but I brought all the ingredients. But who's the girl, Megan? You haven't told me anything."

She groaned, leaning back in the couch. "Because there's nothing to tell. She's interested, she thought I was gay, I'm not, so nothing's happening."

Hannah beamed. "Sure you don't want to give it a chance?"

"If I was going to, it would've been back when you had that crush on me in high school."

She stared, her jaw dropping. "Wait. What? No. How did you know?"

"You're really not subtle," April said. "Not that I was there, but I can't imagine you managing to hide it."

"Yeah," Megan agreed. "I actually thought about it too, but I didn't think I could handle it. Besides, you were already my best friend, and I wasn't going to jeopardize that."

Hannah shuffled her feet as she considered her responses. She wanted to run away and hide in the bedroom, but they were only staying for a little while, and she didn't have time to waste. "Need any help in the kitchen?" she asked, turning to April for a rescue.

"Sure, why not."

Half an hour later, they sat in the living room with mac and blended potato, onion, garlic, and yeast, as well as some garlic bread. "So, I've been trying to give you time, but what is it that's so urgent?" Megan asked. "A week with no word, then you say to come over and that it's important, and you have yet to say anything more on the subject. Is everything okay with you and Emily?" She took a bite, her eyes lit up, and she took another.

Oh, I'm a god. Did I not say? She wondered if saying that would actually go any worse than her actual plan. "It's been really complicated. Not her and me—well, sort of—but we're great. I…" She sighed, touching her forehead to her knees as she tried to figure out any way to not sound insane.

"What?" April asked. They were all on the couch. Maybe she should demonstrate it first and explain everything later.

"Let me show you." Standing, Hannah turned around and bent low, setting her feet firm on the ground as she slid her hands underneath the couch.

"Wha—"

Before Megan could finish the word, Hannah lifted them off the ground. She had to stop short lest she smash their heads into the ceiling. That hadn't occurred to her until it was almost too late. "So. I'm Thor. Reincarnated. Emily is Sif. Our grown-up god kids came to Earth and told us. I figured this would be the easiest way to tell you. Please don't hate me. I promise I'm not on drugs."

Jaw almost on the floor and eyes bulging, Megan seemed at a loss for words as the couch touched the floor again.

"Like, the actual god, Thor? Like, he's, she's…you're real?" April looked almost as startled, but she was taking it better than Megan.

"Yeah."

"You have lightning powers?"

"No." She sulked. "Apparently, that's a misinterpretation of the mythology…history? Terminology is complicated. It's real, though. I've been to Asgard. Well, not Asgard exactly, but the world it was in before it was destroyed. I can't think of the name of it right now. I crossed the Rainbow Bridge." Realization dawned on her. "I can show you. Come on, we can go right now."

Megan shook her head, her mouth still hanging open.

"And you're sure?" April asked, looking between her and the couch, gripping the cushion for support. "I mean, you don't seem any crazier than usual, and you just lifted something pretty heavy."

"I can lift a car, no problem. I just don't have one in my apartment." She looked about the room, searching for anything more impressive to pick up. "Is there anything that would prove it better?"

"If you're sure, I believe you."

"Really? I don't think I would."

Standing, April placed a hand on Hannah's shoulder and stared into her eyes. "Either my best friend has lost her mind in a week, or you know what you're talking about. I believe you. Plus, you could totally beat me up if I didn't."

How did she ever deserve friends this trusting?

"You're not a god." Megan's voice was weak. It almost sounded like it was coming from the other room.

"Call me what you want. I'm Thor."

She shook her head again harder, as if she was trying to wake herself up from this nightmare.

"Megan—"

"I don't know what the fuck is going on or how the hell you did that, but you're not a god."

April rolled her eyes, turning. "Megan, I put up with enough of this shit from you for the both of us. Hannah has clearly been going through some pretty unimaginable stuff, and you will treat her with respect." She took a step forward, seeming to tower over Megan despite the height difference.

"She's not—"

"You've said." Her voice was curt and left no room for arguing.

"Fuck it. Megan, you want proof?" Hannah was on the verge of tears. It was ridiculous. Of course Megan wouldn't believe her. Why would she? But she was Megan. Her best friend. The first person she'd come out to. How could she not accept Hannah for who she was? "Pay for a cab. Please." She caught herself, hardening her resolve. "I'll show you. I just have to take you on the Rainbow Bridge, right? That'll prove I'm not crazy?"

Megan looked between them. It was clear that she couldn't understand why April wasn't on her side. "Yeah, okay."

❖

"This is ridiculous," Megan muttered, slamming the car door behind her.

"It's right up here. Thank you," Hannah said as the cab drove off. She wondered if she'd have handled it better than Megan was. She hoped she would've.

April asked, "You didn't want to have him wait?"

"I'd rather he not see us disappear."

"You two are insane," Megan muttered. "What am I even doing here? I just wanted to have some delicious garlic bread and catch up with my best friends, not go on some insane adventure to prove that the one person who means the most to me in the whole world has finally lost her mind."

"Finally? Did this seem likely?" Hannah didn't think she'd ever come off as particularly unstable. She knew she wasn't insane, but she couldn't imagine why anyone would've expected her to become so.

"You're the only person in the entire world who actually wants to be an accountant."

Hannah rolled her eyes. "Oh, whatever. Are you coming or not? If I'm the most important person in your life, then you can at least humor me."

"This is ridiculous. You two have fun."

Hannah picked her up by her waist.

"Stop it!"

"Come on." With a quick wave for April to follow, Hannah found the spot past Mimir's statue, and walked straight at the fence, coming out in another land. "I am so glad that worked. That would've been so embarrassing."

"What?" Megan spluttered as Hannah dropped her on her ass on the solid structure of light.

"Holy…" April gasped as she appeared through the shimmering gateway. "This is—"

"Yep."

Megan rubbed her eyes, staring out at the new world before her. "What?" she repeated.

"Convinced?"

She seemed to be searching for words. Her mouth opened and closed a few times, but no sound came out.

"If I wasn't already, I am now," April replied.

Megan shook her head, staring unblinkingly at the rainbow they were standing on. "This isn't possible."

Hannah shrugged.

"I…I…How?"

"I don't know."

"I want to go home."

It was a better response than before. At least she didn't think Hannah was insane anymore, or if she did, she had to be mad herself for those mental gymnastics to work.

They took a new taxi back, and the ride was tense the whole way. Hannah tried to think of anything she could say to Megan, but she was just so mad. Why would Megan act like this? Didn't she trust her? The cab dropped Hannah and April off at Hannah's apartment, with Megan staying in it to head back to her place. Hannah hoped that she hadn't lost her best friend, but she comforted herself with the knowledge that she'd done everything she could.

"Want to finish dinner and crack open a few beers?" April asked.

"Yeah." Hannah watched as the car traveled on until it turned a corner in the distance. She just had to give Megan time. Until then, at least she had one more person she could talk to. Plus, April was pretty great, and that helped.

CHAPTER TWENTY-ONE

Emily glared at the bar. The place had been packed all night. All she wanted was some time to be alone and miserable, but instead, work kept offering her distractions so she had to focus on other things and take her mind off her troubles and do everything but sulk in peace.

She shook the cocktail and poured it into two glasses, forcing a smile that she was sure wouldn't reach her eyes. She was probably glaring. If she wasn't a beautiful goddess, that would be pretty off-putting.

Instead, the girls giggled and gave her a massive tip. "I love your hair," one of them said, her words already slurring. "Can I touch it?"

Emily had the most amazing goddess powers. Holding back a groan, she nodded, her smile growing even more forced.

The woman ran her fingers through Emily's golden locks. It felt annoyingly nice. "Wow. It's so sleek."

"Do you need me to call an Uber?" she asked. This girl was beyond drunk.

"Nah, I can still drive." She turned and spilled half her drink on her friend. Great. Apparently, even as much as work was distracting her from everything, she was still too distracted from work to do her job properly.

She cleared her throat and wished again for any power more useful than pretty hair and good farming. "You clearly can't. I need you to give me your keys."

"Don't be silly," the girl's friend said. Her words were less slurred, but she'd had more than enough for anyone who wasn't a Norse god.

"Man, I thought you were cool."

Emily sighed. "I am cool. So cool that I'm going to keep you from killing someone and spending the rest of your life in prison."

She blinked.

"Give me your keys." Emily held her hand out, the other hand on her hip. She was taller than the drunk girl, though not any bigger. "You're here all the time. You can pick them up tomorrow. I'll even throw in a half-price drink for doing me this favor."

The combination of intimidation and bribery seemed to do the trick. The woman hesitated only a moment before fishing her keys from her purse and handing them over. "Can I have that half-priced drink now, though?"

With another sigh, Emily nodded. What was the harm? She'd already spilled half of this one. "After you order your Uber. You can drink it while it's on the way."

"Yes," she shouted, throwing her hands in the air and spilling more of her drink.

Emily helped her order the ride and mixed her another drink. Only when the girl was gone did her mind turn back to the knife her best friend of eight years had been sticking in her back every single time they'd seen each other.

It had all been a lie. Every last word of it. Sure, Alys claimed to care. Hell, they were even willing to take a risk to help with this Hel thing…maybe. That could be another trap. She had no way of knowing. Everything Emily had thought she'd known about Alys was a lie. Their entire friendship. Years of being there for each other. Alys had just been using her. Why wouldn't this time be a lie too?

Hell, how could she even know Hannah was real? What if she was… Emily swallowed the fear.

They weren't together because it was destiny, at least, not entirely. She knew and loved Hannah to her very core. She could trust her. She would always trust her.

And Hannah seemed to still trust Alys.

She gritted her teeth, starting to snarl under her breath, when she found a man staring at her from barely a foot away, leaning over the bar. "Hey," he said, and it sounded like he'd been saying it for a bit. "Christ, are you drunk?"

"No. Sorry." She shook her head. Now work wasn't distracting her enough. It was a fine balance. "Was totally in my own world." She offered a more genuine smile, but she doubted it looked real. "What did you order?"

"A beer."

"Right." That was easy. She poured him his IPA and stared longingly at the nozzle. If she started drinking right then, she'd end up in need of a cab as badly as that girl. She'd wait. She could have all she wanted when she was home.

Why did Hannah trust Alys? They had only been her friend because they were forced to be. Hell, everything they'd said about Hannah had probably been some sort of manipulation too. But to accomplish what? What did Hel want, and what had she done to convince Alys to do all of this?

It didn't seem like they actually wanted to manipulate Emily. Hannah had a point about them not having a choice.

No, she wouldn't forgive them so easily. She couldn't. They'd still gone along with it all. They'd spent this entire time lying to her face every single day. Their entire friendship was based on a lie.

And they got way cooler powers than her too. Hannah was so sweet that Emily could manage to not resent her for lucking out and having all the awesomest godly gifts, plus it was unbelievably hot, but Alys was a manipulative liar and a fraud, and yet somehow, they still got all the cool powers. Emily huffed, crossing her arms over her chest. They could probably even throw fireballs.

It would explain why they were such a good cook.

Emily couldn't do anything cool. What was even the point of being a god?

She poured the drink before the new person could ask a second time, only half paying attention to the action. Maybe she was the goddess of bartending? Wouldn't that be the most useless power imaginable? Of course that was what she would get.

She continued sulking for the rest of her shift. This seemed to do nothing to deter the customers from leaving her tips.

She stayed behind and cleaned up and was the last to leave. As usual. When she was done, she threw herself into her car and slammed the door. Now she could quietly mope at home and try to avoid waking Hannah. That was so much better than doing the same thing at a bar.

On the way home, she swung by a fast-food place to grab a burger. Maybe she could eat her feelings away. It would be faster than drinking them away. She'd try that too, though. Sipping her milkshake, she pulled up to the curb at home, making sure she wasn't blocking the other tenant's car.

Emily hopped out, slurping, the grease-soaked bag swinging at her side as she sulked and walked. She wanted to scream, but that would wake everyone up. It would almost be worth it.

She opened the back door, still angrily sucking on the straw. It would be so much better with some whiskey. She closed the door, more loudly than strictly necessary, but before she could open the actual door to her apartment, it flew open, and Hannah's sleepy face beamed at her. Emily let out a surprised slurp as the straw fell from her lips.

Hannah took the chance to take its place, throwing her arms around Emily and pulling her into a kiss. After several long minutes, Hannah finally pulled away. "I missed you."

"Right," Emily muttered. She hated how bitter she sounded.

"I set my alarm. I wanted to make sure I was here for you when you got home, but then you weren't here."

"I stopped to get food. I wish you'd have messaged me. I'd have grabbed you something."

She offered a little grin. "I did."

"Oh."

"It's fine." Hannah finally released her and gestured inside. "I can make myself something."

"We can split my burger and fries."

She only hesitated for a second. "Well, if you insist."

Emily found herself grinning. "God, I love you."

"I think you mean Thor."

"Dork."

"Love you too, Sif." She giggled. "I love you too, Emily. So fucking much."

The burger was cold by the time she finally got to it.

Chapter Twenty-two

A few days passed while Hannah and Emily continued to wait for any word from their sons. Megan had yet to contact Hannah again, and she was growing worried, and getting to go off and prove her godhood by arm wrestling a Jotunn or something was sounding increasingly amazing. Maybe if she found the king of the Jotunn and proved she was stronger than him, the Aesir would believe her.

Work progressed as usual. Isabel kept making lunch, and they enjoyed the comfortable and beautiful amenities of their company. Hannah crunched numbers, then came home, and Emily went to work.

At Hannah's request, Emily took shifts on her normal days off, Wednesday and Thursday, swapping with a coworker in case they needed to leave that weekend. Hannah still couldn't quite wrap her head around why it mattered so much, but she knew that she had to prove herself. She was Thor, the god of thunder, and none would deny her claim.

Fortunately, her hunch was proven right when Modi and Magni caught her on her way to the car after a particularly long Thursday. "Is everything okay?" Isabel asked, looking concernedly at the two burly men in period attire.

Hannah almost said, "Yeah, they're my kids," but she managed to catch herself. "How was she going to explain this? She'd been terrified when she'd met them, and Isabel had saved her ass. She couldn't just tell the truth, could she? She really should, but she couldn't risk a reaction like Megan's, not when it could cost her job. "Yeah. It's fine. It was just a misunderstanding before."

"It sure didn't seem like it." Her eyes narrowed as she looked them up and down.

Hannah looked between her kids and Isabel, desperately hoping that they wouldn't say something stupid. "They've apologized since then. They're, um…" She tried to think of something that would make sense. She needed to get them some normal people clothes—if pants even existed that big. "They're in my old school's LARP club. I hadn't recognized them at the time, but apparently, they joined up just before I graduated." This was the worst lie. "They were here to invite me to a game, and I totally overreacted."

"Right…" Isabel said.

"LARP?" Modi asked.

"Yeah. Of course. I'm ready." That made sense as a response, right? "So don't worry. I'll be fine."

"Okay." Isabel said, looking particularly unconvinced. "Well, you have fun, I guess?" She kept watching Modi and Magni. Hannah needed to get them away fast before they said or did something that would ruin any chance of her being able to still work there.

"We will," she said quickly.

Isabel's brow creased. "You sure you don't want me to come?" Was she attempting some secret code? Like, if Hannah was in danger, she was supposed to wiggle her nose or something?

"Oh, it's fine," Hannah insisted, a little more intensely than necessary. "You don't need to worry. I'll see you tomorrow. Drive safe."

"Okay," she repeated, sounding even less sure, but she climbed into her Mercedes and drove off, very slowly, watching Hannah the whole way.

"You don't have time to see her tomorrow," Modi insisted.

"Yeah, I do. I'm not getting fired."

"It's not urgent, brother," Magni said. He turned back to Hannah. "We believe we figured out a way to convince the other Aesir."

Modi stared at him. "Of course it's urgent." He swallowed, tearing up as he turned back to her. "She's our father. She deserves to be home."

Magni chewed on his lip. "You know how Mjolnir seems to like you, Hannah?"

Narrowing her eyes, she stared. "You mean the thing you didn't bother to tell me about when you were trying to prove everything?"

Modi looked anywhere but at her. "Right. That."

"There a reason for that?"

"I wanted to be sure before I trusted you with this." He reached behind him, producing a surprisingly small hammer, which was to say, a large hammer with a surprisingly small handle. His hands dwarfed it, but it seemed perfectly sized for hers. "I know you're you." He let it go, and it flew right into her hand.

Hannah stared. She already believed, she already knew, but it had never felt so real. She was Thor. "Does this mean I can control lightning now?"

"No. Why do you keep asking that?" Modi asked.

Hannah shrugged. "I thought maybe…"

Magni shook his head. "The gauntlets, brother."

"Right. Yes. Of course." Modi removed the gloves from his hands and set them atop the hammer.

"These are way too big for me."

He nodded. "Yes. I'm not quite sure what to do about that, but if you can wear them for a moment, then with Mjolnir, Megingjord, and Jarngreipr, there's no way they could doubt you."

Why was she even willing to go to all this trouble? "But I… there's no way I can do any of this. I can't even use a war hammer. Especially if the gloves don't fit." She wanted to be accepted, but this felt ridiculous. She wasn't a warrior, and she didn't want to be.

"You don't need to be able to use it. It will always hit its target and fell them in a single blow," Modi said.

"What? No! Then I definitely can't. Don't give this to me." She tried to shove the items back into his hands only for him to step away. "I'm not killing anyone." The image of that mugger flashed in her mind, and she wanted to hurl. If she'd had this, then he never would've survived.

"You don't have to. If you show up with all three, you'll be the very image of Thor, the very image of yourself. And if that's not enough, then you can save us all."

"Come again?"

With an exaggerated sigh, Modi explained. "Mjolnir, that hammer, and Jarngreipr, those gauntlets, are two of your accoutrements. Without them, you're not the entirety of what you can be. With them, no one will doubt you again. But Megingjord, your belt of strength, was lost in the fight with the Midgard Serpent. If you could get to Vigridr and find it, then everything would work out. And no one will die."

"And, Vigridr is…"

"The island where you died. Where many of us died." His breath was shaky as he peered at her, a pained smile on his face.

"Is it in Asgard? I mean Idavollr?" She finally remembered the name. It had been bugging her for days. She was so proud of herself. Then what they'd said dawned on her. It was a bit more important than finally remembering a word. The gods were going to die? "Wait, what do you mean no one will die?"

Magni shook his head. "No. It's here on Midgard. But it's sealed. Ever since Ragnarok, no one has been able to enter it. I know not how or why, only that it's so."

"I assumed that it was done with Odin's dying breath," Modi said. "Perhaps we could leave the island but not enter it again."

"He was eaten whole. How would he have time for such a thing?"

Modi scoffed. "Because he was eaten whole. Fenrir's stomach acid should be no stronger than any others, despite his size. He'd have time."

"I don't think so. Fenrir would've chewed."

"It's certainly not what I heard."

Hannah rolled her eyes. She'd grown used to the idea of an old her dying. Thor wasn't her, at least not really. That didn't bug her, but these two completely talking past her to go on about mythology was starting to. It was like having two Alyses. "But what about people dying?" she shouted. "You're avoiding the question."

Modi looked chagrined, but Magni only looked sad. He didn't even face her, looking over the top of her head. Not that that was hard. "There's an apple tree that keeps us all young. As I'm sure you've noticed, we're not anymore. Young, that is."

"I thought it made you immortal."

"So you have heard of it." Modi stared into her eyes, his tone growing somber. "Without those apples, we'll all grow old and die. You included. But they're still in Asgard, and the way is blocked off. Idunn has tried growing a new tree, but it won't bear fruit for many decades. The one in Asgard is the only hope, and without your belt of strength, none of us could remove all the rubble."

"I'm sure you and I could do it together," Hannah said. Did she still want to get an apple for Alys? Or was that for Hel? It definitely made it harder to care, but she didn't want them dying either. And she certainly couldn't allow her children to die. That was more than enough reason. It didn't matter how crazy all of this was, they were still her sons, her responsibility, and she couldn't let them die.

He shrugged. He didn't look as if he believed her. "Perhaps. But they'll never let you try if they don't trust you. We need the belt. Modi and I will keep looking. I'm certain we'll find a way into Vigridr."

Hannah chewed on her lip. "I just need to find some island on Earth? And then find my belt? I can do that."

"It's no mere island," Magni said.

"A hundred miles by a hundred miles, according to the prophecies. I didn't have the chance to measure."

"Should be easy to find, then."

"It's not finding it that's the problem. It's getting in and then securing the belt. I just hope nothing has taken up residence in the time since we've been gone."

"If nothing can enter, then how could it?" Modi asked.

Magni ignored him. "Do you have a map?"

Hannah pulled up a map on her phone, letting the two of them marvel at the device until one of them almost snapped it in half. "Hey! Be careful."

"My apologies, Father...Mother?"

"Hannah."

"Hannah. It should be here." Modi handed it back, his finger on a not-insubstantial stretch of water. "But until we figure out how to unseal the boundary—"

Smirking, Hannah said, "Let me know if you find it out, but I think I may have an idea." She neglected to clarify, but they didn't push. That was a relief. They would hate it if they found out what it entailed. Waving good-bye to them, she climbed into Emily's car. "Oh, do you need a ride to the Bifrost?"

Magni grinned. "Yes, that would be much appreciated, thank you."

❖

"Fuck yeah! Does this mean I need to call out?" Emily asked after Hannah had briefed her on the situation.

"No, I figured we'd leave after your shift Friday night. I can't miss work, and I need to make sure my plan will actually work. You sure you're in? Think you can get the weekend off? I have absolutely no idea how long it would take to sail there, and I forgot to figure out how to get a boat. Fuck."

"Hannah, of course I'm in." She chuckled. "Finally, we get to do the cool part of being gods. I want to go on an epic quest."

"And save our kids?"

"Right. Sure."

Hannah sighed. "Emily—"

"Oh, come on. You get all the cool powers and everything, the least I can get out of this is getting to be the hero in a big action movie."

Hannah couldn't help but smile at that. Of course that was why Emily was so pissed she didn't get the kind of powers Hannah and Alys did. She wanted to be like in her movies. "All right. Fine, Conan."

"The Arnold version, right? I can live with that." She grinned. "Wait, you have a plan for dealing with a magic barrier but not one for dealing with a boat? That's kind of impressive."

Sulking, Hannah grumbled back, "I hadn't thought that far ahead."

"The boat comes first."

"Then I hadn't thought that far behind."

Planting a soft kiss on Hannah's cheek, Emily said, "Okay, so what's the plan?"

"Think you can handle spending the weekend journeying to a magical land with your best friend? And your girlfriend, obviously. I'm not missing this."

Shutting her eyes, Emily collapsed into the broken recliner with a massive groan and clutched her head. "Right. I guess we do need the only person we know with magical powers. Are you sure your hammer can't break it?"

She shrugged. She'd left the hammer in the back of the car and avoided giving it further thought. "Don't think so. Besides, if that was all it took, our kids...Modi and Magni," she corrected, since Emily hated saying that. "Would have done so."

"They're not the brightest."

"Well, they didn't have us to teach them for plenty of that time."

"Aren't they like thousands of years old?"

"I'm not actually sure. Try asking Alys."

Her jaw clenched. "Fine. Call them. I'll try to deal with it." She rose from her seat. "I'm going to work. I'll see about getting the weekend off and putting in an extra hour." She sounded pissed, but she still gave Hannah a peck on the lips before she grabbed the car keys from the kitchen table. "Love you."

"Love you too." Hannah sank into the seat Emily had just vacated. She'd never actually called Alys herself, but she had gotten their number. She found it in her contacts and tapped the screen to call.

Alys answered on the first ring. "Hannah?" They were clearly surprised to hear from her.

"Yeah." She wanted to go right in, but after the last time they'd seen each other, she had to ask, "You doing okay?"

A pained laugh echoed over the phone. "Not terribly. I feel like I've made a mess of everything. I've been trying to give Emily space, but I keep looking at the phone, hoping she's contacting me. Though it's nice hearing from you." They hesitated. "Does she know you're talking to me?" They swallowed, and their voice rose in a panicked pitch. "Is she okay?"

"She's fine. We just want to go to Vergooder...Ver...the Ragnarok place."

"You what?"

"Wanna come?"

Hannah could almost picture them staring in annoyed confusion at their phone. Or maybe it was barely contained excitement, as much as Alys loved all this mythology stuff. "Yeah. I'd love to."

"Oh. That was easy." She wasn't disappointed, but she'd been planning a whole speech about how it would maybe win Emily's forgiveness, and it would be a really cool adventure, and they'd get to go on a boat...right, the boat. "I don't suppose you have access to a ship that could handle traveling across the ocean? 'Cause I've got nothing. I'm buying a kayak soon, though." She knew that that wasn't helpful, but she was really excited for it. She hadn't rowed in a while and was starting to miss it.

"I don't think that'll help. Why do you want me to come, anyway?"

Right, the important part. She'd skipped it. "It's sealed with magic, and we can't do magic. Also, I think that it would be a great way for you and Emily to patch things up," she added, trying to make it make it clear she wasn't just using Alys. She really did want them and Emily to patch things up. She knew how important they were to each other.

"Oh." And it sounded like the addition made no difference. They seemed kind of hurt.

"I really do want you there."

"It's fine. I'm gonna see what I can find out about Vigridr."

That was what it was called. Hannah smacked her forehead and instantly regretted it. Ow.

"You two keep me abreast of anything. What was that sound?"

"Nothing."

"Okay." They sounded skeptical. "Hel might have some info. If I tell her I need to help you do this so you can get the apple, maybe she'll stop insisting I kill you and take your place. I don't have superstrength, so I'm still not sure how that's supposed to work."

Hannah shuddered. "Could you maybe not mention killing me so casually?"

"I said I *wasn't* going to do it."

"While that's more comforting than the alternative, it's still not that comforting."

"Kinda does give you more reason to not trust me, huh? I assume the fact that I'm being honest about it doesn't make a difference?"

"Maybe a little bit of one?"

"I have a lot of loyalty to Hel—she was there for me when no one else was—but Emily is my best friend, and you're…" They trailed off. "You're her girlfriend. I promise, hell, I *swear on my life*, I will not hurt you. Unless you're into it." They gave an awkward chuckle, clearly hoping that the humor would break the tension.

It didn't. "Leave off the last part."

"I won't hurt you. I promise."

"Fine. Okay. Thank you. Go talk to Hel, tell her you're not killing me, and see if she has a boat."

"I always do end up captaining her ship, don't I? Yeah, I'm pretty confident I can get us a ship, and likely the spell to get past that barrier too. When are we leaving?"

"Does Saturday at around four a.m. work for you?"

"Sure. I don't work Sundays or Mondays, so I'll put in for Saturday off. Shouldn't be an issue. I hardly ever take time off."

Hannah smiled. Finally, someone understood her priorities. Emily cared so little about making sure she could actually get out of work. "That's very responsible of you. All right, I'll tell Emily the plan when she gets home. You have a good night."

"Think it'd help win her over if I brought food?"

"Well, it'd certainly make *me* love you."

They stammered, and it took a second for the reply to become words. Did Alys have a crush on her? No. Of course not. That would be ridiculous. She was Emily's girlfriend. "I'll do pulled pork. I know it's her favorite, and I'll make sure to bring enough buns for you."

"There can never be enough buns for me." She hadn't meant that to sound at all sexual, but she stood by it.

"Well, I'm gonna go talk to my daughter. Bye." They hung up, leaving Hannah alone to figure out what to expect. This was going to be a very weird trip. Wait, had Modi and Magni said she'd died fighting a giant snake? What else was gonna be there? She wished she could trust herself with that hammer.

CHAPTER TWENTY-THREE

At the docks, as a few workers and fishermen milled about, Emily and Hannah found Alys waiting in jeans and a long-sleeved T-shirt. It seemed they all had about the same idea for clothes, but Hannah wore a tank top and a jacket, while Emily had swapped the jeans for cargo pants. Hannah tugged awkwardly at her jeans, trying to figure out how to get comfortable in them. She was never going to get used to pants.

Alys stood from the cooler they were sitting on and waved toward them. "I was starting to wonder if you were bailing on me."

Hannah yawned, stretching toward the sky. Her morning workout had mostly woken her up, but this was just too early for her. "It took me hours to fall asleep. I'm so tired."

"You can sleep in the boat, honey," Emily said.

"Where is the boat, anyway?"

Alys gestured behind them, and the air shimmered, and the water at the end of the dock was no longer empty. Where there once had been only calm waves splashing against the pier, there was now a small vessel, seeming to sit atop the waves with furled sails on its sole mast and oars in the center. It looked to have room for five people, maybe six if they really squished, but it was more than enough for three.

"The fuck?" Emily asked.

"How…oh, right, magic. Duh. That's kind of why we need you."

Alys smirked. "Neat trick, huh? Wish I could say it was my own. Hel apparently had lots of time to mess with it during her time stuck in, well, Hel. This ship used to be a lot bigger, but now it's magical and can change shape and form for our convenience. It also is completely unaffected by the waves, so it can keep max speed or just stay where I put it without a rope. It's almost more like Skidbladnir than what it was like in legends at this point. I wish I could cast that kind of magic. Maybe in a few millennia." Hannah stared, trying to decide if she should ask for clarification. "There's beer and pulled pork in the cooler, along with some buns, water, and hush puppies. Should be enough for the trip. Sorry there's not more of a variety. Oh, and I brought my old STP so you two can piss off the boat."

"Is the cooler magic? Wait, what's an STP?" Hannah asked.

They stared. "No, the cooler is not magic. It's just a cooler with some blocks of ice. And STP stands for Stand to Pee, you just…I can walk you through it when the time comes, if you really need. You ready?"

"I am," Emily said. She hadn't seemed thrilled about having to see Alys so soon, but after a brief conversation, she seemed to be managing to keep her cool. "Did you bring barbecue sauce?"

"Of course. And I even brought the weird red pepper and vinegar one you love."

"Thanks," she muttered. "Hannah, would you get the cooler?"

She picked it up, almost tossing it over the edge, as it was lighter than she'd expected. "Is this thing waterproof?"

"Somewhat, but let's not throw it in the water and test it."

"If you insist." Obviously, she wasn't actually willing to lose their food, that would suck, but tossing things in the river was fun. Once the cooler was securely placed in the front of the boat, she took a seat in the middle. "How did you talk me into this?"

Emily chuckled as she climbed in. "I didn't convince you of shit. This was your idea."

Right. It had been. She just couldn't let her sons die. She needed to get that apple. And who knew, maybe an adventure would be fun. Just so long as she made it back in time for work. "We need to get the belt. And it sounded fun. It's an adventure. Plus, I've never ridden on any boat that had sails and I've always wanted to. I love being on the water."

Smirking all the more, Alys climbed into the back, propping their feet up by Hannah. "Ready when you are, skipper."

"Is that me or her?" Emily asked, sitting at the front, as far away from Alys as possible on the little vessel.

"The one who knows how boats work."

Unable to assail that logic, Hannah pushed off with one of the oars and began slowly guiding them out of the little channel, heading toward open water. "Any idea how fast this thing should be?" She really needed to make it back by Monday morning. She was not willing to risk this internship.

"That's gonna depend on the wind, I guess. And you. I just asked Hel for a ship."

"What did you tell her?" Emily asked, turning to stare at them.

"I don't remember the exact words, if that's what you want, but something to the effect of 'I figured out how to get your apple. I need Hannah alive for it, but she needs my help. If we can find Thor's belt, the Aesir should believe her enough that she'll be able to go to Idunn's tree and grab what we need. We just need a way to sail there and a way to get past the barrier.' That good enough?"

Emily looked a bit chagrined, not that Hannah got a good look, having to crane her neck for even a glimpse. She must've expected Alys to betray her all over again. "Yeah."

"You have a way past it, then?" Hannah asked. She'd trusted that Alys could do it, but being reassured before they actually traveled all the way there would be nice. No matter how hard it was to trust them, she doubted they'd lie about that. Hell, as up-front as they were being about everything, she had trouble thinking they'd lie about anything at this point.

"Of course. Hel's the one who sealed it."

"Oh." It hadn't been Odin, then. She could keep that little detail from her kids, letting them think their grandfather did something noble with his last breath. If it even was noble. "Why'd she do it?"

"Because having people come across a land full of dead monsters sounded like a bad idea."

With a shrug, Hannah pulled the oars in, propped them up in their holdings, and began to unfurl the sail. Finally! Her whole life, she'd wanted to do this, and now she had the chance. As the sail dropped, it caught the breeze and began pushing them forward, causing the boat to pick up speed. Unseating one of the oars, she adjusted their heading until they were headed what felt like the right direction. She double-checked on the saved map on her phone and verified it. "All right. Looks like it'll probably be around a day."

"That's all?" Emily asked.

"You only got two days off, how long did you think it'd be?"

"Well, I figured it'd be by Norway or something."

Huh. She had a point. Why was it over here? "I don't know. They'd just pointed to this place in the Pacific."

"Maybe they didn't want the fight to be too close to home," Alys said. "Nothing in the myths really suggests where on Earth it was."

"It's still weird. Like how the Rainbow Bridge is in Portland."

"Well, I don't know what to tell you. I could try calling up Hel and asking, but I'm not sure if her projection would be able to keep up with the boat, and I have no idea how she'd react to you two knowing that she existed. So I'm gonna go with that they needed someplace where there wasn't likely to be any collateral damage they cared about. No Norsemen, just whoever the aboriginal people are. Or it moved with the Bifrost. Either way seems as strange. Hell, maybe Hel moved it herself with her spell."

"You'd think they'd want some of their own people to join in," Emily said.

"That's what the Einherjar are for."

"The what?" Hannah asked.

"The dead warriors that go to Valhalla."

"Oh." The matter settled, they sailed on, the waves barely touching the light vessel as it skipped over them. They were making good time. She was hoping to keep the whole trip to no more than fifty-two hours. It would give her just barely enough time to make it to work. They'd deposited the car in overnight parking, so she'd have to make it back around eight, dive in, and head to work. Now, if only she could control the wind, then she wouldn't need to worry about it. "I want my thunder powers."

"Bless your heart. I think movies lied to you, sweetie," Alys said.

"But then I could make a storm and have the wind blow us right there."

"And fill the boat with water. I'm good. I'll take you just having superstrength and a nifty hammer. What's the word with that anyway? Modi and Magni said it wanted to come to you? Have you tried summoning it or throwing it and having it come back?"

"This probably wouldn't be the best place to check, but I didn't bring it."

"You didn't bring the only weapon we have?"

Emily groaned. "I'm sure she had her reasons."

She just couldn't bring herself to take it. "Sorry."

Hannah stretched out, her feet almost reaching Alys, her head lying in Emily's lap. "I'm sleepy."

"I know, honey." Emily stroked her hair. "Why don't you take a nap?"

"But we're sailing, and it's exciting."

"We'll be sailing for a while."

She didn't even remember falling asleep. All she knew was that one second, the sky was still dim above them, and the next the water around them was lit up as the sun beat down. Their Portlander skin was unused to the vicious attack of UV rays. "Morning," she muttered, shielding her eyes from the light.

"Oh, you're awake," Alys said. "Emily didn't want to disturb you, but I'm starving. Also, I think there's some sunscreen in the cooler. I know I meant to pack it, anyway, but I knocked some embers on me when I was smoking the pork butt and got distracted, so I'm hoping it's in there."

"I'm gonna have to get up, hon," Emily said in a soothing voice.

Hannah murmured, struggling to keep her eyes open.

"Could you try?" Alys asked.

Emily sighed, adjusting enough to elicit a whimpered complaint from Hannah, but she managed to pop open the lid, having to hold the cooler in place as a sudden breeze caught it. "I see what I'm assuming is the barbecue in a Styrofoam container." She hefted it out of the bag, grunting slightly and disturbing Hannah. "I did not expect it to be this heavy."

"It's ten pounds of pork shoulder."

"Okay, that's definitely a start to getting me to forgive you 'cause holy shit."

Hannah grabbed the food and sat up, grinning so wide it hurt. "I forgot you cooked stuff."

Alys let out an amused chuckle. "Yep."

"Okay. I'm awake."

"Would one of you mind making us some sandwiches? I'm gonna keep looking."

"You almost never go for sandwiches," both Alys and Hannah said.

She could almost hear Emily roll her eyes. "Seems easier to eat on a moving boat."

"Can't argue with that. I'll make them." Alys snatched the meat from Hannah, who only gave a brief sound of protest.

Emily continued digging, grabbing a few glass bottles of beer, and rolling them over to Hannah. That eased the pain of waking up. Emily then lifted a small plastic tube. "And some fifty SPF sunscreen. That ought to help. I was already starting to burn."

Shrugging out of her jacket, Hannah said, "Come sit with me, and I can do you." Emily didn't even make the obvious joke as she handed over the tube. Hannah squeezed some onto her hands and massaged it into Emily's neck, eliciting a light moan. Damn, one of them really should have made the joke. She followed up on Emily's face, then slid her hand up the shirt to add some protection to her back.

"I can take my shirt off if you want."

Hannah felt her face heat. It was probably sunburn. "That would be embarrassing. Alys is right there."

"They'll live."

"I don't mind watching," Alys said.

Her sudden-onset sunburn only grew worse as she tried to ignore Alys. "Do me now."

"I thought you didn't want me to."

She glared. Of course that was when she said it. "I mean the sunscreen."

"If you insist." She rubbed some on Hannah, dipping her hand below the low collar of the tank top to make extra sure her nipples were adequately protected. "That help?"

"Yes," she muttered. They did have a whole day. Maybe having an audience wouldn't be the worst thing in the world. She always liked trying new things. "Are the sandwiches ready?" If they weren't, then she might have a taste of Emily instead.

For a few brief moments, they enjoyed their food in silence, sipping beer and taking bites as the skiff sliced through the sea. Eventually, Alys broke the silence. "There's a lot more meat if anyone wants any."

"Maybe in a bit," Emily said.

Hannah didn't need the wait and made herself another sandwich.

"Emily?" Alys asked.

"What?" Her tone wasn't quite short, but she still didn't sound too thrilled to be talking to them.

"I really am sorry, you know? I should've told you a long time ago."

"Yeah. You should've. But I know."

Hannah looked between them, offering an awkward smile. "I understand why they did it," she offered when neither of them seemed interested in saying another word. "It was a really tough situation, and there wasn't a great option."

"I understand too." Emily sighed, draining the rest of her beer and grabbing another. "But it doesn't make it easier to forgive them. They hurt me. Badly. Our entire friendship was based on a lie. I think I'm to a point where I've decided that I'm not going to throw it all away over this, but it's going to be a pretty difficult hurdle to overcome."

"You're not...I mean, you won't?" Despite the trickle of tears trailing down their face, Alys's eyes were alight with hope as they stared in disbelief at their friend. "You mean the world to me. I swear, I won't lie again."

"Then let me ask you this, if you won't lie: what are Hel's plans for us?"

They blinked. "If she gets her apple, then nothing. As long as we're alive, Ragnarok can't start again. She's not certain that it'll start back up if we die again, but she'd rather not take the risk. At least that's what she's told me. Though if that really is Baldur in Idavollr—and I can almost guarantee it's not, but she won't tell me who the real one is—then he's the first line of defense against it. As long as he's alive, Ragnarok can't happen. Although who knows, it might be completely done with, I'm just surprised we got a new sun so easily. But if he dies and sets it all off, then Hannah and I die. You actually make it through the whole thing, Emily, so I'm not sure how you died in the first place."

"So I've heard."

"Okay, I really need more info on that Baldur thing," Hannah said. If it really was an imposter, she needed to warn her sons.

"I'll give it when I have it. All I know is that one of your friends was supposed to be him, but Hel won't tell me anything, and I think she's already suspicious from my probing."

"One of my friends?" Hannah asked.

Alys shrugged. "I think so. Maybe. She's never been all that clear about anything. It's possible that was my assumption. I knew Baldur would be brought back, and I assumed it was the same way, but I swear she said that Baldur would be in Portland. And that wasn't even the only backup plan she'd mentioned. I need to find out more. Maybe if this little quest goes well, then she'll be in good enough spirits to answer my questions."

Hannah chewed on their words and her pulled pork. She could hardly imagine any of her old sorority sisters being gods, but she hadn't imagined it for herself either. Megan certainly had the attitude for a Norse god, but why wouldn't she have been contacted by anyone if that was the case? Modi and Magni should've heard something about them too, shouldn't they?

"But anyway, we're not a threat to Hel," Alys said. "At least, she doesn't think we are. With her hubris, she doesn't think anyone is. The other Aesir could be on her radar, but I doubt she'd expect anyone catching on to her anytime soon. I think she just wants to be alive again. I'm not sure she has any plans after that."

Emily finally met their gaze. "And what do you want?"

They shrugged. "I don't know. From the sound of it, she's been lying to me, but I don't know to what degree. I owe her my life, quite possibly literally. She's never said, but as the goddess of death, she's likely how we're all alive." Alys swallowed the rest of their beer. "I'd never really considered what having us brought back might mean."

"Then why can't she bring herself back?" Hannah asked.

"No idea. Maybe her own magic doesn't work on her."

"So if she doesn't mean us any harm, why not ask us for the apple herself?"

With a playful grin, Alys said, "She isn't willing to accept anyone's help. It's why I don't understand what she's up to with Baldur." They held up a hand. "Before you ask, I don't count as help because she's manipulating me even more directly than she is you."

"Are you going to give her an apple?" Hannah asked.

"Do you not want me to?"

"I don't trust the person who made you lie to us this whole time. I don't know what she's up to, but if she keeps suggesting killing me, it's hard to want to help her."

"Then no." They swallowed, not quite meeting Hannah's gaze. "I won't. She's up to something, using me, lying to me. Even if none of us are in her sights, it doesn't make me trust her. I owe her everything, but I don't like being made a fool of. That's my job. Making fools of other people. Not myself. Or maybe both, as I think I'm proving right now."

Hannah rolled her eyes. "You just love being Loki, don't you?"

Alys nodded. "Don't you love being Thor?"

"I think I do." She'd never said it before. She hated how it was impeding her life, but it had given her a whole new family, and it certainly gave her some interesting new experiences. Plus, it was great for sex. "Like, really do. It's amazing. I get to go on awesome adventures, I can bench-press my girlfriend. Hell, I could bench-press her and a semi. Plus, the immortality sounds cool once we get those apples."

"You could do so many taxes," Emily teased.

Hannah gave her a playful slap, and she almost fell out of her seat. "Sorry. I think I've gotten stronger."

Alys smirked. "Now just imagine after you get that belt."

"That's such an easier way to get strong. I've been doing car crunches."

"Did she really do that?" Alys asked.

"Yeah. It was unbelievably hot," Emily said. "She had to carry me to the bedroom, and we barely made it there before I ripped her clothes off."

"Sounds like fun. I'm really missing out."

That strange sunburn returned to Hannah's cheeks. She must need more sunscreen.

"You have no idea," Emily said, and there was something in the tone that Hannah couldn't quite sort out.

Alys's hurt look hardly made sense either.

Emily crossed her arms and stared at the ocean.

Alys cleared their throat. "What's the map say?"

They'd been sailing for a few hours. It was certainly long enough that they should be able to get a better idea of what their pace was going to be.

Her phone showed that they'd made it a little over a quarter of the way there. That was pretty impressive progress from what little Hannah knew about sailing. The wind seemed to only be building. It might take less than twelve hours for the first leg of their journey. Then they had to scour an entire island for a belt. Totally doable. She certainly wouldn't miss work. "Just under a third of the way there." The GPS was being pretty finicky, but their general location matched more or less where they should be. She'd brought a printout of the map, but she wasn't at all versed in navigation. "But the GPS is starting to freak out. I don't suppose you have some skills in navigating at sea that you've been hiding from us?"

"Let me the see the map."

"So you do?"

"Well, no." They took the piece of paper. "But I have magic." Their hands danced over the page, and a purple light began to float over the paper. "I wish this was bigger. It won't be too precise, but it might work better than your phone at this point."

"Okay, that's pretty useful," Emily said.

"Hel didn't want me getting lost. I actually had to use it years ago. My phone had died, and I forgot the way home."

"Can it find the belt?"

"Would that work?" Hannah asked.

Alys shook their head. "I don't have a way to track it. Maybe if you'd brought Mjolnir and Jarngreipr, though I doubt it'd make a difference, so don't feel too bad."

"The one time I forget my magic hammer," Hannah said, trying to sound nonchalant.

"I'm gonna take a nap," Emily said. "Some of us don't deal with these hours."

Alys nodded. "I'd recommend we all do. Who knows what we'll find there?"

Hannah cocked her head. "But the boat—"

"The wind won't knock it off course. It's a very good boat."

They settled in, trying to get comfortable on the practical seats that seemed to have never heard of the word padding. Hannah finished a few beers, hoping it would help. Between sleeping during Emily's shift and her nap when they'd first started out, she wasn't too tired. The excitement for their imminent arrival made sleep that much more unlikely. But she knew she needed it, and she found it at the bottom of the fourth bottle.

Hannah had been awake for a little while, leaning against the mast as she ate. The fruity beer wasn't her usual thing, but it was still pretty good and a pleasant way to start the day. If one could call it starting the day, as the sun had barely begun to slip below the horizon, its pale red light shimmering on the calm water. They were almost there.

"I slept surprisingly well." Alys was still curled up on the floor beneath a bench, their eyes closed. "Are we almost there?"

Hannah glanced at the map, pinned to the floor by a few beer bottles, the condensation ruining the paper at the corners. "Yeah." There was nothing nearby to suggest an island, but according to the map, they were right on top of it.

"This is gonna be exhausting." They sat up, stretching and yawning. "Hand me some of the pulled pork. It's supposed to work instead of a sacrifice."

"Really?"

"I assume the goddess of death would know."

Tough to argue with that. Hannah handed over a bit of food. She really hoped they still had enough to get by.

"Would you furl the sail?"

Hannah did as instructed, watching with great fascination as they prepared themself.

"Give me a minute." The meat sat in their lap, staining their jeans. Their hands moved above it before they finally snatched it up, held it to their mouth, whispered a few words, and finally let it fall overboard. Hannah watched, transfixed. Their eyes didn't open, and they sat there motionless for several minutes, as the boat tossed about in a sudden bout of waves.

Hannah grabbed the oars, trying to still them. Hopefully, their momentum hadn't carried them past their destination. "You okay?"

Alys didn't answer, but Emily stirred, looking between them in confusion.

There was a crackling at the front of the ship, and Hannah turned as the sky began to burn away, revealing a swath of land as far as the eye could see. It blanketed the horizon, but rocks seemed to surround every shore.

Emily stared. "Is that it?"

"Yes," Alys said, climbing back into their seat.

"Where do we moor?" Hannah asked.

"I don't know any more than you do. We'll just have to find a spot."

Hannah started to row, picking up speed until the wind whipped past them again. She could carry them around the whole island if she had to. She just needed to hurry. She was a little rusty, and her form was sloppy, but it seemed to be doing the job.

"Holy shit," Emily breathed.

"I think I'm kind of in love with your girlfriend," Alys said. Hannah could feel their eyes on her biceps.

Emily moved back with Alys to give Hannah room. "Yeah. Not exactly news, but I can't blame you. Holy shit."

"Wait, what?" Hannah asked.

It was finally Alys's turn to be sunburnt. Their face lit up in a bright blush that quickly disappeared, as their hair grew longer and turned pink. "Nothing. Don't worry about it."

Emily chuckled and looked like she was enjoying herself far too much as she wrapped an arm around them. "Hey, you're the one who said it."

"Go sit back with her."

"She's still rowing."

Alys groaned, holding their head. "I didn't think I'd said it that loud."

"It's a small boat," Hannah said.

"There are waves and stuff."

"You weren't joking, were you?"

"About? This island? No. Definitely not."

"Alys, come on."

They stared at the deck of the boat, wrapping their arms around themself. "I'm not great at being honest."

"You can say that again," Emily muttered, removing her arm from their shoulder.

"Actually, you're the one person I am honest with. I only kept the one thing. I know it was a big one, and I get why you're still struggling with it. It was fucked up, but you're the only person I've ever been open with. Well, you and Hel, and I've chosen my side there."

"Oh," Emily said, not quite meeting their gaze.

Hannah picked up speed, glancing around for any sign of a dock, or at least something similar. "That's incredibly moving, and I really want you two to have this conversation, but I need an answer. What did you mean?"

With another groan, Alys finally met her eyes. Apparently, theirs had turned red at some point, so that was a little unnerving. "I was exaggerating because your rowing is incredibly hot." They gestured toward her arms. "It's just a bit of a crush. Nothing serious. Probably."

Hannah forgot to row. They what? Why? How?

"It's nothing new," Emily said. "We have the same type. We even dated the same person once."

"At the same time," Alys said, adding some unneeded specification. "But I'm not trying for that. Neither of you trust me right now, and that's with good reason. Hell, heh, Hel, I'm the one who started Ragnarok and got you both killed." They glanced at Emily. "And I've done far from enough to show that my allegiances have changed. So while obviously you're gay and wouldn't be into me, and probably monogamous, it's not a question I'm trying to put out there. Sorry."

"Oh." Unable to take her eyes off them, Hannah started rowing again, still trying to process what all they'd been saying. She'd assumed Alys disliked her after that rough first meeting, and apparently, couldn't have been further from the truth. It was forcing her to reconsider a lot of things, not the least of which being her own reactions to them. It was a lot to take in. But there were more pressing matters.

They had to go a few miles in uncomfortable silence while Emily and Alys both glanced awkwardly around the boat, before they found an outcropping of cliff that seemed low enough to climb onto. The sun had nearly set, turning the island and the sea their own shades of purple. "Do we have a way to moor it? I didn't think to bring anything."

Alys blinked, patting their sides and looking around. "Shit. No. All I brought is the stuff in the cooler. I grabbed my sword and axe and some climbing gear—went once, hated it—but I forgot about it after I stuffed the cooler in the trunk. I think it's still on my kitchen counter."

"Great."

"Any spells?" Hannah asked.

"Just the one." They patted the mast, and the boat began to grow, rising in height. It didn't bring them quite level with the coast, but it seemed to be sitting more stably in the water.

"I guess that'll do. Am I throwing you, then?"

"Shit."

"You'd break us," Emily said. "Not that that isn't how I want to go, but do you think you could punch some hand and foot holds in the rock?"

Hannah stared at the cliff face. She supposed she could, but she really didn't want to have bloody knuckles. Isabel was going to think she was in a fight club. "Fine, but if I break a nail, it's your fault." She began leading the way up the cliff, making points in the wall that she was sure were too close together for Emily and Alys's comfort, but they could suck it up. It was the right height for her.

As they clambered up one by one and caught their breath at the top, it finally hit Hannah. They were really there. She was going to find her old belt and prove herself as the god of thunder. No one would be able to doubt her anymore. She was Thor, damn it, and they'd know it too. She'd be accepted. She'd have a whole new community to be part of all over again.

They had begun their journey into Vigridr. Now came the hard part.

CHAPTER TWENTY-FOUR

This place was huge. Like, really, really big. Modi and Magni had said the island was a hundred miles by a hundred miles, but Hannah hadn't pictured what that meant. How had it managed to go unnoticed for so long? Surely the spell didn't allow ships to pass through it. Did it? Had it even been there in the first place, or was it a magic island? "Now what?" she asked, looking between Emily and Alys.

"I don't know," Alys said. "I mean, this is all pretty new territory, even for me."

"You know more than the rest of us." There was only a hint of bitterness in Emily's voice.

They glanced at Emily. "Maybe we should set up camp? The sun's going down, and I'd rather not explore the place at night."

"We can't do that," Hannah screamed. "I have work on Monday. We only have like thirty-six hours, er, let me check." She pulled out her phone. "Thirty-eight hours."

"Hannah, we can't go traipsing around an abandoned island in the dead of night," Alys said. "I know how important your job is to you, but we made great time here. We just need to hurry tomorrow. We'll finish it up in a few hours and then have, like, twenty to spare, and we'll make it back in no time."

Crestfallen, Hannah looked to Emily for support.

"As much as I hate to say it, I'm with them. It's not worth the extra risk."

"Damn it." Hannah stomped her foot. "Then why'd you have me row all the way in here? Or have us nap?"

"Because I didn't think it'd be quite this late, but I don't want to be caught here at night. I have no idea what to expect."

Hannah nodded. "Fine. I guess we can have one night of drinking and eating your delicious food, but as soon as the sun rises, we're getting moving."

"Of course." Alys smiled.

Emily wrapped her arm around her.

Alys cleared their throat and took a few steps toward the trees. "Well, I'm going to go get some firewood so our food can be warm. You two have your fun. I'll make sure to announce myself before I'm back."

While Hannah did have the barest inkling of an urge to tell them to stay, she had better plans. Nothing like getting laid after a day's work-out.

❖

Alys was true to their word, announcing themself rather loudly well before they were in view.

"And here I was thinking you wanted to watch," Emily called back, throwing her shirt on.

"I can't believe you really did it. I didn't think you were the type to have sex on a scary magical island."

"Technically, we did it in the boat."

Hannah pulled on her clothes while the two quipped at each other over the cliff.

"Well, those stains are never coming out. Good thing the boat can shapeshift."

"Then why doesn't it have padded seats?" Hannah asked.

"It's not that good at shapeshifting, I guess. Are you two coming up here? The fire's almost ready. And bring the cooler."

"Yeah. Sure," Emily said, sounding far more disappointed than Hannah ever was about barbecue. They used the holes Hannah had made earlier and climbed back up. "You all right?"

Alys stared at her. "Yes. Why?"

"Didn't want you all jealous."

They turned their attention back to the fire, feeding it some more kindling. "I'm fine."

"Okay…" Emily did not sound convinced.

Hannah sighed. "Well, I'd offer you a turn, but I think Emily would kill me."

Emily coughed repeatedly and smacked her chest, taking a shuddering breath. It was completely worth it. "Wait, you're…I mean you, you're…"

Alys had gone white, though that could have been the shape-shifting, but they had not turned their attention from the fire.

"I'm just fucking with you."

"Right," Emily said, looking her up and down.

Hannah shrugged. She hadn't really had time to process the whole thing. Besides, if she survived this, she'd have plenty of time. Maybe even eternity.

Alys grabbed some buns from the cooler and muttered, "Damn, I wish I'd brought butter."

Hannah blinked. "That's all you have to say?"

They shrugged.

"Wait, did I upset you?"

"I'm fine. I keep telling both of you this. All I want is to toast these buns and warm up the meat."

"I wasn't totally against it."

They dropped a bun in the fire. "What?"

"I don't know. It was just sprung on me." She'd certainly checked them out before, but that was before they'd gotten rid of their...assets.

"Of course," Alys said, fishing the bun out of the fire with a stone arm. "Sorry for springing it on you."

"I didn't mean it like that. I'm not blaming you."

"It's fine. I'm fine. This bun is not fine. But I won't mess up the next few. Let's try to relax. We have a big day tomorrow."

"Okay..." Hannah watched them cook, trying to figure out what to say. In the end, the best she could come up with was, "Thanks for the food." And, "It's delicious."

That had to count for something.

CHAPTER TWENTY-FIVE

"Now where?" Emily asked, yawning and stretching. The sun had barely risen, but they'd all been up for hours. Pulled pork sandwiches still made an excellent breakfast.

"We find the belt," Alys said. "If it's where you died, then it'd be near Jormungandr's corpse. I wonder if your body is still there. That'd be weird."

"I'd think that Modi and Magni would've taken my body away. I mean, wouldn't they?" Chewing on her lip, Hannah tried to imagine what it would be like to find her own corpse. Would she even recognize it? It was pretty doubtful that they looked all that much alike, unless Thor was actually five feet tall and a girl.

"Maybe. They did have the gauntlets to give you, right?" Alys asked.

"Jormungandr is a giant snake, right?" Emily asked.

"Yeah, why?"

"Isn't that a giant snake?" She pointed off in the distance. Sure enough, there was a long greenish body. It was so massive that it made it difficult to tell how far it was, but it dwarfed the trees around it, and even the ones closer by. Hannah had originally assumed it was another cliff face or maybe some old wall.

Alys turned, shielding their eyes against the sun. "Yeah. That seems to be a giant snake."

"So that way?" Hannah asked.

They nodded. "Yeah. Would you like to take the lead, oh dear Thor?"

Hannah stared at them. "You're the one who can shapeshift. And you have swords and stuff, so I bet you even know how to fight."

"You can lift a freight train."

"I haven't actually tested that."

Rolling their eyes, they began marching toward the fallen creature. "Fine, whatever." Their muscles grew under the shirt until it clung tightly to them, looking a bit too tight. Hannah knew that problem all too well. Their long pink hair shortened and turned a dark maroon. Next, to Hannah's great surprise, they shrunk a few inches, though their arms grew longer. "I don't feel like getting beaned in the head by one of these branches," they explained. They were all heading into a sparse forest. There were no trails, and the growth was wild and untamed, but there was room to move, and Hannah could see a good distance in front of them.

Emily ducked under a branch. "Point taken."

"So there shouldn't be anything here, right? I mean, it's been sealed off for years, and everything died in Ragnarok, so there's no reason to worry. Right?" Hannah asked. Alys had said there was no way anything could've gotten in. But what if there was? Hannah was on a big epic quest for a magic belt, and that meant monster fighting. She didn't want to fight monsters. She couldn't let herself hurt things again. She saw the mugger buried inside the wall from her light shove. If she let herself do something like that again… She couldn't even finish that thought.

"If that's what you think, then why didn't you want to lead?"

"Just tell me I'm right, Alys."

"I don't know." They sighed and stepped around a fallen tree branch. "Listen."

"To what? You're not telling me anything."

"I mean, listen…do you hear any animals? I thought I heard a bird a little bit ago, but I haven't heard anything since. I think maybe there's a creek somewhere around here, but I've tried messing with my ears a bit, and I can't tell any clearer than that. So keep your ears open, and let me know if you hear anything."

"You can change your hearing?" Emily asked.

"I'm still getting used to it. I've pretty much only ever used my shapeshifting to make myself more androgynous. Other than getting that off my chest, being able to have a dick is really useful at concerts."

"I'm sure you're loving that."

They nodded. "Hel had made me promise not to shapeshift around anyone until I could reveal myself. You have no idea how big a relief it's been finally being able to stop hiding this. Being able to be myself, however I feel like expressing that at the moment, is amazing. Having to keep things from you wasn't fun for me either. I'm still sorry that it hurt you, though. If it makes you feel any better, I kind of hate myself for it too."

They walked in silence for a few moments before Emily finally said, "I don't hate you."

"Well, that's good to hear."

Hannah smiled at the two of them. They'd made some impressive progress, even if they weren't quite back to where they had been and where she hoped they would be again. It looked like their friendship really was strong enough to survive all this. "I swear, we're not getting any closer. It looks just as far away as it did before."

"I think it looks a bit bigger," Emily said.

Alys put a hand to their brow and leaned forward, staring at the giant snake. "I don't know. It must be, but this is probably gonna take a while. I don't suppose we could climb on your back and you could Hulk-jump us around, Hannah?"

"What?"

"Like, jump really far, to make faster progress. Your legs are super strong too, right?"

She glanced at her calves. "They're pretty strong, I think, but that sounds like an easy way to get all of us hurt. If throwing you was dangerous, then jumping all over a forest has to be even worse."

"Then I guess we walk," Emily said.

Nodding, Alys leaned against a tree. "Then can we take a break? I need some food in me if I'm going to be running around a hundred-mile island."

"Yeah, that sounds good." Hannah took a seat by them. "Did you bring the food?"

"Shit." They looked between Hannah and Emily.

Emily shook her head. "Don't look at me."

They both turned to Hannah.

"If I had, would I have asked?"

"Damn it."

Emily stared the way they'd come. "Should we go back?"

Grinding her teeth, Hannah considered their progress and then looked toward the body of the giant serpent. "I don't want to lose all of this walking."

"We haven't gone that far," Alys muttered. "It's only been a couple hours."

"Yeah, but we're in a hurry."

Emily's stomach growled. "Well, I'm starving."

"Why couldn't you have your goats?" Alys ran their fingers through their hair, their sharp nails—or were those claws?—raking their scalp. "We could cook them every night, and they'd be fine the next day. That would be fantastic."

"What?" Hannah asked.

Emily stared.

"I told you before. Thor had magic goats."

"Huh."

"Speaking of magic animals," Emily said, looking her friend up and down. "Why can't you do that? I don't know a lot about Norse mythology, but you're a shapeshifter. Can't you be an animal?"

Alys looked absolutely flabbergasted. "I've only tried a couple times. It's sort of weird. I either have to change my brain too or deal with some oddities...either way has its disadvantages. But in the mythology, I was able to turn into a pretty impressive horse and gave birth to an even better one. I guess I could try it. Or maybe a deer, given the environment." They screwed their eyes shut. "This would be so much easier if I had food."

"The sooner you come back with food, the sooner we can eat. Maybe try being a cheetah."

"In a forest? That's a terrible idea." They shook their head. Their face began to elongate, and Hannah could swear she heard their skull crack. Fur sprouted around their mouth, then on the rest of their body as their bones and flesh narrowed and elongated, shifting into a four-legged form, growing taller. It was as horrifying to see as it was fascinating. Hannah was transfixed as she watched wordlessly. Within a minute, a larger than average deer stared at them.

"Alys?" Emily asked.

The deer smirked, revealing surprisingly intimidating fangs.

"Deer don't have fangs," Hannah muttered.

"Some of them do," the deer said.

If Hannah hadn't already been sitting, she'd have fallen over.

"Be right back. See if you can start a fire."

"I have absolutely no idea how to do that," Hannah said.

Emily stared at the ground before them and gestured at all the fallen branches. "I think I can manage. My father taught me when I was a kid. You know how much those hicks love camping." It was so rare Emily actually brought up her parents that Hannah didn't press her on it.

The deer nodded and sped off, far faster than Hannah was sure deer could move. Magic deer were weird.

❖

After their first warm meal in what felt like far longer than it actually had been, Hannah and Emily climbed onto the increasingly long deer as it grew another set of legs, and set off toward the snake carcass that blocked the horizon.

"Promise not to get mad about your girlfriend riding me?" Deer chuckles were a very strange sound, and Hannah hoped to never hear one again.

"Hey, I'm riding you too," Emily said. "Knew it would happen eventually."

"Please…you're too butch for me."

The group rode on, Hannah and Emily taking in the sights as their deer-friend focused on running. Alys was quite obviously still growing accustomed to having six legs, as they stumbled often, but they never fully lost their balance, and Hannah and Emily were never tossed off onto the ground.

The dead snake finally seemed to be growing closer. It actually felt as if they were making some real progress. Finally.

"Wow," Emily muttered. They were past the serene forest. Now there were rockier planes and plateaus, all overgrown with weeds and vines. Corpses in various states of decay, some several times the size of a normal human, littered the ground. Some still held their weapons, while others must have had them stripped away by a desperate combatant. It was strange seeing what was a battlefield now that it was still and quiet. With all the corpses, Hannah had expected it to reek, but it was mostly an old earthy scent, like going into an attic that no one had been inside in years.

Please don't wake up. Hannah watched each body for any sign of stirring. If watching Megan play those games that she couldn't recall the title of—the ones that had those shitty movies made of them—had taught her anything, it was that dead bodies in mystical locales always rose up and attacked. She knew that this was real life, but as a dead person who had been brought back, she felt that wasn't much evidence against her fear.

For quite a while, the bodies did as she wished, remaining still and restful in their eternal slumber. Unfortunately, about halfway toward their destination, a couple corpses that were slumped against some rocks in what would have been an incredibly uncomfortable position began to stir. One gripped a weapon and took a sluggish step toward them, but Alys was too fast, and sped off into the trees before it could have done anything to them.

"Did you see that?" Hannah asked, tightening her hold on Emily.

With a strangled whimper, Emily managed, "Mm-hmm."

"Sorry." Hannah loosened her grip, hoping she hadn't broken any ribs.

"It's fine." She still sounded pained. "Were those zombies?"

"Draugr," Alys replied, exertion clear in their tone as they hopped along a path taken over by roots and vines, making the footing treacherous for spindly legs.

"What's the difference?"

"Well, they won't try to eat you." They panted, almost losing their footing as their right-middle leg sank into an old root. "Okay, they might try to eat you, but they shouldn't have a preference for brains."

"Will they attack us?"

"Yeah."

"Then they're zombies. Hell, most zombies don't even have a thing for brains."

"Whatever," they muttered back, leaping onto a raised bit of land that seemed clearer of obstacles. Rather than continue, they planted their butt firmly on the ground, causing Hannah to copy them far more forcefully.

"Ow!"

"I'm exhausted. You try doing all this."

"Sorry."

Emily slid into Hannah's lap. "Hey, there." She grinned at her and planted a kiss on Hannah's cheek before rising to her feet and helping her up. "You need a break?"

The deer nodded.

She looked around. "I don't see any more of those things. Rest while you can. Want some more food?"

"I do," Hannah said.

"Me too. Emily, you still have the bag?"

"Yeah, but I think we're gonna have to eat it cold this time."

"That's fine."

They took a brief break, the three of them keeping on constant guard for any signs of their new undead friends.

Feeling a bit restored, they continued on foot. Alys had shifted to a similar form to the one they'd used earlier but with black hair and slightly broader shoulders. "I don't think we're going to find the belt without a fight," they said, their eyes probing the nearby shrubbery for any sign of danger.

"I can't fight," Hannah said.

They stared at her. "You're Thor."

She shrugged. "So? You said my thing was thunder and strength, not fighting."

"But you have superstrength."

"Doesn't mean I know what to do with it."

Emily held out a hand, silencing them. "Well, it looks like you might have the chance to find out."

Following her gaze, Hannah saw two of the corpses walking toward them, still partially concealed by the branches of a nearby tree. They were both brandishing axes. For some reason, this was always how Hannah thought she'd die. "But…" She backed away, holding her hands up as she stared at the zombie-like creatures walking toward her. They weren't even shambling. That wasn't fair.

"Fine," Alys growled. "Get behind me and let me know if anything's sneaking up."

Okay. She could do that. She didn't have to hit anyone, so that would be fine. It didn't matter that they were zombies. She felt sick just thinking about it. She could end up hurting Emily and Alys. Worse, if she accepted that fighting was okay, what would stop her from doing it again? No matter what, she couldn't repeat it. She'd almost killed that guy.

But she could keep an eye out. Swallowing, she glanced around what barely qualified as a clearing, looking for interlopers, glancing over her shoulders every few seconds. It didn't look like any of the other zombies were headed their way. At least, for now.

"What the hell do you expect me to do?" Emily asked. "Aren't I like the goddess of wine?"

"Earth, marriage, and grain, mostly." Alys leapt back as one of the corpses took a swing with the heavy-looking axe. "I don't think we have time for talking." They charged, ramming their shoulder into the creature. The instant they made contact, their arm became a mess of tentacles, wrapping around the body and holding it in place. They tried to pry the axe from its grip, but even in its current predicament, it seemed unwilling to let go.

"Can't you ask your friend about this? She's the goddess of death, right? Shouldn't she be able to stop walking corpses?"

"Try hitting it," they snapped back, growing horns.

Hannah continued her watch. They were still alone, but the other monster was advancing on Emily. She wanted to call out, but Emily could already see it, and distracting her could mean her life. Hannah wished Megan was here. The only other time she'd ever been in a fight before the man in the alley, Megan had pulled her off that poor girl. Alys did it once and Megan another time. What if she fought without anyone here? She'd kill someone. If only Megan hadn't freaked out, she could've joined them, and they wouldn't be unarmed against two living corpses with weapons.

Emily barely dodged a blow from its blade, her long golden tresses whipping by the weapon. It didn't seem to take any hair, but Hannah supposed a haircut was a lot better than losing an arm...or her head. She felt so helpless. She couldn't fight, she couldn't, no matter what, but she couldn't let the woman she loved die either. She looked around again, this time for anything that Emily could use as a weapon.

A loud crack echoed through the clearing as the newly horned Alys's head collided with that of the creature in their grasp. One of the horns caught, and the spray of gore when they ripped it away made Hannah cover her mouth to keep from vomiting. She tried to focus on her task to keep the assortment of pulled pork and beer where it belonged. Her gaze hopped from rock, to branch, to tree, but nothing seemed suitable. She did wonder if she could rip a tree out of the ground, but she didn't have time to play around. She needed an immediate solution.

Finally, she found something. An honest-to-goodness sword was lying by a nearby tree. She ran for it, hoping her departure wouldn't cause Emily and Alys any particular concern. As she rounded the bend, she snatched it from the ground, grinning broadly. She was actually helping, and she didn't even need to fight. She could do this.

A hand grabbed her wrist. Apparently, this sword already had an owner, and the corpse that had been leaning against the tree, out of her sight from where she'd been, wanted it back. The smell wasn't earthy anymore. Now it was like being inside a dumpster full of rotting meat, that someone had defecated in. "Sorry. Can I just borrow this for a minute?" she asked, trying to sound chipper even as the corpse opened its mouth as if it was ready to eat her. She was probably too tough to taste good. Should she tell it that? "I'll give it right back," she squeaked.

His blue-gray face contorted into a horrifying caricature of a smile. "You've the first voice I've heard in many years, Thor."

With a great deal of effort, Hannah managed to swallow the lump in her throat. "Oh?" Her voice was shaky and frail. She could scarcely recognize it as her own.

"The blade is iron. If you'd like it, you may have it."

"Okay?" Shuddering, she tried to pull away, but the Draugr didn't let go.

"It seems you'll be meeting Hel soon. No reason for me to hurry that trip. Though you've been once before, haven't you, Thunderer?"

She nodded.

"Take the blade. It seems my kin have a desire for your friends' flesh. I can see why. It has been so long since I had a meal."

Not desiring to see what the creature was going to do, Hannah ripped free, his hands still clinging to her as she ran back to the clearing.

The two zombies Emily and Alys had been fighting were twice as large as Emily now, making Hannah feel all the smaller. She could scarcely even see where Alys ended and their opponent began, both of their forms were so twisted and misshapen. She heard footsteps behind her and knew that her newest friend must have decided that sending her to Hel did sound worth it. "Emily!" she shouted.

Turning, Emily narrowly managed to avoid having her head cleaved off, but her lips curled into a vicious smile as she saw the weapon in Hannah's hands. Knowing that if she threw it, it would be more likely to kill Emily than the zombie, Hannah ran over and handed it to her.

"Thanks, honey." Her smile grew larger, her teeth showing with a malicious glee as she swung the blade at the creature. "Fucking finally! All this god shit and I finally get to the good part."

It couldn't move its axe back in time. The sword cleaved it in two as if it was little more than a stick of butter. Why would it still be so sharp? "Iron, of course," came a distorted sound near her. The living mass of razor-lined tentacles wriggled in delight, ripping off the skewered head of what had once been a human body as the mass shifted back into the moderately familiar form of Alys—now with gray eyes and red and black hair. "Good thinking. These things don't like iron too much. Cut it a few more times."

"There's another one," Hannah said, pointing toward the armless monster behind her, whose limbs still clung to her wrists, waving uselessly as she gestured. There were so many terrifying things happening around her that the severed hand barely even registered.

Emily charged, winding the blade back as if it was a baseball bat, and took off the thing's head with a mighty blow that sent it flying and caused the body to tumble over.

"Let me see if I can figure this out," Alys muttered, closing their eyes. Hannah didn't know a lot about fighting, but she was pretty sure that wasn't a great way to go about it.

Their hand moved in a strange pattern, and the world around them began to heat up. The corpses, struggling all the while, caught fire, the blaze building from their chests and expanding outward, igniting the grass as it went.

"I'd suggest we run," Alys said, wasting no time in following their own advice.

They sped off, leaving the corpses and the forest around them to the inferno.

As they fled, the body of the serpent grew closer. Hannah hoped it wasn't going to rise up and attack. She'd had more than enough being attacked by undead monsters for the day, and she doubted they'd fare anywhere near as well against that monstrosity.

Suddenly, it was right in front of them. Panting, Hannah leaned against the mound of scales and flesh, finding that it gave more than she'd have expected, and she sank in. She took a deep breath, trying not to think about how gross that was. At least it was comfortable. "What now?" she asked, still trying to catch her breath.

"Now we head to the head," Alys said. "It's not like you died fighting its ass."

She nodded.

"Which way?" Emily asked.

Hannah glanced at Emily and Alys. They both seemed whole. Now that the adrenaline was starting to fade, she'd been worried they could have been injured and not noticed. "Is everyone okay?"

"I'm great," Emily said, sounding a little too excited. "Did you see me back there?"

"My tentacles are gone."

"You got rid of them," Emily replied.

"Oh. Right. Then I guess I'm fine. At least as fine as anyone can be without tentacles."

"You can grow them again."

"It wouldn't be the same." Alys sighed forlornly, dramatically holding their hand to their forehead.

Hannah sank to the ground, using the squishy snake body as a somewhat disgusting pillow.

"So no one's gonna answer my question about the head?" Emily whined.

Alys rolled their eyes—blue now—and smirked. "We go the opposite direction of its scales. It's a snake, it's made to be able to move across the ground."

"Didn't it live in the water?"

"You researched." They grinned. "But no, not originally. After I fathered it, it lived on land until Odin made it eat its tail and threw it in the ocean. My poor baby." They patted the side of the serpent.

"How did you give birth to…" Hannah paused for emphasis, gesturing wildly to the horrifying monstrosity. "*That?*"

"Technically, Angrboda did. I just impregnated her. Well, the old Loki, not me, obviously. I've no intention of fathering or mothering any children. Or parenting at all, for that matter. I'm sorry this all happened. Ragnarok, I mean. My kids don't turn out too well, do they?" They took a few steps back, staring at the body, taking in the size and shape of the scales. "It should be this way. We just need to go find the head. Hopefully your body, or at least your belt, will be around there. Then we can get out of here." Their gaze fell on the burning forest behind them. "Hopefully."

"Are you sure you're okay?" Hannah asked. "I've known my kids for a few weeks now, and while I still have trouble believing it, I know it'd hurt to see them die."

It took a little while, but Alys nodded. "I knew he was dead. And that he killed you. But I also know he's my kid. As is Hel. It doesn't change that they keep choosing to hurt the people I care about."

Hannah wasn't sure what to say to that. Normally she'd hug them, but they were covered in gore, and she wasn't sure what that hug might mean. She should at least think things through first.

They walked on for a few miles with no one disturbing them. Apparently, even the Draugr steered clear of the creature. Maybe they too were scared it would rise up and want to eat them. "Do you think we could ride you again?" Emily asked, turning to Alys. She never had been one for working out.

"Geez, buy a god a drink first."

Hannah grabbed a beer from the bag on her back. "Here, now will you?"

"For you, beautiful? Any time." They drained the can, and their body began shifting back into the form of the six-legged deer. The antlers seemed bigger than they had been the previous time.

They climbed aboard and made good time, though it was still several hours before they finally reached the serpent's head.

Once there, they dismounted, and Alys took the same human form as before. It had been a long day, and Hannah couldn't blame them for not feeling particularly creative. "You're supposed to have died nine paces from him. Walk around in a circle around the head, and if someone finds something, call out. Hopefully we don't have to deal with Draugr Thor because that does not sound like a fun fight."

"I'm sure he'd never attack us since Emily's here."

"I'm not making out with a zombie."

They spread out, searching the ground for the glint of metal or the sight of a skeleton in fancy armor. The sun was almost directly overhead, so it wasn't difficult. "They had the gauntlets," Hannah called loud enough for the others to hear. "So probably they took the body."

"Or the gauntlets fell off and no one found him," Emily said.

"It's only nine steps. He couldn't have been that far," Alys said.

"How do you know it's nine steps?" Hannah asked. "Did Hel tell you?"

"Well, no, but it's what the myths say. It's even what the prophecy said."

Emily replied, "Maybe it was wrong. None of the myths depicted us coming back to life. Did they?"

"Just Baldur."

"Wait." Emily sounded like she was barely holding back her anger, as if this was proof that Alys had lied again. "Baldur *is* supposed to be alive? You don't think that might be why he's in Idavollr?"

Alys shook their head. "I don't think so. I wouldn't imagine you can raise the same person twice. I don't think you can copy a soul or whatever it is that makes us the same people we were, and Baldur was part of her plans on Earth. She'd revive him there, not just release him in Idavollr fine as can be with all his memories. All she wants is to be alive again, to be able to escape from Hel. If she was going to release Baldur, why wouldn't she get the apple in exchange for that? There's no reason she wouldn't be able to do so. It just doesn't make sense."

"They don't have access to it," Hannah said.

"They what?"

"Sorry," Hannah said. She knew she should've told them. It was hard not to feel like a hypocrite keeping secrets. "I was a little worried about telling you, and then it kind of slipped my mind. That's why we need the belt, so I can clear the way to Asgard. The tree is still there."

"Oh." Alys sighed. "Then Hel will be glad she didn't kill you. Shit, she's not gonna like this."

"I thought you weren't working for her anymore?" Emily asked, the distrust already back in her voice.

Hannah glared at her. They had patched things up. They'd been joking with each other a little while earlier.

Alys sounded so hurt when they replied. "I said I was gonna be a double agent. I have to keep reporting to her. She has to think I'm still working for her. I'll make sure she doesn't kill you, but that apple would've been a good bargaining chip."

"Well, now she'll know she needs us alive," Hannah said. "Hopefully, that'll work."

"'Hopefully,'" Emily muttered.

"I'm all ears if you have something better." Alys was currently looking in a bush, so Hannah couldn't tell if they were covered in ears, but she could imagine it. Alys would absolutely do that for a pun. She blinked. Did she really know them well enough to say that? Given how many times they'd made the joke about taking a weight off their chest, she supposed she did.

"I don't know. We'll figure something out," Emily said.

"Well, then, until we do, this is the best plan I've got."

Emily groaned loudly enough that Hannah could hear it from the piles of broken rocks she was sifting through.

Something glittered in the distance. Hannah ran to it. It was definitely metal, but it was covered in a heavy layer of dirt. After a minute or so of digging and brushing it off, Hannah found a metal belt buckle still clinging to a leather and metal belt. It looked familiar, but she needed the expert. "Alys, what's it supposed to look like? I think I found it."

When they arrived, Alys chuckled. "Pretty much like that."

"That's it? You're sure?" Emily asked.

"I am."

"Yes!" Hannah actually jumped for joy. She could prove who she was…she could be Thor. She breathed a sigh of relief. Her life was perfect and exactly what she wanted, but she couldn't just ignore this part of her. She'd ignored parts of herself for too long. She hadn't come out properly until college, and she wasn't okay with hiding anything else. She was a god, and she wanted to be part of the community of gods in Idavollr. Hell, she wanted to get to know her kids. They were family, and she was only now getting to know them. She loved family. Her parents meant the world to her, and so did her sisters, and they were even less blood related than Modi and Magni. She wanted to know her sons, and she'd rather have an eternity to do so.

Glancing over her shoulder, Emily said, "We need to hurry. If we wait much longer, I'm not sure there will be a way back through the fire."

Hannah was still hoping that it'd blow itself out, but based on the smoke towering over the trees in the distance, it wasn't doing so. It didn't, however, seem to be spreading that quickly. The old trees of the forest must have been made of sturdy stuff. "Let's hurry," she said, unsure if it was because she wanted to get back and claim her title or because she needed to make it to work. Or the fire, but that wasn't on the top of her mind.

"Alys?" Emily asked, looking hopeful.

They could all smell the fire, and they were going to have to head right through the part of the forest it had started in.

Alys glanced at her, and understanding dawned on their face. "Fine, whatever."

The deer ran through the forest. There was smoke but still no flames. They knew where to go, even if they had gone southwest a few dozen miles past where they'd come from. Heading northeast, they closed in on the flames, close enough that Hannah could hear them instead of only smelling them. Looking to her left, she could see them. They were still a while away, but a good deal of the forest was on fire.

"Please hurry," Emily muttered.

Hannah could feel her squeezing tight as Alys picked up pace, leaping over logs and moving as fast as six legs would carry them. They ran for hours. Hearing a deer pant was strange, but clearly, they were as scared of being devoured by the flames as Hannah was. Only when Hannah hadn't heard the fire for a good ten minutes or so did they finally slow down.

They seemed to grow slower and slower after that, letting out weird little deer pants. Hannah climbed off to give them a break, but before Emily could do so, Alys began to fall, taking her with them.

Hannah swooped in, lifting them up, and holding the two of them in her arms. "I can carry you from here."

With a quick peck on the cheek, Emily climbed out of her arms, her feet already touching the ground. "It's fine. I can't see the fire, and the smoke doesn't look as bad."

"Maybe it stopped?"

"If so, we might not have needed all that, and then I'd feel bad for Alys, so let's assume it's just slowing, and that they saved our lives."

"All right." Hannah slung the deer over her shoulders. They barely moved. "You okay?"

"I'm all right," Emily said.

"I think she meant me," Alys muttered. "I'm fine. Just tired." They were still panting.

"Rest. I can carry you."

They moved on. At a couple points, they had to wake Alys up to consult on directions, since they were winging it a bit more than they'd hoped, but in three hours, they found the cliffs towering over the ocean, and it only took another couple hours—the first half hour or so spent walking in the wrong direction—before they found the ship they'd left waiting for them.

"Ready to go home?" Emily asked.

"I don't know, I was having fun." Alys was now a human with long silver hair, yawning from their seat on Hannah's broad shoulders. "Let's get the hell out of here."

CHAPTER TWENTY-SIX

Hannah felt beyond gross from her days at sea and running through a forest fire, plus fighting the undead, all in the same outfit. When she woke again to the sight of the empty ocean for miles and nothing but a starry sky above, she found herself wishing for a change of clothes or at least a bath.

"What time is it?" Emily asked, stirring next to her and stifling a yawn.

Hannah had plugged her phone into Emily's portable charger before she'd fallen asleep, so she powered it on and waited for it to tell her. As the home screen lit up, she tried to swallow her dread. "Fuck."

"What?" Looking concerned, she sat up, squeezing Hannah's free hand.

"It's almost five," she muttered, holding back the curses she wanted to add on top of that. They were still a good while from home. Likely seven hours, if not more, judging by their current progress. "Shit, babe, what am I gonna do? I have work in three hours."

"It's okay, honey. We'll figure this out."

"According to the map, we just passed Hawaii," Alys said. "It looks like one of the islands shouldn't be too far from here if we turn back. Maybe an hour. You should have a cell signal there, and you can at least call in. Probably better than showing up at noon with no prior word."

Hannah nodded. They were right, as loath as she was to turn back. Though she doubted she could get a doctor's note in Hawaii, unless she wanted to say she was sick *and* on vacation, but that sounded less believable. "Thank you. You're a real hero."

"That mean I'm forgiven?"

Hannah shrugged, giving them a sympathetic smile. "I wasn't the one mad at you." She'd known Alys for maybe three weeks before they'd confessed everything and betrayed their oldest friend to keep from killing her. It was hard to hold a grudge against that.

Emily grumbled. "Fine. You're at least mostly forgiven. At least enough that I'm willing to stay your best friend."

"Great, then maybe I can join your snuggle pile." Sitting up, they flashed Hannah a winning grin that had no doubt been shapeshifted into perfection. "Actually, you mind turning the boat around? I'm still not clear on how to do all that."

"I'd love to." Hannah hopped to her feet and began her job with the boat, using oars and sail to turn them in the right direction, double-checking with the map. In a little over an hour, they'd find the coast, and then Hannah could call and explain that she was sick. Hopefully, that would be enough to save her job, though she should still get a doctor's note.

"Forgive me for being a bit confused, as I'm apparently the only one who wasn't aware of this, but how the hell are we past Hawaii?" Emily asked. "I don't know much about sailing, but shouldn't that have taken days on its own? We ended up in Vigridr in like fourteen hours."

Alys chuckled. "Magic."

"Right, but really?"

"Yeah, really. Magic. If something with a motor would've been faster than Hel's ship, she'd have insisted I take that and ensured that I had the money to do so if I didn't already. The same magic that keeps the boat from going off course also lets it use the wind, well, a *lot* more efficiently than should be possible. Though apparently, still not as fast as Hannah needed when traveling against it. Hel had gone on about how it worked for a bit. She seemed really proud of it, but I'd be lying if I said I listened to the whole speech. I'm sure Hannah would've been in heaven—though that turn of phrase would result in some very interesting mythological crossovers—but I just don't care that much. What I got was, 'it's magically fast, it can shapeshift, and it doesn't need a constant hand.' Good old *Naglfar* is one hell of a ship."

"'Hel' or 'hell,'" Emily asked, making a second "l" sound.

"Exactly."

Hannah sat by the cooler, watching the other two as she grabbed a drink. She would finally have the chance for something other than pulled pork soon, so she didn't bother with breakfast. "You hadn't called it that before. What does it mean?"

"You don't want to know."

"Why? Is it like the ferry of the dead or something? Does this ship take people to Hel?"

"I don't think the dead need a boat. There's a bridge, to my knowledge. No, this ship is disconcerting for other reasons that I'd rather not trouble you with."

"No, come on. Tell me," Hannah pleaded.

They sighed. "If you insist, I'll tell you when we're on land, and then you can decide if you're up for getting back on it."

"But now I want to know even more." Hannah grumbled, sipping her beer. She'd never cared much about mythology, but it was growing far more personal the more she knew, so she'd rather have all the answers already. "It's not like I'm going to swim to Hawaii."

"Fine. It means nail farer, because it's made of the finger and toenails of the dead."

Her stomach turned. "I want to swim."

CHAPTER TWENTY-SEVEN

Emily sat back while Hannah moored the boat at a dock in Hanalei, and Alys paid the outrageous fee.

When she was finally on dry land, Emily had to stretch her legs and be thankful the ground wasn't moving or covered in zombies before she could properly appreciate the view. Only then did she look at the palm trees, the gentle waves splashing on the white sands, and the handful of locals and tourists fishing in the pre-dawn light. "Wow. It's beautiful."

"It's not bad," Alys said.

"I've only ever been to Honolulu before, and that was at a resort." Hannah looked around, taking in the view. "I'm starving."

"I need a shower," Emily replied. "There's still dead guy blood on me."

"Maybe don't say that out loud," Alys suggested.

"Yeah. You're right."

"How about, since I'm already trying to make things up to you, I get us a room at a hotel? Hannah can call into work on the way, and we can have a shower and spend a nice day in whatever this town is."

Emily shrugged. "Sounds good to me."

"I guess," Hannah said. "But I was thinking I should go to a clinic in Portland today so I can get a sick note."

"Well, I want a shower either way, and a hotel seems like the easiest way to do that."

Alys patted her shoulder. "There's no way you'll need a sick note for one day. Don't worry about it. I know how much that job means to you, but I promise, it'll be fine, and if they're jerks about it, then I'll put a spell on them."

"All right," she muttered, pulling her phone out of her pocket and tapping it a few times.

"Wait." Emily put her hand over the phone before Hannah could hit call. "We're out in the middle of the street. I've called in when I wasn't really sick enough times in my life to know how to do it, and you want to wait until we're someplace quieter."

"I should've called at sea."

Alys snorted. "Yeah, because that wouldn't sound suspicious."

"But it's almost six."

"Which is still early and also might mean we can't get into a room yet," Emily said.

"Then I'll pay for last night and tonight, I don't care," Alys said. "I need a shower too. You have no idea where all of my appendages have been. Shapeshifting has a few disadvantages."

"How about you buy us some new clothes too?" Hannah asked. "I need to get out of this outfit, and I'm sure you two feel the same. I could even go shopping while you shower."

Emily breathed a sigh of relief. "That sounds amazing. Anything that'll fit me and isn't covered in blood is fine."

"Size doesn't matter, just grab me some men's clothes," Alys said. It seemed there were some advantages to shapeshifting too. "I could go with you if you need. I just hate only wearing shapeshifted clothes. I feel naked."

Hannah stammered. "I didn't know you could do that."

They shrugged.

At the advice of a local, they headed down to Kuhio Highway, as it had food, a hotel, and some clothing stores, all within a brief walk from their spot at the Hanalei Pier. They'd had Hannah ask, as she had the least gore on her.

Twenty minutes later, they were checked into the hotel and in their room. Alys had had to pull a few strings to let them check in so early, and pay a substantial upcharge, but they got away without having to pay for an entire extra day. The second they were in, Alys made a beeline for the shower. "But I was gonna do that," Emily whined.

Hannah tapped the still-open call button on her phone. After waiting a moment, she said, "Hi, sorry, this is Hannah Olsen. I'm an intern in the accounting department, and I'm really sick this morning. I was hoping it would go away, so I didn't call in earlier—" The voice on the other end must have cut her off.

The call was too quiet for Emily to hear it all, but she distinctly made out "Do you know how often accountants call out?" and tried not to laugh.

Hannah breathed out a sigh of relief. "Okay, thanks." She added a few more thank yous after each pause, sounding increasingly grateful, until she finally hung up and collapsed into the nearby chair.

"This is your first time calling into work, isn't it? Like ever?" Emily asked. Of course it was. There was no way her workaholic dork had ever been irresponsible a day in her life.

Hannah nodded.

Emily sat on the armrest, wrapping an arm around her and pulling her head to her chest, stroking her hair. She knew how panicked Hannah was. Being an accountant was her dream, it meant everything to her. But a single sick day wasn't going to cost her it. "It happens to everyone. I promise, you don't have to worry."

She nodded again.

"I'm getting blood on you, aren't I?"

Another nod.

Emily jumped up, grinning. "All right. I'm gonna go grab Alys's wallet, and you can buy our stuff."

"Okay. You sure you—"

"They don't have modesty." Emily didn't bother knocking and threw open the bathroom door. "Where are your pants?"

Alys poked their head out from the shower curtain, their short-cropped hair still covered in shampoo. "Over there." They pointed to the corner, opening the curtain some more and revealing nothing Emily was used to seeing in all the previous times she'd seen them naked. "Tell her to order food too. Or you can. Get delivery."

"Awesome," Emily said, collecting herself. She was never going to get used to shapeshifters. The wallet was in their back pocket, as always. "How do you keep these when you shapeshift? You weren't wearing pants as a deer."

"Magic."

Emily shook her head. It was probably the best answer she was going to get. At least it meant she could have food. She took out one of the cards and tossed the wallet to Hannah. "Mind getting us clothes while I order food?"

"Not at all. Get a lot." she said as she headed to the door. After the door swung shut behind her, Emily pulled out her phone to order, only for the door to open again and Hannah to poke her head in. "Can we go get food? Once you've both showered and changed, I mean? I really want to go out on the town."

"Are you not gonna shower?"

"After we all shower, then."

Emily groaned. Collapsing into bed sounded so nice, but it wasn't like she hadn't gotten enough sleep. "Yeah, all right. But pick out some awesome clothes." As gross as she felt, and as badly as she needed to shower and put on something clean, it almost felt wrong. It was her first big adventure, her first real fight. She was a proper hero now. Way cooler than any mythological Sif. But she was also sticky.

"I'll do my best."

When Emily walked out of the bathroom later, Hannah was sitting on the bed, and Alys was wearing a pair of men's swimming trunks with no shirt. Emily had gotten a look earlier, but it was still surprising. They had a fairly androgynous guy's chest with far more feminine abs. "That was quick."

Hannah grinned. "They only had swimwear. I figured we could find more later."

"All right. Your turn." Emily dug through the clothes while Hannah showered. She'd bought way more than they needed. Hopefully, the place had a good return policy. Emily threw on a pair of black board shorts and a gray tankini top.

When Hannah was out of the shower and wearing a seafoam green tube dress, they all meandered out, their sore bodies not moving in any hurry. The store Hannah had gone to was only a couple blocks away and on the way to all the restaurants, so they stopped in and returned the clothes they weren't wearing.

"Holy shit, that place was expensive," Alys said as they left. "I had no idea I was spending that much."

"I'm sorry," Hannah replied. "Should I have tried to find a cheaper place? It was the closest."

"It's fine. I doubt there would be much cheaper that's actually close. I don't tend to spend much, and I make a decent bit. You really don't need to worry. I was just surprised."

"Really? I didn't think stylists made that much. Are you sure you don't want me to pay you back? At least for my clothes?"

"I'm quite happy to spoil you. Besides, I robbed a few banks when I first found out I was a shapeshifter, so I'm pretty flush with cash." They flashed Hannah a smile that would've caused a lesser woman to place a protective arm around her. Emily's was only there for comfort. Alys's smile grew more wicked. "And here I was thinking you didn't get jealous."

Emily glanced at Hannah. "I already said you're welcome to try. Especially if I get free stuff too. She's just so soft and squeezable."

"I'm really not that soft," Hannah said.

"Damn, it's a shame we're in public and that I'm not wearing a shirt, cause then I'd see exactly what I could pull off. Not like I didn't notice her eying my breasts when I still had them. I could include clothes, but that wouldn't attract any less attention than my suddenly having an impressive pair of tits."

"I wouldn't complain," Hannah said. "Wait, you robbed a bank?"

"Yeah, been over the tragic backstory, let's just appreciate how sexy and roguish it makes me."

Hannah chuckled, rolling her eyes, but she was grinning. Maybe even blushing? Damn, maybe Emily was a little jealous. If it happened, it happened, it was just so unlike her to feel this way. Was it Sif? She'd go with that. Fucking shitty wife god, can't even fight zombies and tries to make her jealous of stuff she'd said was fine. "Guess you'll just have to do a sexy cat burglar look to keep in character, then."

Alys smirked. "Maybe later. Right now, I think it's time I do the gentlemanly thing and treat you ladies to some dinner."

Emily rolled her eyes. She was used to this side of Alys. "It's like nine a.m."

"Fine then, brunch. We can have mimosas."

Never ones to turn down food or alcohol, Hannah and Emily offered no protest, and they found a spot nearby that offered what one would assume could be traditional Hawaiian food. In all likelihood, it was more of a bastardization made to appeal to tourists, but there were pineapples and drinks with little umbrellas in them, so who really cared about the authenticity?

They sat on the porch, enjoying the break from pulled pork, as they had round after round of drinks. "It's a shame we have to head back so soon," Emily said, wiping sauce from her lips.

"I'm not missing work," Hannah said firmly.

Alys stole a piece of food from her plate. "No one would ask you to. We know how important this job is to you. Although you're literally a god, so I'm a little curious as to why. All the gold in Idavollr isn't enough for you?"

Hannah pursed her lips, staring. "I know I could just do anything I want, but it's always been my dream. It *is* what I want."

"Why, though?" Emily asked, setting her half-eaten shrimp taco back on its plate. "I like my job, but I would happily give it up and do something else if the opportunity arose. Hell, I'd give it up to live here."

"We're at a bar," Alys pointed out. "You wouldn't have to give up shit."

"Well, I'm sure there're accounts here."

Hannah sipped her mojito. "For years, I've been planning my life around this. I don't want to change it just because my life has changed a bit." She bit into her chicken pesto sandwich and bought herself some more time.

"I can get that. Being stubborn is respectable." Alys flashed another winning smile. Shapeshifting was so overpowered.

"It's not just that I'm stubborn."

"Or maybe it is, and you're too stubborn to admit it," Emily said.

Hannah shot her a quick glare before continuing. "I love my job, and I've always wanted to be an accountant. It feels right, and I love making all the numbers make sense and fighting them until they do. I won't give it up."

"I'm sure you could convince Forseti to let you handle the treasury."

"It's not the same," Hannah said, setting her foot down hard. Metaphorically, or else there'd have been an earthquake. "It's not what I'm trained for, and it's not what I've wanted. Hell, it's not even a desk job then. And I love Muller Trucks. I have an amazing friend there, and other than my temporary boss, everyone is great, and it's just been perfect. Plus, it's gorgeous and has a great view. And there's like zero chance of monsters attacking. I don't think I can get that in Idavollr."

"You got the name right," Alys cheered.

Emily let out a forlorn sigh. "Fine, I guess we'll have to stay in Portland. I hope you accept this is your fault."

Having finished their fish burger, Alys waved to the waitress to get another round of drinks. When she was gone, they said, "I kinda like my job too. Though it would be great if I could freely shapeshift there. But people get all weird when you look nothing like the person they've known for years, and you don't match your ID at all. Bunch of fucking fascists."

Emily tittered. "That must be so hard."

"It's the worst. Thank you for convincing me that I didn't have to keep pretending to have tits, at least, Emily. Though granted, I'm not sure I always hate having them. It can be fun." They winked at Hannah.

"It's not like I never liked being a girl, but I had to do it for so long that it's nice taking a break, and I always appreciate being as androgynous as possible. That way, people won't even try to gender me."

"The waitress did call you sir."

"That's because she didn't have a better term. We'll fix that. Just need to bring *comrade* back."

"Da," Emily agreed.

They finished their food, making a few Soviet Union jokes as they did so, and hung around for a few more drinks before Emily found herself yawning.

"How are you tired?" Alys asked. "You didn't have to do all the shapeshifting or running."

"I still fought."

"And slept since then."

She shrugged. "I'm nocturnal and have had to be awake during the day. It's hard."

Hannah chuckled, hugging her and kissing her cheek. "How about we get you to bed, and then Alys and I can party a bit more?"

"You sure you can do that and still make it to work tomorrow?"

She rolled her eyes. "It's barely past noon, and you know me with alcohol."

"God, I keep forgetting how early it is."

"I know. Come on. Alys, you mind hanging out here for a bit? I'll hurry back."

"Take all the time you need," they said. "Though I might go look at some more stores when I'm done here, see if I can find some proper clothes. Or at least a souvenir. Give me a call when you're looking for me. My phone's charged enough."

"All right." Grinning massively, she tugged on Emily's hand. "Come on and fuck me already," she whispered.

Emily didn't need to be asked again.

❖

Emily breathed in Hannah's scent, holding her naked body. If she'd been tired before they'd started, she was absolutely spent now. "God, I love you."

"I keep telling you, that doesn't work when you're talking to a god."

"By Odin, I love you?"

"He's dead." She wrapped an arm around Emily, pulling closer, the soft chest pressing in and sending a shiver up Emily's spine. Maybe she could handle another round. "I love you, Emily. You're more than enough god for me."

"Fuck…" Emily bit her lip and stared. She had never been more in love with another person in her entire life. She doubted she would be. "You sure about that?"

Hannah cocked her head, sitting up and straddling her hips. "What do you mean?"

Emily shrugged. "It's not important."

"It is." She bounced.

"That is not gonna help me talk."

With a massive grin and reddened cheeks, Hannah said, "I'm sorry." She didn't sound it.

Emily chewed on her lip, trying to focus and not just flip Hannah and pin her down. It was tempting, but she managed to resist. "Alys has been making their interest in you abundantly clear."

"Yeah, but that doesn't mean anything."

She shook her head. "It doesn't have to. And you know that they and I aren't exactly on the best terms right now, but I think we'll get there. And while I wouldn't exactly self-identify as poly, I'm not any less poly than everyone else in Portland."

"Huh?"

"You don't even know what that means, do you?"

"Just because I've only dated one other person before doesn't mean I don't know things," Hannah cried. "I mean, I'm not super familiar with it. But I've heard of it. It's dating more than one person. I just didn't know what you meant with the Portland thing."

"Right. I guess it maybe doesn't come up as much when you're in college and with a bunch of other people who aren't from around, well, there. I almost said here, but…" With a light chuckle, she gestured around them before bringing her hand back down on Hannah's hip. "Monogamy is not all that popular in Portland. Maybe it's just the sort of people I've known, not that I know that many people, but I mean, I'm a bartender, and I spend way too much time in bars, so I hear things. I'm not against my girlfriend dating other people if that's something they want." She meant it. That flash of jealousy earlier had worried her, but it wasn't enough to change who she was. She wasn't the possessive clingy type, and she wasn't going to start acting like it just because she was with her destined lover or whatever.

"Babe, I don't want—"

"Don't just say that. I'm not asking you to comfort me. If it happens, then I hope they don't betray us both for Hel. If it doesn't, cool, but please don't break their heart. They *are* still my best friend."

Hannah furrowed her perfectly arched eyebrows.

"Like I said. Whatever happens, let me know. No keeping it from me."

"I would never."

"Now, that part, I do appreciate." She slid her hands up Hannah's back and pulled her down, pressing their lips together. "I just want you to be happy."

"I am happy."

"Well, yeah, we're on vacation in Hawaii. Hard not to be."

Hannah's nails lightly scratched Emily's arm. "I don't mean like that. I'm happy in general. My life is amazing. Hell, it's perfect."

"Okay."

"Aren't you happy?"

Gritting her teeth, Emily couldn't quite look at her.

"Wait, are you not?" Hannah cupped her cheek and turned her to face her. "Emily, what's wrong?"

She shook her head. "Nothing like that. I love you. I just..." She sighed. "Finding out that my entire friendship with literally my only friend was based on a lie sucked ass. And just...no, it's stupid."

"Emily, what?"

She pulled away, leaving Hannah sitting on the bare mattress—how had they managed to pull the sheet off?—as she pressed back against the headboard. "It sounds so stupid. You two have these amazing powers, and you have your dream job and your degree and are doing everything you want to do in life. And here I am, still just with the job—that again, I do actually like—that I only took because it was an easy and fun way out of my old life, and I had nothing else going for me. I'm the god of being your wife. And that's it. Who the fuck has armored crazy people run up to them and tell them this great truth about themselves and then doesn't get any amazing destiny? I wanted to be Harry Potter or something, and I'm not even Hermione. I'm, what, Ginny?"

Hannah shrugged.

"You have read it, right?"

"Of course." She rolled her eyes.

"You are kinda young."

Now glaring, Hannah crawled toward her. "I'm not that young."

Emily chuckled and pulled her close. "I love you. Hell, I guess I love my life. And probably still my job. But I want more than that. We're literal gods, and I don't get to do anything."

"You killed zombies." Her voice was so quiet. She was taking this way too seriously. Emily shouldn't have said anything.

"Yeah. I did. You're right." It was pretty sweet. She needed more of it. And to not just be a magic wife.

"You don't sound convinced."

Another shrug. "No. I did. It was awesome. But Alys did so much more—"

"They killed one. You killed two."

"Only because you brought me a sword. And if you'd fought, then I wouldn't have gotten to do anything. So thanks for that and the sword, but like, what the fuck am I supposed to do? You have superstrength, and they have magic and shapeshifting, and I'm a good farmer."

"You're more than that."

"I'm the woman you love. I know. But that doesn't mean much for the big mythic stuff we seem to be dragged into. And I want to be dragged into it. I know you do too. You do, right?"

Hannah nodded. "Not as much as you two seem to be, but of course I do. It's exciting, and it's family. It just doesn't mean as much to me as my job."

"You're insane." Emily chuckled and mussed her hair, not like it could get any messier. "I want to be able to actually contribute."

"You do," Hannah said firmly, squeezing her hand. "I'm the one who doesn't help. Like, big deal, I have superstrength. All that means is that I can carry you and row you places. I didn't fight. I grabbed you a sword. A dog could've done that. All I did was get in the way."

"No, Hannah." She tugged on her hand, sending Hannah tumbling into her lap. "You did plenty. I know you're not the violent sort. Let me take care of that. I'll find out how to do it better. No matter what I have to do. I can be your hero. Let me do that."

"But—"

Emily silenced her with a kiss. "No. You don't need to fight. It's completely all right. At least it gives me exactly the purpose I wanted. Let me do that for you. Even if I don't have superpowers, I can still be the hero."

"Okay…" It sounded as if she wanted to say more, but Emily had better ideas in mind.

"Now let me take care of you."

Hannah did as she was told, and Emily went above and beyond the call of duty. And then a few more times. Alys would have to entertain themself for a little longer.

CHAPTER TWENTY-EIGHT

The waves splashed against their feet while Alys lay on the soft sand, watching a few other tourists mill about. "Damn, they really are taking their sweet time." They'd had a few more rounds of drinks before wandering around town and looking in the shops. The alcohol hadn't completely worn off, though they could always change that if need be.

Some sand kicked in their face as someone walked by, and they bolted upright. "Hey!"

"Sorry." Hannah's awkward smile and the wet hair clinging to her face only made her cheeks fuller. "You'd said you were at the beach, and I was looking all over and didn't see you there."

The crush might have been worse than they'd thought. They couldn't even pretend to be mad when looking at that face. "Don't worry about it."

She flopped onto the ground. "You find anything cool to do?"

"Does getting drunk count?"

"You were already doing that before we left."

"Then no. We can go shopping if you want, but other than that, I don't have any ideas."

"We could go swimming."

Her smile lit up the beach. As it was early afternoon in Hawaii on a nearly cloudless day in the summer, that was saying something. An urge to kiss her bubbled up, and Alys pushed it back down. "Sure. Though we don't have anything to change into."

She looked crestfallen for a moment before her face lit up all over again. "Swimming, shopping, then dinner and drinks? Come on, that sounds amazing."

Alys nodded. "Yeah. All right." It almost sounded like a date. But she didn't mean it like that, right?

"What time do we need to leave tomorrow?"

"You're the mathematician. We made it there in like fourteen hours and passed Hawaii in, what, six?"

Hannah nodded. "Yeah, somewhere around there. The wind wasn't exactly in our favor on the way back."

"I don't have the map with me—"

"I do." She pulled out her phone, that heartwarming smile still plastered on her face even while putting off swimming and shopping. "Okay, so it looks like the island…Vigridr?"

"Yeah. Good job."

"I can learn Norse names. It's just hard. I'm an accountant, not a linguist."

"Was that a *Star Trek* reference? Nice. I approve."

"Huh?" She stared, confusion clear on her face.

"Damn. Never mind."

"*Okay.*" She turned back to her phone and tapped on the screen a few times. "So, I think that was somewhere around two thousand miles away. Give or take a bit. The point on the map isn't that precise. I don't know how we'd have found it without you."

"I'm useful like that."

She giggled, and Alys's stomach dropped out. "That means we were probably going like what, three hundred three-thirty knots? Goddamn. How? I mean, magic, obviously, but, how? Oh, that's like three fifty to three hundred and eighty miles per hour."

"Now you're just showing off." She was trying to impress them. That was a good sign.

"Yup." Nodding, Hannah grinned and focused on her phone, her tongue slightly poking out of her mouth as she crunched the numbers. "Probably around ten hours for the trip back? If I'm gonna go straight to work, we can leave at like eleven—so, eight here, or otherwise, we might want to head out around nine—six here? It's a magic ship, so we can sleep in it and not have to worry about keeping on course. Damn, I'm so glad we have that. That speed isn't even possible. Sailboats only go, like, thirty knots."

"I love that you're such a massive dork."

"Hey!" She looked so hurt. Alys absolutely didn't want to brush her hair out of her face, pull her in, and kiss away any pain.

They swallowed their libido back down. "I mean it as a compliment. I'm kind of a nerd. Emily never really geeks out over anything, and it's really nice getting to hear someone talk like that. Especially someone I can actually be myself around." They shrugged and very closely studied the sand. "Sorry. It was just nice."

"Emily says it too. I'm just still not used to that being a nice thing, I guess."

"My fault."

"No, it's not." As Alys looked up, they could swear Hannah was leaning in for…well obviously not that, right? They moved away, clearing their throat as they stood and let out a nervous chuckle. "So we know when to leave. Like, probably around five, then? Sounds good. Let's go get to that shopping."

Hannah stared. "Yeah?"

"Yeah. Definitely. Let me spoil you. I already promised I would."

"I can pay for my own stuff."

They shook their head. "No. Please. I insist."

After a very brief moment's hesitation, she jumped to her feet and grabbed Alys's hand, sending their heart fluttering. "Let's go."

Hannah looked beyond gorgeous in a new little red dress. Alys had gotten to see her try on that, a hula skirt, some jeans—as she insisted that she should totally own jeans only to not get them—and a few other outfits that all looked amazing on her.

Their drink now seemed far too empty for how much they were staring into it. There was so much to process. They were not ready to fall for their best friend's girlfriend. The last time had only been a minor crush, and the relationship had gone terribly, and Hannah and Emily seemed so much more serious than Emily and Claire ever had been. How could they risk coming between them? They had to resist, to stuff their feelings back down. They'd already betrayed Emily enough.

"Up for another round?" Hannah asked, adding yet another empty beer glass to the table. "And maybe some more nachos?"

"How do you even still want pork when we've been living off it?"

"We can get shrimp, then, or fish. I just had to try the kalua pig. That chicken was amazing, though."

"How about calamari?"

"Isn't that cannibalism for you?"

They rolled their eyes. "By that standard, everything is cannibalism for me. We can get more nachos if you want."

"Both?" If she would just stop smiling, Alys would stop giving in to every single thing she said.

"Yeah. Sure."

"Then we can check out that ice cream place?"

Alys couldn't help but laugh.

"What?"

"The gods all eat so much, it's such a huge part of Norse culture and mythology, but I'm the one who's supposed to be the great eater. And I mean, clearly I am." They gestured at the massive collection of dirty plates. "But I can't quite keep up with you. And I'm supposed to be able to eat almost as fast as fire."

"What?"

"You still haven't read the copy of the *Prose Edda* I gave you, have you?"

She huffed. "I tried. I made it through the first few pages. It's just really dry."

"You're an accountant."

"I know." Her lip trembled, though Alys suspected it was a ploy. But why? What was she begging for? Just to not make her read? And why look so adorable? Were they just hoping Hannah liked them, or were they trying desperately not to read into obvious signs that she did?

"Please try to read it. You should read the *Poetic Edda* too."

"Can't you tell me the stories instead?"

"Oh." They couldn't take their eyes off her. "You really want that? It wouldn't bore you?"

"No. I mean, yes, I do want that, and, no, it wouldn't bore me. It sounds funner than reading it. I really like listening to you." She was definitely blushing this time. They weren't imagining it. "I just thought it'd be fun."

Was she making up an excuse to spend more time with them? If she could read through those textbooks, then she could absolutely survive the *Prose Edda*. Or maybe myth—if they could still call it that, just didn't do it for her—but then why have Alys tell the stories? There wasn't an explanation other than wanting that time with them. And maybe even as more than— Alys cut that thought off. "Ice cream sounds great. After another of their local beers and that calamari and nachos."

"Yes!"

Hannah caught the waitress's attention, but Alys almost wished the food would never come if it meant they'd be leaving any sooner.

By the time they finished their meal and the dozen or so beers that accompanied it, that nagging feeling would hardly leave Alys's mind. But they wouldn't give into it. They would only give into ice cream. "Or maybe a milkshake," they said as they looked over the menu.

"What's Hawaiian grilled cheese?" Hannah asked.

Alys managed to hold in a laugh while the clerk at the counter explained it, and Hannah promptly ordered one, along with a sundae. She really was insatiable. Damn it, that thought wasn't going to help. "I'll get a chocolate milkshake."

"Sounds good," Hannah said. "Can I steal some of yours?"

They nodded. "Yeah. Of course. I'll grab another straw."

She shrugged and dragged them to a table. "You have no idea how many looks I got in my sorority for how much I can eat. Especially when I still look like this in the end." She gestured at her body. Alys had not needed the cue to stare.

"I can imagine."

"Like, I loved them all, but there were definitely some not so savory rumors." She stuck her finger in her mouth to indicated what those rumors were. "And I definitely didn't. Apparently, I'm just magically fit."

"I don't think so."

"You don't think I'm fit?"

They pinched the bridge of their nose. How hard was it to not accidentally insult her? "No. You definitely are. Insanely so. But in the myths, Thor wasn't all that fit. He was big and muscular, but there was nothing to suggest fitness. I feel like there was even mention of a belly, but that may have been in some other adaptations. I'm pretty sure that's just you. You exercise every day and have enough energy that you manage to burn off those calories. Though your godhood definitely helped your metabolism. Otherwise, you wouldn't even be able to eat this much."

"Huh." She sucked her teeth as she took that in, only to run to the counter a moment later when their order was ready. "This looks so good." She slammed the tray down on the table and threw herself back into her seat. "Hawaiian grilled cheese. Weird. Want some?"

"Of course."

As they bit into it, Alys had to admit it was interesting. Not worth going out of the way for, but they would have to try upping their grilled cheese game if they wanted to compete, and they absolutely did.

Hannah started digging into the sundae. "I wish we had more time here."

"I know. But you don't want to miss work." They were never going to get over the idea of Thor being an accountant. But it made Hannah happy, so it was hard to find it ridiculous.

"I would never. Er, never again."

As they chuckled, Alys caught themself reaching out, wanting to brush back Hannah's hair. Why did they keep almost doing that? They pulled their hand back and grabbed the milkshake and hoped it would freeze their damn lust. Or crush. Or love. Whatever it was. Ignoring how well they knew the answer, they did their absolute best to think of something as far away from it as possible. "Vigridr was pretty crazy, right? Like, I'd read about it, and Hel told me about it, but I never imagined it as quite that big. I thought a hundred miles was an exaggeration. Hell, most experts did. But pretty sure it was accurate. Though it was supposed to be a field."

Hannah shrugged. "Maybe it used to be? Hel could've moved it."

"But then how would Modi and Magni have known where it was? I guess they could've tracked it with Mimir or something. I don't know."

"Maybe we'll find out."

They nodded, feeling a small smile tug at their cheeks. "Yeah. I'd love that. Getting to learn about all this stuff is half the fun of being a god."

Hannah didn't echo the sentiment, but she did smile back, and that was good enough for Alys. "I'm sorry, though. About Vigridr. The fighting, I mean. I know you were probably expecting me to take care of things. I'm the god of strength and I just—I wouldn't—I couldn't bring myself to do it."

"It's fine. No one's judging you for that. Fighting is terrifying."

"It's not…I guess I was scared but not because of that."

Was it about the mugger? And the time Alys had mind-controlled her. Goddamn it. How could they even be thinking about falling for Hannah when they were still hiding that? Maybe they really were the villain. So many scholars thought that Loki was only made evil to match the Christian influence spreading at the time, but how could anyone who wasn't evil do the shit they'd done to the only people they'd cared about? They got rid of their tear ducts. "I get it. I'm sorry—"

Hannah shook her head. "It wasn't just the mugger. I…" She still had tear ducts, and she was clearly using them. Tears fell into her shake. "I'm sorry I'm so useless."

What? Alys stared at her. That was what she was upset about? "You're not useless. We wouldn't have even made it there without you rowing, and you got Emily the weapon that saved the day. And you carried me when I was exhausted. You don't have to be some big damn hero. You're not Thor. You're Hannah. And I…we don't mind protecting you."

She nodded, still sniffling. "I know. Emily says the same thing. But I am Thor. I have the strength, and I can't even use it. I just couldn't let myself do that. I can't." She was shaking.

What was going through her head? What could they do to help? They wouldn't use magic for it, not when they already had to live with the guilt of messing with her mind.

"I just can't do that. I can't let myself even get close to hurting anyone like that. Not again."

"Hannah?" they asked. What was she talking about? "If this isn't about the mugger…"

She stared at her food, pushing the unfinished ice cream away. "I'm not hungry. Do you want to go back to the hotel?"

"Hannah, please, talk to me. What's wrong?"

"You're going to think I'm a monster."

"I had tentacles yesterday and have repeatedly been told to kill you, and I…I really don't think I'm in any room to judge someone else's monstrosity." Great, they were a monster and a coward.

"It's not the same." She folded her arms over her chest, curling in on herself in the little metal chair. "I can't fight. I won't. I don't trust myself with it."

"Why not?"

She cleared her throat. For a moment, it looked like she might run away, but she didn't quite manage to stand, staring at the ice cream. "It was in high school. I got in a fight with this girl. I don't even remember why. I think she accused me of trying to steal her boyfriend. Yeah, that's right. I was too scared to admit that I wouldn't have been interested in a guy, but she took my hesitation as proof, and set in on me. She hit me and…"

Alys swallowed a lump in their throat. With her strength… It didn't take much to imagine what happened. They could still vividly see the man Hannah had sent into a wall. The man she'd killed. No wonder she was terrified. If only Alys hadn't been too busy with their own guilt to see it.

"I kept hitting her until Megan pulled me off. I had assumed it was the adrenaline, and I never let myself do anything like that to anyone else again. She was in the hospital until the next year. She didn't even graduate in our class. All because I lost control of my temper. I swore

I would never do that again. And then I did. You saw that mugger. I nearly killed him. I don't care if it's monsters or anything. I can't do that again. I won't."

"Hannah…"

"I won't let it happen. And my temper cost me my last relationship, and I never even did anything, and I won't let it hurt anyone else. If I give in and fight someone…I don't know what would happen."

"They were Draugr, zombies."

"I can't let myself think that it's okay. No matter what. I can't fight."

Alys didn't even recall standing, but they rounded the table and took Hannah's hand. "And you don't have to. I'm sorry for pushing you so far that you had to tell me."

"You didn't."

"I understand what it's like to not trust yourself. I could tell you again and again that you could fight and then stop from doing anything more, but I know how little that would mean. So let me just say, you'll never have to. I'll keep you safe."

Hannah nodded, pursing her lips. "Thank you."

"Any time."

"You really don't think—"

"You're not a monster." *Unlike me.* "You're a beautiful, amazing, wonderful woman." Also unlike them, but they were okay with that part.

Hannah started to lean in again, and Alys widened their eyes, licked their lips, and tried to figure out what to do. Before they could decide, Hannah glanced down at their hands, at Alys sitting on the table in front of them, and then at their lips. "I should go tell Emily the story. Thank you for listening."

"It was nothing." They needed to tell her. To confess.

"And for dinner and your boat and everything else. You're wonderful, Alys. And I know we can trust you. Emily is coming back around to that too."

That sure killed the mood. Alys nodded. "Thanks." But they shouldn't trust them. Not after what they'd done.

"Let's go back to the hotel. We can grab Emily and head out. There will be time for more when we're home."

More what? Alys stared, trying to sort out that last bit but not quite able to bring themselves to ask. She hadn't meant… "Hannah, I…" *Just say it.*

"Come on." She tugged on their hand, and they followed obediently. They'd follow her to any of the nine realms or even the roots of Yggdrasil. They had fallen hopelessly.

❖

As the three of them all sat in the boat, Hannah kicked the iron sword from the island. "You kept that?"

"I told you, I'm going to be the hero. I've got to be able to fight, don't I?" Emily asked.

"I could buy you a better sword," Alys said. "One that isn't all old and rusty." Always just trying to buy everyone's love instead of being honest with them. Damn it, the guilt was really killing them now. But Emily might throw them overboard if they confessed now, and they'd deserve it. But Alys could make it up to both of them. They just had to talk to Hel and get the information Hannah and Emily needed. Then they could come clean. They just needed something to offer first.

"Hey, this one kept us alive," Emily said "Besides, Hannah got it for me."

Hannah's cheeks reddened as she stared at the sea, watching the island fade behind them as she rowed. Once they were farther out, she unfurled the sail and let the wind carry them.

Emily reclined against the cooler, sipping a beer, her bare feet resting in Hannah's lap now that she was facing forward again. "It's going to be weird to be home."

"We weren't even gone that long," Alys said.

Hannah leaned against the side of the ship. "It sure feels like it, though. That adventure in Vigridr and then the trip to Hawaii. It seems like weeks."

"With a normal sailboat, it would've been, but *Naglfar* is amazing like that."

"Don't say that," Hannah said. "Now I know what it means."

"This boat is amazing like that?"

"Better," she grumbled.

"You rested up enough for work?" Emily asked.

Yawning, Hannah shook her head. "Apparently not."

"Snuggle pile?" Alys asked, wiggling their eyebrows playfully.

Hannah moved Emily's feet off her and threw herself down onto the deck, resting her head in Emily's lap. "Sure, if you can figure out how to do it in here."

Stroking her hair, Emily planted a soft kiss on the top of her head. "Sweet dreams, honey." They both said I love you, and Hannah drained the rest of her beer before closing her eyes and nuzzling Emily's thigh. That left Alys and Emily with six hours to talk. Normally, that would sound amazing.

"The snuggle pile thing was a joke, right?" Alys asked.

"I honestly don't know," Emily said.

They nodded. "I'm sorry."

"You've said. It's enough. I forgive you. Just stay on our side."

"I will."

"Good, then."

"Throw me a beer?"

If Alys hadn't turned their arm into a tentacle at the last second, a fish would've enjoyed the drink. "Gonna need to work on your throw if you're gonna be a hero."

"Shut up."

They smirked. Maybe things really were back to normal—or something better now that they were all open and themselves.

Emily sighed, swirling her own drink. "She likes you, you know?"

Alys blinked. "Oh?" Had Hannah said something about it? By Odin, they knew better than to think like this already.

"I'm not sure she's quite confident in it yet, but yeah."

"And you're really okay with that?"

"Yeah, but if you hurt her or betray us again, I'm shoving this sword so far up your ass, it'll come out your mouth."

They almost coughed up their beer. "I thought you were just gonna kill me with it. Did not expect the end of that threat."

"That's step two."

Alys nodded. "I won't hurt her."

"And?"

"And I won't betray you. Either of you. I already said. You're my best friend and she's…she's…"

"I know."

Alys blew out a breath and stared at the reddened sea as the little ship drifted over it, barely seeming to touch the waves. It didn't matter how terrifying turning on Hel still was or how dire the consequences could be. They'd keep their word. Emily had been their best friend for eight years. The only person to really understand them and who wasn't even using them for some evil goal. And Hannah was…Hannah.

CHAPTER TWENTY-NINE

The little standing shower in their home was a sad change from the luxurious one at the hotel in Hawaii, but it was good enough. Hannah picked out a cute brown blouse with a black skirt, grabbed the car keys, and headed to work. She promised herself that she'd call Megan when she was done. Maybe now that she had everything, Megan would believe her too. There were only so many magical hammers in the world, right? That had to convince Megan that she wasn't insane.

Arriving at work a little early, Hannah waved to the receptionist and hurried to her desk. She couldn't clock in for a few more minutes, but she wanted to start the second she could; she'd have a good deal of work to make up.

Once she was able to sign in, she found all the accounts she had to settle. It looked like Isabel had taken over a couple but nowhere near all of them. She popped in her earbuds, threw on some good accounting music—Lily Allen—and went to town on the assignments. It felt nice to be back doing what she loved. At least this she could control. And she could fight numbers without any risk of killing anyone. That made her queasy. She blinked, rubbing her eyes.

A tap on the shoulder dragged her back to reality, and Isabel flashed a grin. "You finally stopped to breathe. You look tan. Good sick day?"

"I wasn't…I mean—"

"It's fine. I know you. There's no way you would've missed work if you didn't absolutely have to. I won't push for details. I'd rather have plausible deniability."

"Thanks for taking care of a few things."

"Don't mention it. I would have done more if I'd had time."

Hannah glanced at the list of accounts. "Well, I'm almost caught up with where I should be."

"You go, girl. Are you some kind of super accountant?"

"Of course." Hannah winked. "I'm Thor, god of accounting."

Isabel returned the gesture. "Well, maybe I won't do it for you next time. It seems like sacrilege to steal from your holy bounty, O Mighty Thunderer."

Hannah's eyes widened, and she shook her head. She wouldn't. Right? "Wait, no. Please."

Giggling, Isabel said, "Relax. I'm only kidding. I'm sure you'd do the same for me."

"Anytime. As long as you don't mind an intern doing your work."

"Your work is absolutely perfect. Anyone would be lucky to have you take over for them. I hope I didn't mess things up for you."

"I'm sure you didn't." She checked the clock in the corner of her screen. It was earlier than she'd thought. She was almost ahead in her work. "I skipped breakfast. Want to maybe go grab a coffee and a bagel? My treat. I owe you for last week."

"Your check came in?"

Hannah checked her bank account on her phone. It had, in fact, come in. That was a relief. "Yep."

"Coffee sounds great." She yawned, stretching. "I could use it."

Hannah treated her to an espresso and a scone and had a Danish and hot chocolate for herself. She liked coffee fine, but she didn't need caffeine so much as she needed a break.

"Are you sure I'm not in trouble for yesterday?" Hannah asked as they sat outside. It had been weighing on her mind since she'd called out. Hawaii had been nice, and in some ways, much needed, but she wouldn't risk losing her internship. And she wanted to keep Isabel as a friend.

"Miranda came back. I guess you missed her."

"Oh no. That's my actual boss, right? She must be so upset with me."

Isabel laughed. "Come on, love. Don't be absurd. She spent the whole day getting reacquainted and taking pumping breaks. I don't think she even noticed." She leaned back, dark brown eyes staring over the rim of her cup. "You don't need to worry. Your receptionist friend relayed your message and sounded as adorably pathetic as I'm sure you did, and Miranda couldn't have cared less. I talked about you a little and showed her some of your work, and she's really impressed."

"You're sure?"

"I'm sure. The other intern is already gone. You really think calling out sick is gonna cost you anything?"

"Maybe." She pouted.

Isabel kicked her under the table, causing her to spill some of her hot chocolate.

"Hey!"

"That's what you get for having that attitude. Now, come on. Let's introduce you to your real boss before you have a panic attack."

"But—"

"Shove the Danish in your mouth and drink the cocoa at your desk. I'm not letting you sulk another minute." She waved for Hannah to follow and marched off.

Hannah rushed after her, trying to finish her Danish as she ran. Through her godly might, she managed to succeed, and saw her boss for the first time with pastry crumbs all down her blouse. "Hi." She waved, a nervous smile plastered on her face as she stared at the tall, severe, black-haired woman who was walking back into the office at the same time as they were, carrying a small leather bag.

"I take it this is Ms. Olsen?" the boss asked, turning to Isabel.

"Yep."

She looked her up and down. "I'm Mrs. Ravencroft, but you can call me Miranda. It's a pleasure to meet you." She extended a hand, and Hannah took it eagerly.

"I've heard great things."

"Compared to Brian? Even a sponge would be a good boss."

Hannah held her tongue.

"I saw your work. You're learning the trade very quickly, and I don't have any feedback for you other than good job, and I'm glad we could finally meet. Just don't go calling out sick too often."

Her cheeks burned, and Hannah gave a deep nod. "Of course. I'm sorry, ma'am. I didn't mean—"

"It's fine. You're still an intern, so try not to overuse it, but if you're sick, you're sick. I don't want you spreading it around the office. You sure you're feeling better?"

"Of course, ma'am. I'm fine."

"Like I said, call me Miranda."

"Right, Miranda."

With a playful chuckle, Miranda saluted her. "At ease, soldier. You don't need to be so formal. The fact that you even want to be here is more than enough for me to want to keep you around. Add to that that you're actually competent, unlike a few of the people whose names I won't mention. So relax, enjoy your coffee, and stop stressing so much. It'll make your work suffer."

"Yes, ma'…randa."

"Good catch." Patting her shoulder affectionately, Miranda walked across the room to her office, leaving Hannah to sigh in relief at not completely bungling that introduction.

Isabel studied her. "Feel better?"

"A little."

"Good. Let's go finish up, and then I brought lunch again, in case your check hadn't gone through."

"Great." They sat at their desks, and Hannah tried to finish her hot chocolate and focus on her breathing. She'd been so terrified, but everything was fine. She could do her work and hang out with her friend. Alys was right. She had been worrying over nothing.

❖

As she left the office, Hannah was a little disappointed when she didn't find her sons waiting for her. She needed to get them cell phones or something. Would those work in Idavollr? Probably not. There had to be some way to reliably communicate. Magic pigeons?

She waved good-bye to Isabel and climbed into the old Nissan, heading home. She was tired of waiting. She wanted to run off and prove herself right now. It had been weeks since she'd found out who she really was, and still, she hadn't been accepted. If the last time she'd come out had gone this poorly, she might have gone right back in the closet. Other gods were still having trouble believing it, let alone her friends, and she couldn't take it. She'd go there and show them everything. She just needed to have Emily with her.

"You awake?" she asked as she walked down the stairs.

"Yeah," a voice said from the living room. "I should get going."

Right. She had work. Damn it. Hannah refused to encourage her skipping work any more than she already had. "Do you have tomorrow off?"

"Yeah."

"How about after I get off work, we head to Idavollr and show them everything? I'm so tired of waiting. Please?" She bit her lip, staring at a very exhausted Emily. She'd slept in the boat. Hannah had no idea why she was still this worn out.

Emily stared back, eyes closing as she yawned. "Fine. Maybe they'll actually have some idea of what I can do."

"Make the perfect beer. Duh."

"I guess it's better than nothing." She snatched the keys from Hannah's hand and planted a soft kiss on her lips. "I love you. I guess tomorrow, we officially become gods."

"I think we already are."

"Queens of Idavollr?"

"I'm not taking the throne."

Emily sighed, glaring. "Then clearly, nothing happens, and there's no reason to worry so much about it. I'll see you soon. Have a good night."

Once she was gone, Hannah decided to follow through on her earlier promise to herself. She called Megan.

"Hannah," Megan began.

"Hold on. Please."

"What?"

"I know you don't believe me. I—"

"That's not it." She could hear traffic going by. Megan must've been waiting for a bus, or maybe she was walking home. Hannah wished she had her own car. She'd offer to pick Megan up, and they could talk everything through. "I *do* believe you, but I don't know how to handle this insanity."

"Oh." Hannah deflated in her chair. She had been so certain that once she had everything, she'd be able to convince Megan, as well as the other gods. Of course it wasn't that simple. Megan had already seen the Rainbow Bridge. Her issue couldn't have been disbelief.

"What did you want?"

"I'm going to Idavollr tomorrow, and I thought maybe later this week, we could all hang out and celebrate that I'm officially Thor."

"So, what, it's your godhood quinceañera?"

"Basically. Though I don't think I'll have as pretty a dress as you did."

"Mine would fit if you want to borrow it."

"Yes!" Hannah sat up, grinning like an idiot. She was glad Megan wasn't there to make fun of her. "Please?"

"Fine. I'll bring it."

"So you're coming?"

"How can I miss my best friend's quince? Of course I'm coming."

Hannah blinked away tears but couldn't fight back her smile. "Thank you."

Chuckling came from the other end of the phone, then the telltale squeak of a Trimet bus. "I've gotta go, but I promise I'll be there. I'll bring the dress and maybe some champagne."

"I can't wait." Everything was finally perfect. She could have all of her friends, and she had Emily and… Well, it was perfect.

Megan hung up without another word, but Hannah could hardly blame her if she was rushing to the bus. Didn't want to hold up the line. She was amazed by how easy that had been. She'd been ready to cry and plead. Megan was important to her, and she'd been terrified that she'd lost her after the other night. "Thank Odin," she muttered with a giggle. She still hadn't done much research on the subject, but she was pretty sure that was the right god. It looked like she was going to have a pretty exciting week.

Chapter Thirty

Emily and Hannah sped across the Rainbow Bridge in the old car while the bright light shone from the road. Hannah had said repeatedly that they had to make sure they were back in time for work, and who knew what all the gods would ask of them, so Emily was hurrying.

When they pulled up before the castle, Modi, Magni, and an older woman ran out. She was shorter than them, with long gray hair halfway down her back. "You're here," Magni called. "Does that mean you found it?"

As Hannah emerged from the car, Modi swooped her up into a massive bear hug. "Oh, it's so good to see you. I wasn't sure what would happen."

"Why did you fear?" Magni asked, giving his brother a hearty pat on the back as he snatched Hannah, pulling her into another embrace. "You knew full well that our Hannah was unbeatable. Even if Jormungandr himself was still alive, she'd thrash the bastard."

Hannah doubted that killing Alys's kid would have gone too well.

"No hug for me?" Emily asked, coming around the car as she beeped it locked.

Modi obliged her. "You are well? Did you accompany her? I was terrified to lose you again, as well."

"I'm fine." She chuckled, hugging him back lightly, letting out a pained groan when he squeezed tighter.

"Who's this?" Hannah asked, as she was finally put down.

"Is it true?" the woman asked, looking at her with an expression somewhere between terror and ecstasy. She seemed nervous. Her head hung low, but the hope in her eyes was unmistakable. "Are you really our father?"

Offering a faltering smile, Hannah gestured to the belt she was wearing over her pink dress. She didn't need to throw on guy clothes or anything of the sort to prove herself. She was Thor, and they had to accept that she was. The head of Mjolnir stuck out over her right hip, while the gauntlets dangling from her hands caught the brilliant sun overhead. Apparently, not having air pollution really did make a difference. "I seem to be. Assuming that you are Thor's daughter and that I'm not incredibly confused."

She nodded. "I am. I'm Thrudr. It's so weird to introduce myself to my own parents. Mother, I can certainly see." She gestured at Emily. "She barely looks different from when I last saw her, but—"

"Not used to your dad being a girl?"

"I'm not used to him being so small." She laughed and finally giving her a hug. "But I can see it in your eyes…and in your hammer. You really are him, aren't you?"

Hannah hugged her back, hiding her doubts in Thrudr's shoulder. "I think so."

"Well, surely they can't doubt you anymore," Magni said, releasing Emily. "Let us talk with Forseti. I'm sure he'll be irritable, but he can't deny you now."

"Why?" Hannah asked. "Couldn't anyone wield these things?" Magni had been using the hammer when they'd met. They'd insisted this would prove it, and she'd gone along, but it didn't make sense.

"No one else would look that good in that dirty old belt," Emily said, receiving an eyeroll from Hannah and another giggle from Thrudr.

"It's good to see you, Mother," Thrudr said.

"Please, call me Emily."

"Emily, then." She grinned. "Ullr will be so excited to see you. If he ever gets back from his hunting trip. It's been two years now."

"Should we be concerned?" Emily asked, sounding as if she genuinely was, despite having no idea who that was. Hannah liked to think that it was because she was finally accepting who they were.

"No, he's been gone for decades at a time before. I don't know how his wife puts up with him."

"Father was gone far more often," Modi pointed out.

Hannah muttered, "Thanks."

"Let's go." Emily gestured with a jerk of her head toward the castle. "You know how Hannah is. If she ends up missing work just to prove she's a god, she's never going to forgive any of us."

"Father finally learned responsibility?" Thrudr asked. "I suppose later is better than never."

Hannah decided to lean into it. "It only took dying."

A booming voice echoed over the courtyard. "I said you could stay one day." Forseti stood on the parapet above them, looking down at the family reunion.

"She—" Modi started.

"I have proof," Hannah called, letting her voice ring out louder than Forseti's. It didn't have the same basso vibrations, but it carried more than well enough. She held the hammer high above her head, staring in shock when it grew in size. She guessed it was excited, then immediately regretted that image. "I have Mjolnir." She'd practiced the next two names in her head, she'd rehearsed this all day yesterday, and she could get it right. "Jarngreipr." She let her gauntlets reflect the light. "And Megingjord." She used her free hand to indicate the belt, hooking her thumb behind the buckle. "I am Thor, daughter of Odin, and I dare you to deny it a moment longer."

That felt good. Fortunately, he was too far away to see her shaking in her Uggs. Alys had helped with the speech, though Hannah added the last bit herself. She never could turn down a challenge. Well, she never turned down races when she was on crew, and she'd never turned down a drinking contest in her life. That had to count for something. She just had to see if Forseti was the same way.

It was a long while before he spoke. He stood, unmoving, watching, waiting. For what, she didn't know. Perhaps the first excuse that came to mind. "You rode across the Bifrost in that contraption. If you were really Thor, you'd be able to step foot on the bridge yourself."

"You could've brought this up last time." That would've been way easier than having to miss work and risk life or limb against a bunch of zombies. What if she'd been fired? All for something that she could've proven by walking on a fucking bridge? That dick. "But let's go. I'll walk on it right now." At least the belt was supposed to help with the apples. But she could've brought Valkyries or something.

"You will?" He sounded nervous. She could barely hear him.

"Okay, this is getting ridiculous. Come down here if you want to talk."

He did. Apparently, he no longer felt he had the upper hand. When he was downstairs, he said, "Well, you could still be Loki."

"Don't be ridiculous," Modi scoffed. "That traitor would never have the courage to come here. This is Thor. I'll swear any oath you need."

"Let's take a walk," Hannah said, her hand resting on the hammer now securely back in the belt of power. Her confidence was growing by the minute. They could scream that she wasn't Thor until their faces were blue, but she'd prove them wrong, whatever she had to do.

"Well, I—"

"If you don't want to walk a few miles, I can tell you," Magni said, "She picked up that car—that's what it's called—and set it on the bridge herself. We all walked onto the Bifrost together. I'll vouch for her, as will my brother and my mother if you'll believe her word."

Emily waved and offered a shit-eating grin. "It's true."

"Do you intend to challenge me for the throne?"

"For the dozenth time, no!" Hannah shook her head, kicking the courtyard ground. "I just want a community. If I'm a god, I'd rather be able to talk to other gods about it and not have to hide that part of myself. This is my home too."

He sighed, but finally nodded gravely. "You're right. I'm sorry. After everything, I've been scared to trust anyone. Even Father has been under constant surveillance."

Hannah started to say something, but Emily slid an arm around her hip and whispered, "Save it. We're barely trusted as it is."

"So we're welcome?"

"Is that really Mjolnir?" he asked.

"How can I prove it?"

"Throw it."

"At what?" Hannah looked around. She didn't want to hurt anyone.

"I'd normally say Father, but he's understandably skittish since the last game of it killed him." He pointed toward a small ash tree in the corner of the courtyard. "I'd like a nice fire tonight. If that's Mjolnir, it should be able to fell that tree in a single throw and return to your hand."

She knew she should've practiced. She hoped never to get in another fight, so any skill with the weapon would be unnecessary.

"Alys says it can't miss," Emily said quietly, sliding her hand away and taking a few steps back.

Fine. She'd come this far. She certainly wasn't going to turn back now. Drawing the hammer, Hannah took aim at the tree. There was no way she'd be able to hit this. It was too far away, and the hammer was too oddly weighted.

She flung her hand forward, and the weapon hurled straight at her target, demolishing the base of the tree and a good several feet up, causing the rest of it to crash against the far wall. "Oh." Her jaw dropped as the hammer landed back in her outstretched hand. That had really worked. She was so lucky the hammer was magic.

An ecstatic Emily pulled her into a kiss. She'd done it.

"Very well. If it was only the one of you, I'd doubt it, but even I can see the resemblance. You are who you say you are. This is your home. Come, stay for a meal. Stay forever. Help us get back to Asgard."

It finally sank in. Again. She was a god. She was Thor, no matter how strange it still felt. And she could be accepted by people like her. She'd finally finished coming out again. Or mostly finished. Isabel could find out after Hannah had been hired. Which left her parents, but she could rationalize her way into waiting for that. It had been a long month.

"Thank you. We'll stay for the meal. But we'll be back to help with Asgard." Hannah wanted to hurry home and tell everyone, but she never turned down food.

Emily dragged Modi and Magni away from the festivities after they'd had half a dozen drinks and their fair share of goose and goat. Hannah followed once she'd finished draining her drinking horn. They gathered at the top of one of the towers, and Hannah saw out over Idavollr for the first time, and found herself speechless.

In the very far distance, the land still smoldered where Asgard had once stood, but everything before and around it was so beautiful. It was overgrown, with massive trees, vines, and piles of rubble, but there was a serene beauty to it, abandoned as it was. There were crystal-clear lakes—or maybe they were fjords—green hills, icy mountains, and a few large animals, which seemed distinct from what she'd find on Earth.

The sky was a whole other beast. When the sun was up, it looked almost like home—well, her other home—but it was setting now. She'd never seen so many colors in a sunset. She wasn't even sure what a few of them were called. Above it, the stars were already starting to shine, and they were larger and brighter than any she'd seen in Midgard. It was like they were right there. She felt as if she could leap up and touch them. Maybe she could.

"Beautiful, isn't it?" Thrudr asked. She hadn't been there a moment ago. How long had Hannah been staring? "I saw you all sneaking off. If I'd known it was just to watch the sunset, I wouldn't have worried. I'm so glad we managed to find a new sun. So few were willing to volunteer."

"What?" Hannah stared.

Thrudr chuckled. "She was eaten during Ragnarok. We had to find a new sun to take the role, but fortunately her daughter volunteered."

Hannah blinked. "What?"

Modi clapped her on the shoulder. "It's true, Father. Fenrir ate her, just as he prophesized he would do, but the world couldn't go on without a sun, so we found a new one."

"Huh," Hannah said.

Emily shrugged. "It's not any weirder than anything else we've learned."

"Was that all you wanted?" Magni asked, looking to Emily. "To take in the view from up here?"

She shook her head. "Would you like to tell them, or should I?"

"You can," Hannah said.

"All right." She sighed, taking in a deep breath before she spoke again. "That guy back there isn't Baldur. At least, we don't think it is."

"What do you mean?" Thrudr asked. She was family too, and they'd already told her. Hannah had to accept that they could trust her.

Still, she bit her lip. How much should they reveal? Even if everyone here understood, based on what they'd said about Loki, it wasn't the best idea to reveal Alys. At least not yet. Should they admit that Hel was trying to break in? "It's just a hunch. We don't have anything to go on. Not yet, at least. But we don't think it's really him."

"Why wouldn't it be?" Magni asked. "I know Baldur, just as I know you." He sucked on his teeth, his eyes narrowing as he looked between them. "Well, he has been a little odd since he came back, but it's been decades. Surely, if it wasn't him, he would have done whatever he'd wanted by now."

"Unless he's after an apple. He can't get into Asgard any more than you can. We need to expose him first."

"You speak madness," Thrudr said. But the words lacked conviction. She must've noticed something off too.

"I know you think he's one of you, but please don't trust him. We'll have proof next time." If Alys managed to get any. "But don't try to get to Asgard without us. I don't know what he's planning, but I promise it's not good."

They all remained silent for a long time, but Modi finally nodded. "I trust you, Mother. If you say he's not who he says he is, I believe you. I'll be on guard."

"Thank you."

"And you will hurry back?" Magni asked.

"This weekend. Definitely."

Emily nodded. "I have more sick days to burn anyway."

"I don't know what that means," Thrudr said.

"Don't worry about it."

They all hugged again and started heading out, avoiding the rest of the crowd and walking toward the car. "So, Thrudr, tell me about yourself," Hannah said. "You're Emily's and my kid too?"

She looked up between her two burly brothers. "Unlike Magni here." She laughed, giving him an affectionate slap on his exceedingly large bicep. So he wasn't Sif's kid? "But yes. You really don't remember anything?"

Hannah shook her head. "I'm sorry. The three of you feel kind of familiar, and when I first gave them a chance to explain, it all felt right, but I don't know if that's only because I wanted to believe it."

"It's because you're you," Magni insisted.

Thrudr looked her dead in the eye. Hannah was surprised to see that, beneath the long gray hair, her own eyes peered back at her. "I'm sure you're my father. Or mother, if you prefer. Granted, you never seemed all that concerned about gender in the first place. At least, that's what Uncle Tyr always told me."

"What do you mean?" Hannah needed this information. It was her life. Her history. Maybe it would start to make sense if she knew everything.

"You were quite quick to pretend to be Freyja once."

"I did what?"

Cackling, Magni said, "It was only to get Mjolnir back."

"Then why was Loki only the handmaiden?" Thrudr asked.

"He tricked Father, obviously," Modi said.

As the three continued to bicker, Hannah let that sink in. Not that she used to be a crossdresser—that was weird, but it was hardly troubling as she was a girl now—but that Loki had been part of it. Everything she'd been told made Loki sound evil. Granted, she didn't seem much like Thor herself. Could it be that he wasn't actually that bad? Or at least that he hadn't always been? "You don't think Loki could've been trying to help?"

They looked at her in utter shock. "Of course not," Magni bellowed. "That rat bastard."

"You don't remember, but there's no way. You couldn't trust that monster as far as you could throw him." Modi spat on the ground. And Hannah could throw things pretty far.

Thrudr looked at Hannah with a sad expression. "If you knew the things he's done...If not for him, you'd never have died. He started Ragnarok. Forseti is justifiably traumatized and terrified by it. I can't blame him for being paranoid, even if it does sometimes mean that he behaves the way he did with you."

This only raised more questions, but as they were already at the car, she just thanked them for the information. She'd ask Alys about it. Maybe they could fill in more blanks. If she kept talking to her kids about Loki, she'd give something away. "We should get going."

"Of course." Modi asked. "You'll be back soon?"

"You couldn't keep us away."

They hugged and parted, with Emily and Hannah making their own way down the path as the others seemed to fall back into debating their father's life.

She hoped Alys would have the proof about Baldur in time to stop whatever he was planning.

Chapter Thirty-one

The door was already open, so Hannah and Emily went right in. Alys wasn't inside, and Hannah could smell smoke coming from the back. Emily led the way to the back door. "Hey, Alys, you out there?" she called.

"Oh, hey. Is it seven already?" they asked. "Sorry. I'll be right in."

"What're you smoking? When will it be done? Is it for me?" Hannah asked.

"It's always for you if you want it." That cocky playful smirk that they seemed to have perfected played across their face. They looked different today. They always did, but despite the long purple hair, they looked more like when Hannah had first seen them, though a bit taller. Hannah tried not to unashamedly stare at their returned—and apparently upgraded—chest, and settled on only glancing occasionally. "How are my two favorite ladies?"

"We'd be better if you had that information already," Emily said.

"Sorry." She reacted before Alys could even finish looking hurt. "It's good to see you. I'm just worried about…Goddamn I hate saying *our kids*."

"But you're getting used to it," Hannah said, beaming.

"I suppose."

Alys sighed. "I'm working on it. I can't seem too overeager. She wants to have Baldur's help clearing the rubble, and I tried insisting that was pointless. I think she's lying and seeing what I'll do. It's why I'm trying to be patient."

"Patience sucks, though," Hannah said. "Can't we hurry up and do something? Like if you have any proof, then we can expose him, and then we can get the apples together."

"I don't think I'll be welcome." They paused for a moment, and that cocky grin returned. "What if I go as Baldur?"

"That still wouldn't give us proof," Emily said.

"Well, yeah, but…Damn it. I really want to see the cool magical stuff. It's not fair that you two get to go, and I don't."

"I know." Hannah pulled them into a hug. "I'm sorry. We'll work on that. If you can expose Baldur, it'll be a big first step."

They nodded into her shoulder.

"Try talking to her again tonight?" Emily asked.

"I'll try. I just—"

"Don't want to seem overeager. You said."

Alys pulled out of the hug and blew out a breath, giving a weak smile. "Let me just…" They pointed at the smoker. "If we're gonna be talking a bit, I need to add some more chips and maybe a little more sauce."

"Sure, take your time." Emily said.

"You still haven't said what it is," Hannah said.

"Brisket. Figured I'd make it to celebrate. Or are we not throwing a party? Oh, and it'll be done tomorrow. Hadn't answered that either."

"I have work," Emily grumbled.

"We can party in the afternoon, then."

"You have work," Emily reminded them.

"And so do I," Hannah said.

"Well, I guess I'll just have to look after Hannah myself." They offered as lascivious a grin as they could, which, as a shapeshifter, was pretty impressive.

"Saturday? Lunchtime? If you have the proof by then, we can go to Idavollr after."

"I suppose." With a dramatic sigh, they stepped over to the smoker. "Give me a minute."

Five minutes later, they were all gathered on the couch. Hannah hooked a foot around the coffee table, pulling it close enough that she could use it as a footrest. "If you are…well, overeager…" Alys had said it so many times, it was starting to not sound like a word. "What do you think would happen?"

"Oh, I'm sure she'll only kill me a little. Maybe flay me alive. I don't know. She needs me, but…Oh."

"What?" Emily asked.

Alys shook their head. "It's nothing. I'm just leaping to conclusions."

Hannah reached over Emily and rubbed their shoulder. "It doesn't sound like nothing."

"She's already suspicious. Especially with how badly I don't want her to kill you. It's possible she'd use either of you as a bargaining chip. Perhaps killing you to get me to do something or kidnapping you or saying that she'll kill you. I don't know what pieces she has on the board—that's kinda the problem—and I don't know what she can do. It's why I can't just opt out. As much as I'd love to ignore her at this point, we'd never know about Baldur, and she might have someone else kill us or do it herself. She's very cagey about her resources."

"Then we'll be careful," Hannah said. "I'm really hard to kidnap."

Alys shrugged. "If you say so."

"I have superstrength."

Emily patted her back.

Hannah sulked.

"Look, I'm trying. I'll let you know when I know more." Alys sighed. "I'm gonna go grab a drink. You two want anything?"

"Always," Emily said.

Immediately coming out of her sulking, Hannah voiced her agreement.

A few minutes later, a soft smile on their face, Alys returned with a six-pack in hand. "It was easier than carrying just the three, and I knew I'd have to get these in a bit anyway." They popped off the cap on the coffee table and leaned back, propping their feet next to Hannah's. "How did they react when you told them? About Baldur, I mean, though I'd love the story for your whole coming-out thing."

"Oh, that was great." Emily beamed at Hannah, squeezing her hand on the back of the couch. "She shouted across the courtyard at Forseti and challenged him to dare question that she was who she said she was. And he made her destroy a tree with Mjolnir."

"I'm sad I missed that." They glanced at Hannah, likely trying to picture her doing it. Hannah supposed she didn't exactly look the type. "I still can't believe Forseti is in charge. Especially with Baldur, whether fake or not, being around. Why would his son be in charge? I mean, sure, he's the god of justice and mediation, so he could be a good ruler, but there are plenty of older gods left. Is Freyja not there? I assumed she was in charge in her husband's stead."

"No idea," Hannah said helpfully.

Emily set the empty bottle on the table. "We still haven't gotten much in the way of introductions. I think they assume we should already know. We are Aesir, after all."

"Yep, we're a couple of asses." Hannah grinned, setting the empty bottle down and grabbing another.

Alys smiled back. "You remembered."

Hannah tried not to grow too distracted by the smell of the food cooking outside. Neither of them had bothered to eat before heading over, as Alys always cooked. But it wouldn't be ready until the next day. She couldn't survive. "Is there food?"

They looked over, and Hannah promptly pouted. "All right, fine, I'll go fix something." Swinging their legs off the coffee table, they left yet again.

"You could've asked when they were grabbing the drinks," Emily said.

Hannah shrugged. "I forgot how hungry I was."

"How?"

Hannah sighed. The discussion about Loki yesterday still weighed heavily on her, but she couldn't see Alys as that person at all. There were a few words she could think of to describe them, but "rat bastard" was pretty far from any of them. "I need to get April to cook something for lunch Saturday too."

"You just like letting people spoil you."

"Who doesn't?"

"Well, you *are* royalty."

Letting out an ungraceful laugh, Hannah leaned against Emily, resting her hand on those ridiculous abs. "So am I a prince or a princess?"

"Princess," Alys called from the kitchen.

"You're in the other room. You can't hear us," Emily shouted back.

"You're not that quiet."

"Hannah, Princess of Asgard," she muttered. "Er, Idavollr, I guess."

"Princess of Portland?" Emily offered.

"I love it. Hannah, Princess of Portland."

"Sounds like an eighties cartoon," Alys called.

Emily pulled Hannah closer, resting a hand on her hip. "I'd watch it."

A loud thump sounded from the other room, followed by a couple expletives. Emily sat up, staring concernedly in the direction of the kitchen.

"I'll go check," Hannah said. When she reached the kitchen, nothing seemed amiss. There were no pans scattered on the floor, the oven hadn't fallen over on top of Alys—so she sadly wouldn't get to show off her strength—there was nothing. Alys even had a somewhat exaggerated smile on their face, but there was a slight shimmer on their cheek as they tried to shift something away. "Were you just crying?"

"No. Of course not. Don't be ridiculous. I'm fantastic." Their smile grew even less convincing as they turned to the fridge. "Anyway, I was thinking, how about tacos?"

"Tacos sound great." Hannah rested her hand on their shoulder. "But first, I want you to tell me what's wrong."

When they turned, Hannah noticed that the outfit didn't seem to be fitting as well, and it didn't take her long to see why. The distractions she'd been staring at earlier were gone. It made the clothes loose, but it gave her a decent idea of what the problem must have been.

"Nothing's wrong. What sort of tortillas do you want?"

Okay, if Alys wasn't going to take advantage of that taco setup, then clearly something was really getting to them. "I'm your friend, right?"

They nodded. "Yeah. Why?"

"You can be honest with your friends." They choked back a sob. There went any possibility that Hannah was crazy. "Tell me what's wrong."

"God, you're stubborn."

"Is that a Thor thing or a Hannah thing?"

"Both." They grumbled but pulled themself onto the counter to sit. "Fine, I'll talk, just stop giving me that look."

"What look?" Hannah blinked.

"Never mind. I think that's just your face." Was that a good thing or a bad thing? "It was mostly dysphoria," they said, but it didn't sound quite honest.

"What's dysphoria?"

"Right. You're not used to that. It took Emily a while too. Though, of course, I had an easy fix for my dysphoria that I was hiding that entire time. Because I am such a great friend." They banged their head against the cabinet but didn't seem to notice. "I've made it pretty clear that my breasts bothered me. Normally, I'm not against using them for more interesting reasons, like messing with people or wooing or having someplace to put my phone if I don't have pockets, but with you, right now..." They sighed. "It's not an all-the-time thing. Gender can be fun to play with as a way to express myself. Hell, nothing's quite as awesome as pulling off a femme look in a masculine body or a masculine look in a feminine body, but I tend to be a lot more comfortable being androgynous. Christ, I hate being honest. Can I just strip instead or something?"

"As fun as that would be, I want you to go on. Please."

They managed to flash a slight smile, though it still looked incredibly pained. "Emily said my flirting with you was fine if you were into it, and I know you prefer…never mind. I think that part's obvious." They sucked on their teeth. It was painfully obvious how much being this open hurt them. They couldn't even meet Hannah's eyes. "I'm sorry I've been being such a creep."

"You're not—"

"Oh yeah, I am." They finally turned back, purple eyes meeting Hannah's for a moment before they turned away again. "To be honest, I've never really had a serious relationship or any friends before. I had Emily for the last eight years, but until a week ago, that was all a lie. And I've dated maybe two people for a combined total of two months. Hel is the only person who has ever really known me, and I wasn't allowed to be honest with anyone else. Now I have this cute girl I'm spending all my time with, who actually knows who I am and is totally my type, and I've been making a complete ass of myself."

"What exactly is your type?" Hannah asked. "I'd always kind of assumed you and Emily had—"

"No, never." They sounded almost offended. "I like femmes and femininity, no matter what the person's gender is. Plus, you're a total badass, and that doesn't hurt." They jumped down, using some tendrils that hadn't been there a moment before. "But that doesn't excuse how I've been acting about you. Just because I'm slightly masc-of-center and guys are total creeps doesn't mean I should be too. I'm better than that." Their smile was more genuine as they looked at Hannah, brushing hair out of their eyes. "Ground beef sound good? I have some leftover pork, but I assume you're kind of sick of it."

Hannah wrapped an arm around them, pulling them down a few inches until they were finally in range, and leaned in. Alys stiffened but immediately moved into the kiss, their lips meeting. For a long moment, neither of them breathed. It felt so right. It was honestly shocking. It wasn't the same as it was with Emily—though not better or worse, at least that she could tell without a few dozen more tests—but there was something indefinably different. Maybe because this was a romance that only she had chosen, without any influence from Thor. She could handle that destiny might be the reason she was with Emily, but it felt amazing to know that this one was all her.

"Pork, then," Alys finally said when they pulled away.

Hannah rolled her eyes. "Or chicken. Or fish. I don't care."

"Of course, fish tacos...now you're *trying* to set me up for that joke."

"That really all you have to say?"

They blushed a bright pink and nodded. "I need a minute. I liked it. I want more. I just...Go cuddle with your girlfriend. I'll have your euphemisms ready in, like, fifteen minutes."

Hannah started toward the living room but hesitated. "You do know that if your behavior was bothering me, I'd have told you, right?"

"Getting that now."

Grinning, her own cheeks heating, she grabbed a beer from the fridge. "Use that fancy white Mexican cheese in your fridge, please, not just the taco mix. From April's experiments back when she ate meat, I can say it goes a lot better with fish."

She left them there, taking a moment to appreciate the genuine smile adorning their face. If that was all that was bothering Alys, Hannah was glad to have set their mind at ease. And fortunately, telling Emily was surprisingly painless. She barely even blinked. She mostly rolled her eyes and teased. "Of course my two massive dorks would end up making out."

Hannah plopped down next to her, sulking anew. "We didn't even make out."

CHAPTER THIRTY-TWO

A dull knock on the front door awakened Hannah and Emily, who had managed to fall back asleep after some early morning fun. "Fuck," Emily muttered, pulling the sheet away from Hannah.

"Hey!"

"Fine, you can get the door. I needed something to cover myself with." She tossed the sheets back.

Grumbling, Hannah checked the time on her phone. It was only eleven. They'd invited everyone over for noon. Though she should've set an alarm once she'd realized she was gonna take that nap. Her morning workout always seemed to get Emily in the mood. She threw her nightgown back on and ran to the door, throwing it open and grabbing the back door. "Hey, sorry." As it swung, she found April waiting, her light blond hair pinned up in a fashionable bun.

"Sorry, am I too early?" she asked, glancing at the frilly pink gown.

"A little, but it's fine. It's great to see you. Come in." Hannah's eyes fell to the bag in her hands. "Please say that's your hummus."

Smirking, April replied, "Of course it is."

"Then absolutely come in. Let me go get dressed. Maybe a shower."

"Take your time. I was hoping to use your oven. I didn't get to cook, since, despite there being almost no one there this summer, someone has been hogging the oven all week."

"You're kind of one to talk."

She looked hurt for a moment before conceding the point. "Okay, well, maybe, but I only have two classes right now, and I want to cook to work off the stress. We're barely into the term, and grad school is already so much more work. I thought I'd get a head start and be able to take it easy later, but no, if I'm in my room, I have to be studying, and—" She paused. "I should let you shower. Suffice to say, it's been exhausting."

"I can understand. I'm sure you're kicking school's ass though."

"Well, I do have a god on my side."

"At least two." Giving April a smile, she ran down the hallway for a quick shower. After throwing on a blue maxi dress and putting on some light makeup, she found April already hard at work over a boiling pot in the kitchen and Emily leaning against the counter talking to her. As weird as it was to see her two worlds colliding, how could she ever complain about finding her two favorite blondes? "What's up?" She knew they'd met before, but that was when they thought they were normal humans. How could it not be different having your goddess wife meet the president of your sorority?

"Just telling April every embarrassing thing you've ever done."

"I already know all of that." April giggled. "I'm far more interested in finding out more about you, Emily. You've been stealing my best friend, and I still don't know near enough about you. I did have Megan run a background check on you, though."

"Wait, you what?" Her eyes opened wide as she stared, slipping off the counter to take a step toward her.

April turned, biting her lip. "She's still in academy. She can't even do that. But I can't believe I didn't ask before." She groaned, obviously kicking herself for the oversight. "You have a record? What was it? Tell me."

Hannah stared at Emily. Did she? "You do?"

Emily groaned. "I managed to get arrested for having pot when I was like twenty-four. Literally weeks before they voted to legalize it. It was just a slap on the wrist, but it's still on my record. Misdemeanor."

"Oh." April deflated. "The way you looked there, I thought it'd be something worse. Sorry."

"It's fine. You're trying to look after Hannah. I'm the same way. Hell, I…" She turned to Hannah, "Wait, she knows right?"

"Yep."

"Just a few days ago, I was fighting zombies to protect her. It was literally the coolest thing I've ever done in my life. Like, holy shit."

"Wait. What?" April glared at Hannah. "You were in that kind of danger, days ago, and you didn't even tell me? What the fuck?"

Hannah's jaw dropped. How could someone be mad at her for this? She was Thor. Wasn't she supposed to do that sort of stuff? "But I'm Thor."

"Yeah, and I'm your friend, and if the living dead are trying to eat my best friend, I deserve to find out as soon as possible, not days later from someone else."

"She's fine," Emily said.

"But she might not have been. When was this?"

"Saturday?" Hannah replied, trying to double-check in her mind.

"An entire week ago? I can't believe you. I would have come. You could at least tell me. Where was this? How did it happen?"

Emily stepped between them, rescuing Hannah again. "Really? That's the part that bothers you? Not the zombie thing?"

"If there are gods, I don't see why there can't be zombies."

"I think the word is actually Draugr," Hannah offered helpfully.

"You better keep her safe." April took a step, staring at Emily with a fire Hannah had never seen in her eyes. "I can't believe this." As she turned back to Hannah, her gaze softened. "You're sure you're okay?"

April was really that worried about her? It hadn't even occurred to her. "I'm kinda unbeatable."

April punched her.

"Ow!"

"You're not Superman. Take care of yourself, okay? Please? I don't know how I'm supposed to focus on my urban studies classes when I'm worried about you being eviscerated off in some magical kingdom."

"It wasn't a kingdom, but fine. I promise I'll tell you, and if you don't have too much homework, I'll even let you come." How hadn't she thought to mention it? Was she just too used to hiding it? Wow, she really was a bad friend.

"Damn right you will." She wrapped her arms around Hannah, pulling her into a tight hug. "Please don't get killed by zombies. Draugr. Whatever."

Hannah had been so focused on exploring this new part of her that she hadn't even thought about how it could affect the people close to her. She'd always compared it to being accepted into the queer community and to coming out, but it wasn't really. Sure, being gay could be dangerous, but people didn't tend to have to fight actual monsters.

Hannah could hear Emily escaping behind her. "I'm gonna go shower. You crazy kids have fun."

Sounds came from the stairs. "Damn, you're here early." It was Megan's voice. "The door was unlocked. Hope you don't mind."

Hannah pried herself free from April's grasp only to throw her arms around Megan. "I was worried you wouldn't come."

"I told you I wouldn't miss your quince." She pulled out the quinceañera dress that Hannah had managed to forget about. "Want to go change?"

Snatching it from her hands, Hannah nodded. "I'll be right back."

When she returned in the sparkly red and white dress with a red skirt so poofed out that she could barely fit through the door, Emily had finished her shower and was sitting on the couch with Megan wearing jeans and a sports bra. Hannah couldn't take her anywhere.

"It's really all real?" Megan asked. From the sound of it, Emily was still bragging about fighting zombies.

"Of course. I took on three zombies single-handedly. If that doesn't prove it, I don't know what does."

"Single-handedly?" Hannah asked.

Emily grumbled. "Fine. *Two* single-handedly. Alys took care of the other one."

"Who's Alys?" Megan asked.

Hannah hadn't introduced them yet. And they'd already kissed. April and Megan were gonna flip.

Hannah glanced at the door. "They should be here by now. They're the one bringing food you'll actually eat."

"Wait, you mean if she doesn't show up—"

"They," Emily and Hannah both corrected.

"Then there's no meat?"

Chuckling, Emily said, "'Fraid so, officer."

Hannah rolled her eyes. "Like you're any better."

"I can put up with not-meat."

"Sure you can." Hannah held on to the doorway to the kitchen, leaning in to call to April. "Food almost ready?"

"Yeah. I just finished the pad Thai. I hope that doesn't clash too much with whatever your other friend is bringing."

It wasn't like April would be eating it. "It's fine. I love your pad Thai, though."

"Pad Thai isn't vegan," Megan called.

April smirked and whispered, "Don't tell her."

"Then you'll love it," Hannah called back.

The four of them gathered in the living room, Hannah sitting next to Emily and Megan on the couch and April taking the chair. "To the new god of thunder," April said, holding her beer up.

"Fuck it. Fine," Megan grumbled.

"And the goddess of…" Hannah faltered, trying to recall. "Grain."

"Yeah, go me," Emily muttered. They drank, Emily downing hers.

"Are you going to move to Asgard?" April asked.

"Asgard is gone." Hannah took a bite. It was even better than the last time. She was just sad that she hadn't gotten to the hummus yet, but there'd be plenty of time for that. "But we're not moving to Idavollr. Our lives are here. We'll be involved over there, but that's it."

Megan looked at her in shock. "Really? That's a relief."

Was she really that scared of losing her? Hannah studied her. A few weeks ago, it had seemed like Megan didn't want anything to do with her. "I promise, I'll never vanish on you. And I'll keep you informed on anything dangerous I end up involved in. I don't have any intention of fighting, so you don't have much to worry about."

"Seriously? Aren't you like the god of war?"

"Strength and thunder and also oak trees, but not war. You remember high school. I can't do that again. Especially now. I could hurt someone too easily, and I'd be giving into my anger. Besides…" She shook her head, flipping her hair dramatically to emphasize the statement. "True strength is in finding another solution."

April beamed at her. "Maybe you *are* Superman."

"You're sure doing the Boy Scout thing right," Megan muttered. She paused, staring. "Is that weird? Having been a guy? You don't—"

"You've literally seen me naked."

"Just making sure." Megan held up her hands in surrender. "You know, what happened to Holly doesn't mean you can't fight other people. Especially if they're zombies. That are trying to eat you. Violence works perfectly fine as a solution."

April stared at her.

"Says the pig," Emily muttered under her breath.

"What was that?" Megan asked.

"Just joking. I love the cops. Blue lives matter."

Megan glared. "You use violence too. Weren't you just saying that you were fighting monsters with a sword?"

Emily leaned back, a mischievous grin on her face as she met Megan's eyes. "It's in the bedroom if you still want to see it. I didn't need a badge for it. I have nothing against violence. Just don't like getting arrested."

Hannah found herself praying for Alys to arrive. To herself, she supposed. Or maybe to Alys. Being a god was weird.

"Anything in here I should be arresting you for?" Megan asked.

"Why? Do you have a warrant?"

"Weren't you two getting along a second ago?" April asked.

"Who says we're not?" Megan replied, still glaring at Emily.

Emily chuckled. "Are we, like, gonna make out, or what? Because you could cut this tension with a knife."

Megan threw herself back against the arm rest, eyes wide. "What? But you're Hannah's...Stop it!"

"I'm gonna go grab another beer. Anyone want one?"

They managed to make it through the pad Thai without any more issues. Hannah was still unsure if Emily and Megan were actually getting along, but at least they weren't at each other's throats anymore. Though they'd be hot together. Hannah tried to focus on the show they were watching and on the delicious hummus-covered tortilla chips, rather than the idea of her girlfriend and her first crush. Fortunately, Alys picked then to finally arrive.

"Sorry I'm late," Alys called. Apparently, no one needed to knock anymore. "Could I borrow you two for a moment?" They pointed at Emily and Hannah. "Hi, people I don't know. Introductions later. I'm sure we'll need them." They opened the door to the bedroom and turned back to Emily and Hannah, who hadn't moved. "Now."

In the bedroom, Alys shoved the door shut. Raising their finger, they said, "Okay, first thing's first. Why are you wearing a quinceañera dress?"

Emily stared. "So that's what it is. I've been wondering the same thing."

Hannah could feel her cheeks burning. "Because I'm Thor?"

"That adds up, actually. Okay, second thing." They looked toward the sword leaning against the wall. "Emily, I need you to promise not to stab me."

"Why?"

"Please?"

"Is there a reason I would stab you?"

They waved off the question. "I have mostly good news. I just need your word. We've made up. You're my best friend. Please don't stab me?"

"Fine, whatever. I won't stab you."

"Okay, great." They breathed out a sigh of relief. "I have good news. I don't have to kill Hannah."

"You'd already said you wouldn't."

Hannah squinted. "What do you mean you don't have to? Don't all of Hel's backup plans involve me dead? Did she finally tell you?"

"She did. Absolutely." They grinned. "And the best part is, I don't have to kill you."

"Why?" Emily glanced at the sword.

"Because I'm supposed to kill you instead."

"You what?" Emily stared at them, her jaw dropping.

Hannah watched them, certain she looked just as shocked. There was no way Alys would do it, but why on Earth would Hel suggest it? And did they really think Emily would be that quick to stab them?

"She wants me to take your place. She's decided that Hannah's an even bigger weak point than you. Not sure it's actually true, but I played up that it was. That I'd do whatever it took to keep Hannah alive. Even if I had to kill you."

Hannah's mouth went dry. She wasn't that weak. And why were they being so serious?

Emily shook her head, taking a step back. "You're not going to—"

"Of course not. You're my best friend. I'm not breaking that trust again."

"I'd call murder a little more than that."

They shrugged. "I'd have brought you back anyway. Assuming that's possible. I don't know anyone who's died twice yet, but I would try."

"Really not making the stabbing thing seem less appealing."

Alys nodded. "Okay. Not okay to the stabbing. Still, please don't. But she needs to think I'm taking your place. At least until we can do something about it. She suspects I'm going to kill Baldur, and she gave me more than enough information to get him out of the way. I don't know what other plans she has in motion. There have to be other people in her employ who'll make sure I don't do anything too stupid, but I'm going to anyway. I'm telling you everything. That's as stupid as it gets. And I'm not killing you. Just means I might need to live here…Since she'll think I'm dating Hannah."

"I assumed that would happen anyway," Hannah said.

Alys appeared to malfunction, blinking for a few long seconds.

"They're still telling us the important part, Hannah. Couldn't you have waited to break them?"

"I'm fine," they shouted, far too loudly. "I just…wasn't expecting that. I, I mean…you, she…we."

Emily chuckled. "Not sounding less broken."

They were lucky they were adorable. Damn, being adorable while talking about murdering her girlfriend was quite a feat. "I'll kiss you again after you finish telling us everything."

"Right. Yeah. Sorry. Um, she needs to think I've killed and replaced Emily. She has to think she has the upper hand. That I'll do what she wants."

"What does this mean?" Emily asked.

"I didn't plan it all out. It only happened an hour ago. But she told me who Baldur is. Walked me through part of the plan. Not anywhere near enough, but she was trying to convince me that my bargain is working. Naturally, I'm betraying her, but she doesn't have to know that."

"Then what? Am I going to have to go into hiding or something?"

"We'll sort it out. I knew you'd never let me set this all up if I told you first, but I also knew that if I didn't agree to something desperate, she'd enact some other backup plan, likely killing both of us, or she'd order me to kill Hannah. Believe me, I tried insisting that we needed Hannah to get the apples. It's when she moved to this idea. So I have to kill you, just you know, not for real. I needed a way out, and it was the only one I could find. I swear, I won't betray either of you."

"All right." Emily shrugged. "I guess there'll have to be two of me."

"Emily, you mean the world to me. You're the first friend I've ever had, and I love you more than I even thought I was capable of. And I may have a slight crush on Hannah," they added, muttering.

"Slight?" Hannah snorted. Maybe Alys really was a dork.

Even Emily laughed, some of the tension easing out of her body. "That's a word for it."

"You don't need to keep trying to sell us on it," Hannah said. "We trust you."

"We have a guest room," Emily said.

"Oh, great, you can sleep in there, then." Alys flashed that grin. Sighing, they sat on the foot of the bed. "Thank you. Fuck. Right, so there is something kind of important that I should've led with, but I didn't want to say any of this."

"Baldur?" Hannah asked.

They nodded. "The Baldur in Idavollr is a spy, made to look like the real one by Hel's magic. He was supposed to have grabbed an apple for her ages ago, but well, you know. He can't get into Asgard."

"We have to go tell them," Hannah shouted, reaching for the door.

"Wait. There's more. God, now I'm an infomercial."

She turned, staring. "What else could there be?"

"There're more gods here. Including the real Baldur, which might give your claims a little more merit."

"Here on Earth?"

"Here in this apartment." They stood, glancing at the door. "They were the backup plans. It's why Hel wanted you dead. She knew how protective of you Megan was."

"Megan's Baldur?" Hannah almost screamed, probably loud enough for them to hear in the other room.

"No. She's Tyr. One of your other brothers. I assume the other girl is April? Well, I guess they could be other random people, I'm sure you have more friends, but it would be weird if your best friends weren't here for what's apparently your quinceañera."

Hannah rolled her eyes. Of course they couldn't resist making that joke right now. But what were they talking about? How? What? There was no way Megan and April were gods. "How did Hel know they were my best friends? Wait, so April's Baldur?" It sounded so absurd.

"Yes. And she made sure they're your best friends. She had me set it up so that they'd end up at Portland State with you. Hel even performed spells on you to draw you together. I didn't know the last part, and I didn't know who your friends were, or I'd have told you that earlier. I'm sorry. Hell, I still don't even have all the details. Megan was supposed to keep you safe since Hel had given you a life that would make you passive and weak so you wouldn't get in her way—and you're not, by the way, she fucked up—and I guess April was so the other gods wouldn't find Baldur if they sent someone to make sure he wasn't in Hel? She really didn't tell me shit."

Hannah stared, the words barely making sense. "Does that mean our entire friendship—"

"I don't think so. Well, partly. You all have free will, you're your own people, but she set up your lives. Just like she set up mine so that I'd have parents who would never accept me, and she could swoop in and be there for me. She didn't tell me that part. I just realized it. Holy fuck." They sat, their eyes wide. "I need a minute."

"But—"

They shook their head, staring at the floor. "Okay, I'm gonna assume that we all have free will because if we didn't, her plan would've worked. If everything had gone perfectly, then she wouldn't have needed me so much, and I wouldn't be betraying her." They turned to Emily.

Emily sat next to Alys, wrapping an arm around them. "Alys, there's no way anyone can control you. You're pure chaos."

"Thanks."

"I mean it."

"But…" They turned back to Hannah, blinking away tears. "She set everything up. Even had me make sure you all ended up at the same college." They bit their lip, their eyes twitching. "She told me how she'd picked out your families, guiding things with the occasional spell. There's no way that doesn't include me. She really did do that."

"I'm sorry."

"I'm the one who should be sorry. That means the only reason you had your childhood, Emily, was so I could more easily befriend and manipulate you. I'm so sorry."

Emily nodded, blinking away tears.

Hannah chewed her lip. This was insane. Hel had made her weak? But she was so strong. Oh. Had Hel made her afraid to fight? Had Hel made her want to be an accountant? She'd been so scared about how much her past life controlled her, and it hadn't occurred to her that it could be someone else controlling what she did. Who even was she? "I'm gonna give you two a few minutes while I go tell April and Megan." She could focus on that. It was doable. It wasn't a full existential breakdown. "I don't feel right keeping this from them for a second longer than I have to."

"I'll be okay," Alys said. "I'll explain everything I can."

"Take your time."

"Wait," Alys said. "There's one other thing I put together. I was really tempted not to say this one."

Hannah turned back, narrowing her eyes. "What could be worse than all that?" How much more could there even be? Her entire life was a lie. Again!

They wet their lips, staring at the floor. "I think I kept you out of prison in high school. Hel had me pay off a few people in Seattle when you were that age. One of them was the DA. I didn't know who it was for or why."

"You…" Hannah gasped as understanding dawned on her. "Oh."

"Yeah."

"That's a good thing, isn't it?" Emily asked. "You didn't mean to hurt that girl, Hannah."

"But I did it anyway. I've always wondered why nothing more happened. I wasn't even suspended. I tried to move past it. But I knew that girl was suffering because of me. I couldn't even bring myself to visit. Maybe I should've gone to prison."

"No." Alys's voice was firm. "You didn't know about your strength, and you didn't deserve jail."

"It was an accident," Emily said. "And if Alys hadn't acted, we'd never have met. This is the one good thing Hel did to you."

"I paid off that girl's hospital bills too," they said, sounding defensive. It made sense. Of course Alys had hung on to what must've felt like one of the only good things they'd ever done.

"Still kinda the same thing," Emily said. "Not giving you that one as a separate good deed."

Hannah took a deep breath and nodded. "All right. Thank you for telling me. I'm gonna go tell everyone else."

Emily got to her feet. "Let me."

Hannah waved her off. "No. You two still need to commiserate and work past all this. I finally have an answer. Or more answers than I ever fucking wanted. Thanks for that. I might even be sincere. Now, let me give my best friends their answers."

"Wait," Alys said, their voice scarcely more than a croak.

Hannah turned back, leaning in. She'd already had her entire existence shaken. How could there possibly still be more?

"This one's all me. Not even Hel. Um…" Alys turned to Emily. "Any chance I can have a minute alone with Hannah?"

Emily stared. "After that lead-in?"

"You did promise not to stab me."

She gritted her teeth, meeting Alys's gaze without a word.

Hannah said, "Emily, please. You two can talk after. This sounds important, and I don't have the energy to fight, not after everything I just learned."

Emily sighed, crossing her arms. "Fine. I'll go grab another beer. You want one?"

"Yeah."

She stared at Alys.

They blinked. "You're offering me one?"

"If I'm not stabbing you and you're not killing me, it means you're still my best friend. So beer?"

They nodded, wiping their eyes.

Once the door closed, Hannah sat on the bed right next to Alys.

She could take this. How bad could one more revelation be? "What is it?" she asked after a long silence.

Alys gulped, took a deep breath, opened their mouth, closed it, then tried again. "I mind-controlled you. One time. Just to make you go home."

Hannah couldn't even blink; she just kept staring. "You can do that?"

"Only if someone is very weak willed or compromised. You were freaking out, and I was trying to protect...no. I'm lying to myself now. I was trying to make sure my asset wasn't compromised. I want to believe it was because I already cared about you, but I'm not willing to give myself that. You'd killed that mugger, and you were freaking out, so I gave you my keys and put a quick spell on you, telling you to drive home so I could deal with the police and keep you out of trouble. Apparently for the second time."

"You what?" The words weren't even registering. The mugger had died? No, not had died. She'd killed him? "I what?"

"Hannah..." Alys reached out.

She scrambled away, putting her back to the wall as tears streamed down her face. "I ki...ki..." She couldn't even say it.

"Fuck." They screwed their eyes shut and nodded. "That was part of this confession too, but I didn't mean to blurt it out like that. He had a gun on us, and you were standing up for me. You didn't do anything wrong."

"I ki..." She could say it. She had to. He deserved that much, didn't he? "I killed him?" She blinked away tears, but they wouldn't stop coming. "But this is why I don't fight. This is why I can't be trusted. I..." She'd lost control twice in her life. The first time, she'd nearly killed an innocent girl. The second time, she had killed a mugger who was in the wrong place at the wrong time. Maybe he'd have killed someone else. Maybe she'd saved someone's life. But even that idea felt hollow. She was a murderer. What right did she have to judge anyone else?

"I'm so sorry. I swear, it was the only time I ever mind-controlled you. And I'll never do it again. And I won't keep anything from you ever again. It's why I'm saying all of this. I don't have any more secrets."

Hannah wanted to punch them. She felt bile rise in her throat. There was that temper. The one that had cost someone their life. "Can she still walk?"

"Huh?" Alys blinked and shook their head. "Who?"

"The girl I did this to. You paid for her hospital bills. Is she okay?"

Alys bit their lip. That wasn't a good sign. "Fuck. I'm not lying to you again. I just said that." That was a much worse sign. "When I saw her, she was in a wheelchair, and she had brain damage. The doctors said she'd be able to live a normal life, but she wasn't likely to make a full recovery."

Hannah nodded. The god of strength had bashed a teenage girl's head in. Of course she was brain damaged.

"I'm so sorry."

"For what?" Hannah asked. "You're not the monster here. I am."

"No, you're not." Alys leapt to their feet and took a step but seemed to think better of it. "You didn't know what you could do. Hel is the one who made you and didn't tell you a thing. She's the one who controlled all of this. I'm the one who did everything. Blame me. Blame her. None of it's you."

"You were just her pawn." That sounded so mean, but she couldn't take it back. It was true. "You did what she forced you to do. She didn't force me to do anything. I've never met her. Yeah, she's a monster who manipulated my entire life. But I'm the murderer."

"She's also a murderer. She's killed lots of gods. Though I'm sure you could put some blame on Odin…Not the point. None of it is your fault."

Hannah shrugged. "Tell me that when we don't have an imposter god to deal with. I don't have time to process any of this, and there's way too much." She headed for the door. She needed to tell Megan and April everything. That was what was most important.

"You're right. So does this mean you…Nope, I'm just being a selfish asshole, as usual. Never mind. Let's go save your kids."

"You're asking if I still want you?" Hannah asked. "I'm barely staying afloat right now. I don't know if I want anything. I don't even know if I'm mad at you."

They nodded. "You have every right to be."

"One thing at a time."

"Okay."

She opened the door. "Emily, they're all yours."

Emily gave her a concerned expression and looked her up and down. "What happened?"

"Just more Hel stuff," she said. And it was the truth. Hel was the one who had orchestrated all of this. And Hel was the one they couldn't let come back to life. Who knew how much more damage she'd do?

Emily nodded. "Yeah. That was tough to hear. The bitch gave me homophobic parents. I really hope I get to stab her."

Hannah forced a smile. "I'm sure you will."

Emily grinned back. "All right, I'll go talk to Alys. You sure you don't want help?"

"Yeah. I'm sure. They're my friends. I should be the one to tell them." She closed the door behind her and tried to prepare herself to explain everything.

April and Megan looked incredulously at her.

"Tell us what?" Megan asked.

"What was all that about?" April added, moving toward Hannah.

Hannah opened her mouth and closed it again. She tried to focus. It was a monumental task, but eventually, she managed. "You're Baldur."

"What?" April reached up to her hair as if checking it was all there.

"No. You're…" Hannah gave a dry chuckle. "My brother. Wow, we really are sisters. Hel did set that up well. You're Baldur, and Megan is Tyr."

"I'm who?" Megan asked.

Hannah felt like a terrible person to give this news. She still barely knew anything about mythology. Hell, she couldn't even pronounce half the names. "I don't know. My brother as well, apparently."

"I don't want to be a boy."

"I feel you."

"What are you talking about?" April asked.

Hannah swallowed the lump in her throat. She'd do the best she could. "Hel, the goddess of the underworld, set it up so that both of you, Emily, Alys, and me all came back to life and ended up meeting. I don't know what all it means, but you're the real Baldur, and there's a fake one in Idavollr, and we need to tell our kids, unless that's also what Hel wants."

"Bullshit," Megan scoffed, staring as if Hannah had gone insane. Again.

Hannah opened the bedroom door and peered in. "Alys, any way I can prove it?"

They nodded, looking up from their knees. "April, have you ever been hurt?"

She shook her head, taking a step back. "Plenty of people haven't been hurt."

"Hannah, punch her."

Hannah glared at Alys. *Really gonna suggest that now?* Maybe she was mad at them. "That could kill her."

"It won't."

"Can Megan punch her?" She looked to where Megan still sat on the couch.

"Sure."

Megan shrugged. "If it'll make you all stop with this craziness, fine. Not like I haven't wanted to before anyway." She took a few steps toward April and gave her the lightest punch possible.

April seemed unimpressed.

"Did that hurt?" Alys asked.

"No."

"Try harder?"

"But...Fuck it." Megan pulled back and slugged April in the stomach as hard as she could.

April was still unmoved. "That doesn't mean—"

"Hey, Megan, want to try out Emily's sword?"

April looked between the four of them, terror in her eyes. "We can't just—"

"You'll be fine."

Megan stared. "I'm not gonna stab her. What if you're wrong? Or what if it only works on punches, and I end up hurting her?"

"Yeah!"

Hannah looked at Alys. "Are you absolutely certain?"

"I wouldn't say it if I wasn't."

Goddamn it. This was exactly the opposite of what Hannah should be doing. But she needed to save her kids. She punched April. It wasn't the hardest she could go, but it wasn't something any human could simply walk away from. She hated herself doing it, but it wasn't really violence, and she wasn't angry at April, so it didn't count, right? She wasn't giving in to her worst impulses. She wasn't the same monster she used to be. The same monster Hel had made her to be. She wanted to believe that, but even if she wasn't becoming a monster again, she doubted it was really Hel's fault. No matter what Alys said. It was simply who she was. Who she'd always be. "Did that hurt?"

Shivering, April shook her head again. "Well, no."

"You've seen what I can do. That should've done more damage than a sword ever could."

"But..." April stared at Hannah's fist still pressed against her shoulder. "I can't be."

"Alys, any chance you're up for talking yet? I think we're all having our own existential crises."

They stumbled to their feet and walked into the living room, Emily following close behind. "She…that is to say, Hel, my daughter, hasn't told me much until recently. I didn't know why she had me do the things I did in the past, and there were enough random weird tasks that I never guessed who was who. I vaguely recall Megan's name when Hel made me delete her application at Harvard."

"You what?" Megan took a step, her hands clenched into fists.

"Sorry. I don't think I ever did anything with April, but I don't know for sure. There was a lot. Hel wanted to make sure everyone got into PSU, and she took care of most of it. I only needed to interfere occasionally, since she isn't capable of leaving Hel. Her domain. It's named after her."

"Yeah. I've been doing some reading," April said. "But just because I'm invincible—"

"I will find some mistletoe if I have to."

"Okay, fine." She sounded scared.

Hannah looked at her, confused. What would mistletoe do?

"She's weak against it." Alys sighed. "So, sorry, I'm a terrible person and have probably ruined all of your lives."

"It was Hel," Emily said.

Hannah wanted to echo the sentiment. She did agree with it. But she couldn't quite get herself to say it.

"I actually like my life," Megan said, visibly starting to calm down. "If I'd gone to Harvard, I wouldn't have had my classes with Hannah, and I wouldn't have done nearly as well without her help. School was a lot of work for me."

Hannah blinked. She had a point. "I love my life. I have the four most amazing people in it, and I have those crazy kids and my dream job, and I'm a fucking god." And a murderer, but she was trying really hard to see the bright side.

Emily slumped onto the couch, patting Alys's knee. "I'm still pissed at Hel for the families she gave you and me, but right now, I wouldn't change a thing. Well, that's not true. My powers fucking suck. I mean, fine, I'll make the best beer ever and become a world-renowned brewer or something, but I want to be a badass swordswoman or something. Is there a goddess of war?"

"Yeah, but it's Megan."

"Damn it."

"I am?" Megan pointed at herself. "Fuck yeah. Anything else?"

"Justice and law," April said.

Emily chuckled. "Wow, it's like you were made to be a pig."

Megan rolled her eyes. "Fuck it. I guess I'm fine, then."

"Can you or Hel make me have already finished grad school?" April asked.

"Afraid not."

"Well, I guess being invincible is far from a bad thing. Especially with some of the changes I want to try when I get into politics. What if someone tries to assassinate me? Oh, that'd be amazing. No one would ever believe what happened." April beamed at Alys. "This is wonderful."

"She gave you all way better lives than she did me," Alys said. "I really thought she cared. She was the only one who seemed to."

Hannah squeezed Alys's hand. *Just say something nice. Tell them you care. It shouldn't be this hard.* "We care about you," she managed.

"I don't actually know you, and you made it so I couldn't get into Harvard...Ow!" Megan glared at April, who'd just elbowed her.

"I do too," Emily said. "You're my best friend, and I love you." She squeezed Alys's other hand.

"Now, let's go tell Modi, Magni, and Thrudr before Hel's fake Baldur does something."

"There's not really any rush," Alys said. "We just have to stop Fake Baldur before we get to the apples."

There was absolutely a rush. Hel was pulling way more insane shit, and Hannah wouldn't have time to process any of it if she still had to worry about her kids. "I want to tell them now. As you pointed out, they are my family, and I won't leave them with a spy hanging around them."

"I was a spy."

"And that's precisely why we need you to tell them."

"Wait." They stared, neon green eyes wide with panic. "No. I'm not going to Idavollr. That's insane. They'll kill me. Besides, remember the whole thing about Emily? I'm supposed to be her now."

"They'll have to go through me." Just because Hannah didn't want to fight didn't mean she couldn't stop people. If she lifted someone off the ground, there wasn't a lot they could do. "You helped us find the belt, you put yourself at risk to find out about Baldur, and you're..." She still liked them. That kiss had been amazing. But she couldn't bring herself to say that right then. "You deserve to be accepted there as much as any of us. Come with us, talk to them, explain everything, and if they don't want you there, they can throw me out too because you're family." Damn, she hadn't expected that last part. How much did she like Alys back? It was starting to seem like a lot if she was already calling them family after they'd admitted to mind-controlling her and covering up the murder she'd committed.

"Family is a weird term. Even as Loki and Thor, I'm not your family at all, but okay. Sure. Fine. If you insist. But only because you keep looking at me with those ridiculous eyes, and I may actually melt if I don't do what you tell me."

Hannah managed a smile and dragged them to their feet. "Then let's go."

"I guess I'm calling out of work," Emily muttered. "Damn, just when having two of me was starting to sound useful."

"Do we have to go?" Megan asked.

"Yes. Obviously." Hannah gaped at her. "Do you not want to go to the magical kingdom and be a god?"

"I don't have academy until Monday. Fine."

"I'm in," April added.

"Can we at least eat the meat I was promised?" Megan asked.

"I forgot it," Alys said. "Sorry."

"We can pick it up," Hannah said. "Maybe a peace offering will help them believe us."

Alys added, "And not kill me."

So Idavollr it was. They swung by Alys's, then headed for the statue of Mimir and the Rainbow Bridge.

Hannah chewed her lip as Emily drove. This had to go better than the first time. Right? She was Thor now, and they'd accepted her. Surely they'd believe her. She had proof that was pretty difficult to deny. Hopefully, it would be enough for Forseti.

CHAPTER THIRTY-THREE

Hey, I know this is a weird question, but where do my kids live?" Hannah asked of the first familiar face she saw. She couldn't recall his name—assuming she'd ever known it—but she recognized him from Forseti's hall.

"They don't all live together."

"Okay, where's the closest one?" Hannah had had the foresight to grab Thor's crucial items, but she hadn't thought to change out of her poofy dress—which had been hell to fit in the car—and she could imagine that being a strange distraction. She hoped it would distract this guy enough that she wouldn't have to explain who Alys, Megan, and April were. Were they allowed to bring guests?

"Who are all these people?"

There went that hope. "Just friends. I'll tell everyone later. It's urgent, please, I need to see my children."

"Thrudr and her wife both live right over there, in the hall of the Valkyries." He gestured behind himself.

Great, the kid she'd just met. But it'd do. Wow, she really did not know her kids that well. Did that mean no one cared about the lesbian thing? "That's fantastic. I'll go find them. This way?" She pointed toward the long building in front of the castle.

"That's it."

"Thank you." She waved for everyone to follow and charged on. If Fake Baldur knew he'd been found out, he'd likely think better of pulling anything when he saw Thor running in his direction. At least, that was the hope.

They charged through the hall, prompting curious gazes from Valkyries in various states of undress. Hannah tried hard not to enjoy the view. Who knew if more of them might be her kids?

"Thor?" someone asked. She looked vaguely familiar. Oh, Hannah knew this one. Shit, where was she from? That was it, she'd been there at that first feast.

"Yes, hi. Where is my daughter? I was told she lived here."

The Valkyrie chuckled. "She's right down this way, second to last door on the left."

"Thank you," she called, and they ran that way. It didn't matter that Alys said it wasn't urgent, it was. She needed to keep her family safe. And she needed to stop the bitch who controlled all of their lives.

"Father?" Thrudr asked, looking up from a book. She was lying in bed next to another woman whose long black hair was pulled back in a tight bun. Her own gray hair fell over a nightgown. "Mother? And... I'm sorry, I don't think I know you."

There were important matters at stake, but Hannah couldn't pass up this opportunity. "Aren't you going to introduce me to your wife? I just found out I have a daughter, and now I have to learn I missed her wedding."

"Oh. I'm sorry. This is Hildr. She used to serve ale with me in Valhalla."

"I thought the Valkyries were warriors," Emily said, stepping alongside Hannah. "So you're..." She paused. "Bartenders?" Did Emily want to be a Valkyrie now? Hannah could get into that.

"We're both."

"I relate."

Hannah rolled her eyes. "It's a pleasure to meet you, but I'm afraid I have some important business that simply can't wait. Okay, one last question, actually, did I get to go to your wedding, or was I dead?"

"It was after you both died. She helped me deal with it." She looked to her wife, clutching her hand. "We'd known each other for centuries, but after everything that happened, I really needed her." So she had missed the wedding. She felt awful.

"That is so beautiful, and I'm so sorry I wasn't there to walk you down the aisle."

"What do you mean?"

"Not how marriages work here," Alys whispered.

"Oh."

Thrudr rose, smiling softly. "What's the news? Is there anything I can do?"

Emily said, "Well, how about I show you what the problem is. April, you cool?" She gestured toward the sword on her belt. Hannah had tried to talk her out of taking it, but Emily had fallen in love with that thing since their trip to Vigridr. Apparently, everyone found love there.

"Not like it hurts."

"Okay, so this is the real Baldur." She drew the blade and promptly shoved it at April's belly. It didn't so much bounce off as seem to entirely ignore April's presence. It went through and then was simply not inside her. "I assume that's pretty good proof?"

Thrudr's eyebrows shot up, and she nodded. "My love, let's get dressed. I believe there's a man in our court who needs to answer a few questions."

Megan chuckled. Of course she was enjoying this. She got to play supernatural cop before she even became a real one. Maybe that would be enough to get her to not beat up Alys over Harvard. "Well, as Tyr, wouldn't that be my duty? I mean, all I've been told is I'm the god of law and justice."

Thrudr cocked her head, staring. "How about you all explain everything before we go? I'd like to not have any more surprises."

Alys cleared their throat. "Are you quite certain you need me here? I may be one surprise too many, and you already have all the proof you need, right?" They started to walk away, but Hannah grabbed their hand.

"No. You're staying. You've more than earned your place back here."

"Okay, I'm sorry," Thrudr said, "but could you please just tell me who she is?"

Alys grumbled. "I'm not a she." They stepped in front of Hannah and Emily, a charming smile on their lips. "Nor am I he, at least not anymore. But, uh, oh fuck." They glanced in the direction of the swords on the opposite wall, then to the daggers poking out from under the pillows. "Promise not to kill me?"

"No," Thrudr growled.

"April, stand in front of me?"

"I'm still pissed at you for manipulating all our lives."

"April," Hannah shouted, glaring. "They were being manipulated themself. It's not fair to blame them for everything, especially after all they've done for us."

"Like what? They haven't done anything for me."

"Okay, maybe Baldur was a bad person to ask for help," Alys mumbled.

"April, please. They taught me everything I know about this

world, and they kept me safe when zom…Draugr were trying to eat me, and they're my, well, we're kind of dating."

"You're what? I thought you were with Emily."

"It's not official yet."

"I was going to say," Emily said. "Bit of a surprise to me."

"Me too," Alys said, not taking their eyes off Thrudr.

She had just said that, hadn't she? She'd kind of thought she'd imagined it. "Well, there's stuff there, and I'm gonna ask them out when we're all done with this, so could you please make sure they survive?"

"You don't tell me anything anymore." Grumbling, April stood in front of Alys. "Fine. I don't approve of violence anyway. Alys is a horse, after all, and I don't support the killing of animals." Hannah remembered Alys telling that story. Okay, definitely not the time, but she was so proud she knew a Norse myth someone brought up.

Eyes locked on Alys, Thrudr gripped a dagger as Hildr made her way to a pair of swords. "A horse. And you've pissed off Baldur. From the sound of it, you've pissed off just about everyone. Isn't that right, Loki?"

Hannah could see a smile tugging at Alys's lips. That was not helping. They didn't have to look so damn proud of themself every time they were called out for being him. "You seem to have found me out. Here I was about to introduce myself, but it appears I don't even need to. It's a pleasure to meet my dear friends' children. Your mother and father are my dearest friends in the world. And apparently, more than friends, starting later today, if you don't kill me."

Thrudr eyed April, likely judging if she could make it to Alys in time. "We'll see about that."

"Thrudr, please," Hannah shouted.

"Stop it," Emily demanded.

Thrudr shot upright, staring. "But, Mother, it's Loki. He's responsible for all of this."

"Loki might have been. Alys isn't. They've proven their loyalty, and they're the one who found out that the Baldur here isn't real, and they helped us restore Tyr and Baldur to you. Without their help, Forseti would never have believed we're Sif and Thor. You don't have to forgive Loki, but accept that Alys isn't the same person."

"Then you're not my mother."

She shrugged. "I don't remember being your mother, so in a lot of ways, I'm not. But I'm proud of you for what you've made of your life, and I would really appreciate you not murdering my best friend."

Hildr glowered. "Thrudr, don't tell me you believe this nonsense."

"She's still my mother." Thrudr sighed. "I'll help you confront Baldur, but convincing everyone not to kill that traitor is entirely on you." It was something, at least.

"Thank you," Emily said.

Hannah watched Emily, wondering what it would have been like to actually raise their children together. She was such a good mom. Hannah held her hand. "That's all we can ask."

Thrudr turned to Hildr, giving her the most convincing pout Hannah had seen in her life. There was no way she hadn't spoiled Thrudr as a child. "Please, my love. I'm sure we'll have a chance to execute him after they talk to Forseti."

Hildr looked between Thrudr and Alys, her grip on the swords loosening.

Someone yelled in the hall. "Woo! He sure can drink."

Hannah glanced at the door. Was living in a Valkyrie hall always like living in a sorority? Of course it was, what was she thinking? That made perfect sense.

"Keep it down," another voice whispered loudly. "Some of our sisters are sleeping."

Emily opened the door. "Are you coming?" she asked Thrudr. "You believe us, right?"

With a heavy sigh, Thrudr nodded.

Hildr looked to her, but finally gave in and set her weapons down, then leaned in and kissed her, lingering for a long moment. "Let us get dressed," Thrudr said.

The rest of them headed back into the hall.

"I swear," one drunken woman said, her voice still loud enough to wake the dead. "I don't recall Baldur being able to keep pace with Magni before."

Hannah felt the world freeze in her gut, her heart, her veins. Her son was drinking with the spy she was there to denounce, and Hel was suspicious of Alys. It was why she'd told them to kill Emily. It had to be a test. It was the only thing that made sense. Why else would she insist Alys had to kill their best friend? She was testing their loyalty. Which meant she was expecting them to do something like this.

A door on the opposite side burst open, and a Valkyrie in full armor, with metallic wings, held a sword as long as Emily's arm. She didn't say a word as she stalked toward them, head forward, her posture hunched. She looked more like a predatory animal than a warrior.

Another door swung open, and two more came out. One had a spear, and the other held two axes. Their eyes were blank, staring like sleepwalkers.

"Mind control?" Alys asked. "Does Hel know we're here? Can she even do magic from Hel?"

"What's going on?" Megan asked.

Alys cleared their throat. "They're under Hel's control. But it—" The one with a sword took a swing. Apparently, the Valkyries didn't like lectures any more than Megan did.

Alys caught the sword in their hand with a metallic clang. "It could be Baldur. I don't know. This spell shouldn't work from a range, not if it's the same one Hel taught me."

"You can control people?" Emily asked, drawing her sword, just in time to block a thrust from the spear.

The Valkyrie charged forward, flipping the weapon upward, and Emily leapt back, blood spurting from a cut on her cheek.

Hildr and Thrudr's door opened, and Hannah turned, ready for more of the new mindless zombies, but they still looked the same, just armored and armed. "What in the nine realms is going on?" Hildr asked. "Geirahod, why are you attacking Mother?"

Emily narrowly dodged another thrust. "Someone's controlling her. We think it's Fake Baldur."

Thrudr caught the spear in midair and snapped it over her knee. "Or Loki."

"Goddamn it," Alys muttered. "This isn't me. I swear. Would I attack myself?"

"It wouldn't be the first time."

An axe flew at their head, and they dodged. Hannah threw herself to the floor and looked up, to find the axe held by Alys's tentacle. "I would never let them hurt Hannah." They charged in with more limbs, trying to wrestle the sword from the first Valkyrie, but the axe-wielder charged, her mouth hanging open in a silent cry as she swung at their back.

Thrudr smacked the axe-wielder on the back of the head with the broken spear, then dropped it and grabbed her shoulder, throwing her to the ground. "Herja, control yourself. I know you're in there."

Herja's jaws clamped on Thrudr's wrist with a sickening groan of bending metal, and Thrudr let out a pained cry.

Hildr hauled Herja off, pinning her to the wall and drawing her sword.

"Don't hurt them," Alys cried. "It's not their fault. They don't know what they're doing."

"She'd willingly give up her life," Hildr snapped back, but she sheathed her sword.

Alys's tentacles wrapped around the three Valkyries, holding them in place. Geirahod dropped, boneless, slipping out of the tentacles and picking up the two halves of her spear. Alys pressed down with their tentacles fighting to hold her.

"Let's get out of here," Hildr shouted.

"I can hold them," Alys said. "Go."

Hannah wasn't willing to watch her soon-to-be-partner sacrifice themself before they'd ever even have a proper date. She grabbed them up with a single hand and ran like mad, the Valkyries chasing after them.

None of the other doors opened as they charged the entrance. Maybe that was it. Maybe Fake Baldur could only control three at once.

The two drunk women were still talking by the front door, but there was no one else. Baldur had to be at the dining hall. Unless he was at a tavern or something, but Hannah had never noticed one.

As soon as they reached the door, the drunken Valkyries drew their weapons.

"No," Thrudr shouted. "Don't attack our sisters. They're ensorcelled."

But one of the Valkyries leapt at April, sword swinging for her neck and burying itself in the wall instead.

The other jumped on Megan, but she grabbed her hands, keeping the weapons away while Emily tried to pull the Valkyrie off her.

Alys dragged them away, and they ran out the door. Who knew how many more ensorcelled warriors would be after them? The Valkyrie den sat just outside the castle. They could make it there.

They sprinted for the gates, the Valkyries hot on their tails, and ran up the front steps. The doors were already open, and loads of people staggered away, all drunk, and no doubt ready to be taken over by Hel or Baldur at a moment's notice. But they didn't have any other options.

They ran right through.

"Hannah?" Modi was sitting at a table with Forseti, Magni, and the fake Baldur. As glad as Hannah was to see their familiar faces, this was terrifying. Hildr and Thrudr slammed the doors behind them, holding them closed. But no one banged against them.

Because Baldur was there. And he was trying to keep his cover.

"What's the meaning of this?" Forseti asked.

Hannah looked at everyone. What could they even say? They'd sound crazy before they could get their accusations out.

"Father has something important to tell you," Thrudr said. "And someone is trying to stop her." She glared at Baldur, her hands on her hips.

Magni stared. "Sister? What has happened?"

Forseti had only just accepted she was Thor and had known the imposter pretending to be his father for decades. How on Earth would Hannah get him to believe her? Hannah racked her brain for a way to deal with this.

Forseti looked between Alys, Megan, and April. "Who are these people?"

"Want me to handle this?" Megan asked, slipping past everyone else.

Hannah stared. "What do you mean?"

"You're invincible, right?" she asked the fake Baldur. What the hell was she planning? They had to be subtle. There were so many ways this could go wrong.

"I am." His eyes trailed over each of them, but his focus seemed most taken by the Valkyries and the swords at their hips. "I don't like showing off. It was a very traumatic moment."

"Bullshit," Hildr shouted. "The real Baldur was stronger than that. And he certainly didn't know magic."

"What are you talking about?" the fake Baldur asked, looking concerned. And confused. Was he really not responsible?

"Just open the doors," Hildr said. "They were right behind us. We'll have proof."

April opened the doors, and the Valkyries were all there, looking around and talking. "How did we get here?" one of them asked.

"I was just in bed," another said.

"See?" Hildr asked, sounding desperate. They really did seem crazy.

"That proves nothing," Forseti said.

Megan smirked, her hand sliding under her jacket. Hannah took a step to find out what the hell she was doing, but the sound of a gunshot stopped her. The man who'd claimed to be Baldur clutched his shoulder. "I'm so glad I already passed my polygraph. This would be so awkward to explain."

"What?" April mouthed.

"You—" Hannah managed, cutting herself off.

Emily just stared.

"Nice," Alys said.

Thrudr gaped at Alys. "You were telling the truth."

Hildr stepped toward the fake Baldur, her hand on her sword.

Magni and Modi looked confused, glancing between Megan and Baldur.

Forseti rose, looking ready to bellow, but Alys spoke first. "Obviously, that isn't the real Baldur." They smirked.

"I am," he cried, clutching the bleeding wound. "That *thing* must have been mistletoe."

"It was lead, I assume," Alys said. "And as my newly dear friend ascertained, this was the quickest way to prove it."

Hildr grabbed the fake Baldur by the back of his head and slammed it into the table. "Release my sisters. Now."

"I don't know what you're talking about," he cried.

Alys's smirk wavered. "Megan, I think it may be beneficial if we showed them who the real Baldur is before they cut our heads off."

Megan looked to April. "I don't feel great about this."

"Oh, for heaven's sake." April stared. "Are you really going to make me do it?" She drew Emily's sword and shoved it through her own abdomen. She was suddenly holding it at a weird angle away from herself. "Does that prove it?"

Modi continued to stare, perplexed and alarmed.

"I love your new friends, Father," Magni said. "They seem even more interesting than your old ones. Or *are* they the old ones?"

Alys nudged Hannah.

"Right. Um. These are my brothers. Sisters? These are my sisters: Megan is Tyr, and April is Baldur." She gave an awkward smile and tried to process what had happened. She hadn't thought Megan would shoot him. She'd wanted to be a cop her entire life. *Cops aren't supposed to just shoot people!* Then again, Megan was trying to be a Portland cop. From everything she'd said about them, that was about how they'd treat someone claiming to be a Norse god.

Megan waved, holstering the gun under her jacket.

"Why do you even have a gun?" April muttered, giving her own wave. "Hi. I guess I'm your uncle."

"I wanted to practice for my firearms certification. Oregon doesn't let you rent one if you don't already own one."

"Seriously?"

"Yeah. It's a ridiculous policy."

April's eyes narrowed. "No, I mean, you seriously bought a gun for that? Your class would teach you. Do you even have a concealed carry permit?"

Half-smiling, Megan avoided her question and turned back to the table.

"You're my father?" Forseti asked.

"What? Me?" Megan replied.

"He means me," April said. "Yes. I am. I'm sorry that..." She stared at the bleeding man and covered her mouth, taking a few deep breaths. "That...I'm sorry I wasn't here." She turned away, screwing her eyes shut. Hannah understood how she felt. She just kept being responsible for this stuff. She was the one who dragged Megan along, and another person had gotten hurt. Even if they were a bad guy.

"No, I'm real," the fake Baldur insisted. "I'm your father. Believe me."

Hildr tightened her grip. "The real Baldur was nothing like you. He wasn't a coward. And he would never control the wills of my sisters."

"What—"

Thrudr set her hand on the fake Baldur's shoulder, prompting a pained whimper. "We'll get to the bottom of this. Find out who you are and who sent you."

"But—"

Hildr's hand silenced him.

"And who's that?" Magni asked, pointing at Alys.

Thrudr's lips curved into a vicious sneer. "That would be Loki. I'm still not convinced that they're not the one who cast this spell."

"For fuck's sake," Alys griped.

"Would someone tell me what is going on?" Forseti shouted, jumping to his feet.

"Someone cast a spell upon the sleeping Valkyries," Hildr said, her voice scarcely more than a snarl. "They attacked us mindlessly. They moved like puppets. Puppets controlled by this monster." The fake Baldur let out a mewling whine as she shook him.

"He has been with me the whole time," Forseti said. "I'd have noticed him cast a spell."

"Then it was Loki," Thrudr said.

Alys groaned.

"Of course." Forseti narrowed his eyes, looking Alys up and down. "I didn't do a thing," Alys said.

"I didn't either," the imposter yelled.

Hildr smacked him again. "Loki tried to protect Father. I don't think it was him."

"Them," Emily corrected.

Thrudr stared. "They've committed enough crimes. We can't trust them."

"At least you got my pronouns right," Alys muttered.

"Then kill them," Forseti said. "Loki was banished and turned against us."

"No killing Alys," Emily shouted.

Not this again. "Alys is a dear friend." Hannah and Emily did their best to explain to Modi and Magni how important Alys was and what all they had accomplished for Idavollr, stopping only briefly to explain what guns were.

"I can't believe you're going to date the sworn enemy of Asgard. Then again, he always was great at making you forgive him," Modi said.

"Except when he killed..." Magni's eyes fell on April.

"Just because he helped you doesn't mean we can trust him," Hildr said. "Loki is only ever out for himself."

Alys sighed. "I have nothing but Hannah and Emily's best interests at heart."

Forseti leaned forward, staring into Alys's eyes. "Give me one good reason I shouldn't have you killed. Something you haven't already told me."

"What more can I say?"

"Your help now is not enough to make up for what you've done in the past. If it wasn't for you, everyone would still be alive. The fact that you're trying to make up for it has given me enough patience to hear you out, but you murdered my father, and you started Ragnarok. Why should I forgive you?"

Alys swallowed, their gaze not leaving his. They nodded. "You shouldn't." Finally looking away, they leaned back, staring at the ceiling some fifty feet above their heads. "I'm not the same person, but I'm not entirely different either. That's why you want these other four, isn't it? No matter how much they've changed, they're still the ones you lost. Well, I'm still the one who betrayed you." They turned, looking past Emily to Hannah. She could hardly even bring herself to meet their eyes. Alys was going to offer up their life? For what? They hadn't done anything wrong. "I betrayed Thor, time and again. I don't remember it, and I'd like to say I wouldn't do it again, but after everything I've done to my friends just in this life, I can't blame you for wanting to kill me."

"That was all Hel," Hannah said quickly, pleadingly, desperate for Forseti to believe her. "She was controlling you, lying to you. It's not your fault."

They shrugged and offered her a weak smile before turning back to Forseti, their expression hardening. "And Hel must be the one who did all this tonight. It doesn't matter that I didn't help this time. I've done far too much for her. I'm sorry for everything I did in this life and my last. If you're gonna kill me, please make it quick. No tying me up under a venomous snake or anything."

"What?" Hannah said, tears blinding her. Of course they were going to make a reference to another myth she didn't understand, even while talking about their execution. "Alys…" What could she say? She'd just met them. She couldn't lose them now.

"The hell they will," Emily said, her voice low as she reached for her sword. "I won't let anyone lay a finger on you."

Magni eyed Emily curiously. "That reminds me, since when did you start carrying a sword?"

"Is that really that important right now?"

"I can wait," Alys said.

"I just thought that, maybe, it'd be fun if I trained you," Magni said. "Modi and Thrudr would be happy to help, I'm sure. I never really had the opportunity to spend time with you doing something I was good at. Or much of anything after I trampled your garden."

Was this really the time? Wait, no, it obviously wasn't, unless he was up to something. Magni was trying to break the tension, to cool people's tempers. Was he trying to save Alys?

"Sure. I'd like that," she said, trying to force a smile. "But first, please talk Forseti into not killing my best friend."

"Does he really mean that much to you?" he asked. That was what it was. He didn't care about Alys, but he cared about his family and the people who mattered to them. It was the same reason Hannah had risked her job to prove herself and to help get the apples that would keep him alive.

"*They* do."

Magni leaned to his right, whispering in Forseti's ear.

"You can't be serious."

He whispered again.

"Very well. Thor," he called, his voice ringing throughout the hall.

"Yes?" Hannah asked.

"Sif."

Emily huffed, crossing her arms. "What?"

"The two of you plead for me to spare Loki, despite him having done more to harm you than any other, save for my father. If you will vouch for him, put your lives on the line alongside his, then, and only then, can he be forgiven and allowed back into Idavollr."

"Don't," Alys shouted, jumping to their feet. "I'm not subjecting you to that. I won't. This is my problem, and I deserve it."

"I'll do it," Hannah said. She couldn't lose Alys. Maybe she really had forgiven them.

"Any day," Emily added. "They, not he, mean the world to me, and if one of us was going to end up hanging, I always assumed it would be together."

"All right, then. Thrudr, Tyr, is this acceptable?"

"Me?" Megan asked.

"You better behave," Thrudr snarled at Alys. "If you bring harm to my parents, you'll wish you only had a venomous serpent to deal with."

"Noted."

"Can I hit them a few times first?" Megan asked.

Forseti nodded. "I have no objections."

"Hey!" Alys stared at Megan for a moment before dropping their hands to their sides. "Yeah, fine, I deserve it."

"At least look like you'll put up a fight."

"Fuck that. You can hit me or not, but I'm not making it a game for you."

Glaring, Megan slugged them a single time in the jaw, hard enough to send them back a few paces, rubbing their rapidly forming bruise.

"Ow!"

"Want another?"

"No."

Megan smirked and took a seat. "I feel better."

Forseti grinned and gestured for the Valkyries who had stuck around to come inside. "Very well. If we're to have more Aesir, we should have drinks."

Hannah gulped. They'd been trying to kill her a few minutes ago, but they seemed normal now. And she'd been mind-controlled too. Who was she to judge?

Hildr looked so relieved, she hugged the Valkyries. "I'm so glad you're okay."

Thrudr beamed at them. "That was terrifying."

Forseti sighed. "Take my father…take this imposter to the dungeons." He gestured to the fake Baldur.

They'd really managed to take care of it. They'd saved the day. And they could finally have that celebration.

❖

"Thank you for the drinks, and the goat, but we really do need to leave." Hannah dragged Emily to her feet. It was already too late to make it back in time for her shift, but Hannah wanted to make sure that Emily would be ready for the next day's. "And thanks for not killing Alys."

"Other than that last part, it was our pleasure. Though I will admit, that traitor's cooking was far better than any attempts in his last life. I suppose letting them live for now isn't quite as painful as I'd expected," Forseti said, grasping her wrist. "Is there no way I can convince you all to stay? Tyr, we need you more than ever now that we've been infiltrated. And we need to make it into Asgard."

"We'll be back," Hannah said. "We have plenty of time to get to Asgard. And it sounds like it's going to take a while."

"Yeah. Lots of rubble to clear and all that," Emily said. "I'll be a big help."

"I'll swing by from time to time," Megan said. "Maybe I can bring the criminal justice system up to contemporary standards."

"So more abusive?" Emily asked.

"Even better standards, then."

"Father?" Forseti asked. He looked to a decidedly tipsy April. "Must you leave? The false-you was my closest adviser. I don't know what to do without you."

She set a hand on his shoulder and almost fell as she tried to climb off the bench and stand next to him. "You'll be fine. I believe in you."

"Will you visit?"

She nodded. "Of course." She looked around, managing to trip on nothing. "How could I not?"

"But we need to leave for now," Hannah said.

"Surely we have more to offer you here," Thrudr said. "This is your home."

"So is Portland," Emily said.

"But you're welcome to visit," Hannah added. "We'll get you

phones, and we can all drink and have Alys's and April's cooking, and we can introduce you to modern technology. I bet you'll love television."

Magni clapped a massive hand on Thrudr's shoulder. "We'll be there. How about tomorrow?"

"Emily has work, but what about Wednesday? We'll find some board games."

"Very well," Modi said.

"I can't wait," Thrudr added.

Magni grinned. "I'll bring our beer, and we can see which is really better."

"But why?" Forseti asked. "What's keeping you there?"

"Internet and people not wanting to kill me?" Alys offered.

"Not you!"

Hannah squeezed Emily's hand. "I have a job I love and a life I'm not willing to leave behind. I promise, I'll always come back, but my other life means just as much to me." She tugged on Emily, guiding her closer, so she could reach Alys, and took their hand too. "There's too much to leave behind." She hoped that wasn't part of Hel's plans. Who knew what was or wasn't? Maybe Hel wanted them to take over and stay in Idavollr, or maybe she wanted them as far away as possible. All Hannah could do was what she felt was right. It was her life.

"Father?" he asked.

April leaned against Megan. After a few drinks, she'd either be unable to stand or dancing like a madwoman. It was never consistent. "I have grad school. I'm gonna change the world. Just like you're trying to." A look that could only be described as parental pride appeared on her face. Hannah had seen it enough times to know it. They were both politicians, or were at least trying to be. It made sense. And it was April's life too. Though it would really suck if Hel had managed to manipulate her into politics, but if that was the case, Hel would no doubt want those politics to be in Idavollr, not Portland.

"I think you have this place well in hand," Megan said. The evidence seemed to suggest otherwise, as the new people had caught the spy, but Hannah decided not to make that point. "I have two years of experience I have to earn before I can apply to the FBI, so I can't go running off. I don't think they'll accept you as a reference. Pretty tough to run a background check in another world."

"What about you, Mother?" Magni asked. "Maybe you could stay, at least for a while. You did want to train with us, right? We'll make you into an even greater warrior than Father."

Hannah felt the urge to object, but she had no desire to be a warrior. She just hated turning down a challenge. The rest of it dawned on her a few seconds later as she realized Emily seemed to be seriously considering the offer. "You wouldn't. Right? You wouldn't just leave." She'd gone to all that effort a few minutes ago to keep Alys around, and she could lose Emily? Granted, Alys would've died. and Emily would be a couple hours away, but it was still really bad.

"Of course not." Emily beamed at Magni. "I promise, I'll come back. Often. If it'll let me be strong enough to protect Hannah, then I'll train every single day. But I think Hannah would kill me if I stayed."

"I wouldn't..." she whispered. She wouldn't kill anyone. Not again. Never again. But she couldn't hide her relief that Emily was staying with her.

Emily laced her fingers between Hannah's. "I'm not running off anywhere. I'll just commute a bunch."

"We can train on Midgard as well," Thrudr said. "It gives us all the more reason to visit."

"And it'll give you time to try my beer," Emily said. "Did I ever make beer before?"

Modi shook his head. "You made wine."

"Well, I'm gonna learn to make beer."

Thrudr hugged her, the handle of her sword. "I can't wait."

She hugged her back. The whole affair devolved into a hug fest. It took a considerable amount of work to pry Forseti away from April, especially since he was the main thing keeping her upright, but they finally managed and bid a tearful farewell before they all climbed into the car and made their way back to Earth.

The car ride was silent for the better part of an hour. "Well," Megan finally said. "That was fun."

"You shot someone," April said, shock still clear in her voice.

"You shot someone," Alys repeated, sounding impressed.

Hannah turned in her seat to look back and saw Megan nod from her spot in the middle. "Yep. Didn't think I'd actually get to do that. You know, most police officers never fire their gun."

"Good," Emily muttered.

"Did we just save the world?" April asked.

"It doesn't really feel like it," Hannah said.

"I shot someone."

"We are well aware." April's tone showed even more scorn.

"He's fine. At least until they interrogate and execute him. I mean, he will have to verify that he was working for Hel. The other gods wanted me to do it for them." Megan reclined, lacing her fingers behind her head. "I almost did. Would've been interesting. Now, that's some on-the-job experience you can't get these days."

April stared. "Do I need to have you checked into a psych ward? You should be less okay."

"Again, I didn't kill him. But he was some undead monster who was trying to trick our—I guess—family into reviving the evil goddess who manipulated our entire lives. Forgive me for not caring about his fate."

Hannah opened her mouth and closed it again. When she put it like that, what the hell was there even left to say? Maybe they really had saved the day. They'd stopped a villainous plan in Idavollr. They'd prevented someone who was willing to kill them from being brought back to life. And they'd kept Alys from being murdered. They'd even managed to avoid hurting any of the mind-controlled Valkyries. Plus, now that she had the belt, they could start heading into Asgard and get back the apples to keep the gods alive. It had been one hell of a crazy month.

"You did good," Alys said. "I honestly didn't think this would work so well. Especially that bit where they were gonna kill me. That part really had me on edge."

"Right?" Megan agreed.

April shook her head and let out an exasperated sigh.

"I wouldn't have let them kill you," Hannah said. She hated the edge her voice had. What would she have done to stop everyone? Could she have hurt her family? She seemed capable of almost anything.

"They'd have to get through me," Emily added. She brought the car to a stop. "Mind carrying us the rest of the way, honey? I'd rather not smash into the curb."

"Right! Sorry." Normally, she was already hopping out of the car the second they got close. Picking up cars was just so fun.

The world shimmered and shifted as she carried the car through the portal, and they were back home in Portland, where everything was normal, and bridges weren't made of light. It was always bittersweet leaving that place, but this was where her life was.

"So," Emily asked as Hannah climbed back into the car. "Where does everyone want me to drop them off?"

❖

Emily pulled the Nissan into its usual spot in front of the run-down little house on Eighty-eighth. They'd dropped Megan and April off at their homes downtown, so Alys, Emily, and Hannah climbed out of the car. The house looked even smaller after they'd turned down yet another invitation to live in a giant castle.

As Hannah caught up to Emily and took her hand, she noticed something different about her. There was a long red cut running from the right side of her jaw up to her brow. How had she missed it? Had she been too busy staring at Alys all night? "Emily," she said, way too loudly for the middle of the night outside their landlord's window. "What happened to your face?"

"Huh? Why?"

Alys snickered. "'Cause it's killing me."

"That doesn't even work with how I phrased it." Hannah glared at them and gestured at Emily.

Emily pulled out her phone and stared at it. "Oh. Wow. I look badass."

Hannah faltered. That was her response? She wasn't even a little worried?

"Damn," Alys mouthed.

"But you were hurt," Hannah said.

"It's fine. I was fighting Valkyries. They're a lot better at this than me. It just shows how much I need training."

Alys slapped her on the back. "Great way to view it. You'll be a Valkyrie yet."

Emily grinned, and Hannah rolled her eyes. She would never understand this macho crap.

"How're we going to do this?" Alys asked.

"Go around back, head inside," Emily said.

They rolled their eyes. "You know what I mean. This place. With the three of us. We could go to my place. I'm sure that wouldn't be suspicious. I know it's a small house, but I own it."

Emily groaned. "All the times you could've offered, and you wait until I'm halfway through a year-long lease? Wasn't even worth the deal for a free week, but I wanted to make sure the fucker wouldn't raise the price on me one month."

"Well, in my defense, I had to keep my rendezvous with a manipulative goddess secret."

"Not much of an excuse."

Hannah chuckled. "Possibly the worst excuse."

With a heavy sigh, Alys turned to look at Hannah, running a hand through their rainbow-colored hair. "Well, I'm trying to be better now. I'm sure it would be believable having us live there. Maybe."

"It's fine. You don't need to worry."

"Do you still need to pretend to be Emily?" Hannah asked. It made an easy excuse to have Alys around, but she wanted it for more than just a cover. Damn, was she falling for them already? Maybe it hadn't been Thor. She really did just fall in love fast. "Hel is kinda stuck in Hel now. What does it matter?"

Alys shook their head. "She may have mind-controlled Valkyries in Idavollr, and who knows what else she can do? She had a backup plan she'd never even mentioned to me. There might be dozens more. She had decades to prepare, and there are so many things I did for her that I've heard nothing more on since. No, I'm not letting her know I betrayed her. Not if it means she'll kill you."

"You don't think she already knows?" Hannah asked.

Alys shrugged, looking defeated. "You can't see what the people you mind-control are doing. But I'm still hoping it was Baldur casting that spell. I don't know. This entire thing doesn't make sense. I was never able to do it from a range, I've tried. I don't know how either of them would. So either she's holding out on me—which she absolutely is—or she has more people that I don't know about. But no matter what the answer is, it's not safe. She'll try to kill us again if she suspects a thing, and we have no idea what she knows. I should stick with what she told me to do, and then we can see how she reacts."

"What if Fake Baldur tells her?" Emily asks.

They gave the faintest smirk, which was more disconcerting than it should've been. Their mouth hadn't been quite that large a minute earlier. "Your daughter will be taking care of that soon. As much as I pissed her off and with that look in her eyes, I've little doubt of it. He won't have the chance to say anything, and Hildr will be watching him until then."

"What did you do?" Emily asked.

"Me?" Hand over their heart, their smile far more innocent as their mouth shrank back down. "Whatever do you mean?"

"What did you do?" Emily repeated.

"Not a thing." They started heading for the door, leaving Hannah and Emily to run after them.

"You don't even have a key," Hannah called.

"Then let me in."

"What did you do?" Emily repeated.

Only when Emily had closed the door behind them and Alys had handed them both beers did they finally say, "Well, I did have to practice impersonating you before we got back to Earth, didn't I?"

Emily groaned. "For fuck's sake."

"I just told her to make it quick. Not even to make him suffer or anything. You know she'd have never listened to me. And I needed to make sure Hannah was safe."

Hannah stared at them. After all this, had they seriously arranged a murder? Or an execution? It was just wrong. "You didn't…Won't that send him straight back to Hel?"

"Okay, I may have said a little more than to make it quick. Just what she'd have to remove to make sure he couldn't contact Hel while they kept him imprisoned indefinitely." Their expression grew bashful.

Emily drained her beer.

Hannah followed her example. "You can't just…we…" She gave an exasperated sigh.

"I know you don't like it. But I will do anything it takes to keep you safe. And I completely understand if that makes you change your mind about what you wanted to ask me."

How was Hannah still into them? Alys had mind-controlled her, covered up murders, and instructed someone to hurt a prisoner while pretending to be her girlfriend. And they'd done it all to protect her. She shook her head. "No. It doesn't, though it definitely should. You really need to not manipulate people so much."

"I know."

"You could've asked me to tell her," Emily said.

They stared for a long moment. "That didn't even occur to me."

"That's a great sign," Hannah said. "I have amazing taste."

"Yeah, I'm the worst." Alys sighed, draining their beer. "You should probably back out now."

In a single quick motion, Hannah pulled Alys to her. "I already made my decision. Emily is okay with it, and you're living with us anyway. Go out with me."

They nodded their head, gaping. "Okay."

"Good." Their lips met in a heated kiss, with none of the comfort and fear of their first one. Hannah needed to finally make it real. It didn't matter how bad an idea this was. It didn't matter how many horrible things Alys had done for Hel. Hannah was falling for them. And she needed to see where it could go. They didn't pull apart until Emily cleared her throat.

"I get one too?"

"Of course!" Hannah plopped into her lap and grinned before kissing her.

"Damn, and I thought she meant me."

They ignored Alys's joke, deepening the kiss, Emily's hands running down Hannah's back. She'd known months ago that she was finally having her dream come true. She was going to be an accountant at one of the most reputable businesses in the city. She'd just had no idea what else that dream had in store.

About the Author

Genevieve McCluer (http://genevievemccluer.com) was born in California and grew up in numerous cities across the country. She studied criminal justice in college but, after a few years of that, moved her focus to writing. Her whole life, she's been obsessed with mythology, and she bases her stories in those myths.

She now lives in Arizona with her partner and cats, working away at far too many novels. In her free time she pesters the cats, plays video games, and attempts to be better at archery.

Books Available From Bold Strokes Books

Secret Agent by Michelle Larkin. CIA Agent Peyton North embarks on a global chase to apprehend rogue agent Zoey Blackwood, but her commitment to the mission is tested as the sparks between them ignite and their sizzling attraction approaches a point of no return. (978-1-63555-753-4)

Journey to Cash by Ashley Bartlett. Cash Braddock thought everything was great, but it looks like her history is about to become her right now. Which is a real bummer. (978-1-63555-464-9)

Liberty Bay by Karis Walsh. Wren Lindley's life is mired in tradition and untouched by trends until social media star Gina Strickland introduces an irresistible electricity into her off-the-grid world. (978-1-63555-816-6)

Scent by Kris Bryant. Nico Marshall has been burned by women in the past wanting her for her money. This time, she's determined to win Sophia Sweet over with her charm. (978-1-63555-780-0)

Shadows of Steel by Suzie Clarke. As their worlds collide and their choices come back to haunt them, Rachel and Claire must figure out how to stay together and, most of all, stay alive. (978-1-63555-810-4)

The Clinch by Nicole Disney. Eden Bauer overcame a difficult past to become a world champion mixed martial artist, but now rising star and dreamy bad girl Brooklyn Shaw is a threat both to Eden's title and her heart. (978-1-63555-820-3)

The Last First Kiss by Julie Cannon. Kelly Newsome is so ready for a tropical island vacation, but she never expects to meet the woman who could give her her last first kiss. (978-1-63555-768-8)

The Mandolin Lunch by Missouri Vaun. Despite their immediate attraction, everything about Garet Allen says short-term, and Tess Hill refuses to consider anything less than forever. (978-1-63555-566-0)

Thor: Daughter of Asgard by Genevieve McCluer. When Hannah Olsen finds out she's the reincarnation of Thor, she's thrown into a world of magic and intrigue, unexpected attraction, and a mystery she's got to unravel. (978-1-63555-814-2)

Veterinary Technician by Nancy Wheelton. When a stable of horses is threatened, Val and Ronnie must work together against the odds to save them and maybe even themselves along the way. (978-1-63555-839-5)

16 Steps to Forever by Georgia Beers. Can Brooke Sullivan and Macy Carr find themselves by finding each other? (978-1-63555-762-6)

All I Want for Christmas by Georgia Beers, Maggie Cummings & Fiona Riley. The Christmas season sparks passion and love in these stories by award-winning authors Georgia Beers, Maggie Cummings, and Fiona Riley. (978-1-63555-764-0)

From the Woods by Charlotte Greene. When Fiona goes backpacking in a protected wilderness, the last thing she expects is to be fighting for her life. (978-1-63555-793-0)

Heart of the Storm by Nicole Stiling. For Juliet Mitchell and Sienna Bennett a forbidden attraction definitely isn't worth upending the life they've worked so hard for. Is it? (978-1-63555-789-3)

If You Dare by Sandy Lowe. For Lauren West and Emma Prescott, following their passions is easy. Following their hearts, though? That's almost impossible. (978-1-63555-654-4)

Love Changes Everything by Jaime Maddox. For Samantha Brooks and Kirby Fielding, no matter how careful their plans, love will change everything. (978-1-63555-835-7)

Not This Time by MA Binfield. Flung back into each other's lives, can former bandmates Sophia and Madison have a second chance at romance? (978-1-63555-798-5)

The Found Jar by Jaycie Morrison. Fear keeps Emily Harris trapped in her emotionally vacant life; can she find the courage to let Beck Reynolds guide her toward love? (978-1-63555-825-8)